The Scouring

By Valerie Watson

First Edition: September 2013

The Scouring

Edited in part by E.M. Ragland

A special thanks to Erika Howard, Brandi Morini, Tyler Sylican, and Barry Girsh for their contribution to the cover art.

ISBN-13: 978-1491071496 (paperback)

For information for to www.facebook.com/TheScouring

A note to my family and friends:

You will undoubtedly recognize names, places, characters and situations that were taken from my real life, from you. Thank you for the large amounts of inspiration! And I have done it in tribute to you. However, please take into consideration that many things have been exaggerated, added and changed to make the story more exciting and interesting. You may be reading and notice that you believe a character is you. Then, based on what you read you may think that I personally have a certain opinion of you. Please don't do this! Remember, I have exaggerated, added and changed to make this a good read. I love you all!!

Valerie

For Eve

*You insisted that I write the things that were
bouncing around in my head, real and imagined.
Then you stayed by my side through the whole thing.*

You know the rest…

Snow Globe

While looking through the glass, I observed her, and I observed him.

She was born on the wind. She seemed to have volumes of energy intertwined with laughter and tenderness, shooting from her presence in a spiral of bright white light. It was with her everywhere she went, going out into the world, when she was out in the world.

He was born of the earth, connected to it. His energy was under his hands, close to him, surrounding and moving him. All who touched his life became a part and were carried with him in his power. Protected.

No one could see her light. Her energy rushing out to meet – no one. Many took her light for granted and so it diminished for a time.

He remained singular. Surrounded by love, but alone in his center. Sometimes his singularity begets anger or confusion and so his power feels wasted. No purpose.

I saw through the glass as time passed, and so it went.

Later, she found strength in her light for herself. Resolved, refined, joyful. But, not content.

He resided within himself. Steadfast, unwavering, he had arrived. But, was not fulfilled.

What would the connection of these look like, from outside the glass?

The slice of space where these two touched... ah... like a small, singular ignition. A flash and a small steady glow. He saw her light and dared not deny its existence. She felt his power and was unable to resist its draw.

And then – space between them. She was here, and him there. Too far... nothing could reach that far.

But, as I gazed into the glass, I beheld the white light, stronger than ever, billowing toward the glass. But not out in random dissipation as before... It began to bend, drawn strangely down. Back to earth, to him. Her energy touched his; it changed, reverberated and became rich with warmth and color. The arc created was stronger than anything earthly and though it could be passed through, it could not be broken. It shone like the sun. The circuit was complete that linked the wind with the earth. Forever alive.

Through the glass I observed - them. Connected.

1

Raisa lay in the grass under a tree that could only partially shade her. The breeze was blowing the sparse leaves of the young magnolia so that the sunshine would blind her one second and leave her blinking the white splotches out of her eyes the next. She could feel the grass tickling her bare arms and she wondered if there were ants or any other little creatures that might be considering her a mountain to defeat. She smiled to herself for the Gulliver's Travels reference. Normally the thought of bugs would at least move her to an upright position but not today. She was exhausted and her body was begging for sleep. If she could only turn off her brain she could rest. She knew she was alone in the park and the odds of anyone disturbing her were slim.

Might as well try again. I didn't sleep at all last night, she thought. Raisa had been plagued with this problem all of her life, over-active thoughts, not enough rest. As she lay in the warmth of the afternoon she began a "stress-relief" exercise that she had used since she was eight years old to ward off bad dreams, fend off the uninvited wicked voices, clear her mind of the maddening internal rhetoric, and reach for that ever illusive state of unconsciousness. It was actually a little funny that the voice she always heard in her head when she did this sounded like Ricardo Montalban, but it was comforting too. She knew she was the one putting the voice there when it sounded like her faithful Ricardo... who else would do that?

You are a-laying on the a-white sand of a beautiful-a-beach-a. The temperature is-a-perfect. When you open your-a-eyes you can-a-see in the-a-distance a small-a-boat with its-a-sails a-blowing in the-a-gentle-a-breeze-a. Birds fly-a-gently over-a-the-a-shore-a and you are-a completely at-a-peace. Now you close your-a-eyes again-a, and you a-feel-a so relaxed that you-a-almost-a-float-a. Breathe the-a-salty-a-air-a, feel the-a-gentle-a-warm-a-breeze-a. Now you concentrate on the-a-muscles in your-a-feet-a. You feel-a-them relax-a, as-a if they were-a-melting. Now your-a-calves, they are-a-soft and supple and you-a-can touch the-a-muscles and they relax to your-a-touch-a. As you-a-move your-a-thoughts to your-a-thighs-a……… your-a… calves are-a…. melting… thighs………

◆◆◆

"AHHHHH!" Evert yelled as he lurched from behind the corner and clawed at Raisa as she walked down the dark hall to her room. The scream she tried to produce jammed at the top of her throat and she froze where she stood with nothing but a sputter escaping her mouth. Her brother laughed without remorse at his prank. "You're so stupid, Raisy. Who did you think it was, the boogey man?" Evert delighted in tormenting his little sister; it seemed to be his favorite pastime.

Flip, flip, blur… flip…

"Raisa, what are you doing?" Evert sneered. Raisa didn't understand the question because she wasn't doing anything at all. "I can't believe you're six. You act like you're two."

Flip, flip…… blurrr… flip, flip…

"Ow!" Raisa began to cry as her hands landed in the broken glass on the floor that she was trying to clean up.

Evert snickered thinking it was hilarious that he had kicked her in her rear-end. *She makes this too easy,* he thought. *It was a perfect target sticking up in the air like that.*

"Mom, Evert pushed me down and made me cut my hands," Raisa yelled toward the stairs that led to her mother's room.

"She's a baby and a tattletale!" Evert yelled in the same direction.

Their mother came down the stairs, passing both of them without surveying the situation, or even looking at either of them.

"She's only seven years old, Evert," she sounded annoyed at best.

Flip, blur… flip…

Raisa sat on the floor outside her sister's bedroom door, her ear pressed to the crack.

"Evert needs to cool it with Raisa," Aileen exclaimed. "He's going about it all wrong…"

What do they mean? Raisa wondered.

Flip, flip, flip, flip… blurrrrrrrrrrr….. flip, flip, flip…

Evert had been in his room with the door closed for most of the day doing who-knows-what. Raisa knocked softly on his door, "I know you're in there, Evert… I made a card for you… can we please make up and start over?"

"Go away. I'm sleeping, Raisa," Evert responded groggily. "What's a worthless card going to do anyway…"

Blurrrrrr….. flip, flip…

Raisa sat under the kitchen bar counter where no one would see her. *I wonder how long before someone would wonder where I am?*

Flip…

Raisa shifted, trying to ease the pain from sitting for so long. She stood and looked at the clock. It had been three hours.

Flip, flip... blurrrrrrrrrrr ..... flip, flip, flip...

Raisa lay on her back in the dead of night, staring wide-eyed at the ceiling and counting her heartbeats. *What was that sound!* She gasped. She didn't dare to get up.

Flip, flip, flip...

Raisa was in her room - again. No one seemed to notice. Or care.

Should an eight year old feel so alone? There are 6 people living in this house and no one ever speaks to me. I hear them talk 'about' me sometimes but I don't know what they are saying. Sometimes it feels like they are pretending to talk in secret but that they expect me to listen, to make me scared. It's a puzzle...

Flip, flip...

It's all part of the plan. I can tell! They want me to believe that they are my family, that they care about me, but I think they are just playing. All of them, my family, my teachers, people at church and school, all of them.

Flip...

Raisa slammed her radio off as she paced the floor of her room.

Flip...

They're planning it, I know it. She lay awake at 3am, imagining dark shadows crawling across her ceiling and not daring to shut her eyes.

Flip...

As Raisa lay in her bed she fought to stay awake but lost. She dreamed a dream that came to her almost every night.

She wore a white dress and sat at a white bistro table decorated with a single vase that held a pink daisy in an expanse of white nothingness. The scene seemed peaceful but something was pending. Then the white nothingness was overcome with a rolling fog and black nothingness. The darkness unrolled like thick smoky batting and it was full of dread. There was no air to breath into her lungs. The lack of sound was maddening. It rolled over her and the table and the flower in silence and simply replaced them.

She woke choking violently with tears streaming from her eyes.

Flip...

This is a game to them, especially Evert. They are tormenting me. Trying to convince me that life is going on like normal. But I know... I know their secret. Just when they think that I am the most happy I can be and when my back is turned and I don't suspect anything, that's when it will happen. They will capture, torture and kill me. They will laugh at me for being stupid, show me to the entire world and kill me. It has to be true... it's the only thing that makes sense!

Flip...

So... tired...

Flip...

When will I die?

Flip...

I don't care anymore... just want this over.

Flip...

Let them come!

Flip... flip, flip, flip...

Raisa sat in her living room on the carpet in the corner, knees pulled to her chest, rocking and crying, and not caring who heard.

Charlotte, Raisa's sister, was the only one home. The story was that mom and dad where out and she was told to stay home and babysit. No one else stuck around for a boring night with the brat. Charlotte heard Raisa's hysterics and came into the room.

"What is wrong with you, Raisy?"

Suddenly Raisa wasn't so sure if she was ready to die at this moment.

"Nothing, I'm fine."

Charlotte could see the horror in her sister's eyes and persisted.

"My gosh, Raisy, I've never seen you like this. You're scaring me!" She tried to move in to comfort her little sister but Raisa flinched at her touch. Charlotte was shocked at the response and tried to speak softly and reassuringly, but her voice was wavering with what sounded like concern, "I would never hurt you, Raisy... please... please tell me what's wrong. I can't help if I don't know..." her voice trailed off. Then her voice resolved, "Look, Raisy, I know that we... well, I guess I, am not always that nice to you, but I really do love you and I don't ever want you to feel frightened. *Please* tell me what's wrong."

That did it for Raisa. Enough was enough. *Whatever is going to happen is going to happen now!*

Raisa spent the next hour telling her sister how she knew of the whole plan to kill her and that she could tell it was true by everything she had seen and heard. Her shoulders were squared and she was prepared for the end of the charade, like tearing down a set to a stage play, ending the ruse. She expected everyone in her life to saunter into the room, all at once, grinning and laughing at her and tormenting her. They would tell her about their plan and how it was a shame that it had ended so soon since they were just getting started with the fun. And Raisa's anguish was so entertaining.

But that didn't happen. Charlotte turned and went to the phone on the wall in the kitchen. She didn't call the others or even mom and dad. She called the Pastor of the church – at 11:45 at night – and told him that she was bringing Raisa to him immediately. They lived only two small blocks down the road.

Raisa had always thought that their close proximity was a little too convenient. The Pastor was in pajamas and a robe when he opened the door but he seemed genuinely unconcerned that he had been woken up in the middle of the night. Raisa's big sister prodded her to tell the whole story again. When it was done, Charlotte looked at the Pastor as if to say, *"What do I do?"*

Raisa eyed the Pastor. *He* does *look very concerned.* Real or fake, she couldn't tell. But he "blessed" her and sent them on their way.

Raisa's head was buzzing and dizzy for the rest of the night.

She did feel a little lighter somehow though. It had been good to say it all out loud, regardless of what would happen now. She suspected that they were just scrambling to rewrite the script. She had thrown them a curve ball and it might take awhile to recover and put a new plan in place – to kill her. Maybe there were some "rules" to it. *Maybe it is a requirement that I am fooled or surprised,* Raisa thought.

Flip, flip, blur…

Raisa was looking at her sister Charlotte in the mirror while she did her makeup. It had been three weeks since the whole "incident". *Maybe there is a chance that it was all in my head; maybe I'm just totally insane!*

Flip, flip… blurrrrrrrrrrr….. flip, flip, flip…

Raisa was at school… recess in the sixth grade. Garik was the meanest boy in school. He had a naturally villainous face that always looked like he was in the throes of plotting his next hideous deed. *Why does he have to be in my class?* He caught Raisa's eye and shot her a glare, not unlike most days. Raisa's best friend since forever, Corliss Fairchild noticed the exchange.

"Raisy, what's his problem anyway?"

7

Raisa shrugged. "I don't know, he's always hated me, but I have never been able to figure out why. Just naturally evil I guess."

Raisa looked at Corli and was considering how her friendship might fit into the whole "plan of death" thing. She had never considered Corli to be one of the "bad guys" but that could be a trick too. Or maybe there were actually some "good guys", people on her side, although she highly doubted it. Raisa sighed out loud. Or maybe she was just some broken kid with a fantastical imagination. Raisa had just looked down and started fumbling with her snack in her lap when she felt a quick burst of air and saw a flash of a brown t-shirt from the corner of her eye. She snapped her head up in surprise. Garik was standing in front of her, his face only inches from hers. Raisa could swear that she saw a small glint of green fire escape his eyes. He was close enough that she smelled the dirt and sweat on him and he was wearing that same sneer on his face.

Raisa's heart was suddenly pounding hard. "What do you want?" she said, trying to sound brave.

"Just thought I'd tell you," Garik sounded almost like he was growling, "that you were right the first time." Raisa could only stare. "Stupid girl," his smile widened, "you *will* die!"

♦♦♦

Raisa woke up so suddenly it felt like crashing in a car. She pulled herself up in confusion. Had she actually gone to sleep? She only remembered as far as calves, or was it the-a-thighs-a. She laughed a short *huh* to herself and tipped her head in thanks to Ricardo. The sun was setting on top of Catalina Island in the distance and the reservoir below her had turned black in the shadow of the hills around it. She had always wanted to go down to the water and see if it seemed fresh or stagnant but had always been deterred by the thought of weeds, thorns and mosquitoes. While she contemplated the water, thoughts of what she had been dreaming seeped into her conscious mind. The dream was actually the memory of her childhood. That's when she had realized that she saw other things in this world that others didn't, and that she might be some kind of target. She still felt, after all these years, like there were two realities: normal life, and the paranoid delusional one she had worked up in her head. But somehow she knew they were both real... not that she had figured out who was after her or why, but she could feel it in her chest. There was more going on than what meets the eye. Raisa's throat tightened. Nothing really made sense to her right now. Life should be joyful and wondrous... shouldn't it? She could only hope that someday she would find some answers.

She shook her head to clear the images, picturing the way you shake an etch-a-sketch, and pulled herself up to her feet. Her jeans were cool in the breeze where the grass had made them damp. She checked for bugs, tiny ropes and stakes, and headed for her car parked a few yards away on the street. She checked the clock on her phone and realized that her timing was perfect. Corli would arrive at the Taco Shop at about the same time she would.

2

With the sun set, a slight chill was in the air. But Raisa threw her hair up in a rubber band and left her windows down anyway as she drove down the hill just to make sure she was all the way awake. She held the steering wheel in place with her knee and flipped through her home-made CD's trying to figure out what kind of music she was in the mood for. Nothing sounded quite right. Music was her soul and because of that, if she ever felt down about something it was difficult to play anything... five notes and she'd be crying her eyes out, an emotional mess. It was a double-edged sword. She needed music like air to live but if she couldn't afford to crack, she couldn't listen to it. So tonight she drove in silence.

As she pulled into the strip-mall she could smell the corn tortillas and oil wafting through the air. *Yum*, she thought as she parked, *I LOVE Taco Tuesday!* Corli saw her through the window, stood up on the rung of her bar stool and waived excitedly but didn't move from her seat. It was rough to get a table on Tuesdays.

"You scored!"

"I know, right? And we are close to where the entertainment will set up too!" Corli waived her hand with her best Vanna White impression. She was wearing that big happy smile that always made Raisa a little more at ease. "Now, since I got the table, I get tacos first." She hopped off her stool and headed for the taco line. Raisa settled in, checked her phone for any messages and ordered mango iced teas from the waitress. Corli

10

walked back not two minutes later with two plates of tacos and plopped one in front of Raisa.

"Corli," she complained, "I can buy my own dollar tacos you know."

"I know. It's just the least I can do since I can't *do* anything. How is your dad anyway?" Corli's smile had faded into thin lips and a crinkled brow. "And you! You look half dead! Have you gotten any sleep at all?"

"I just took a nap in the park. Does that count?" Raisa tried to sound cheerful but she could feel the short lived energy draining from her just from trying to fake it. She took a big bite of taco and tried to get most of it down before going on. "My dad is the same." Raisa's voice was small but even. "Not awake much and even when his eyes are open it's hard to tell if he is really "there". I left when my mom got there at two."

"Raisa, you got there at 6am yesterday." Corli had a very disapproving tone. "And I know you... you can't sleep in a chair."

"I know but I always feel so guilty when I leave... I don't want him to be alone. I'm afraid that my mom will leave and not tell anyone. I couldn't handle it if he... was alone."

Corli reached over and laid her hand on Raisa's. "I don't think he will be, Raisa."

Raisa's back straightened a little from her slouch. Her chin lifted and her head turned slightly. Suddenly, Corli felt like Raisa was looking through her instead of at her.

"You know, I think you're right." Raisa looked as though she were someplace else. "My mom told me a couple of days ago that he opened his eyes, smiled and started talking for the first time in days. He told her that John and Lyle were there and asking him to come with them. He gave my mom's hand a squeeze and went back to sleep. I thought he was just wacked

11

out from the pain meds and my mom didn't seem astonished or anything. She acted like it was just another comment."

"Who are John and Lyle?" Corli asked carefully.

"John is my dad's oldest brother that died five years ago and Lyle is his youngest brother that died just a few months ago from cancer."

Raisa and Corli sat unmoving and quiet. The noise of the restaurant seemed far away. Corli was watching Raisa and trying to keep from spilling the tears that had welled in her eyes. Raisa was staring through her tacos.

Vincent will be fine. Raisa heard the words as if they were piped directly into her brain and though she could see the Taco Shop around her, a picture had been superimposed over her sight. She saw her uncle's, John and Lyle, standing in front of her in white suits and warm smiles. Their arms were at their sides and both had their palms facing her as if that was what was holding the image there. Raisa felt a sensation of peace wash over her and then as quickly as it had started, she saw them lower their palms and the picture was gone. The sounds of the restaurant flooded back and she heard Corli saying her name.

"… Are you okay? Where did you go just now?" Corli still had a wrinkled brow.

"I… I'm fine… really." Raisa at this moment couldn't bring herself to tell Corli what had just happened. Because she wasn't even sure she had it straight in her own head. Even though she had always told Cori – almost - everything and she had never once laughed at her or doubted her. "I think I just need to finish eating." Raisa promptly devoured the rest of her chicken tacos.

As if on cue to lighten the mood, two boys in their early twenties sat down in the area reserved for the musicians. They had only a guitar, an amp and a mic a piece and began jointly tuning their guitars. In unison Raisa and Corli automatically straightened their posture, fluffed their hair, brought their hands up under their chins and snuck a sideways glance to see if they were cute or not. As they looked back at each other with wide-eyed affirmations, Corli let a giggle slip, her hand flying to cover her mouth. Raisa rolled her eyes. Girly-girl behavior was something that she rarely condoned. She was more of a "if-you-want-something-from-me-you're-gonna-have-to-work-for-it" type of girl. She turned to check and see if Corli's outburst had been noticed. Sure enough... the boy closest to her friend was looking at Corli and grinning.

"Settle down," Raisa whispered without moving her mouth. "Be cool..." and with the slightest head tilt let Corli know she should turn and smile.

Corli turned to look at the boy as if she was casually noticing him for the first time. No one was buying it, but it was cute. "Hi," she said with a bit of a blush covering her face. The boy winked. He didn't really have time to speak because his partner had started playing. He only missed half a beat and joined in with a beautiful harmony. Raisa looked at her friend and the boy as if she were framing them up for a picture and noticed a slight haze in the air between them. It was as if some free flowing static was trying to materialize and connect the two of them. It had a warm yellow glow to it. She wondered if anyone else *at all* ever saw this stuff. She glanced around the room and found that most people were only interested in who they were sitting with or their tacos.

She turned back to look at the boys and enjoy the music. They were expertly picking out a Crosby, Stills and Nash song. She noticed that they were playing a whole verse before they started to sing. Raisa new the song very well, but she was surprised to hear it. It was one of the many songs that her sisters Aileen and Charlotte sang. They would sit on their beds in the

13

room they shared and play and sing for hours. But that was
many years ago before they had married and left home. Raisa's
eyes closed, and because she really couldn't help herself, she
began singing along so softly that only Corli might be able to
hear her.

> *Helplessly hoping*
> *Her harlequin hovers nearby*
> *Awaiting a word*
> *Gasping at glimpses*
> *Of gentle true spirit*
> *He runs, wishing he could fly*
> *Only to trip at the sound of good-bye*
>
> *Worthlessly watching*
> *He waits by the window*
> *And wonders*
> *At the empty place inside*
> *Heartlessly helping himself to her bad dreams*
> *He worries*
> *Did he hear a good-bye? Or even hello?*
>
> *They are one person*
> *They are two alone*
> *They are three together*
> *They are four for each other*
>
> *Stand by the stairway*
> *You'll see something*
> *Certain to tell you confusion has its cost*
> *Love isn't lying*
> *It's loose in a lady who lingers*
> *Saying she is lost*
> *And choking on hello*
>
> *They are one person*
> *They are two alone*
> *They are three together*
> *They are four for each other*

Corli watched and listened to both Raisa and the boys. She heard Raisa singing different harmonies with each verse and she knew every single word. "How do you *do* that? I've never even heard that song and you're singing all the words and fancy harmonies. You really should make a career out of this you know." She turned back to acknowledge the boys with a big smile and some slightly over-animated clapping.

Raisa barely heard what her best friend was saying. She had gotten lost in the song, lost in the words, and started to feel something bubble up in her chest. When she felt her eyes begin to burn, she realized that she needed to leave, quickly. Corli would understand. She grabbed her bag, stood and stepped around the table. "I'm gonna take off."

"Noooo…" Corli whined.

Raisa threw an arm around her and gave her a squeeze. "You stay and introduce yourself to guitar boy. I have a good feeling about it." Raisa pecked her on the cheek and headed for the door.

The noise from the restaurant shut off as the door closed behind her and she paused to take a deep breath. The cool air outside helped clear her head. *No music, no cracking*, she said to herself as she stepped off the curb and headed out. As she came closer to her car she could hear the voices of some boys that seemed to be just hanging out in the parking lot. *Boys talking crap*, she thought. *How original.* They were gathered under a small tree that was directly under one of the light poles a few yards from her car. The light was so bright that the shadows were very strong under the tree and she could barely make out how many there were. It looked like three or four. Their banter hushed as she got closer. All of a sudden she felt very uneasy as if she was way too vulnerable out in the open. *You're being overly paranoid, Raisa. What can they do to me in this busy*

15

parking lot with all this light? But she sped up anyway. Once she was safely in her car with the doors locked she felt better. But as she started the engine and pulled out, she could not help but try and get a better look at whom or what had frightened her that much. As she strained her eyes to separate the shadows, she saw, or she thought she saw, two flickers of green light. Raisa sucked in a startled breath and punched the gas to get moving. As she felt the extra adrenaline pumping her heart she started talking to herself to try and calm down. "Don't be ridiculous, Raisa. That had to be a light from someone's cell phone or any electronic device for that matter." But she couldn't shake the feeling that it was more than that. She drove away trying to leave it all behind. She had enough to handle with her dad sick and in the hospital. Now was not a good time to delve into her theories. *But it would make sense,* she thought. *Corner me while I'm distracted.*

The porch light was not on when she pulled up to her house. *That's good, mom's at the hospital.* But the darkness was creepy. So Raisa positioned the front door key in her hand and looked carefully around before she got out. She darted to the door, unlocked, swung open, ducked in, slammed and locked the door in record time. *You're such a woos...* she couldn't help but feel foolish. Raisa called her mom's cell and they had a fifteen second chat. Mom verified that Raisa was home. Raisa verified that mom was at the hospital.

"How is dad doing?" She had to ask before she hung up.

"He's the same, Raisa." Her mother sounded tired and resigned... but not panicked. *Not that I would know what my mom sounds like in a panic*, she thought.

"Okay, bye."

Maybe I'll get some sleep. Unfortunately it sounded more like a question than a statement in Raisa's head.

Raisa peeled off her jeans and plopped on her bed, too tired to wash her face and change into her typical tank top and pajama bottoms. She knew she would regret it... she could never get all the way comfortable without completing the whole ritual. She just couldn't bring herself to lift her body off the mattress.

She drifted off to an uneasy heaviness. She knew she wasn't really sleeping since she could measure every half hour on her alarm clock with its neon green numbers. Two images played back and forth in her mind, one of her father, lying in his hospital bed, and the other of green fire-like eyes glaring at her from a shadowed face. She could see her father's labored breathing, the IV in his arm, and his heart-beat rumbling through his chest, working so hard that it created waves across his body. He was in a dark room and the light over his bed had a spot light effect, barely spilling enough illumination to see anything beyond his arms. Raisa shook the image from her mind, trying to think of something else that would be less painful to her heart. She checked her clock. The numbers blurred and morphed into eyes. She found herself trying to look past the light of the green smolder to see the face. She couldn't tell whose face it was but had the feeling that she knew it. *Is someone trying to tell me something?* And then the image changed back to her father. The light had expanded in his room a little. *Where is mom?* She couldn't help but wonder since she could not see her in the room with her father. *Stupid, this is a dream...* back to the shadowed face and green eyes... *or are they numbers?* Raisa heaved a sigh of disgust as she reached up and batted at her clock to turn it around.

What seemed like minutes later, Raisa heard the garage door open and close, which meant her mom was home. She looked toward her clock, not willing to move or open her eyes very far. She remembered turning it around but noticed a slightly lighter color air in her room. Assuming dawn was not far off she closed her eyes. *Just a few more minutes and I'll get up and go to the hospital...*

♦♦♦

The courtyard in the middle of the old Mediterranean-style house was full of warm sunlight. Raisa sat at a small, old, worn and rustic dark wood table across from a boy. His hair was loosely curly, dark but sun-kissed and his skin was the color of light maple syrup. He wore a plain white t-shirt that accentuated his coloring... and his toned muscles. Raisa looked to his face but it was as if she was looking through a camera lens that she couldn't focus. He was smiling though, at her. She knew that. The stucco was the color of cantaloupe and she could see into the richly decorated kitchen, living room and through to the windows in the front of the house. Raisa felt happy and peaceful. She tried harder to see the face of the boy but she could not bring it into focus. Then without warning, everything changed. The feel of anxiety pressed on the air, like the music in a movie had just turned sinister. They heard gunshots ringing from the front of the house and men shouting in the street. The front door crashed open and for a split second she saw green flames licking up from the men that entered the house. Raisa felt herself pushed down by a strong and warm arm. Then it wrapped around her protectively. The boy who just a moment ago had been staring into her eyes and now was holding her tight to his body, produced a gun, seemingly out of nowhere, and returned the gun fire that was now splintering through the walls across the courtyard from where they were.

"We have to get out of here!" he yelled over the deafening noise. But they were trapped.

18

Raisa peered around the corner to see if she could figure a way out. The distance to the next place that might be safe from the gunfire seemed miles away. She looked frantically for something they might use as a shield. Her goal was a front window that was farthest from the front door. She looked around the corner again and her eyes flew wide.

"*DAD?*" Her father was standing there, in the middle of this battle, exactly where she had wished there was a wall.

Everything went still as if the only two people that existed now were her and her father. He was smiling… *and he looks… younger…*

Raisa felt no fear but she had to warn him, "Dad, get out of the way! You'll be shot!"

"I'm fine, Raisy. I'm here for *you.*" He looked at the boy by her side and smiled even wider. He looked back at Raisa and she thought she could *feel* that he liked this boy… he approved. "You can get out this way, Raisa." And he pointed to the window she had been considering. "I'll protect you."

She heard a ringing sound, like a phone… but that didn't make sense. Then the violence of her surroundings came back into focus. But her father was still standing there, arms held wide, a smile still on his face.

Raisa grabbed the boy's hand from her arm. "Let's go!" She had to practically shriek over the noise. The boy didn't hesitate even though she was pulling him in front of the screaming bullets. As soon as they reached the window and before they jumped out, Raisa turned and looked back at her father. He nodded his head and was gone.

Raisa and the boy started running…

◆◆◆

19

Dad! Raisa's eyes flew open. She jumped up and threw on the jeans she had been wearing a few hours ago. She was expecting it to be light out but it seemed to still be dark. Darker than when she had heard her mother come home. *That's odd.* She shrugged, chalked it up to delirium and flew down the stairs. She was just about to run out the door when a figure sitting straight as a pin at the kitchen table caught the corner of her eye. She had to grab the wall to stop her momentum. And then she felt a low thudding shock in her body that started in her stomach and emanated to her fingertips. It was her mother, sitting in the kitchen, perfectly still, in the dark.

Raisa glanced at the clock over the stove as she moved slowly to sit next to her mother. It was 3am. "Mom?" Raisa could barely get the sound out.

"I got home at 1am." Her mother's voice sounded like she was reading a storybook to a five year old. "Dr. Inouye said, *you don't need to be here for this.* He told me to come home, so I did. They called just a bit ago." Raisa couldn't see anymore. "He's gone home, Raisa. He's gone home."

3

You're alone now Raisa Coen. The voice sounded as if it were smiling and poisonous at the same time. *How does it feel to be 19 and fatherless… poor dear… poor dear…*

Shut up… SHUT UP. You can have no *part of this day!* Raisa squeezed her eyes shut so tight that it hurt. She had realized within the last year that a voice may pipe in unannounced but she had control over whether it stayed.

Raisa suggested to her mother that it would be best for her to drive but her mother insisted that she was fine. Of course. So Raisa was in the passenger seat of her mom and dad's old Buick station-wagon as they drove to her father's memorial service. Just sitting in this car brought back so many memories of her father. For one, this old bucket-of-a-car had the coldest air-conditioner on the planet. It would form icicles on the vents during family road trips. She was sure this had something to do with the fact that her father was a brilliant engineer and always tinkering with cars, planes and lawn mowers. Whenever he was in the garage on a Saturday, Raisa felt like he expected her to sit there with him and wait for a request for a tool, in silence. It was the only way they got to spend time together so Raisa didn't mind so much. Her dad could fix everything and never hired anyone for anything. No plumbers, electricians, painters, carpenters and certainly not mechanics. He even taped together Evert's chin when he split it open nearly two inches wide from a motorcycle wreck.

21

He also had a stern side. Each kid in the family got the belt – once - just to make sure they knew who was boss. Raisa's turn occurred at three years old when she stepped into the street to retrieve a ball. He said she didn't look for cars but even at that young age, she distinctly remembered looking both ways. That incident would forever stay ingrained in her memory… and her rear end.

Raisa also remembered some small kindnesses. They had a pet mountain quail that her dad had rescued during a family camping trip. It lived almost ten years with them. When the bird got sick, probably from old age, her father stayed up all night trying to save it. And on one very rare occasion, her father gave her a loving hug and soft words of encouragement when she was upset and crying about a boy. But even with all of these memories, she didn't ever feel like she knew the person that was her dad. They never talked… about anything. Raisa was just a quiet observer of this man's life.

As they pulled into the church parking lot Raisa was drawn from her reverie by the sight of all the cars.

"Are we late? It looks like everyone is here already." She checked her phone and realized that they were still a half hour early. She and her mother parked and walked through a back doorway and down a hall to where the viewing was to be before the service. Typically, this was reserved for family, but as they got closer, they saw at least fifteen people milling around outside the room and the number of hushed voices from inside the room and echoing down the hallway sounded like dozens.

"Who are all these people?" Raisa was asking her mother but she had walked too far ahead to hear and disappeared into the room. Raisa came near the door and her feet stopped walking. *I can't go in there… I don't want to see this.* She suddenly had a sick feeling in her stomach and her palms were getting sweaty.

There's no law that says I have to go in there. I'll just wait for the service. She moved forward and without looking in the room, she passed it and walked to the chapel foyer, and sat on one of the couches there. For a moment she wondered whether or not she should be crying. How should she act as a mourning daughter? *This whole thing is ridiculous! My dad should not have died! He was only sixty-five years old... he should have fought harder... he didn't care about his family or he would have fought harder!* Raisa was vaguely aware of the tears streaming down her face. *And he was alone... I should have been there! I shouldn't have left! I can't take that back! I... I can't...* She was sobbing now but somewhere in the back of her mind a picture grew, like something coming closer in a stream of water... her father... walking arm in arm with his brothers.

"Raisy?" Her sister Aileen had come to find her. She was gently touching Raisa's shoulder and speaking so tenderly, so compassionately that it could only be pain and love that was in her voice, nothing else. "Raisy, you need to come in. We're waiting for you. *Dad* is waiting for you."

"I don't think I can..." Raisa felt like she was broken into a thousand pieces and it was an illusion that she was still in one.

"Yes you can, Raisy... we're going to say a prayer as a family, and we need you. Come on, I'll be right next to you."

"Okay," was all she could say. Aileen held her hand out to help Raisa up and then to her surprise, did not let go.

They walked into the room. Raisa's eyes took in the scene. The room was full of people. Unwilling to look at the casket, she first looked at Charlotte, who was looking back at her with red puffy eyes and a sympathetic smile. Next to her was Evert, who Raisa could tell, saw no one at all. He was hanging on to their mothers arm, head cast down with his face so contorted, she couldn't decide if it looked like anguish or anger. Her mother,

23

Lona, with glassy moist eyes, (who she could tell could not look at the casket either), had perfect posture and an even voice, thanking those that had come to pay their respects. Her sibling's families were sitting behind them listening and watching. They had expressions on their faces that seem to say, 'I'll catch you if you fall'. Then Raisa looked at her father. She had expected to feel the sensation of drowning, but she felt... the same. Nothing was different.

Raisa let Aileen's hand drop and walked quietly over to the beautiful wooden casket where her father lay. *He would have liked this*, she thought as her hand brushed over the dark manzanita burl with inlays of light birch. She looked to his face lying there against the glossy white satin pillow and paused as if waiting for him to say something to her. "He's not here," she said with quiet wonder in her voice. "This was his shell, but he's *not here*." Raisa looked over to her family with a gentle smile. Their expressions changed into those of peaceful repose as if Raisa was able to push a comforting energy around them. Even Evert's pain seemed to vanish from his face. Aileen gave a beautiful prayer, and the casket was closed.

Walking down the hall following the casket as it was wheeled to the chapel, Raisa heard in her mind, *I love you Raisy.* And in her mind's eye she saw her father's smiling face.

"I love you too, Dad."

Her mother heard her, and smiled.

As they entered the chapel Raisa caught her breath. It was completely full short of the two rows in front that had been reserved for immediate family. Looking around, she realized that she probably only knew a third of them. When she saw Corli sitting in the back row coming up on her left she had to fight the urge to run to her.

24

As they came closer to each other, Raisa held out her hand and wiggled her fingers. She mouthed the words, "Come on, come sit with me *please*."

"Are you sure?" Corli whispered as loudly as she dared. Raisa bobbed her head up and down, so Corli scooted into the line of people and caught up with her. "Can you believe all these people?"

"No, I can't," Raisa said flatly.

They all barely fit into the two pews. Raisa sat with Charlotte on her left and Corli on her right. The opening song, "Nearer My God to Thee", was all it took for Raisa to maintain a consistent flow of tears down her face for the entire service. It made her feel proud to hear a list of her father's accomplishments: his service to his country, his church and his work. But it wasn't until the podium was opened for those that wanted to add their thoughts that it became overwhelming. A line formed, at least twenty and growing, of people that wanted to thank Vincent Coen for helping them in some way.

After the first eight had spoken, Raisa turned to Charlotte with nothing short of shock on her face and whispered, "I had no *idea*. Did you? I mean, when did he do all this stuff? Built a fifty-yard fence... visited every week for a year... took my husband to the hospital... saved my dog...? Why didn't we know about any of this stuff?"

Charlotte had a similar wide-eyed look on her face. "Maybe that explains why he was never available for Back-to-School-Night," she whispered back with the slightest amount of sarcasm.

An hour passed and the line never dipped below six people, but the officiator looked like he was getting anxious. He finally stepped up to say that there was no more time. The woman that he had stepped in front of set her hand on his shoulder and seemed to plead for her chance to speak. With a nod and a wave forward he let her step to the microphone.

She was a fair skinned woman with full lips, light hair and eyes. She looked like she might be in her early forties and had a very graceful way about her. Raisa couldn't imagine where her father would have met her. She didn't quite fit in with the rest of the "church goers". As Raisa looked up at her, she saw a delicate sunshine colored glow begin to spread above and around her. "My name is Gloria Castaneda," she said in a quiet but strong voice "and Mr. Coen saved my life, and my son Devon's life. I will never be able to repay the great kindness that he showed to me and my son. But I will pray for him and his family every day for the rest of my life. Thank you." She lowered her eyes, smiled and made her way back down into the congregation.

Raisa couldn't help but watch her as she walked to the back of the chapel and came to stand next to... *is that her son?* Raisa saw a boy, a little over six feet, dark wavy hair, beautiful light brown skin, an angular jaw and stunning deep-set eyes. He was wearing jeans, a dark shirt and dark jacket. Raisa would have blushed at how handsome she thought he was but instead she gasped at what else she saw. He had a visible energy around him in fading rings of coppery light that increased in size as they came nearer to the ground. They seemed connected to the ground and they seemed to move with him and because of him, under his hands. It was vivid to her eyes, not like the faint mists that she had seen gathering around others. It was mesmerizing to the point that it was all she could do to stay in her seat. She had the strongest desire to go to him...

"Raisa!" Corli was tugging on her arm and breathing into her ear as Raisa snapped her head around. "Close your mouth!"

"But do you see...?"

"Yes, I see, but the song is almost over and you have to go to the cemetery next. Just a few minutes more." Corli entwined her arm with Raisa's and left it there to try and keep her "present".

During the last prayer as everyone else had bowed their heads, Raisa turned to look at him again. The energy around him smoothly pulsed, almost like it was in time with the beat of his heart. As if in answer to her gaze, he slowly lifted his head and looked directly at her. Then above her into the air. Then back to her face.

4

Devon tossed his coat over the back of a chair as he entered his apartment and fell into the couch with a heavy sigh. He had just dropped his mother off at her condo after Mr. Coen's funeral. His roommate and best friend, Penley Gray, was at work, a local pizza joint, so he had the place to himself for a few minutes at least. He pulled a can of coke out of the mini-fridge they used for the base of their makeshift coffee table and turned on the game console. While he waited for NBA 2K11 to load, his mind wandered back to the service and the girl he had seen sitting in the second row with the rest of Mr. Coen's family. She was beautiful. Her coloring reminded him of his own mothers. But she had long curling golden hair. Her face was shaped like a heart that gave her a child-like look, but her pale blue eyes were electric and almost fierce. That would have been enough to catch his attention but when he saw her, there was a light. A bright white plume of energy streaming up in rays and spirals toward the ceiling that seemed to change with each of her breaths. It seemed to connected to her it at her chest and neck. And though it dimmed slightly like wisps of smoke as it went up, it *felt* like if she were outside, it could reach the heavens. When the service was over he tried to get to her but there was a battalion of her family separating them and he knew they were headed for the cemetery. *I'll see her again.* There was no doubt in his mind. *It'll be soon,* he had determined.

The apartment door crashed open and startled Devon out of his thoughts. He realized that he had been watching a loop of his game and had never actually started playing. "Pen, could you be a little louder? I don't think the nice people at the end of the complex heard you."

"Sorry, I couldn't reach the door knob," Pen said with a half smile. "Can you grab some of this stuff?" His arms were full with a guitar case, amp, lunch box and several paper bags with unknown contents. He hadn't left himself a way to put anything down.

Devon jumped up and grabbed the precariously perched amp and lunch box. "You could have made two trips…"

"What, and let someone walk up and steal my stuff? No way!"

"Why do you haul all this crap around with you anyway?" Devon knew the answer. Pen would feel like only part of a person if he didn't have his guitar with him. But he had to chide his friend, it was his job.

"Because you never know when you might meet someone that will break into song and need some back-up," Pen said brightly. "Life is a musical my friend. Hey, thanks for your help."

Pen began to scatter his belongings around the apartment, as if the amp *belonged* on the kitchen chair, no-one would trip over the guitar in the entry way and the bags he set on the kitchen counter had reached their final destination. Devon rolled his eyes. He loved Pen like a brother but he knew that as long as they lived together, he would be the tidy one.

Pen peeled his t-shirt off and shook his blond, California sun bleached hair out of his eyes and headed down the small hallway. "Hey Dudley," he yelled back from his room. Pen called him that when he wanted to tease him about being mopey. "I'm jumping in the shower, but I've got a gig tonight over at The Rabbit Hole.

29

We're just opening for the headliner but it should be cool. You should come with."

Devon pushed the start button on the controller. He had no intention of leaving the apartment tonight. He felt a familiar dark flare of pressure at the edge of his mind and systematically pushed it away.

A half hour later Pen emerged in a fresh t-shirt and jeans and damp hair. Devon was in the second quarter of his basket ball game and losing terribly. Just as he was going in for a lay-up, Pen exclaimed, "Dude, you suck!"

Devon missed the shot. "Thanks for that..." he paused the game, stood up and stretched. He headed for the kitchen, opened the cupboard and pulled out a bag of fried pork rinds and started munching.

"*Bleck*, how do you *eat* that stuff?" Pen's face contorted playfully.

Devon held the bag out. "Here, try one..."

"Not if my life depended on it." Pen laughed.

"Then don't knock it."

Pen's face smoothed from joking to hesitation. "Hey, I know you don't want to go out tonight. What with that guy's funeral and how your job has been going..." not that he wanted to open up the subject, he just wanted Devon to know he got it, "but it's Saturday night. You know...," and then Pen's smile reappeared. "*Saturday night's the night I like. Saturday night's alright, alright, alright, whooooo...*"

Wow, he's singing already. Devon leaned down to put his elbows on the counter, popped another cracklin' in his mouth and sighed a little while he was chewing. He didn't think he could be jovial for his friend tonight. "I don't know man, I think I'm just going to hang out here and play vid's tonight. But thanks for the offer."

30

"Your loss." Pen knew when not to push, but he wasn't quite done. "I met a girl though." Devon stopped crunching and looked at him unblinking, more to tease him than out of shock. "And she said she would come tonight." Devon stood up straight. "And…" Pen garnered a crooked smile and raised one eyebrow, "she said she would try and bring a friend." Pen wasn't sure if this would work *for* or *against* him.

"No, man, I'm not ready for *all that* tonight." Devon suddenly lost his appetite and tossed his nearly empty bag back into the cupboard.

Pen's shoulders dropped. "That would be 'against'," he muttered under his breath. "Okay. But you know where I'll be if you change your mind." Pen finished getting ready, re-gathered his music gear and was walking out the door within fifteen minutes. "Bye, Dudley." He grinned and ducked as Devon chucked an empty coke can at the door, and was gone.

Corli sat on the bed watching Raisa stand at the window. Raisa looked out over her family moving around in the back yard. The sun had set and Corli had been searching for the right things to say to Raisa since they had returned from the cemetery. It made Corli consider their friendship and how she had always felt the need to protect and comfort her. This was a strange notion since Raisa had always seemed like the strong one to her. Raisa had always dealt with her problems head on. She always considered everyone's feelings, made a plan and systematically worked things out. She always seemed calm and cool, even at the worst of times. Like now.

Raisa turned and looked at Corli. "Thank you Corli."

"For what? I feel like a total lamo…"

"Just for being here and being you. I don't know what I would do without you." Raisa moved to the bed and gave Corli a hug.

Corli squeezed the tears in her eyes so they wouldn't come out. "I'll always be here for you... I love you."

"Huuoooh." Raisa threw herself back on the bed. "It's all so *emotional*. I just don't want to think about it anymore."

Corli saw her chance. "Well, I wasn't going to say anything but if you want to get out of here, I have a great idea!" She couldn't help herself. A smile crept over her face along with a blush. Her eyes went to her hands and she started twirling the tassel on a pillow.

Raisa sat up, her eyelids lowered and her head tilted as she looked at her friend. "What's going on?" She asked curiously.

Corli bounced on the bed once. "Well, like I said, I wasn't going to say anything, you know, on a day like this... you would never want to go out or anything. I mean, your whole family is here and everybody is so sad, and it just wouldn't be right to leave, and I would never go - "

"*Corli*," Raisa grabbed her friend's hands. "What?"

Corli blushed again. "Remember guitar boy?"

"Oh, yeah. I haven't had a chance to ask you about that... It seems like a month ago but it's only been a few days. Well?"

"His name is Pen, that's short for Penley, isn't that cool? And he is really nice. We talked for two hours at the Taco Shop after his gig was over. He is *so* cute. And I thought I was making a fool of myself, I was saying the stupidest things, until he asked me if I wanted to come to a show he is opening for tonight. He said to bring you along. Of course, that was before..."

"Hmmm… I don't know. The timing isn't great…. But I'm so stoked for you! You have not *really* liked anyone since Tommy Snodson in ninth grade!"

"Don't remind me…" Corli made a gagging sound.

Raisa went back to the window and looked down to see her mother talking with Charlotte. Things seemed to be wrapping up. "Who am I to stand in the way of true love? Come on, I'll ask my mom and see what she thinks. I'll only go if she seems okay with it. But you *have* to go."

They locked arms, walked down the stairs and out the sliding glass doors to the back yard. Raisa's mother gave them a warm smile as they approached. She hugged them both, which caught Raisa off guard. Her mother was very rarely openly affectionate, and *never* the instigator.

"Mom, this is no big deal," Raisa started to feel awful for even asking, "but I was wondering if I could go with Corli to – "

"Of course you can, Dear. Go. Get out of here and relax a little. You've been shouldering too much of this. Besides, music will do you good." She turned them both around and gave them a little shove.

Raisa was vaguely aware that her mouth was skewed as she processed her mom's actions. Corli looked at her as they walked back up to her room. "Hey, how did she know we were going to listen to music?"

"Good a guess as any, I suppose." Raisa was wondering the same thing when the smiling face of her father flashed across her vision.

Raisa closed her bedroom door behind them as Corli looked down at her 'church appropriate' dress. "Ugh, I don't want to wear *this*. I didn't bring anything to change into though…"

33

"I'm just wearing jeans and a t-shirt." Raisa wasn't in the mood to have to think about an ensemble. "You're welcome to anything of mine."

Corli rolled her eyes. "Like anything you have would fit me."

Raisa gave Corli a once-over. She had always been jealous of her shiny brown hair, curvy figure and the fact that she was the perfect height, five-five. Raisa, on the other hand, was basically the opposite of curvy and five-eight, which basically made her taller than eighty-five percent of all boys she met. "Actually, a bunch of stuff I have will fit you." She pulled out a black shirt that had gathers around the waist. It was too short for her but too cute to get rid of. And a skirt that she didn't feel comfortable wearing since she had graduated from high school because of how short it was on her now. "These will be perfect."

Corli changed into the outfit and looked at herself in the mirror on the back of Raisa's door. "Wow... who knew?"

"You should come shopping here more often." Raisa said with a smile as she pulled on her skinny black jeans and a white t-shirt.

When they finished their outfits off with flats, earrings and a couple of bangles, Raisa grabbed her bag and headed for her bedroom door, Corli on her heals.

Raisa felt a little lighter now. As heavy as the day had been, she knew that her dad was okay where he was and she thought her mom knew it too. As they headed down the stairs, suddenly Raisa stopped short. So abruptly that Corli almost ran into her. *What a horrible daughter you are to leave your mother tonight, Raisa.* The voice was more nasty and disdainful than normal. Raisa felt tears instantly surface.

"Whoa, are you okay, Raisa? What's the matter?" Corli asked.

Raisa turned and looked at her. "Are you sure we should go? I mean, maybe I should stay with my mom."

Corli took Raisa's hand. "You heard your mom… I don't know but I think she *wants* you to go…"

Raisa thought about what a contradiction her mother's actions were to the voice and realized that it was trying to play her guilt. It had a reason that it didn't want her to leave the house. She *knew* it somehow. *No*, she replied to the voice, *you won't make me feel bad for this*.

As they pulled away from the house Raisa still felt conflicted but vowed to herself that she would let it go.

Corli grabbed the CD case. "Can I pick the tunes?"

"Sure, go for it."

Corli knew this collection well. She skimmed quickly through and popped in her favorite dance mix. "Atomic Dog" started playing and Corli started snapping her fingers and dipping her head to the beat.

Raisa smiled. Corli had always been with her whenever anything important happened. She thought of Corli at the service just a few hours ago… *Oh! What was his name? Devon!* Raisa was shocked that she had let the image of the boy with the coppery rings slide so far in her memory. Now the memory of him came back like a flood. She let her mind wander and wonder what he was like, and if she would ever see him again.

"Hey, Corli, do you remember that boy – "

"Wait! You just passed it!" Corli pointed and bounced in her seat.

Raisa made a U-turn and came back to the driveway for The Rabbit Hole. It was aptly named because it was a basement of a building that no longer existed. Only a small ten by ten building with Broadway style lights on the outside was there to sell tickets and issue entry to the staircase that spiraled down to the venue.

They were in an industrial area a block from the beach. Raisa took a deep breath as they got out of the car to taste the moist, salty air. She loved the beach, especially at night.

Pen had left their names at the door so all they needed were their neon pink wrist bands indicating that they were under drinking age. "These are so embarrassing," Raisa whispered to Corli.

They carefully descended the staircase into the dimly lit club. They stood at the bottom for a few seconds so their eyes could adjust. Both of their eyes went round and Corli took in a staggered breath. "What are those eyes, Raisa –" Suddenly Corli was jerked off the ground and lifted away from her.

"You came!" Pen appeared from seemingly nowhere and embraced Corli in a spinning hug.

Raisa blinked several times, looked around the room and at Corli. What had seemed like burning eyes lining the entire room were now only strings of twinkling green Christmas lights. Corli had disengaged herself from Pen and was awkwardly searching for a response to his welcome.

Pen, suddenly aware that his greeting may have been a bit overzealous, threw his hands behind his back and smiled sheepishly at Raisa. "Hi, I'm Pen." He held his hand out to Raisa.

"Great to meet you, Pen. I'm Raisa."

"The best friend," he said warmly. "I've heard a lot about you."

Corli smiled a toothy grin and shrugged her shoulders. "It was all good, I promise."

Pen slid an arm around Corli and waived a hand at Raisa. "Come on, I saved you guys a seat. It's not at the front, sorry, but it's still good."

Still slumped on the couch, Devon's mind kept wandering from the game, which kept his score at an all time low. His brain toggled between his work situation and the girl from the funeral… his mom mixed in there every once in awhile. He switched the game off without saving and turned on the TV. As he clicked from channel to channel he was struck by how much bad news there was. News had always been generally negative, but now it seemed excessive. It seemed like at least once a month a natural disaster or terrorist attack would monopolize all the stations for a week at a time. He thought it was no wonder that the voices he heard spoke of him being worthless and small. Who could possibly make a difference in this messed up world? What was left to save?

Indeed, Mr. Castaneda. Devon didn't push the wicked voice away this time. *You think that your petty little accomplishments make you a leader but you are mistaken. You will never amount to anything. You are too afraid to –* "Enough!" Devon switched the voice off. "There you go with your morbid curiosity…" he said cynically to himself. "Talking to yourself again, Devon……… I need to get out of here."

Devon made a snap decision to take up Pen on his offer. He took a jacket out of the coat closet by the door, grabbed his keys and locked the door as he left the apartment. He also didn't feel like driving. Instead he decided to walk the two blocks to the shuttle that would take him down to Main Beach and walk the block back into the venue.

As he looked through the windows of the shuttle bus he saw people on the sidewalks walking in different rhythms, in front of the beach town storefronts. Couples, families, friends with friends… and he thought about Pen. He was really the only person he had ever been close to. The only one that had stuck around. He didn't think that Pen actually knew him all that well, but they did have a connection. Simpatico. He thought about the girls he tried to date over the years and he could honestly not put one name with one face. So he'd given up on that type of relationship a while ago. Not that he didn't have offers -

A green flash caught the corner of his sight from a crosswalk outside and he spun in his seat to see if it was what he thought it was. A boy not ten years old was staring back at him and sneering with green fire in his eyes. Devon held his gaze as long as he could but the bus had moved to the next block. Then he saw a man weaving in and out of other pedestrians as if he were trying to keep up with the bus. Just before he dropped out of view he also turned to gawk at Devon with the same smoldering look. "This is weird," Devon grumbled. "Two in one day." The shuttle arrived at Main Beach and he got off with everyone else. He looked around as he stepped to the pavement as if he expected to see a dozen pairs of fire-lit eyes waiting for him. But there weren't.

The walk to The Rabbit Hole from there was uneventful but all the same, Devon could feel his body wound tight as a spring in anticipation of a confrontation.

His name had been left at the door and he thought about how nice it was that he didn't have to wear those awful wristbands anymore since he had turned twenty-one a couple of months ago. He made his way to the bottom of the steps. As he lifted his face to the dark club he instantly saw at least nine pairs of glinting eyes in shadowed faces that appeared to be placed strategically around the perimeter of the room. The alarm that coursed through his veins increased his heart rate. He immediately looked to the stage for Pen and with a shot of relief, saw that he was already performing with his partner and seemed oblivious to any danger at all. As he looked back to the crowd a light flashed in his eyes so bright that he had to raise his hand as if he were out in the noonday sun without sunglasses. The light subsided and he readjusted his eyes. "It's *her*." He moved, almost with a will not of his own, toward the girl. He felt an overwhelming need to protect her. She had no clue that there were so many "undesirables" in this place.

His stride was cut off by two sneering, green-eyed men. "Where do you think you're going?" they said almost in unison.

Devon's stance was steady and almost menacing. "I was just coming to tell you and your pals to go find somewhere else to hang out. We wouldn't want to start anything here, would we?"

"We have as much a right to be here as you do, Boy." The man spit through his teeth as he spoke.

Devon's fists tightened at his sides as he stepped into the two men, preparing to fight.

"Now let's not be hasty gentlemen…" Someone, a boy not much younger than Devon, slid in between him and the snarling men. He had to look up at Devon but didn't seem to be intimidated in the least by his own smaller stature. His eyes glinted and his face looked mischievous, although, Devon could not imagine what in this situation would conjure that type of expression. He addressed Devon, "Unless you want to involve your friends over there, "tipping his head to the table where Corli and Raisa sat, "I suggest we take this outside."

"Fine." Devon was willing enough to take the full brunt of the situation. He knew that as soon as Pen realized what was going on, he would be at his side, regardless of the odds. And the girl… he had to get them away from her.

"Oh, by the way, I'm Garik. Come along." He casually passed Devon, sauntered to the stairs and began climbing without looking back. The two men, now smiling wickedly, turned him around roughly and shoved him toward the stairs.

Devon turned to look behind him after climbing the first few stairs. The remaining six were falling in behind them. *Good, they're all clearing out.* Now he only had to worry about how to get *himself* out of this spot, not his friends. He listened to the music from the club, Pen's music, as if it were miles away. *Wanted Dead or Alive, the Bon Jovi song... how strangely appropriate.*

As soon as they were outside the front doors, several hands were on him and dragging him, with quite some effort, across the parking lot and behind a building to its loading dock. Devon wasn't sure what kind of business it was but the stench there was overwhelming. It had a chemical and rotten eggs sort of smell.

"Far enough." Garik had turned and held up his hand.

"What now tough guy? You gonna have your thugs beat me up?" Devon was anxious to get free for just a moment. He could see that most of these people were cowards. Now that there was more ambient light he realized that two of them were even girls. No matter what the voices said, he was not afraid of a fight.

"What a *brilliant* idea." It sounded like Garik was commenting on art or poetry. Then with a tip of his finger, six men and two women bore down on Devon like a pack of wild dogs. They kicked and punched and bit and clawed at him. Devon defiantly landed a few punches but there were too many of them. He felt warm blood on his face, dripping down his neck and sharp pains in his ribs, they were broken, he thought, almost for sure. After a few minutes there was not a place on his body that wasn't affected. They began to tear at his cloths. Devon thought that the only thing keeping him conscious was the reek of chemicals. But he couldn't hold on much longer. Just as he was about to go under, he heard Garik say something, though he couldn't be certain what it was. Everything was running together... words, laughs, grunts, color, flame, darkness. But it

40

must have been, "stop", because there was no one touching him now.

"Now..." Garik was bending over him. He was close enough that Devon could feel his hot breath. "Maybe now we can have a little chat."

"What," was all Devon could muster in a low rasp.

"After all this time you must be wondering what we are." Garik began, sounding suddenly light hearted. He straightened up and flourished his hand in the air.

"I know you bleed." Devon spit out the blood collecting in his mouth and did his best to clear his head. "I've gotten a piece of your kind before. And honestly, I don't give a sh -"

"Of course..." Garik continued with a half chuckle, ignoring the comment he had cut off. "We're completely human... with a few benefits. But we are chosen. Chosen by... let's just call him The Great One for our purposes tonight. I'm one of his favorites actually," he added as an off-hand note that seemed to please him just to say it. "To keep the likes of you in check. Keep tabs on you, as it were. Don't get too full of yourself, Mr. Castaneda. It will only hurt you and the ones you claim to love. And one last bit of information for your pathetic little brain... a simple request, really." Garik's voice dropped to a rasping whisper as he knelt down and raised his fist in the air. "*Stay away from Raisa Coen, or you'll regret it.*"

As Devon saw Garik's fist coming towards his jaw, all he could think was, *Raisa, that's her name.* And then all light went out.

5

It was still and dark, all except for the floor lamp clicked to the lowest setting in the living room, as Raisa quietly unlocked the door and stepped into her house. The clock above the stove in the kitchen read 12:36am. It felt a little different somehow knowing that her father wasn't upstairs in bed, hearing her come in, and then turning over to go to sleep. Sometimes he would pick that time, just as she came in late at night, to get up and have a glass of milk toast, just to let her know – no conversation needed - that he knew she was home. Her mother, she knew, was sound asleep.

She stepped lightly up the stairs and into her room. Raisa let her mind wander as she brushed her teeth, washed her face and changed into her tank top and pajama bottoms. She thought about the music tonight and how much it lifted her soul, how happy Corli seemed to be with Pen and how cute they were together. Not to mention the amount of static they collected out of the air when they were near each other. It was such a visual thing for Raisa that it was almost hard to believe that no one else could see it. Pen was actually an excellent guitar player and had a pretty good voice. All of his songs were covers though, and she wondered if he had any original stuff. It would be fun to sing with him... not in public – just the thought of that made Raisa's heart beat one panicked beat – but just hang out and work on some harmonies.

Feeling perfectly prepared for sleep, Raisa slid into bed. The coolness of her pillow on her face felt wonderful as she closed her eyes. Sleep took her quickly for a change.

♦♦♦

The courtyard in the middle of the old Mediterranean-style house was full of warm sunlight. Raisa sat at a small, old worn and rustic dark wood table across from a boy. His hair was loosely curly, dark but sun-kissed and his skin was the color of light maple syrup. He wore a plain white t-shirt that accentuated his coloring... and his toned muscles. Raisa looked to his face but it was as if she was looking through a camera lens that she couldn't focus.

Wait... I'm having the same dream! Raisa's heart sped... she could feel it in her chest as she lay in her bed as well as while she sat at the table. She felt determined this time to see the boy's face. She looked at him across the table from her and willed his face to become clear. But, no matter how hard she tried she couldn't see him. He was still smiling at her though. She looked around her at the cantaloupe colored courtyard.

"Dad!" He wasn't in the same place he had been before, creating a wall of protection for her and the boy to escape. This time he was standing in the sun. There was no feeling that this dream would turn into anything bad. "Can you help me, Dad? I want to see his face. I need to know who he is." Raisa's voice was happy but pleading.

"I'll show you Raisa, but you must understand. This is both important and dangerous." His voice was almost musical. But Raisa couldn't help but think she heard something there that she had never heard before, an edge that almost sounded like – fear.

43

"You must promise me that you will be careful. And always listen to me."

"Of course I will, Daddy." As she looked at her father she realized that she had so many questions for him. Was this real? Did he know about the people with the fire in their eyes? Why does all of this happen to her? Just as she opened her mouth to ask one, he raised his hand, gesturing to the boy, smiled the most loving smile she had ever *felt*, and vanished.

Raisa's heart skipped a beat. Now she could feel the boy's gaze resting on her and she knew that when she turned to look at him, she would see his face. But... didn't she already know who it would be? Why did this feel like *the* most important moment of her life? *And I know this is a dream.* A barrage of emotions crashed down on her all at once like a wave of the ocean catching you off guard. Her eyes moved away from the sunny patch of terracotta where her father had stood and into the shade of the table where they sat. "*Devon*," she said, her mind reeling.

"Raisa." The sound of her name coming from his mouth almost stopped her heart. He took her hand gently in his and raised it to his lips. She watched his long dark eyelashes as he closed his eyes and kissed her hand, his broad strong hands tenderly holding hers. Slowly his face came back to look at hers and as he smiled at her, a warm electric current swam through her entire body.

And that was all. The dream was over but Raisa held on to that last frame securely and let it float through her mind. She imagined them talking to each other about anything, laughing together and singing together. She added music to the background, Anthony Hamilton, "The Point of It All". Why not? It was her dream. She knew it was silly – almost like it had been when she had induced dreams about Heath Ledger when she was eleven years old. But she didn't care… it was a happy place to rest.

♦♦♦

The glow in Raisa's room when she woke up proved that she had slept well. Early morning could light up her bedroom like a photographer's studio but this light threw only soft shadows. A peek at her clock confirmed it was just after ten. She hopped up, set her iPod to the blues genre, plugged it into her speakers and cranked up the volume. She knew her mother was still at church so she sang as loud as she wanted while she showered, dried her hair, threw on long shorts and her number forty-eight white t-shirt and straightened her room. Stevie Ray Vaughn's version of Red House was just finishing up when she heard the garage door open and shut.

"Hi, Mom," Raisa called as she made her way downstairs to the kitchen. She grabbed a leftover dinner roll out of the fridge and sat down at the table with her mom.

"Good morning Raisa. You look rested today. How was your time with Corli last night?" Lona looked perfectly groomed as she always did, especially so when she went to church, in a modest straight skirt, low pumps and a white silk blouse. She was looking at some paperwork that had been on the table for a few days while she spoke to Raisa.

"We had fun… the music was pretty good. The best part is that I think Corli has a boyfriend now." Raisa smiled wide as her mother looked up and over her reading glasses.

"Well, that's wonderful for her. Is he a good boy?" It was difficult, Raisa thought, for her mom to ask a question like this without sounding judgmental… but she did try.

"He's a really good guy, Mom. And he's a musician!" Raisa expected more scrutiny about Pen after *that* comment.

45

From what she could tell, all parents thought musicians were freeloading troublemakers. Instead, her mother completely surprised her.

"Oh, how nice for you to have a new friend that's a musician! That will be so fun for you to have someone to sing with." Was her mother being serious? "But, what about you? Did you see anyone... what I mean to say, is have you met anyone recently?"

Raisa was barely processing the comment about Pen being a new music buddy and now her mom was asking if she had met someone? *What does she know? But she couldn't... nobody knows about him. No one could! At this point it's make-believe.* Raisa decided to change the subject instead of walking into *that* minefield. Her mom didn't truly seem to be looking for an answer anyway because she was still reading her paperwork. Raisa thought about her father since it seemed that *he* knew about Devon, whether in her dreams or for real, she didn't know. "Mom, do you ever feel like Dad is... with you?" Raisa half expected her mother to nervously brush off her question.

Her mother took off her glasses and smiled a very sweet and wistful smile as she looked through the window and spoke. "Last night when I laid down to go to sleep... well... do you know the spoon position?" She held her hands up and demonstrated with them as she looked at Raisa. Her expression would have been the same if she were asking if the dishes were clean.

Raisa had unconsciously covered her face with her hand and was now peering at her mother between her open fingers. Sure that her face resembled a tomato, she said, "Um, yeah, mom. I guess I do."

"Well," she continued very matter-of-factly, "that is how we used to sleep, so now I know he is here when I feel him curled up to me." Her eyes started to go glossy.

Watching her mother's eyes tearing up helped Raisa quickly overcome her embarrassment. "That is really so very sweet Mom." She couldn't imagine how hard it was for her mother to be without her father after so many years. Raisa expected that she must be in shock. Just as Raisa was considering talking to her mother about her father in a little more depth and the present tense, the phone rang. The caller ID flashed as she picked up the phone. "Hey, Corli."

"Hey, Girl! How are you? I'm fantastic, by the way…" Corli giggled and Raisa laughed back with complete understanding of what had Corli so giddy.

"You're *spun*, Corli," Raisa teased her.

"I *know*, isn't it cool! Hey, why don't you come over for lunch? My dad made a huge antipasto salad. It could feed China."

Raisa chuckled. "Okay, I'll be there in a few."

Pen woke up with the biggest smile on his face he could ever remember. As a matter of fact, he didn't think he *had* woken up smiling… ever. *Who wakes up smiling?* He laughed to himself at how ridiculous he felt. He immediately wanted to tell Devon about his night, and about Corli… *She is so cool.* He pulled on some drawstring pants and ventured out of his room to see if Devon was up. Devon's neon lit NHRA clock in the hall said it was 12:45ish. He knew it wasn't exactly right, but he couldn't remember at the moment if it was fast or slow. He thought to himself how glad he was that he didn't work on Sundays. His 'roomy' wasn't in the living room or kitchen so he started back to the hall to try his bedroom. "Hey, Dev…" Devon's door wasn't pulled closed so Pen gave it a little push. He was preparing to do something snarky, like yell or jump on Devon's bed, when he realized Devon wasn't in his room either. "Devon?" He called a little louder. "That was stupid," he mumbled. "It's not like he would be hiding in his closet." He checked anyway. "Nope. Not in there."

Pen made his way back to the kitchen and poured himself a bowl of cereal. He was trying to remember if he had missed something about Devon's plans last night. It wasn't as if Devon always told him what he was doing, but he usually had some idea of where he was. *Oh well*, he thought. *I'm sure he's somewhere sleeping it off. He'll miss me soon enough and come home where he belongs*, he joked to himself. *Maybe I'll call Corli and ask her over...* he looked around the apartment, *after I've cleaned this place up a bit*. He dug into his cereal and started to contemplate how exactly he would go about cleaning. It wasn't something he did often.

Raisa was sitting on the porch swing in Corli's backyard listening to her gush about Pen.

"... and then he *kissed* me! Just a peck, but can you believe it? It was *so* sweet. I hate it when guys try to eat your face right off the bat, don't you? I was *so* happy that he wasn't like that."

"That's so awesome, Corli. Just remember to take it slow, okay? You know how you get sometimes... your enthusiasm knows no bounds." Raisa gave her the "tone" but with a smile.

"I know... don't worry. I think this is really different. I feel like we were destined to be partners in... something." She sounded a little serious for Corli.

"As long as it's not partners in crime," Raisa teased. Corli's expression didn't lighten. That never happened. "What's wrong, Corli?"

48

"I wanted to talk to you… about those… at The Rabbit Hole last night, remember those people when we first got there? The ones with the flickering eyes? I only saw them for a second and then they were gone. But those are the ones, aren't they? The people you have been talking about all these years. I didn't think you were crazy or anything, but after all this time… I had never seen them before. Why did I see them last night?"

Raisa felt stunned. Years of her "burden" or "gift", she wasn't sure which, flew through her mind the way they say your life does when you are dying. There was a mixed feeling spreading in her heart. On one hand, she no longer felt crazy and alone in the universe… just like that, confirmation that she was not seeing things all this time. On the other hand, if more than one person can see it, it is very real… and it probably means they are in some kind of danger. She took a deep breath and brought herself back to Corli. Now that she was looking *at* Corli and not *through* her, she realized that she had never seen Corli so affected by anything. That being said, she was actually impressed with how well she was handling it. Raisa wasn't sure where to start. "Wow…okay… um, I remember you saying something, but then Pen grabbed you – scared the crap out of me by the way, I thought you were being abducted – and then there were the strands of green lights so I wasn't sure…. I don't know why you can see them now. Maybe it was because there were so many. The most I've ever seen at one time is two, but it seemed like there were at least ten of them, didn't you think?"

"Yeah, I think so…. Did they leave or just disappear?" Corli was starting to wring her hands.

Raisa hadn't seen Corli do that since Raisa had broken her arm in the mountains when they were fifteen. "I think they were still there for at least a little while. I can kind-of feel them… it's like they make me feel depressed. I think our brains just don't want to process something that's not normal so we block it out," Raisa took another deep breath. She was so worried about whether or not Corli was going to be able to deal with... whatever this was. She had been dealing with it all her life... but now.... She steadied herself.

Raisa decided that it was time for this to be a completely open topic between her and Corli. After all, it would be the safest thing for Corli, now that she could see. "I think something is happening, Corli. I don't know what, but I can feel it. I think that is why you can see them now, why there were more of them and why other things are happening to me too." Raisa joined Corli on the blanket they had spread on the grass.

"What other things, Raisa? You have to tell me everything."

"I know, from here on out we will both tell each other anything that happens, okay? "

"Deal." Corli grabbed Raisa's hand, more for security than anything else. "So what else?"

"Well, the one thing that has been going on almost as long as the green eyed guys is the voices. I know they don't come from the same place... I think the green-eyed guys are just evil people. But the voices I hear in my head, the bad ones, are forceful, demeaning and demanding. They try to manipulate me into doubting myself, into thinking I'm the most horrible person in the world."

"That's awful Raisa! Why didn't you tell me?"

"Well, you hadn't seen any little green men so I didn't want to add to how crazy you already thought I was."

"*Raisa, I would never – "*

"I know... Corli, you are the only person I have ever really trusted in this whole world. You know that right? Remember Garik back in the sixth grade? I knew I could trust you back then when I told you about him."

50

Corli was looking squarely at Raisa. "Swear? We stick together on this right?" She felt more than ever, Raisa was going to need her.

"Swear." They hugged on it. "Oh, and there are good voices too! And…" Raisa broke into a big smile, "my dad."

Corli's eyes widened. "What do you mean "your dad"?"

"He comes to me, in my dreams and in my head. It started the night he died, I guess. Or maybe not really for a few days… the first time he spoke to me while I was awake was at the service. He's going to look out for us… I know it."

"Sounds like you might get to have a better relationship with your dad now than you did when he was alive……….. Sorry, that was pretty terrible of me to say." Corli was cringing at herself.

"No, it's okay. It's probably pretty accurate." Raisa made eye contact with Corli so that she would know she wasn't upset with her.

"So, is there anything else?" Corli was determined to get all the information necessary and be brave about it.

Raisa was trying to figure out how to explain about Devon when Corli's cell phone rang.

"It's Pen!"

It was obvious that any other conversation along these lines would have to wait. Corli chatted and giggled for a couple minutes and then hung up her phone. "He wants us to come over to his apartment and visit him! Oh, Raisa, come with me… *please.*"

Pen hung up the phone. He had just turned to look at the living room in case it needed any more "cleaning" when he thought he heard his name being called from outside. He pushed the blinds aside and squinted out the window to see if he was hearing

51

things. There was a man, slouched and leaning on a post near the driveway to their complex with his head down. It looked like a homeless person had had too much to drink. As he tried to decide if he recognized anything about the slumped figure, he raised his head, cried out again for Pen and crumpled to the ground.

"*Devon!*" Pen was out the door and sprinting. He slowed his movements as he approached Devon, wrapped his arm around him and helped him up. "Shit! Damn-it Devon! What the hell happened to you?" Devon didn't speak as they slowly made their way to their apartment door. Once they were inside, Pen took Devon straight to his room and eased him onto his bed. "What do you need first? God, should I take you to the hospital?" Pen looked Devon over. He realized that if he wasn't dead at this point, he would probably be okay. But Devon was a mess of shredded cloths and dried blood. Pen tried to re-group and took a deep breath. "Dude! What is that smell?"

"Water. And ice." Devon ignored the last question. He knew that he smelled like rotten eggs and chemicals. He should go back to that place sometime, he thought, and find out what that business was. They could bottle the smell and use it as a weapon. He was glad to be home. Just the feel of his bed under him was already helping.

Pen was back in a flash with a bottle of water and two bags of frozen peas, purchased for just such an occasion. While Pen cleaned Devon up – making many trips to the bathroom for wet towels – Devon held the peas in the most necessary spots and relayed the events of the previous night, leaving out the part about Raisa and her friend being there… and the part about Garik's warning to stay away from Raisa. He felt bad withholding information but he hadn't told his best friend about the girl from the funeral yet.

Pen was obviously upset. "Why didn't you yell at me? Screw the stupid gig! I could have helped you! Kept you from getting your ass kicked! Those weird green eyed idiots have never been able to touch us when we're together."

"Don't sweat it. What doesn't kill me makes me stronger." Devon didn't want Pen to feel guilty. Since he hadn't told him about Raisa yet he wouldn't understand that he just wanted to lead them away. "It's not that bad... I got a nice long sleep last night... I'm feeling better already." It was his best effort at keeping it light. He sat up slowly. The pain in his ribs was the worst but he thought it was bearable. *Cracked but not broken*, he thought. "Help me get some cloths on and let's go out to the living room. I'm starving."

Devon was settled on the couch and Pen was bringing him random items from the kitchen to eat, some trail mix, a dried out piece of pizza and a yogurt. "Yogurt? Really?" But he was almost done with it.

Pen was about to tell him that he was lucky they had any food at all, when there was a knock at the door. At first Pen was puzzled – then, he closed his eyes and smacked his hand to his forehead. "Oh, *crap*. I *totally* forgot. I invited Corli and her friend over right before you got here." Pen hurried to the door and pulled it open. "Hi guys." He didn't sound very inviting but it was the best he could do under the circumstances.

Devon decided that he should probably move off the couch and retreat to his room so as not to scare Pen's guests. He was trying to get around the couch and into the hall before they came in, but he didn't make it. He looked up, planning to give a short apology while on his way, but he froze in his tracks. His heart jumped into his throat and stuck there rendering him momentarily speechless. When he did find his voice again, he sounded completely out of breath. "*Raisa!*"

"*Devon!*" Raisa's legs almost gave out from under her and she had to steady herself with the back of the couch. Her heart was pounding so hard that she was sure everyone could hear it.

The light bulb in the table lamp sizzled, popped and blew out.

Pen's mouth was hanging open. "What's going on here? You two know each other?"

Corli looked from Devon to Raisa to Pen. "Your roommate is Devon Castaneda?"

Devon came to his senses first, but with it came panic. "*Shut the door Pen,*" he ordered. Pen instantly did as instructed. "Raisa, what are you *doing* here! *You shouldn't be here!*"

Raisa's mouth dropped open in shock. They had never even spoken… and how did he know her name… so what could possibly make him so angry with her that he would behave this way. This was definitely not even remotely close to what she dreamed their first meeting would be like. Anger seemed to be good for snapping you out of shock and Raisa could feel the blood starting to burn in her face. "Well, if me being here is *that* much of an *inconvenience*–"

"No…." Devon realized how he must have sounded. He stepped toward Raisa and grabbed her wrist to keep her from turning and leaving. "No, wait." His voice was soft and apologetic.

Devon was standing inches from Raisa. The touch of his fingers and the tone of his voice, now, melted away any indignation she was feeling just a moment ago. She felt like there was a magnet in her chest trying to pull her closer to him. She wondered if he could feel it too. She finally noticed his injuries; it had taken a minute to see past the shifting copper

54

light. His lips were swollen and split, black blood was pooled under the skin around his eyes and all of his body that she could see was covered in cuts and bruises. "What *happened* to you?" She reached up to touch his face but pulled her hand back once she realized what she was doing.

Devon wanted the world to go away so that he could have this first moment with Raisa but he knew that wasn't going to happen. He reluctantly let go of her arm and turned to look at Pen. "We have to get out of here. We have to leave. All of us, it's not safe." Devon went to the window and peered through a crack in the blinds, searching for any sign of Garik and his goons.

"What is going on here?" Corli demanded.

"I'll tell you later... right now we have to leave. Pen, drive you and... I'm sorry, what was your name again?" What would have been a smile under better circumstances curved the edge of Devon's mouth.

Pen stammered. "Oh, sorry. Dev, this is Corli and... apparently you know Raisa."

"Right. Corli." He turned to look at Raisa again. "And, Raisa, if you could drive..." He wasn't willing to let her out of his sight right now, "Pen, you follow us."

No one had any arguments. They quickly helped Devon on with his shoes and jacket and were out the door.

Raisa listened to Devon's directions through her ringing ears. The whole thing felt surreal. Devon was with her... in her car... speaking to her... and just one day after she had first seen him. She rolled down her window to feel the rush of air to confirm that she wasn't dreaming. They were driving through residential streets toward the hills. Devon was diligently looking around and behind them, obviously to make sure that they weren't being followed. But she had no clue by what. Corli and Pen were in

Pen's car following closely. Raisa was watching the road. Suddenly she could feel Devon's eyes resting on her... a familiar feeling, she thought. As she turned to look at him, just as she had in her dream, he looked away.

Devon began studiously surveying Raisa's car. Raisa couldn't tell if it was to avoid looking at her or if he really knew what he was looking at. "Nice ride. Seventy-four?"

"Seventy-five, actually." Raisa's Mustang was her favorite worldly possession. "It's a V8. My dad rebuilt the engine and restored it for me. He bought it from a junk yard. You should have seen it when he had it towed to our house. He had to use a flat-bed... it wouldn't even roll. It was a mess." Raisa bit her lip as it dawned on her that she sounded like an idiot... going on about her car when Devon was clearly very alarmed about something and had been through an obvious trauma.

"Your dad was a great man..." Devon seemed to be having a memory of some kind but quickly let it go and resumed his watchfulness.

Raisa wasn't sure how to respond to that. It certainly brought a lot of questions to her mind that she hadn't thought of before now. This definitely wasn't the time though. "Yeah, he is pretty great."

They rode in silence for a while, Devon only speaking to give directions as needed. There was so much he wanted to say... so many questions... he wanted to know everything about Raisa. But, now wasn't the time. "Turn left here." Devon pointed to a street named Cleveland.

It was a brand new street on the edge of what was obviously a growing community nestled at the foot of some rolling hills. As they turned, Raisa saw house after house in various stages of construction. But the unfinished development looked as though it had been abandoned. Raisa gauged by the discoloring of the wood framing that it could have been weeks or even months.

"Pull into the first driveway up there." Devon pointed. There were four large model homes coming up on their right. The one he pointed to had a three-car garage. Raisa turned in and Devon pulled himself carefully out of the car. He limped around the corner of the house and reappeared a minute later. Raisa guessed that he had turned on the electricity main. He went to a keypad on the frame of the door and punched in a code. The double garage door opened and he gestured for both Raisa and Pen to pull in. As they all got out of their cars, Devon pushed the button by the door that led into the house and the garage closed. He pulled his keys out of his pocket and unlocked the door.

As they were walking into the house, Pen stopped and looked at Devon. "I thought you said things weren't going well at work?"

Devon looked back at Pen with a slightly crooked smile. "I said that things weren't going how I planned, not that it was going badly." He led them to a stairway that led down to the basement. They all stopped at the bottom of the stairs to adjust their eyes to the dimly lit space. The small high windows must have had blackout blinds on them. Devon clicked on a light.

"Oh *wow*." It was Corli that spoke first. "This place it sweet." They all looked around them at the lavishly furnished and very large room. There was a pool table with a large bar, mini kitchen and stools at the far end, and a huge sectional couch with a low round coffee table across from a big screen TV and media wall nearest to them.

"Okay, guys," Devon had seen this type of thing plenty of times and wasn't distracted. "We need to talk." The four of them sat down on the couch.

Devon led the conversation. He recounted his experience with his evil voices, the guys with the fiery eyes that he and Pen had encountered in the past, the ones that seemed to be following him yesterday and the attack at The Rabbit Hole.

"I hear them too... the voices." Raisa cut in.

Devon looked at Raisa in surprise. "Wow... okay... do you know how to keep them out?"

Raisa felt so strange talking about this with someone that understood, "I can't anticipate them, but I can shut them off."

"Well, maybe we can work on that together sometime." Devon looked at Raisa. And she looked at him back. Now he knew that this was something they shared, the voices. He felt like they were almost consoling each other, with that look.

"I hear good voices too though." Raisa was glad to have something good to contribute, and something to break her gaze with Devon. "My dad especially, ever since he died..." she trailed off. Before anyone felt awkward she moved on. "You said the guy that attacked you told you his name. What was it?" Raisa asked.

"He said his name was Garik," Devon replied.

Corli gasped. "Do you think it is the same Garik?" Corli asked Raisa with wide eyes.

"It has to be.... It makes sense since he has lived in this area for so long." Raisa told Devon and Pen how she had been able to see the green glint thing since she was in grade school and that Garik had been the first she had seen. "He has been around me a long time... I think he has been watching me and trying to scare me my whole life."

"Those green-eyed people... whatever they are, are creepy. They are such brutes!" Corli was frowning.

"Garik said they were just regular people, with "benefits" though. I would guess that they have an added amount of cruelty

58

because of this *one* guy that they follow. And possibly some telepathy since hearing voices in your head seems to be an integral part of this."

"We should have a name for them," Pen piped in. "Something to identify who we're talking about without having to describe the green, glinting, fiery-eyed, now-you-see-them, now-you-don't guys."

Corli was nodding in agreement with Pen and crinkling her brow in thought. "*I* know, they are brutes and cruel… let's call them bruels." She sounded pleased with her creativity.

"Hmm… not bad." Devon nodded. "Bruel it is. So let's go over everything we know again. One, the four of us can see bruels. Two, we know that the bruels are after us, watching us and reporting on us to this *one* bad guy. Three, for some reason, that we don't know yet, they don't want Raisa and me to be together." Raisa felt herself flush. "Four, Raisa and I hear disturbing voices that seem to be in league with the bad guys. Five, Raisa also hears good voices and has direction from her father." Devon dropped his head and stared at the carpet. He wondered why he didn't hear any good voices, guardians that cared for him. *Now is not the time to feel sorry for yourself, Devon.* He chastised himself and raised his head again. "Now, the big question is – why?"

All four of them sat in silence, bewildered.

"Well, it's something we all need to think about." Devon stood and went to one of the windows to make sure they were completely covered. "If anyone has any ideas, no matter how stupid it may sound, make sure you speak up. Nothing, obviously, is outside the realm of possibility."

Pen stood up too. "Maybe the two of you are going to save the world!" Pen gestured with both his hands to Devon and Raisa and grinned.

59

Everyone laughed a little and the tension in the room seemed to ease just a little.

"We should stay here until it gets dark." Devon was checking the only other basement window. "No one followed us here. I'm certain. This will be our emergency meeting place. Never turn on any lights but here in the basement and always park in the garage and close it. I'll have duplicates of the inside garage key made for everyone. You have to turn on the main power on the side of the house before the garage will open. I'll leave a flashlight on the ground right below it in case it's dark. The code for the keypad is Two-thousand-twelve."

"Referring to the end of time on the Mayan calendar... cute." Pen smirked.

"Nothing so momentous," Devon replied with his own grin, "it was just the target completion year for the housing project."

"I have a question." Raisa raised her hand like she was in class and looked at Devon. "Won't we... or you, get in trouble for being here?"

"Good question." He smiled a full smile at Raisa for the first time and saw her blush because of it, which made him blush. Although he didn't think it was as visible on his skin as it was on hers. He cleared his throat.

Pen was watching Devon. It was odd for him to see his friend flustered, but in a good way.

"Uh, yeah, since the housing slump, this whole place has kind-of closed up. I'm running a skeleton crew to work on the houses that have been sold, and if there is any new interest, I am also in charge of showing the model homes on a case-by-case basis. So... we should be fine." Devon looked embarrassed, and it didn't help that no one had anything else to add.

"Hey, since we're going to be here for a couple more hours," Pen was always good at fixing awkward moments, "I'll show the girls some self defense moves… can't hurt, right? Show you how to beat the crap out of those bruels."

As long as you both remember," Devon looked at Raisa and Corli sternly, "first, *run*… only stand and fight if you have no other choice. Got it?" Both girls nodded quickly.

"I'll start with Corli." Pen held his hand out and pulled her up. He showed Corli some basic evasion tactics and showed her how, if she had a knife in her hand, it worked even better…" Raisa watched but had a hard time keeping her eyes from drifting back to Devon. She gave up.

"Here," Devon reached out his hand toward Raisa. She froze, not completely sure what he was asking for. "Let me see your phone. I'll program my number and Pen's into your speed dial, number four and five. And I'll put your number in mine… if that's okay."

"Oh, of course." Raisa wished that she would stop getting flushed. She handed her phone to him. Their fingers brushed each other. They both felt a static *snap*. Raisa sucked in a quick breath.

Devon reached his hand out and almost grabbed hers. "Are you okay?" He actually looked concerned, like a little shock would have hurt her.

"I'm fine." Raisa smiled without blushing for the first time. *Thank God*, she thought. "I'd hate to see us in an electrical storm. We might blow something up." Devon smiled a beautiful smile at her and she had to remind herself to breath. "Devon," she started a question before she was even sure of what she was going to ask. *Crap*! She moved a little closer to him on the couch to stall and looked up at Pen and Corli in the process. *Okay, I got it.* "There is something else." Devon's brow wrinkled. "Oh, no, it's nothing bad… look over at Pen and Corli." Raisa pointed at them and Devon turned and looked.

Raisa continued in a low voice, almost a whisper. "Do you see anything when you look at them? Maybe in the air above them, or between them?"

Devon squinted his eyes a little, which wasn't hard to do with how swollen they were. "Wow... there's... um... a smoke, or a mist. Its kind-of around them." He turned back to look at Raisa. "You see it too?"

"Yes. I've seen it around Corli before. And I saw it the first night they met. It comes and goes. I think it is strongest when they are... being... well, close. And I have seen it around another person." Raisa's eyes dropped to her lap.

"Who?" What Raisa was saying had Devon thinking about the light shining from her. He had gotten used to it now so it was almost like he just saw through it. But it never went away. Now he wondered if *she* knew it was there.

"Your mother, at the church when she was talking at the service." Raisa looked up to see Devon's reaction.

That was the last person Devon had expected Raisa to name. "What? *My* mother? Wow. I wonder if I just haven't been paying attention."

They didn't speak much after that. Raisa switched between watching Pen teach Corli and watching the copper light reverberating around Devon. It was beautiful, and mesmerizing. But she could look past it now if she wanted to so that it didn't distract her. A lot like focusing and un-focusing your eyes.

Quite a bit of time passed and Raisa decided that she had better try some of the defense stuff. When she stood up to start mimicking Pen's moves, Corli said that she was going to find some glasses for water and headed over to the bar. Pen started from the beginning with Raisa.

Devon thought that he could look at Raisa forever. Just having her in the same room with him lifted his heart to a feeling he had never experienced before. It made him feel lighter and more confident... like he could accomplish anything... he thought it was odd that he felt that way when they had known each other for a whole three hours now. He watched as his best friend worked with Raisa and Corli, and the afternoon stretched in to evening.

"It has to be getting close to seven." Devon started thinking about what he was going to have to say to Pen, Corli and Raisa next. He wasn't looking forward to it, especially with Raisa. He checked the time, got up and looked out the window to see if there was any daylight left. "It's dark now," he said. "One more thing before we leave..." Corli and Raisa had worked up a sweat and gladly abandoned the impromptu self defense class. The three of them gathered closer to Devon. "Pen, you'll drive us, and Raisa, if you could take Corli home."

Pen started to object. "Hey, Corli and I were – "

"Here's the thing, guys... we can't see each other." He looked heartbroken as he stared at Raisa. "It's the safest way. They can't know that we know."

"Do you really think it's that dangerous?" Raisa's eyes were stinging but she willed them to stay dry. *This is stupid*, she thought. *Why am I so emotional... could it be because you've only said five words to the literal man of your dreams?* Raisa asked herself. *Oh, I don't know...* Raisa started to answer herself then shook her head. "There's got to be another way..."

Corli's started biting her nails in anticipation.

"Can't we just meet here?" Pen questioned. He hated to go against his friend but he agreed with Raisa.

"No." Devon was stern but not unkind. "We need this place to stay secret and if we are coming here all the time, that won't last. It's too risky. We can only come here for extreme

63

emergencies. We can talk on the phone, but only when you are sure that no one is listening. It has to be this way," he looked straight at Pen, "to protect the girls."

The group broke up. Devon told them to drive away in different directions. Everyone, including Devon, was unhappy.

"You're right, Devon," Pen sounded sympathetic as they drove home, even though it was just as difficult for him. "It's the best way."

"I hope so." Devon was having a hard time discerning his feelings. Did he feel so rotten because he was selfish and wanted to see Raisa every day, regardless of the danger it would put her in? Or, was it because he wasn't truly positive that this was a good idea?

Raisa pulled into her driveway and turned off her car. She sat for just a minute, convincing herself that this whole day was not a dream. The thought that she could not see Devon again made her nauseous. She sighed heavily and got out of her car. Just as she was crossing the corner of the lawn to get to the front door, she saw something dart from behind the bushes out of the corner of her eye. She was going to run but it was too late. She was knocked over from the side and thrown to the ground. She had the wind knocked out of her and began to roll to her back. She was instantly pinned to the ground by someone that jumped on top of her. She looked up. "*Garik!*" He was holding a knife and he raised it over his head.

"I *told* you that you would die, Raisa!" Garik sneered as he brought the knife down hard into Raisa's chest. "Nosh will be so proud of me," he grunted with the effort he had put into the blow.

Raisa heard the sick, sliding suction sound as Garik pulled the knife free from her body. She watched him stand, triumphant over her, and then turn and run into the night. Her vision darkened and blurred, but she saw one point of light. "Daddy?" Her eyes closed.

6

Lona heard Raisa's car drive up and park and waited for her to come in the house. When several minutes passed and the front door hadn't opened, she looked out the window to see why. She saw the car parked in the driveway, but no Raisa. She looked out to the street and then over to the front lawn. *"RAISA!"* She tore open the front door and ran to her daughter laying flat on the grass. She saw the dark blood on Raisa's chest that was spreading and soaking her shirt. *"Oh dear God, no, no NO!"* With tears streaming down her face and a strength she didn't know she had, she lifted her daughter in her arms and carried her limp body into the house. She set her down gently just inside the front door and pulled Raisa's cell phone from her jeans pocket. With one hand she pressed down, hard, on Raisa's wound and with the other dialed 911. She held the phone just long enough to hear that someone was on the way.

As she pushed on her daughter's chest with both hands now, she whispered to her, "Raisy, do you hear me? You can't go, honey... you can't." Her tears dropped onto the back of her hands and mixed with her daughter's blood. *"Vince... Vincent... Help her! Do you hear me? Help her!"*

Lona heard the sirens coming up the street. "Just a few minutes more, Raisy." She could still feel the faint heartbeat under her hands. "You can do it." The paramedics rushed in the door and took over for Lona, swiftly lifting Raisa to a stretcher and whisking her out of the house. Lona looked down at her hands, covered in blood, and felt the ache in her arms from being

66

in their clamped position for so long. She absently regarded the space where Raisa had been and wondered how to get blood out of hard wood floors.

A paramedic appeared and wrapped a blanket around her. "You're in shock, Ms Coen. Come on. Let's get you into the back of the ambulance with your daughter and get you both to the hospital." The young man in the emergency services uniform guided Lona on, behind the stretcher and up into the vehicle. As soon as they were on their way, Lona reached into her pocket, pulled out Raisa's cell phone, and called Corli.

Nosh was a handsome man; he knew it was true.

The penthouse floor of one of the tallest buildings in downtown Portland had been gutted and turned into one massive, open concept office. Three walls were completely paneled, along with the floors with coffee colored wood. The third was solid, glass windows overlooking the lights of the city. The ceiling was pressed copper. The oversized doors opposite the glass were the only way in or out to the elevator behind them. There was very little furniture. An ornate chaise lounge on top of a Persian rug was positioned in front of a grand fireplace where low flames burned. Next to that a bar was set into the wall. It held a nineteen thirty-seven bottle of scotch and several cut crystal glasses. On the opposite side of the room sat a large mirror that leaned against the wall there. Centered in front of the window glass but facing inward was a single oversized mahogany desk. There were no chairs in front of the desk, just one behind. It was night, and the only light came from the city and one single alabaster banker's light on the left hand side of the desk.

A thick and sickly green haze hung in the air of the room. Nosh sat at the desk, his eyes closed, a fiendish smile on his face.

67

In the shadows of the room, twenty-four women were arranged in a large, open circle. They were barefoot and dressed the same, in loose, thin, black robes that hung to the floor. They stood, statue-like, with their faces cast down.

One spoke, in a low, monotone voice. As she did, a small, smoldering, greenish-black flame sputtered alive above her. It gave off the smoke that did not dissipate. "Sir, it's Marlow. I am watching the boy, Curtis. He is still not aware of his Lasteire." The woman speaking didn't move.

"Good. Carry on." Nosh sounded indifferent. The fire that had been attached to the woman lowered and went out.

Another woman spoke then, but her voice took on a depraved quality. The flame above her spiked alive. "It's Garik....... I have stabbed Raisa Coen in the heart! She is *dead*."

Nosh stood, his hands on the desk. *"Eeeexcellent."* His voice sounded like slithering snakes. "You've done well, Garik... so far. If what you say is true, we are victorious! Continue watching the boy. I may....... don't kill him just yet."

Corli grabbed her mother's car keys and flew out the door. As she drove toward the hospital, she had to remind herself that getting in an accident wouldn't help Raisa, so she slowed down. "I need to call Devon." Just the thought of saying out loud what had happened to Raisa compressed her throat and instantly brought rivers of tears to her eyes. "No!" She had to get a grip. She wiped her face with her sleeve and opened her phone. She was very glad at this moment, as she was driving, that Raisa had put Pen and Devon's numbers in her phone on speed dial. She held down the number four.

"Corli? What's up – "

"*Devon*," Corli was instantly sobbing again. "It's Raisa. She's been stabbed in the chest. I'm… I'm on my way to the hospital… hurry!"

Devon heard the dial tone in his ear but it didn't compute. "What? I just saw her…… this can't be right……"

Pen walked into the living room where Devon was standing, unmoving. "Dev, what's wrong?"

Devon looked over to his friend, pain and regret written all over his face. "Can…… you drive me to the hospital? It's Raisa."

Pen quickly gathered his keys, phone and wallet, took Devon's arm and left the house. He thought to himself that this must be what it looked like when someone was in shock.

Lona sat in the emergency waiting room, the blanket that the paramedic had given her still wrapped around her shoulders. She had been praying and begging for her daughter for the last fifteen minutes and didn't see the doctor until he was standing right in front of her. She looked up at him with pleading eyes but couldn't make her mouth form any words. She stood up instead.

"I've never seen anything like it, Ms Coen," the doctor began, "the place that your daughter was stabbed should have killed her instantly. But it's as if the weapon slid perfectly between her vital organs and large arteries and veins. She has lost a lot of blood and we need to go in and do some repair work, but I think she is going to come out of this just fine. We're prepping her for surgery right now." The doctor placed a hand on Lona's shoulder and smiled. "That's one talented guardian angel she's got there."

Lona hadn't realized that she was holding her breath. Now, as the doctor walked away, she let it out, half laughing, half crying as it came. She sat down again before her knees gave way. *Thank you, Vincent.*

Devon could barely breathe as he sat in the passenger seat of Pen's car on the way to the hospital. "This is my fault," his voice was barely audible. "I made the wrong decision. I should never have let her go home alone."

"You could never have known that this would happen, Devon. You were doing what they wanted, to keep her safe." Pen knew he was grasping, that Devon would never forgive himself, but he had to try.

"They're evil, Pen. I should have known that what they say makes no difference. Oh, God… if she… you don't understand, Pen. If she… - "

Devon. Stop. It's going to be okay. Raisa is going to pull through. Devon felt a warm rush cover him from head to toe. He felt peace and comfort overpower the despair that had threatened to overtake him. He bent his head and let the knowledge that he could hear Raisa's father, Vincent, wash over him for several moments. "She's going to be okay, Pen." Devon looked up at Pen, his face wet and filled with relief. "It was Raisa's dad. He just told me. She's going to be okay."

Pen looked at his friend. He felt, just at this moment, gratitude for 'the powers that be'. Devon deserved to have the good things in life too, not just the bad breaks he knew Devon had experienced since he was small. They pulled into the parking lot at the same time Corli did.

The space that Raisa saw around her as she sat in a small comfortable chair was light and airy. There didn't seem to be any walls but she didn't feel like she was outside either… she wondered how that could be. In the next instant, or several

70

minutes later... she wasn't sure which, her father was sitting beside her, smiling and reaching for her hand.

"Hello, Raisy." Vince sounded ultimately happy and all-together worried at the same time as he spoke. He took Raisa's hand in his.

Raisa took in a short breath, "I can *feel* you." She looked at her father with wonder.

"Pretty nice, huh." He gave her hand a little pat and chuckled.

"What am I doing here, Dad?" Raisa felt confused.

"It's just a visit, Sweetheart. Don't worry."

"Okay." She didn't feel like she should worry. As a matter of fact, she was having a hard time grabbing onto any solid thought at all. Everything felt washed away and peaceful. She could have been content sitting here forever it seemed.

"Raisa...... Raisa," her father called her back to his attention. "You have a great task ahead of you. I want you to promise me that you will never give up. Okay?" His eyes were searching hers.

"Never give up... I promise." Raisa felt her father's hand squeeze hers. The light space slowly faded away and it was dark now. But she could still feel him holding her hand.

Raisa's eyes ached and felt like they were glued shut. She tried to open them but was not having much success. She still felt the pressure of someone holding her hand but it didn't feel like her fathers. This hand was firmer and larger, and very warm. Raisa's heart sped up a little and she became aware of a beeping sound that matched it. She finally willed her eyes open and Devon lifted his head from the side of her bed, having heard the change in her monitor. He smiled a tired but grateful smile and

Raisa thought she saw his eyes well up for a second. But they were still a little swollen and bruised so she couldn't be sure.

"Hello, Sunshine," he whispered quietly as he moved closer, never letting go of her hand.

"How long have I…" Raisa's throat felt like it had gravel in it. She tried to clear it but was slammed with a pain in her chest for the effort. She winced.

Devon's free hand flew gently to her cheek. "Are you okay?" His voice lowered and his forehead wrinkled. "Water… I'll get you some." He let her go and picked up the mauve plastic pitcher and cup on the hospital nightstand.

Raisa watched his steady hands as he poured the water and brought the cup to her lips. She took several sips. "That's better," she whispered.

"Why don't I talk and you listen." Devon sat and took her hand again. "Then you will only have to ask questions about things I don't cover." Raisa gave a slight nod and smiled. "Well," he started, "this is your third day in the hospital," Raisa's eyebrows arched. "Yeah, they actually kept you asleep so you could heal better… your mom is here. She's down stairs getting breakfast." Devon looked down appearing to study the threads in the blanket on her bed and smiled with a slight chuckle, "I think she likes me." He looked back up at Raisa.

"What's not to like," she whispered with a smile. Her eyes went to her hand in Devon's.

He saw where she was looking and reactively let his hands fall away from hers. "Sorry… I… I've been here a lot. And, I guess I've been doing that a lot." He repositioned himself sitting back in his chair.

Raisa thought that she could deal with that. After all, he was here. That was enough in itself to make her happy. She used her eyes to signal to Devon to tell her more.

"Okay." Devon wasn't sure what Raisa remembered and didn't want to alarm her so he stuck with the easy information. "Corli has been here a lot, of course, and Pen too. I think I heard your mom talking to your brother and sisters and they will probably show up today." Raisa pinched her eyes shut for a second; suddenly thinking that she must look entirely awful after lying in this bed for three days. "They took you off the medication that was keeping you asleep early this morning so I've……. we, have just been waiting for you to wake up. I guess that pretty much covers it." Raisa gave him the 'yeah, right' expression, but she didn't push for more.

"Raisy, you're awake!" Her mother came into the room and straight to her daughter's side, bending to kiss her forehead.

On her heals followed two nurses. They began fussing around Raisa, taking blood pressure, asking her how she felt, telling her that she needed to get up soon and use the restroom on her own. *How embarrassing*, she thought and glanced sideways at Devon.

Devon took his cue, pointed to the door and mouthed that he would be back.

In the flurry of activity, Raisa learned that if she got out of bed and did well, that the doctor could choose to release her as soon as the following day, with the strictest understanding that she would not be allowed to do anything strenuous for quite some time. Thinking of home then, brought back the mental picture of her front yard at night, the feeling of being knocked to the ground and of Garik sinking that knife into her. Her chest tightened and her monitors started to sing. Devon's face instantly appeared in the doorway as the nurses scurried to her side. Her mother brought her hand to her mouth.

"I'm okay." Raisa stated a little unevenly. The nurse taking her pulse noted that it was slowing again and Devon disappeared, again. "So, can I get up and get cleaned up? And I'm pretty hungry." Raisa was still speaking very quietly but moving around a little was helping her feel stronger.

One of the nurses looked at Lona, "Are you okay to help her?" Lona nodded. "Okay, just give us a buzz if you need us, and take it slow." They cleared out, taking the haphazard energy and clattering noises with them.

"Mom," Raisa wanted to get this discussion in before too much time passed, "what happened... I mean, I remember what happened. I suppose I still need to tell you about that. But, how bad was it?"

Lona looked relieved. She could tell by the tone in her daughter's voice that she was going to be okay with everything that transpired and that she didn't need to keep anything from her. "I found you on the lawn, maybe only a minute after... it happened. I called 911 and we were here within fifteen minutes, I would say. The doctors say that it is a miracle... your wound is here," she softly touched the spot over Raisa heart on her chest, "and they said that you had a guardian angel because nothing vital was cut."

Raisa smiled, "I know, I saw Daddy. It was him."

That was just a little bit more than Lona could handle. Her eyes pooled up. But she quickly sniffed, dabbed her eyes and stood. She went to her bag, pulled out a pair of sweat bottoms and turned to Raisa with a smile.

"Oh, Mom... that's fantastic."

It was late afternoon and Raisa sat tilted up in her bed. She had learned very quickly in the last few hours what *not* to do. Don't cough, bend over, raise your arms, swallow large bites of food, take deep breathes, lay flat or sit too straight up for too long. Basically, move as little as possible. But when she wasn't

74

moving, there was actually very little pain. Raisa had watched the 'changing of the guard' when Pen had shown up, talked to Devon outside for a few minutes and taken his place in a seat right outside her hospital room door. Devon had explained that he had to go to work for a few hours but that Pen would not leave until he got back around 5pm. Raisa had started to protest, saying that she would be perfectly safe here in the hospital, but received a look from Devon that told her that she might as well save her breath. Her mother sat in a chair by the window quietly reading her Readers Digest and Corli split her time between Raisa's bedside – switching the channels mercilessly with the TV remote – and chatting with Pen outside until he would shoo her back into the room so that he could pay attention. There were several times that Raisa saw Pen stand and study something or someone for several minutes before he sat down again. Corli noticed it too. One time when this happened, Corli and Raisa looked at each other and both knew what the other was thinking. Pen was a great guy, a wonderful friend to Devon, a perfect specimen of a boyfriend for Corli, a fast friend for Raisa, but most importantly, someone you could trust with your life.

"Is anybody home?" It was Aileen peering around the door frame and hesitating before she walked in, holding Raisa's two year old niece, Kristy, on her hip. Charlotte followed right behind. "Raisa, we're so happy that you're ok –"

"Raaysee!" Little Kristy tried to dive off Aileen's side to get to her Auntie. Aileen stopped her but not before Raisa flinched, and in turn reeled with pain.

"*Ah*, that would be another 'don't' Raisa..." she gasped to herself, her voice completely breathless, "no flinching."

Aileen was mortified and walked out with Kristy, looking back apologetically at Raisa as she went.

"Hi, Sis." Charlotte took Aileen's vacated spot by the bed. "You look pretty good."

Raisa was still a little breathless but regaining composure. "Yeah, Mom helped me get cleaned up. Thanks."

Raisa expected questions about the attack and was dreading it. She was trying to formulate answers in her head that would deflect more questions. She didn't want to talk about any of it with her family.

But Charlotte had a completely different line of questioning in mind. "So who is Devon?"

Everyone went silent and looked at Raisa. Even Corli and Pen from outside the door turned to look at her through the half window.

Raisa flushed and sputtered. She could feel the blood pulsing through her veins around her injury. "He's a boy... I met... on Sunday...." She couldn't believe how ridiculous it sounded. *He's the man of my dreams and quite possibly my future husband.* She managed an impish smile.

Corli and Pen grinned and turned back to monitoring the hall. Lona was smiling too but when her daughters looked at her, as daughters often do – because moms have all the answers, it vanished and was replaced with the 'don't-look-at-me' face.

Charlotte looked at Raisa again. "Well?"

Just then Evert walked through the door. Raisa gave a little sigh of relief.

Corli stood up and walked in behind him. She didn't trust Evert. She knew how mean he had been to Raisa growing up. She stood at the foot of Raisa's bed with her arms crossed, eyeing Evert.

Raisa saw Corli's posture and half expected to look over at Evert only to see that he had sprouted green fire in his eyes. But, they were solidly brown – like chocolate. He had a little bit of

76

that tortured look on his face again and Raisa felt an impulse to comfort him. "Hi, Evert. You don't need to worry about me, I'm fine."

"Good," was all he could muster.

Aileen and Kristy reentered the room and Raisa's family started talking to each other. Corli relaxed. Raisa felt happy that they were all there for her. Quite a difference from how she felt when she was a kid, she was thinking. A white patch appeared in her vision and Raisa saw her father standing in front of her like someone had pulled a transparent movie screen down in front of her. With the palm of one of his hands turned toward her, he spoke. "Do you know why Evert was so rough on you all those years?" Raisa nodded her head slightly back and forth. "It was all meant to be, Raisa. Everything was to prepare you. Evert made you tough, so that you wouldn't shrink away from trials. He also helped you to see that just because someone does something unkind; it doesn't mean they are evil. Everyone has their trials, Raisa." He turned and looked at Evert. Raisa could tell that he wished he could comfort his son the way he could comfort Raisa. He turned back and they smiled at each other. Her father dropped his hand to his side, and he was gone.

After awhile of visiting, a nurse came in and remarked that Raisa needed her rest. She took her vitals as she unhooked her IV and several of the monitors, leaving only the one for her heart that was under the bandages. "There… that should make you much more comfortable tonight. I don't see any reason why you won't be able to go home tomorrow. Provided you *rest*." She looked around the room to drive home her point.

The point was taken. Raisa received her cheek kisses from Aileen and Kristy. Evert patted her hand; it reminded her of their father. And Charlotte told her that she wasn't off the hook about Devon as she winked and waved goodbye.

Raisa startled awake, forgetting where she was. In seconds, however, it all came back. She yawned – carefully. *Who knew visitors and dinner could wear you out.* Devon was sitting in the hall now instead of Pen, Corli had fallen asleep curled up in a chair and her mother was simply sitting and looking out of the window. She asked her mother how long she had been asleep and Devon, hearing that Raisa was awake, walked into the room.

He came to the side of the bed and smiled. "Pen said, 'if you want a pizza just let him know what kind and he can bring it by when he gets off.'"

Corli sat up and stretched. "Ooooo... bacon and pineapple, yum. I'm going to go get a soda." She walked out and Devon stole her seat.

"Hello..." There was a knock on the open door. Lona, Devon and Raisa looked over to see two fully armed policemen standing there. One had a metal note pad and was writing something down. They stepped into the room. "I'm Officer Stevens and this is Officer Miller. We have to file a report whenever there is a criminal incident reported by the hospital. Do you mind if we ask a few questions?"

Raisa and her mother nodded mutely. No one had thought about the police. Raisa realized how odd that would be if the situation were normal. She also wondered why she wasn't surprised that her mother hadn't involved them.

Officer Stevens addressed Raisa. "Do you know who did this to you?"

Raisa was trying to think fast but everything was jumbled in her brain. She obviously couldn't tell them the *whole* story... they would lock her up in a loony bin. She quickly decided that as little information as possible without lying would be the best

78

option. "Yes… well, sort-of. I know his first name, that's all. It's Garik."

"Do you know Garik?" he asked flatly. Officer Miller was still taking notes.

"I know *of* him. I've seen him in school before, when I was younger."

"Do you know of any reason why he would want to hurt you?"

Raisa's heart skipped a beat. She wasn't sure how to answer, but then she realized that the simple truth was perfect. "No, I don't."

The officers continued asking questions but of a more generic nature, addresses, times, things like that. It sounded as if they were wrapping up when they asked one more question. "Do you know of any other trouble that Garik has been involved in?"

Raisa glanced at Devon but tried not to look obvious about it. Devon, ever so slightly, shook his head. "No." She lied.

Lona decided that was enough. She stood and gestured that the officers should follow her as she spoke. "Let me tell you what I saw while I walk you out." They followed her out the door.

Corli, soda in hand, passed them in the hall and came back into the room with her teeth clenched. "Wow, guess we should have seen that coming. Did it go okay?"

"Yep, she did great." Devon winked at Raisa. "I think they are going to go the 'gang' direction." Lona stepped back into the room. "Good work, Mrs. Coen, you handled that nicely."

"It was just time for them to go," Lona brushed the front of her skirt with her hands. "All in a day's work." She cracked the slightest smile.

Devon looked at Raisa then. A long look. Corli could tell with a girl's intuition that Devon wanted to talk to Raisa, but not with any great purpose, and not with an audience. It was time for her to clear the room. "Wow, it's getting late… and I bet my parents won't recognize me when I go home… so I think I'll go surprise them. Besides, you're not fooling me anymore, Raisa. I bet you could do one of your perfect cartwheels right out of this room."

"Cartwheels?" Devon sounded perfectly primed to tease Raisa. He and Raisa barely noticed as Corli grabbed Lona's purse and handed it to her. They said their goodbyes and Devon and Raisa were alone.

Devon turned off the bright overhead light and moved his chair so close to the bed that he had to sit on the edge of it and angle his legs straight down. He set his hands at the edge the bed. "Raisa, can I hold your hand… again?"

Raisa raised her hand up and set it in his. "You don't need to ask… you can take either one of them anytime you want." Raisa felt like she was on a first date with someone she had been admiring for a year. She was grateful for the low light in the room. With no makeup and a hospital gown for a shirt, she didn't feel like she was anywhere close to pretty. At least her mother had helped her do her hair. Devon, on the other hand, looked gorgeous in a black t-shirt and jeans, even with the still present but healing cuts and bruises she could see on his face. She imagined that he would look good in a potato sack too. She looked at his face with its rich color skin, exploring his endless eyes, his high and prominent cheekbones, the lines of his jaw, and the perfect soft skin of his neck. One of the feelings she had felt in her dream started to spread through her… she felt heat erupting in different parts of her body. She started to feel woozy, almost drunk. *Easy, Raisa… don't want to set off your heart monitor.* She collected herself and looked at Devon's whole face, not the individual pieces.

He was watching her with amusement.

"What?"

"All we seem to do is stare at each other. Not that that's a bad thing… how about we get to know each other? You know, talk about the normal stuff." *Because I* need *to know everything about you.* Devon was wondering at this feeling that was building inside him. He had never wanted to commit to memory everything about a person like he did right now. Even in a hospital gown, there was something about Raisa that was almost… regal.

"So what would you like to know?" Raisa felt no reservations. She had a feeling that she could tell him anything and he would get it.

"Hmmm…" Devon wanted to make it relevant, "what are your three most favorite things in life?"

You, you and you? Okay, this is important… be serious Raisa. "First is music… for sure. I think it is what keeps my soul alive… hard to explain. Sometimes I feel like singing my life, at random, like I'm in a musical or something. Then I have to remind myself that people would think I'm nuts."

This made Devon happy. "You know you have a kindred spirit in Pen, right? "

"Yeah, I have actually been thinking about asking him if I could sit and sing with him, kind-of like I used to do with my sisters. And I love all music, rock, alternative, R&B, hip-hop, jazz, classical, even a tiny bit of country. But my favorite is blues. Nothing like the blues to stir your soul…" Raisa wondered if she might sound like she was getting carried away with the topic so she let the sentence die.

"So… number two?" Devon's eyes were smiling.

Raisa put her head back and closed her eyes. "The ocean, especially at night. The moon on the waves, cold sand in your

81

toes, the roar of the waves crashing, and the taste of the mist... it's majestic."

Devon felt her reverence for what she was explaining. "You make it sound wonderful. We'll go together sometime. And, three is?"

Raisa wasn't exactly sure how to make this one clear but she didn't want to over think it, so she dove in. "The spirituality that is in the world and in me and in everything... how it is all connected. You know how everyone is always quibbling about what religion is right, science verses religion, is paranormal real or a scam? Well, I believe that it's all one thing. Individuals are given opportunities that make sense for them and they have the free will to pay attention or not. But I see that people are confused. I think there is so much more going on than our small brains can comprehend. I think that if we could see the big picture, everything would make sense. So we have to have faith... that God loves us and it will all work out." Devon was staring through Raisa. "I haven't explained it right... it sounds like nonsense - "

"No..." Devon was taken aback. He had always questioned the world and everything going on in it. He had always felt that there seemed to be no purpose with how divided everyone was. But what Raisa had said, seemed to give definition to the chaos for him. "No, it makes more sense than you can imagine." Devon sat quiet for a minute processing everything that Raisa had just shared with him. He loved how her mind worked. It was so uplifted, so optimistic and... contagious.

"My turn. Tell me your three." Raisa was anxious for this part. Devon was still such a mystery. And she felt like an open book.

Devon hadn't really thought about the fact that his brilliant question would be turned on him. "Oh, wow, I guess that is fair isn't it." He thought about it for a minute and wondered if his list would sound silly compared to Raisa's. He knew she wouldn't see it that way though. "Well, I like fixing things, and making things, working with my hands. The smallest thing can be fulfilling, from replacing a faucet on a sink to carving an eagle out of a piece of wood. It's lame, I know…"

"Not at all! It's nice to know you're handy," Raisa quipped.

"Okay… that's good. Uh… next would have to be nature. In general, I guess. The mountains, streams, fishing, billions of stars that you can only see from up high and the fresh, pine air… when I was younger I thought about just disappearing into the wilderness. But I decided I couldn't part with my mother's paella." Devon smiled, "food is too important to me."

"Well, you're in luck. I'm an excellent cook." Before Raisa had even finished vocalizing this thought, she could feel her face flush from how presumptuous it was. Devon obviously thought it was cute because his smile widened to show his beautiful white teeth. *Moving on, quickly…* "So what is number three?"

Devon's face took on a more serious cast. "I guess it would be helping people, whether it's individually or in a group. I like to see a problem or a goal and help those people realize and accomplish it. I love it when people feel good about themselves, when they have done something that they didn't think they could do. You know the saying, 'Give a man a fish; you have fed him for today. Teach a man to fish; and you have fed him for a lifetime.' It's kind of my truism." Devon looked at Raisa, trying to read her expression. He wondered how he had done.

Raisa was considering everything that Devon had said. It struck her that it could have been a description of her father. With the exception of the foodie part – her dad would eat tree bark and be happy about it. *Well, they say that you look for your father in the guys you like… guess it's true.* She couldn't decide if that was good or weird. "So is there anything else that you need to know about me?"

"What's your favorite color?" Devon's face looked too serious for such a simple question. Raisa didn't immediately respond. When Devon looked up to see why, he broke into a gentle smile. Raisa was perplexed by the question.

Copper, she thought. "I don't really have a favorite... I like all colors." *But copper is my favorite.* "I guess I would have to say white... but that isn't really a color is it?" *Copper for sure.*

"Actually, white is a combination of all the colors mixed together so it makes perfect sense." *And it just happens to be my new favorite color too.* Devon glanced just above Raisa's head and back to her blue eyes. "Is there anything else you want to ask *me*?" He leaned closer to Raisa. He felt like there was a lure pulling him in.

Raisa bit her lip. She wanted to ask *the* most important question. Most girls cared most about money or intelligence or looks – not that those weren't important things, they were – but Raisa had always dreamed that the person she would spend her life with would be able to *sing* to her. *That* was the most romantic thing on the planet. So she carefully asked, "Do you sing?" and unconsciously held her breath.

"No... well, I don't know actually, I've never tried, not for real anyway." Devon was distracted and barely considered the answer he gave. Something much more important was happening. Something he felt he had little control over.

Raisa let her breath go and would have been sad about his answer if he weren't slowly moving closer to her. She tried to keep hold of her train of thought. It wasn't easy. "Would you try... for me... sometime?" Her entire body tensed and her head swam as she watched him leaning closer and closer to her.

Devon's reply was just a whisper, his beautiful face just an inch from hers. "Absolutely." His eyes closed and his lips were parted as they touched Raisa's ever so slightly. He didn't move away. With his face next to hers, so close that they were breathing the same air, he moved so that he was sitting on the bed. He touched his forehead to hers and brought one of his hands to Raisa's neck, and then up into her hair. He gently pulled her mouth onto his and kissed her slowly, almost carefully. Raisa felt like her whole body would melt away if it weren't for the electric current that seemed to be holding her together. He was still kissing her and her breath started coming shorter. She lifted a hand to his arm, feeling the hard muscle under her fingers. Just as she felt that she would break into pieces if she didn't get closer to him, he gently pulled her face away from his. "We don't want to ruin any of the good doctor's work," he said breathlessly as he dropped his hand to Raisa's heart. He felt it beating strongly under his hand.

The room was strangely quiet. Raisa, still trying to catch her breath, looked over to the machine that she had heard beeping out her heartbeats ever since she woke. It was completely quiet and no lights were lit on it anymore. "We blew up my heart monitor," Raisa laughed softly.

Devon smiled at Raisa. He wondered at how happy he felt. His moment that he was hoping for with Raisa had happened. The spark was lit and the connection made.

85

7

Raisa opened her eyes and immediately looked over at the chair near her bed. Her heart sank a little to find it empty. She looked around her hospital room to find that no one was there and the door was shut. Her heart sped a little so she looked over at the window into the hall. She saw Pen's sandy blonde hair and let out a sigh of relief. The wire to the monitor beside her bed hung, dangling to the floor. *Someone must have detached it,* she thought. The memory of the night before came back, filling her entire body with a warm tingling sensation. She couldn't help the smile that crept onto her face. She slowly pulled her legs over the edge of the bed and stood. *Hmmm, I feel pretty good.* She wondered if her father had anything to do with that.

Pen saw Raisa through the glass, heading back from the bathroom to one of the chairs in her room. He knocked softly on the door to the room and pushed it open as Raisa waived him in. "Hi, Raisa. You look like you are doing pretty good."

Pen's voice was always cheery, *just like Corli's*, she thought. "I feel pretty good," she replied, "I'm just getting tired of that bed," she let out a little huff as she sat in the chair. "So, where is everybody?"

"Your mom and Corli are on their way here and Devon... he's... checking things out. He wants to make sure that everything is cool at your house and stuff. He'll meet us there." Pen stood up straighter and lifted his fist to his chest. "I've been assigned the task of getting you home safely."

Raisa didn't like all the fuss. At the same time though, she knew that without Devon and Pen looking out for her, she would probably be scared stiff. "You know, it seems like everything is pretty quiet. I haven't heard any nasty voices for days." Raisa was surprised at how she was just now realizing this.

The doctor gave Raisa her release; the nurses changed her bandage from one that wrapped around her entire torso to a small four by four piece of gauze. She tried not to look at her injury while it was laid bare, but she couldn't help herself. She glanced at her bare chest with the black, ugly stitches poking out everywhere. She thought it was funny how nakedness in a hospital was not as unnerving as it was back in gym class. And she thought it was funny that looking at your own wounds was nothing like looking at someone else's. Just a scraped knee on someone else sent a shock through her body, but hers, as ugly as it was, was only interesting, and seemed oddly placed on her chest.

Lona and Corli arrived and helped her get dressed. Raisa was longing for her own room with her own cloths and her own bed. The minutes seemed to drag like hours, but eventually they were ready to go.

Pen walked in. "Corli, can you drive my car? I need to ride with Raisa and Mrs. Coen." Corli nodded and took his keys.

They caravanned out of the parking lot, Lona in front and Corli behind. Everyone was on edge, expecting to see things jumping from behind bushes at every turn. Pen was in the back seat, diligently scoping their surroundings as they drove the five or so minutes to Raisa's house.

"I feel like I'm in the witness protection program." Raisa was only half aware that she spoke out loud.

They pulled into the driveway to see Devon standing on the front porch. Raisa caught her breath, and was astonished that he still had this effect on her. She wondered if things would be awkward after last night. Maybe he wouldn't be the type to show affection in public. Or worse, not want to let anyone know about them. She tried to read the expression on his face. *All business... but of course he is all business, he's worried about my safety. Don't over-think this Raisa.*

Devon came over to Raisa's door and helped her out and quickly into the house. "Wow, you're moving pretty well, are you on pain meds?" He kissed the top of her hair.

Raisa felt her heart skip a beat but remained outwardly calm. "No, none actually. It only hurts a little if I move wrong." Raisa was glad that she would not be on 'invalid status' now that she was home.

The four of them went into the living room and sat down. "I'll get some drinks and bring them out to you," Lona called as she walked from the entry to the kitchen.

"So, what's the scoop?" It was Corli, surprisingly, that wanted to dive into the status of their surroundings.

"Everything seems quiet," Devon began, but not lightly, he was very intense. "But almost too quiet. We can assume that they may have thought that Raisa was dead..." that word as it pertains to Raisa almost choked him, "but they will realize soon enough that that isn't the case. I looked everywhere I could think of for Garik or any of the other bruels but came up empty. I didn't try to hide either in case one wanted to show themselves to me - I could have grabbed them and beat some answers out of them, but... nothing."

"I haven't heard any voices... except my dad – I mean the bad ones, have you?" Raisa asked Devon.

"No, I haven't. It's like they gave up. But I have a feeling it's more tactical than surrender. Until we figure this out, we need to stay together. Corli, do you think you could stay here?"

Corli smiled, "Like that would be much different than normal."

Devon was glad that Corli could joke. That meant that she wasn't afraid. "Great. Pen and I will do the same as we did at the hospital, and take turns tracking some bruels too."

Devon felt a familiar pressure on the edge of his mind and was curious so he didn't push it away. *You're a good man, Devon.* He took in a short breath. It was Vince that spoke in his head. For the second time now, he felt the peace that came with a 'good' voice. He looked up at Raisa to see her eyes welled up. She had heard it too.

Lona stepped into the room with a tray of drinks. "Lemonade anyone?"

Garik was certain that Raisa was dead and resumed watching Devon as ordered from a safe distance so as not to be seen. When Devon continued going to the hospital though, dread filled him. He cursed to himself consistently for four days. He cursed the Lasteires and their rallys. He cursed the world. He cursed Nosh. He cursed himself. He camped out, hidden, near Raisa's house, waiting and hoping that it wasn't true, that she wasn't alive. He agonized at the thought of having to tell Nosh that he had failed, that he had spoken too soon. He imagined over and over again in his mind all of the different punishments that Nosh might impart on him. He almost wished for death instead, almost. He saw Devon, searching around Raisa's house, only narrowly escaping discovery, and then felt a cold sweat and nausea ripple through him as he watched Raisa arrive home. She was surrounded by her and Devon's friends and her mother, rendering an attack nearly impossible and at best, foolish. In despair, Garik ran away and found a place to groan and wail where no one would hear.

It was day and a wall of metal shutters was drawn in the sprawling penthouse office to keep the appearance of night inside. Nosh paced back and forth in the center of the space, screaming at the voices that were transmitting through the captive women at the edge of the room. The stifling green sludge that hung in the air was thicker than it had ever been as one report after the other came in that told Nosh that his plans were not going well. All of the couples had paired now and were searching for the reasons for what they could see and hear. Some had even made it to The Assembly. He could not comprehend how he could not bring down twenty-four pairs of mere children. The men and women that he recruited into his control far outnumbered the rallys that were protecting them. Just as Nosh had finished sneering orders on how to trap and kill a boy named Nico, the woman that channeled Garik sparked to life.

"Master," the woman's voice clearly denoted fear. Nosh instantly began to shake with fury as he turned and walked toward the unsuspecting woman. He knew the only reason that Garik would feel fear instead of arrogance. "Master, I am in awe of your graciousness, I beg for your mercy, but I have – "

"SILENCE! You worm." Nosh stood over the small frame of the woman, the fire above her licking his face with no ill effect. He reached back as if there was something behind him that he could lay hold of, and then plunged his fist forward into the center of the woman's body. The strength with which he did it picked her up off the ground and hurled her five feet backward and into the wall. She hit it with such force that as she slid to the ground she left a trail of smudged blood from her head. She whimpered and slumped. Then, as if she were regaining consciousness, she stood, face still cast down, and resumed her position in the line of women, blood dripping from her. "You have no idea of the level of your stupidity. You had within your grasp the greatest honor for taking down this one little girl, but *now*........" Nosh paused and pushed his anger down a level. He reasoned to himself that he might as well get all the use he could from this impudent pawn. "I will give you one more chance to kill Raisa Coen, and add to it a most significant task. Once she is dead, bring Devon to me, here. Then and only then will I consider leniency. If you are not successful, kill yourself, worm, for it will be a much better death than what will await you here."

"It will be done." The woman was coughing blood as she said it. The fire above her went out.

Nosh remained standing in front of the same woman. "*Ivan*," he barked.

The flame reappeared and the woman spoke again in a lower tone, "Yes, sir?"

"Follow Garik. See that he kills Raisa Coen. If he does not, kill him and the girl. Then report back to me."

"Yes, I will do as you say. Thank you, sir." The voice sounded happy and absolutely corrupt. The fire went out again and Nosh walked slowly back to the center of the room, ignoring the other voices that were begging his attention.

Garik lay doubled over in the dirt coughing up blood. He dragged himself to his feet, feeling proud that he was still alive, and started walking. *You will die, Raisa Coen.*

Pen sat sideways on the couch in front of the window that looked out to the front of the house. He watched vigilantly for any activity, any sign that the house was being approached, by

91

anyone. Devon, knowing that Pen was on guard, sat staring at nothing, trying to work any possible plan over in his mind. "If we only had more information," he had said out loud to no one in particular. Corli had gone upstairs with Raisa to help her, if she needed it, while she showered and changed her cloths. Lona sat in the kitchen, also looking out of the window to the front of the house, trying to imagine anything that she could do to help.

Raisa and Corli came down the stairs together and back into the living room. "I can't tell you how good that shower felt," Raisa remarked as she sat down in her dad's old recliner.

Devon looked at her and his face transformed. He stood and walked over to her, held out his hand for hers, took it and kissed it. He smiled, let her hand go, and slowly walked back over to the seat he had been sitting in, his pensive mood quickly returning. Raisa wanted to say something but couldn't scare up a comment if her life depended on it. Corli just looked at Raisa with her eyebrows peaked.

Just before sitting down, Devon quickly turned on his heel, looking like he had had an epiphany. "Two things." He had everyone's attention. "Do you have any weapons in the house?"

Everyone was silent. The question even surprised Raisa. She was trying to think of what that meant, exactly... knives from the kitchen? An ice pick? ...when Lona appeared in the room dangling a key from her hand. "Follow me."

Devon instantly followed, with Raisa not far behind. Lona led them upstairs and into her bedroom. She pushed aside one of the closet doors and then several feet of clothes hanging on the rod, to uncover a cabinet. She pushed the key into the lock on the front of it, swung open the door and stood back.

"Of course..." Devon smiled with another 'I'm having a memory' look on his face. He looked at Raisa who had come in behind him. "Do you know how to shoot?" The question was full of nervous energy.

Raisa looked at the gun case now with strange recognition. She knew it. It used to hang in the bedroom that had been converted into a study years ago. She had never realized that it was gone, and she had not been shooting with her dad for so long that there had not been a reason to miss it. "Yes, I do." A memory of target practice when she was about twelve in the desert with her dad and brother popped into her head. She had totally forgotten about that.

"Which one are you most comfortable with?" Devon sounded almost eager.

"The three-fifty-seven," she half mumbled. Raisa was having a hard time thinking that this conversation was real, especially with the implications it carried. She couldn't imagine pointing a gun at a person.

Devon looked a little surprised at her choice. "Okay then." He pulled out the revolver and handed it to Raisa. He began searching for the ammunition. Lona saw what he was looking for and reached over to open a panel. There was plenty. He grabbed a box that worked for Raisa. "Mrs. Coen? How about you?"

"Call me Lona... we're handing out guns for goodness sake." Devon chuckled and nodded. "I'm a shotgun girl myself. Hand me that Remington, it's my favorite. Have you seen 'Annie Get Your Gun'? No... I suppose you haven't."

Devon chose one more, smaller, nine-millimeter handgun, gathered ammo and closed the cabinet. He left the key in it but pushed the clothes back to cover the case. He turned and saw that Raisa seemed to be in a little bit of a daze. He noticed that she did, however, have the presence of mind to hold the gun properly. "Raisa, it's okay, you can do this." He bent and kissed her cheek.

"Yeah, I'm good." She said absently. Raisa felt the gun in her hand. It had been a long time, but it was familiar.

Corli went wide-eyed and Pen smiled as they watched the three of them coming down the stairs with a full complement of weapons. Devon checked all the chambers and clips of the guns. He couldn't help but reminisce back to the times he had spent with Vince, learning how to properly care for firearms. It was a strange feeling to connect everything together now, knowing that Vince was Raisa's father, and wondering if he knew he was teaching Devon something he would need to know in the future. He spent a few minutes making sure that everyone was familiar with the feeling of actually shooting each unloaded gun before he loaded them. They decided together where they would be stowed around the lower level of the house. Only the small handgun was easily accessible on the mantle of the fireplace behind a picture frame of Raisa's family.

Pen stood up. "Hey, I have these too." He pulled two small switchblades out of his back pocket and handed one to Corli and one to Raisa. "Remember your training," he smiled, then turned to Devon. "So what is number two?"

"We're quitting our jobs," he said flatly. He looked at his cell phone for the time. "I'm going to head in right now. I'm going to tell them that I can't run the crew but that I can still show the models if they need me to. When I get back you can go in to your work. I'll cover you financially, bro... we both really need to be here."

Pen was shaking his head, "I don't even need to go in. A phone call will do it. Maybe I should go pick up pizza first though," he joked.

Everyone, including Lona settled in the living room. Corli asked her about her rifle shooting days. It was fascinating. She hadn't ever imagined Lona, or her own mother for that matter, as a young girl like herself.

Pen, as always kept watch at the window, until Devon went to him, touched his shoulder and gave him a nod. Raisa noticed and took it as a guy thing. But Devon turned to her and held out his hand. He helped her up and pulled her into the kitchen.

Raisa felt a tingle that she chalked up to nerves. This was all so strange. Yes, her life had been more unusual than most, but in the last week, everything had changed.

Devon positioned Raisa with her back against the counter. Just as she was about to ask him what he wanted to talk to her about, he took her face in his hands and kissed her. This wasn't like the careful kiss from last night. Raisa lifted her hands to Devon's hips. She felt the bottom edge of his t-shirt and had the sudden urge to feel his skin. She slipped her hands underneath and placed her hands softly on his sides. He moaned quietly against her mouth and moved his body closer to hers until they were touching. She felt his tongue brush her lips as he twined one hand that had been on her cheek in the back of her hair. The other moved down the side of her body and around her waist. Her whole body felt like it was coming unhinged. He began kissing her more urgently and pulled her slowly, tighter to his body. Raisa took a short breath in. "Oh God… I'm sorry!" he breathed on Raisa's cheek as he loosened his arm around her. "What was I thinking… are you okay?" He pulled back and held her face in his hands again. "If I've hurt you – "

"No, I'm fine… really." She almost hadn't noticed the pain, and it certainly didn't hurt now. She let her hands fall to the top of Devon's jeans as she caught her breath. She looked up into Devon's beautiful dark eyes. She saw for the first time that they had flecks of copper that shined in them. "Thank you," she said, not really knowing where the comment came from.

"For what?" Devon's mouth turned up slightly.

"For… the kiss…" Raisa felt embarrassed and dropped her eyes from his.

Devon brought his hand under her chin and raised her face back up. He looked intently into her beautiful blue eyes and whispered. "Oh, no… the pleasure was entirely mine." He rested his lips gently on hers and left them there, feeling the warm current that ran through them together. He pulled back then and drank the sight of her in. He took his hand and placed his palm gently over Raisa's heart.

Raisa was acutely aware that this was very different than when he had touched her chest it in the hospital. She was bound in bandages then and now she could feel his fingers touching her skin. His hand felt hot through the thin material of her blouse. "Raisa," he spoke as if something was twisting him inside, "I swear that you will never be hurt like this again. I will protect you… you can count on it."

"I know." Raisa had no doubt.

Devon was only gone for a couple of hours and brought back food with him. Pen was sitting on a planter near the front porch and reported that absolutely nothing happened in his absence. Devon sent him into the house with a bag full of tamales, carnitas with freshly made tortillas, beans and salad. Devon stayed out front to watch for a while. He couldn't shake the gnawing feeling that everything was too quiet, like the calm before the storm. He tried to cover everything he knew about their situation in his mind and he kept coming up with the same question. Why? If he had the slightest idea why he and Raisa were wanted separated, or dead, maybe he could *do* something about it.

Raisa, he thought. A lightness came to him just thinking about her. How different it was to have someone in his life. He had always thought that people that fell for each other so quickly were just fooling themselves, that it was rubbish, that maybe that kind of love didn't really exist. And maybe some of them were... delusional. But this was different. They obviously had some purpose, together... *And her touch*! Devon dropped his head in his hand. His mind swam with the idea of touching her, feeling her skin under his hands as his own skin warmed under the silkiness of her fingers. He let his mind start to wander. *Snap out of it, Devon!* He lifted his head and did a quick survey of the yard. *Keep your game tight, don't go all soft*, he smiled to himself.

The front door opened. Raisa had a plate of food and started to bring it up to where Devon sat.

"No! You shouldn't......." He stood up with alarm, moved as if to shield Raisa, and quickly pushed her back into the house.

"Sorry..." Raisa looked hurt. *How stupid of me!* "I just wanted to bring you some food... it's really good..." her voice trailed off and she looked down and started picking at a piece of lettuce.

Devon exhaled and put his hands on her shoulders. He bent to level his eyes to hers. "It's okay. Thank you. That was very thoughtful." He took the plate from her hands and stood up straight, looking toward the kitchen. "Pen, can you take the front again?" he called.

Pen bounded to the entry, wiping his hands on his jeans and swallowing a bite of food. "Sure!"

"I'm so tired of being indoors," Raisa groaned. She felt like a whining five year old, but she couldn't help it.

Devon grabbed her hand, "Come on, let's go into the back. It's pretty blocked off back there." As they opened the slider and walked into the back, Corli watched them, calculating their destination. She changed her positioned so that she was looking through the door and had a view of the whole backyard. Devon noticed her tactics, nodded and smiled at her. "Corli is a good friend to you, isn't she. She has picked up on this protection thing pretty well."

"Yeah, it's a whole side of her that I've never seen. Although, I think I've always known it would be there. I feel... honored, I guess is the word, that she cares so much for me that she would get messed up in this whole thing with me." Raisa watched Corli sitting inside the house. The yellow mist was solidly visible above her now. "Do you see?" Raisa nodded toward Corli.

Devon looked up from his plate of food and over to Corli. "Oh, wow, yeah, it's bright! You know I haven't seen my mom since you told me about her having it too. I kind of want to check it out. Maybe when this all settles down." Devon took another bite of food.

"I've wanted to ask you something." Raisa thought this might be a good time to ask some questions that were wearing on her. Every other time she didn't want to risk ruining the mood. "What is the story with my dad and your mom? I mean, how did they meet, and how was it that my dad saved you?" Raisa was a little uncomfortable, the question felt so personal for some reason.

Devon was done with his food so he pulled his chair close to Raisa's so he could touch her. He grabbed one of her hands in his.

Raisa sighed.

"Well," Devon started, "I was just a baby, only about nine months old when your dad rescued us... so I don't remember any of it. My mom has told me the story, but I couldn't really do it justice. I know my father was horrible." Devon lowered his eyes solemnly. He seemed to get lost for a minute. Raisa watched the different expressions cross his face and tried to decipher them... remorse, anger, shame? "And that my mother is the most loving and giving woman in the world. She ran............ You know, I'll tell you what. We'll go see her tomorrow morning before she goes to work and you can get the whole story first hand. You should meet her anyway." Devon kissed Raisa's hand very quickly and without his eyes meeting hers again, stood and walked to the center of the backyard and looked up at the sky.

Raisa knew that he wasn't really looking at the sky. She had obviously touched on something way too personal for Devon to talk about. For the first time since they had met, Raisa felt unconnected from Devon.

It was dark now and the mood was heavy and anxious in the house. Small conversations came and went. Lona was somewhere upstairs. Pen was outside again and Devon was sitting on the couch in front of the window, staring out of it. Raisa decided to turn the TV on low. She clicked through the channels and stopped on a program that she had watched before, 'Edward Brayden and The Assembly'. It was just starting. She had it set to tape new shows and none had taped in quite awhile so she knew it would be a re-run. She enjoyed watching them over again though. He was a psychic, of sorts, that could talk to your loved ones that had passed, bringing back messages to help the living cope. She laughed a little to herself. She was now living proof that it was possible. Corli joined her in front of the television.

Edward walked onto the stage in front his small audience. He began the little speech he gave about how it all works.

"Hey," it was Corli, pointing to the screen, "Raisa, do you *see* that?"

Raisa had glanced over at Devon, noting that his expression had not changed for at least an hour. She turned to see what Corli was referring to and stopped breathing. In the air, hovering above Edward Brayden was a mist or dust with a purplish tint to it. It had rays that spoked out from its center. It went with him anywhere he moved. "I've never seen that before…" she had to force her voice to make the sound. "Devon, look at this!"

Hearing the urgency in Raisa's voice snapped Devon out of his thoughts. He stood and came closer to the TV to see what the girls were so excited about. "Turn it up," he said quickly.

They listened to the show without making a sound. When a commercial came on, Raisa spoke. "I've seen this one before but I definitely didn't see *that*! You know what else is weird? Some of the things that he is saying seem like they have a different meaning than they did before, but I can't quite figure it out."

Corli went outside to fill Pen in on what was going on. He came into the house.

Devon reached for the remote and paused the TV. "Pen, let's get this place locked up." They checked every door and window to make sure the house was secure and turned most of the lights out so that they could see outside of the windows. Raisa had the sensation she used to get when she watched scary movies late at night with her girlfriends. This, obviously, was much more dramatic, and realistic. Pen settled back on the couch but he could still see the TV from there. Devon started the show again. Raisa could see the concentration on his face. When the show was over, Devon turned it off and let out a long breath of air. "There is a sort of rhythm to what he is saying, certain words that seem to have special meaning. I am certain that this is connected to… to us. But without watching more of these, I

100

don't know that I will be able to figure it out. I wonder when the next one is on."

Raisa was smiling from ear to ear. She leaned over, with a short grunt, and grabbed the remote. "No need... voila!" She clicked on her recorded programs. It showed twenty-four taped shows.

8

Raisa lasted through two episodes of Edward Brayden. Devon paused the TV and crawled over to where she had fallen asleep laying across the wrong way of the recliner, her head inclined to what looked like an uncomfortable position on one arm and her feet dangling over the other. He smiled, watching her for several minutes. It was strange, he thought, how he was in her house, watching her TV, protecting this place like it was his own. He had always attached the desire to be somewhere to his material surroundings, not the people he wanted to be with. *I have to be near her.* The realization was startling, and comforting at the same time.

He stood and woke Corli who had fallen asleep curled up next to Pen on the couch. He asked her to lead the way to Raisa's room.

"Come on, Sunshine," he whispered as he lifted Raisa into his arms and carried her, still asleep, up to her bed. Under different circumstances he would have wanted to stay in her room for a while but there were several reasons why that wouldn't happen tonight. Corli plopped on the bed next to Raisa and Devon pulled the door closed to a crack before he went back downstairs.

Pen sat, still bright eyed on the couch. "How are you doin' Dev?"

"That's what I should be asking you," Devon replied as he returned to the floor in front of the television. He pulled his knees up in front of him and turned to look at his friend. "Hey, I

102

want to thank you for... everything. You've never questioned anything I've asked you to do... you've been automatically 'on board' for everything. That's huge."

"I'll send you my bill." Pen smiled. He knew that Devon was grateful. "So, you were looking a little more introspective than normal a couple of hours ago. Did something happen with you and Raisa?"

"No, not really." Even as Devon said this, he knew he wouldn't get away with it.

"Did she ask about your dad?"

Devon raised his eyebrows high. "You know me better that I thought."

"Devon," Pen spoke with strength in his voice, "a man that knows he is not an island is a good man. You are not your father."

Devon didn't reply. He and Pen sat in silence. He felt humbled by what Pen said, and privileged to have him as a friend.

"Why don't you get some sleep, Pen," Devon finally said softly. "I'm going to watch a few more episodes and see what I can come up with."

"Sounds good." Pen slouched into the couch, put his head back and closed his eyes.

Devon pushed play on the remote but glanced back over at Pen. There in the dark, just above Pen's head and chest, a soft yellow glow moved up and down with his breathing.

By 7am Lona was in the kitchen making breakfast. Pen was awake on the couch and Devon was turning over on the floor, brought out of his slumber by the smell of bacon.

"Oh, that smells amazing!" Corli was sliding her socked feet lazily across the floor from the stairs.

Devon sat up and looked toward the stairs. "Where's Raisa?"

"She's right behind me." Corli waved her hand casually behind her back.

In the ten seconds that followed, Devon felt panicked. Until he saw her walking carefully down the stairs. He felt overprotective but justified to himself that the situation merited it. *I hope I'm not always like this*, he frowned.

Lona brought the pancakes and bacon into the living room so that they could all eat together.

Raisa was staring at Devon, wondering when he would talk to her again. She sighed to herself and decided to speak so that she would be spoken to. "So, what did you find out last night? Sorry I fell asleep on you."

Devon's lips were thin. "Well, I decided that the main message to us is that we're not crazy. He talks a lot about how if you are in tune to the other side, you can get signals, hear voices… stuff like that."

All business today… okay. "So why do you think the message is something special for us and not everyone?"

"He kept saying things like, 'you'll see and hear things that others don't, but he would slide it into another context that made it sound normal. There was one other thing he said that really felt like a message. He said it exactly twelve times per episode. 'You are not alone.'" Devon looked at Raisa and her beautiful white spirals. The fishing lure was back. If he didn't know better, he would have thought that he actually was moving toward her. Raisa felt a zing through her and caught a subtle burnished glow from Devon's eyes. Their re-connection was a tangible thing.

"So what are you saying," Corli chimed in, "that he knows that there are four of us, or - "

Raisa broke in with a dazed tone, "there are other people like us... in other places." She didn't break her gaze with Devon. She felt like she was being written into a fairy tale. But she knew it was the truth as soon as she heard herself say it.

It took several minutes for that to sink in with everyone, all of them formulating new questions in their minds. Slowly they began eating their breakfast again. The boys finished and Lona gathered their plates. Devon broke the silence. "Anyway, I only watched five episodes so there are a lot more to go. I'll check them out tonight. Right now, we need to get ready to go."

No one had expected that. But Raisa had hoped.

"Where are we going?" Corli said. Pen thought it was cute that she was always the vocal one.

"To my mom's."

As Raisa left the house, Pen and Corli in front of her, Devon behind, she had a strange feeling. She turned around and looked at her mother standing in the doorway. "Bye Mom... are you going to be okay?"

"I'll be fine, Honey," she waved her off, "I'm going to the store in a few minutes anyway. I'll see you later."

They quickly piled into Devon's truck and took off.

When they pulled out of the neighborhood everyone felt a little more at ease. Raisa was sandwiched on the bench seat between Devon and Corli. She was happy to have any part of her body touching his, even if it was only happenstance. A small smile curved her lips. "Nice ride... sixty-nine?"

Devon looked at her sideways and smirked, "sixty-eight actually."

Corli and Pen both saw that they were missing something, an inside joke maybe, but left it alone. Pen took the opportunity to kiss Corli on the cheek. Corli blushed but repaid him with a peck on the lips.

Garik paced in the dirt at the bottom of a gully near the Coen house, creating a dust cloud with his clumsy footsteps. He had a deranged look on his face and was chewing his fingers as he talked to himself. "Get in, get out… get in, get out." He stopped walking for a moment and let out a noise that sounded like an animal being beaten. "I have to do this. By myself. Yes, it will be better that way. *I* am supposed to kill her. It is the purpose of my life! I'll show Nosh." He began pacing again. "I'll wait till later. They'll think that nothing is going to happen. I'll watch and catch her in a room by herself… but that other bitch is always with her…" He howled again. "No, no, NO… Yes… yes… get in, get out…."

They pulled into a very richly landscaped, gated community that had a fountain in the front. The guard tipped his cap at Devon and pushed a button. As the gate slid to the side, Raisa felt the equivalent of a rock drop into her stomach. *What if she doesn't like me?* Devon drove to a spot near the back of the complex and parked. There were many tall leafy trees that served as a barrier from the road on the other side and more that filled the landscape. It made Raisa feel like she had come into another world, a place that felt far away and protected.

Devon held out his hand to help Raisa from the truck. "You look a little green," he almost snickered.

"You're so funny," Raisa replied with a fake smile as she climbed out.

Devon didn't want to let on that he was actually very nervous too. Not for the same reason Raisa was… he knew that his mother would love her. *What's not to love*, he smiled to

106

himself. As they climbed the stairs to his mother's unit on the second level, Devon felt the anxiety kick in harder. He wanted Raisa - no... he needed Raisa to know everything about him and his past, good and bad. But what if, after she found out the truth, she didn't want him? He decided not to think about that anymore.

Pen stopped at a low gate a few feet from the front door. "Hey, Dev, Corli and I are going to sit out here on the terrace for awhile. We'll come in, in a little bit." Devon nodded.

Just as Devon went to try the doorknob, it turned and the door opened. Devon looked up with a smile. "Hi, Mom." He forgot himself for a minute because as he looked at her standing in the doorway, there it was, plain as day, a lighted mist above her in the air. He turned to Raisa who was standing next to him, waiting patiently while he found his voice. She knew what was causing the delay. He remembered himself again, "Sorry, Mom, this is Raisa Coen."

Raisa stepped forward with her hand extended. She noted in the back part of her brain the low music she heard coming from somewhere in the house. *Luciano Pavarotti.* "It's wonderful to meet you, Mrs. Castaneda."

"Please, call me Gloria." She smiled and gently took Raisa's hand with both of hers. She looked deeply into Raisa's eyes and held on to her hand as if she were sensing her, pulling knowledge of her from her touch. "It is wonderful to finally meet you. Your father spoke fondly of you." She kept hold of Raisa's hand and began pulling her through the door. "Come in, you two." She led them into the kitchen and motioned for them to take a seat at the small round kitchen table. It was positioned in the nook of a bay window and the morning sun was streaming in. Devon and Raisa sat while Gloria poured tall glasses of iced tea.

"So, to what do I owe the pleasure?" She smiled at Devon as she set the drinks in front of them and sat down.

"Sorry that I haven't been by lately. Things have been... a little crazy," Devon apologized.

"It's okay. I know you have been watching after Raisa." She turned her eyes to Raisa. "And how are you? You look fantastic considering the ordeal you've been through."

Raisa felt the caring in her voice and saw it in her eyes. She wondered though, how much she knew. She wished she had asked Devon beforehand. She figured she'd just go with it and see what happened. "I'm doing inexplicably well. You'd never know that... I... was hurt so badly. Thank you for asking."

Devon was torn between wanting to get on with the conversation and wanting it to never happen. His mother and Raisa were waiting quietly. "Mom, last night Raisa asked me about her father and how he helped us. I was going to tell her my version, but I thought that you should do it. She needs to hear.......... everything." Devon's eyes dropped to his iced tea.

"Well," Gloria spoke calmly, "everything is quite a lot, isn't it."

"It's not all that necessary." Raisa felt so intrusive. "I don't– "

"No, he's right, Raisa. You do need to hear everything. Let me make a call and I'll be right back."

Gloria stepped out of the room. They heard her talking to her work, telling them that she wouldn't be in till after noon.

Raisa set her hand on Devon's wrist. Her touch seemed to ease some tension in him. He pulled his forlorn face up to meet her searching eyes. She tried to read this expression. The closest she could get to a matching emotion was anguish. "Are you okay?"

Devon's features softened. He lifted her hand and kissed it.

Gloria stepped back into the kitchen. She delicately set a picture frame down in front of Raisa. "This is Miguel Castaneda, Devon's father."

Raisa's eyes filled with surprise. She wasn't sure why she expected Devon and his father to look nothing alike. Maybe because it was obvious that Devon despised him, so their likenesses would *have* to be different. But they were not different, they were shockingly similar. Miguel's features were just slightly more rounded, lacking the precision of Devon's face, and the eyes... something different about the eyes that Raisa could not put her finger on. Only that looking at this man's eyes gave her the creeps, and looking into Devon's eyes felt like protection and love personified.

"I guess I'll start at the beginning.... I was very young and shy when Miguel found me." Gloria looked sad as she began to recall the memory. "Within a few weeks he became my entire world. He was charming and kind. He made me feel that we had a very special connection, that there was not another two people in the world that shared what we did. Against my parent's wishes, we married.

"We were living in a very small apartment, but we were constantly discussing our dreams of a better life. He had very grand ideas... I became pregnant. My morning sickness was unusually difficult but he took care of me, never left my side. One morning, just a few days after my sickness had subsided I woke to find our bags packed. He said that he had a better place for us, a place that we would be happy and free and where our child would grow and thrive. It was very exciting, I loved him so deeply.

"We drove for hours. The road turned from highway to a winding road and then to dirt trails. I had no idea where we were other than that we had climbed considerably in altitude and were

109

in the mountains somewhere. We came to a clearing and I saw what resembled a compound. As we pulled in and stopped the car, several women came to greet us. They were very happy to see Miguel. The regard they had for him bothered me, but I didn't voice my displeasure. One of the women showed me to a room that had been prepared for me. I couldn't quite wrap my mind around what was happening so I just went along with it all. I assumed that Miguel would come to me right away and give me the explanation that would silence all my fears and doubts.

"I didn't see Miguel for seven days or nights. Then on the eighth night he came to my room and took me... he was very rough and unkind. I had never seen that side of him before. When he was finished, he told me that we were part of a very important family now and that if I tried to run he would kill me. Then he kissed me, told me that he loved me with all of his heart and for a moment I felt the connection that we had shared before, but now it was tainted and twisted with a feeling I had not recognized before... a powerful manipulation." Gloria paused. She took a drink from her glass and checked Raisa's expression to see how she was fairing with the account of her story. *This is a lot, but she needs to know,* she said to herself.

Raisa sat with her gaze fixed on Devon's mother. She was hoping that Gloria couldn't see the horror she was feeling on her face.

Devon sat quietly, still staring into his glass of iced tea, lost in his own version of the images of this nightmare his mother had shared with him before.

Gloria continued. "Every Saturday this group of women and their children, he had fathered nine children by this time, would gather in a room that was designated as our meeting place. Miguel spoke to us from a podium, told us of our calling to be with him as he accomplished great things. He demanded our

110

loyalty in one breath and the next would speak lovingly of our devotion and sacrifice for the cause.

"I tried to befriend the women to see if I could gather any to stand with me and defy him… or escape. But they couldn't imagine why I would want to do such a thing. It was as if they were under a spell. They adored him. They would tell Miguel of my descent and he would beat me."

Raisa saw Devon flinch out of the corner of her eye. Her eyes had been glossy and now they spilled over freely. But her gaze remained fixed and she didn't dare speak.

"I bore the circumstance as best as I could. Devon was born and Miguel seemed to take a particular liking to him. My life was my son and I became more and more desperate to break free. I needed to protect him from Miguel. But I didn't know what to do.

"One Friday evening Miguel called a special meeting. It was hours long. He told us that during our regular meeting the following day, we would be given the opportunity to show our devotion to him, give ourselves over to him completely. He said that we would die together……… I was frantic but I dared not show it.

"The next morning, just as the sky was starting to show a little light, I bundled Devon, tied him to my body and left. I didn't know where I was going but thought that if I headed down and kept off the main trail I might have a chance. Within an hour I could hear barking dogs behind me; I didn't know he had dogs. Just as I felt I could run no more and I knew I was about to be overtaken, I broke into a clearing. There was a single truck there, a deer tied to the back, and one man sitting by a low campfire making his morning meal. It was your father.

"He said nothing, but instantly came to me. I collapsed with Devon into his arms. He put us into his truck and drove.

111

"I don't know how long we were driving because I fell asleep. I woke up to see Devon with a seatbelt and blanket made into a makeshift car seat sitting between us.

"He never asked me a thing about what or who I was running from. He brought me to your home and your gracious mother attended to us. Your father helped me to begin my life, found me a job and a place to live. He has checked in on me a few times a year ever since then, and occasionally spent time with Devon.

"I lived fearfully, thinking that Miguel would find me again. I watched the papers to see if anything would tell me of the fate of those women. About two months after I had left, a story was printed in the paper about a compound that was found with several women and children that had drank poison and died in a cult fashion. They said that there was also one man. They couldn't identify all of the bodies, including that of the man because animals had ravaged them and they had decomposed for at least a month before they were found. I know that I should have been relieved. But I had very mixed emotions. A part of me still loved Miguel. And a part of me cared for those women. But mostly I was glad that no one else would suffer at his hand."

Gloria placed her hand gently on Raisa's. "Now you know everything," she said softly. She stood and looked down at her suffering son and the girl she knew that he already loved, and smiled reflectively. "I'm going to go say hello to Penley and meet his girlfriend... you two finish your tea." She gracefully walked through her living room and outside, shutting the door softly behind her.

Devon couldn't bear to lift his face for fear of what he might see in Raisa's eyes. He couldn't even make himself respond when she put her hand on his arm. Then like an angel coming to save him from himself, he felt her soft lips kiss his cheek. He slowly looked up.

Her voice was tender as she spoke. "I'm so sorry, Devon. I can see how hard it was for you to hear that again. Your mother is an amazing and brave woman... but......... I don't understand why you look as if it was *your fault*."

"Don't you see Raisa? I have spent my life trying to be nothing like him. But no matter what I do, I still see him in me."

Raisa's face twisted. "*No*, I *don't* see! How could you think that? You are *nothing* like him. You are kind and caring and... *good*."

Devon looked into Raisa's eyes and saw that she believed what she had said. He thought that if she believed it, maybe he could believe it too, one day.

Gloria brought Pen and Corli in for a glass of tea. After they chatted for a while about nothing in particular, Gloria stood to make an exit. "I have to get to work, but you kids are welcome to stay here if you like."

Raisa stood up too. "No, I would really like to get back home and check on my mom... but thank you... for everything." She turned to Devon. "Is that okay?"

Devon abandoned his chair and came to Raisa's side. "Of course, we'll get going." He stepped over to his mother and put his arms around her. "Thank you, Mami, I love you so much."

Garik snuck up to his hiding place where he could see the front of Raisa's house. His chest rose and fell unevenly. When he settled and peered through the bush, he choked. The only car there was Raisa's. Devon was not there. "This is my chance!" he squealed.

Garik pulled a knife from his belt, the same one that he used to stab Raisa before. "You will feel this blade more than once this time, Raisa," he spit the words from his mouth. He ran to the front door and smashed through it.

113

Lona was sitting in the recliner reading when she heard the door rip open. She gasped and her eyes flew wide as she saw the crazed boy crash into the room, holding a knife high in his hand. She dashed to reach for the shotgun she had stowed behind the recliner she was sitting in. But she wasn't fast enough.

Garik lunged, brutally back-handing Lona and knocking her to the floor. When her chest and face began to sting she realized he had struck her with the knife.

"*Where is Raisa?*" he snarled as he brought the knife to rest at Lona's throat.

"She's not here." Lona's voice was shaken, but not with fear.

"*Liar!*" Garik screamed as he kicked her with all of the force he could muster. He left her on the floor, satisfied that she wouldn't move, as he ran through the house frantically searching for the Lasteire he was going to kill.

Devon turned his truck into Raisa's neighborhood and his brow wrinkled.

"Something's wrong." Raisa said as she sat up and grabbed the dash.

Devon drove slowly up to Raisa's street. They all sat taught as a piano wire in the front seat of the truck. As they turned the corner to Raisa's house, a quick scan revealed several bruels, not quite hidden but on the fringes of the street watching the house. The truck had not come to a stop before Pen had opened his door and broke into a run. He pulled a switchblade from his back pocket as he approached the nearest bruel.

Devon threw his door open as well. "*Corli, the basement!*"

Corli hopped up and over Raisa into the driver's seat before Raisa even had time to think. Devon swung the cab door shut. Just before he had the chance to run and engage the next nearest bruel, a loud *BANG* came from the house.

114

"*MOM!*" Raisa screamed, but Corli had already flipped the truck around and was speeding away.

Devon instantly shot full speed toward the front door of the house, his own blade appearing in his hand. As he ran he heard, *What is it you think you can do Mr. Castaneda? You are not strong enough to stop this... you are weak and afraid to be a man... you can't............* The voices continued, but Devon simply ignored them. He was going to get to Raisa's mother and save her, or die trying.

Devon reached the open door just as Garik was pulling himself off the floor. He was bleeding in several places, pieces of flesh hanging from his arm and leg, but he was not mortally wounded. As he began his stride to escape, he came face to face with Devon.

Devon barely paused and didn't hesitate. With a baleful smile on his face and a gleam in his eyes, he twisted around Garik, locking him in place. In the same motion, he brought his blade to Garik's throat and cut him deep. A gurgling sound escaped Garik's mouth as he dropped to his knees, then to the floor and was silent.

Devon rushed to Lona's side where she lay on the living room floor, the shot gun still smelling of freshly burnt powder beside her. The wicked voices were now screaming in his head, and he continued to ignore them.

Raisa was shrieking at Corli, "*Turn around! My MOM, I have to get to my mom! Corli, PLEASE!*"

"*No*," Corli said firmly. "No we can't. We have to get you away from them. Sorry Raisa. You are the reason they are there. I won't hand you to them."

The flood of voices began. *Running away Raisa? Leaving your mother to die? You are so pathetic and weak...* they

115

continued without mercy. Raisa dropped her face into her hands and screamed.

She was numb as they walked into the peaceful basement of the model home. She sat down on the couch and held her hands to her ears. "Stop!" She finally turned the voices off. She was wracked with despair over her mother and lifted her eyes to the ceiling. "Dad... Daddy?" She felt her body heaving as if she were crying but there were no tears.

Raisa, I can't... don't worry... She heard her father's voice, but it started weak, was clear for only a moment and then faded away again.

"Lona, Lona can you hear me?" Devon was bent over Raisa's mother, checking her pulse and her breathing. *She's alive!* He surveyed her for injuries. Her shoulder and face had shallow slices across them that had already stopped bleeding and a bruise was surfacing around her cheek and eye. He took a second to shut out the clamor of the frustrated evil voices.

Lona coughed and opened her eyes with a grimace and held her side. "I'm alright. Raisa?"

"She's safe. Don't worry, she's not here. She's with Corli."

Devon, Pen needs you. It was Vince. He paused for only a second.

"Go!" Lona said.

He grabbed the pistol from the mantle and raced outside. Pen stood blood streaked and dirty, arms spread and eyes darting from one assailant to the next. He had dispatched two bruels but now he was trying to hold off the remaining three. They were crouched around him, ready to spring. Devon shouted something that sounded like 'I'll hucking hill you' as he ran to Pen. The three men turned on their heels at the sound. They saw Devon's face, with its fury and determination as he charged them, the gun held steady and pointed in their direction. It took only seconds for them to cower. With a sound like scattering hyenas, they quickly gathered their wounded and fled.

Pen dropped to one knee and sucked air into his lungs. Devon tucked the gun into the back of his jeans and offered him a hand up. "You alright, Pen?"

"Yeah… good…" he managed between breaths as he clapped his hand into Devon's and rose up. "Raisa's mom?"

"I think she's alright," Devon answered as they walked back to the house. They both surveyed the area as they went making sure they wouldn't have any other surprises. "They're gone… I can feel it." Devon threw his hand to the back of Pen's shoulder as they walked to the door.

"Except this one," Pen regarded Garik's lifeless body that was laying face down in the entry, an expanding pool of blood around him. They carefully stepped around it.

Lona had pulled herself up and into the recliner and was dabbing her face with a tissue. She was still somewhat bent to protect a pain she felt in her lower abdomen where she had been kicked. "You boys okay?"

Devon quickly knelt in front of Lona and took her hand. "We're fine. I'm going to call an ambulance for you."

"Don't be silly." Lona went to stand. Her intention was to demonstrate that she was perfectly fine, but the movement twisted her stomach and caused her to wretch.

Devon, instantly filled with a greater alarm, reached for his cell and dialed 911. After being told that an ambulance and the police would be sent immediately, he hung up and returned his attention to Lona. His brow wrinkled with concern.

All is as it should be, Devon. Events have been set in motion that will change everything as you know it. Have faith, Son. Stay the course. Be the man that you are meant to be.

117

Devon looked up toward the ceiling, his hand still holding Lona's, and nodded with strength and resolve in his eyes.

The silence was excruciating. Raisa almost wished for the evil voices over the debilitating numbness of not knowing what was happening.

She kept seeing visions in her mind of different scenarios of the scene at home, her mother being shot, Devon and Pen being attacked and overtaken. She thought of the fearlessness in Devon's eyes, knowing that he would die before giving up or giving in. She watched her vision with horror as she saw Devon fall to the ground, his rings of copper fading, then disappearing as he died.

Just when she thought that she might run screaming out of the house and into the street, she heard a single word. *Sing.* It wasn't her father's voice but a beautiful and peaceful voice none-the-less. The words of a hymn that had always brought her peace trickled into her mind. She initially fought the urge to hear the sweet melody, thinking she preferred despair to the serenity the song might bring, but that thought went against her heart and how she truly felt. Raisa decided to do it for her mom. She let it come and slowly, softly, began to sing.

> *I need Thee every hour, most gracious Lord;*
> *No tender voice like Thine can peace afford.*
> *I need Thee, oh, I need Thee;*
> *Every hour I need Thee;*
> *Oh, bless me now, my Savior,*
> *I come to Thee.*
> *I need Thee every hour, stay Thou nearby;*
> *Tempations lose their pow'r when Thou art nigh.*
> *I need Thee, oh, I need Thee;*
> *Every hour I need Thee;*

118

Oh, bless me now, my Savior,
I come to Thee.
I need Thee every hour, in joy or pain;
Come quickly and abide, or life is vain.
I need Thee, oh, I need Thee;
Every hour I need Thee;
Oh, bless me now, my Savior,
I come to Thee.
I need Thee every hour; teach me Thy will;
And Thy rich promises, in me fulfill.
I need Thee, oh, I need Thee;
Every hour I need Thee;
Oh, bless me now, my Savior,
I come to Thee.
I need Thee every hour, most Holy One;
Oh, make me Thine indeed, Thou blessed Son.
I need Thee, oh, I need Thee;
Every hour I need Thee;
Oh, bless me now, my Savior,
I come to Thee.

Corli sat for several minutes with glassy eyes after Raisa had finished the song. Though there was still sadness and anxiety in the air; there was also calm and hope.

Her phone rang. She said 'okay' several times and hung up, all the while looking at Raisa's anxious stare. "Everyone is… okay. We can take you home now. Let's go."

9

Two ambulances and three police cars were parked haphazardly in front of the house as Raisa and Corli pulled up and parked a couple of houses down. As they reached the front lawn, a gurney with a covered body was being wheeled from the door. Raisa's heart stopped and her sight threatened to leave her. Her legs gave out from under her and Corli caught her just before she reached the ground.

"It's Garik, Raisa. Not your mother," Corli whispered quickly.

In the next instant, Devon was beside Raisa, wrapping his arms around her and lifting her up. "I've got her Corli. Thank you." He gave Corli a heartfelt look. She nodded and hurried into the house to find Pen.

"I thought…" Raisa couldn't complete the sentence.

"I know, it's okay, your mom is inside. I'll take you to her." Devon spoke with such gentleness that she knew her mother must be hurt. The first ambulance pulled away from the house and Raisa saw the word 'coroner' written across the back.

When they got inside, Lona was laying on a gurney, a paramedic attending to her. He was tightening the last strap when she saw Raisa. "Honey, you're here." She held her hand out for her daughter and Raisa moved quickly to her side, eyes already welling up. "I'm fine, honey… don't you worry."

Raisa saw the dried red blood of the cut and the purple and black rippling bruises down one whole side of her mother's face. She couldn't find any words… they all choked her before they could come out. She reached across her mother to hug her and laid her cheek on her mother's chest. It was a gesture that reminded her of being a very young girl, sitting in her mother's lap and snuggling her head under her mother's chin, her cheek in this exact place, to be comforted over something that had made her cry.

"We have to get going." The paramedic broke into Raisa's memory.

"We'll meet you over there." Devon's hands were on Raisa's shoulders, gently pulling her back so they could wheel her mother out.

The ambulance and one police car pulled away. Two policemen stood in the living room, one writing and one casually talking with Pen. Corli was at Pen's side, looking him over and assessing his injuries.

"Glad you got here when you did," the officer gestured to Pen and Devon, "and that no one was hurt any worse. Well, that should do it for us." The note taker slapped the metal top closed on his tablet. "Thanks for your cooperation. There won't be any problems with this. Can't say I'm not glad that there is one less hoodlum out there on the street. Good job, Son." He reached out and shook Devon's hand.

As the officers left, Devon replayed the moment in his mind when he killed Garik. It was so easy to end his life; to take vengeance on the man who tried to kill Raisa. He took pleasure in it. It made him feel strong and powerful, and that bothered him. *And I got away with it. No suspicion on me at all.* Devon was surprised at this and wondered if the police were susceptible to suggestion, like the bruels, and if it was a good or an evil suggestion that they were following. Either way, he was grateful. He pushed the now rickety door closed, though it would not latch. Part of the doorjamb was missing. "I'll fix that first thing…" He looked over at Raisa, who was now sitting on the bottom of the stairs. "Are you okay? This is a lot to handle all at once. Do you want to go to the hospital now or get some- "

"Yes, as soon as possible." Raisa stood up. Devon was right. This entire day had given her a lot to take in. But, every day lately had been like that. She didn't know how to feel… about anything… right now.

Devon took her hand and pulled her to him. He closed his eyes as his arms circled her. Raisa felt the sensation of a warm blanket wrapping her from head to toe. She was torn between wanting to stay like this, and needing to get to her mother. She didn't have to decide. Devon dropped his hands, too soon, to take hers and pulled her into the kitchen.

Pen sat in a kitchen chair, his face tilted back and smiling, his hands on Corli's hips. She was standing, facing him and cleaning his face with a wet cloth. She had several first aid items scattered on the table next to her and was working studiously on Pen's injuries.

Devon's lips turned up slightly at the sight. "We're headed over to the hospital… but I think you guys should stay here, especially since I can't lock the front door right now. Besides, I think tonight will be quiet."

"No argument here." Pen turned to Devon and smiled. Then he touched Raisa's arm. "You give your mom our love, okay?"

"You sure you don't want me to go, Raisa?" Corli was already stepping away as if she were preparing to go with Raisa to the hospital.

"No… no, we'll be fine." She smiled at her friend. "You two stay here and take care of each other."

Devon and Raisa rode in silence to the hospital. Raisa had her knees pulled up, resting on the side of Devon's legs, her head on his chest with his arm securely around her. Raisa thought that this was the only place in the world that felt safe.

Daylight was waning and the shutters would soon be open to allow the night lights of the city to spill eerily into the room. All that could be heard at the moment was the labored breathing of some of the women that were injured during the reports from the day. Nosh had ordered silence. He sat with his face cast down on the surface of his desk, his fingers laced through his hair and clawing at the back of his head. Only five Lasteire pairs had not discovered their calling. Fortunately that included the boy and girl that were the most critically important to the group. The failure of the Assembly depended on the failure of these two most.

A flame leapt to life. Nosh raised his head to see who had defied the stillness.

"Master, I have a report for you."

Nosh rose to his feet and slowly approached. His eyes squinted in anticipation of the news he would hear. "Go on."

"Garik is dead. It was Devon that killed him... I apologize that it was not me... he slit his throat."

Nosh stopped short. "So, the boy is capable of taking a life. How utterly extraordinary!" His eyes flickered to life and a menacing smile spread across his face. "This *is* encouraging," he crooned to himself. "And the girl?"

"She was not with him."

Without changing his expression, Nosh completed the steps to the woman addressing him. He ripped her robe open, exposing her naked body underneath, and pushed his fingers into the skin under her ribcage. Her body contorted to allow for the displacement of the skin but she did not cry out. His hand came around her heart.

123

"I will continue to..." Ivan heard a sound like a water balloon bursting. For a split second he wondered what it was.

Lona's hospital room felt like a family get-together and had for the last five days.

Raisa's siblings and their families treated it like a special occasion. She saw them more in the last week than she had in the last six months. Her frustration was starting to crack through the calm exterior she was trying to keep for her mother's sake. "Has anyone talked to the doctor today?"

Aileen handed Kristy to Charlotte and ushered Raisa into the hall. "I spoke to him earlier, why?"

"Well, did you get any answers today?" Raisa felt like her family purposefully left her out of the loop on everything. Whether it was because she was the baby and they thought she couldn't handle it or wouldn't understand, she wasn't sure. They would probably see her as an eight year old for the rest of her life.

"They said that they would try to take out mom's feeding tube tomorrow," Aileen replied. It seemed a perfectly reasonable response to her.

Okay, so maybe they don't feel the need to keep things from me, they just don't care to find out even for themselves... wow. "But why does she have the feeding tube in the first place? What is *wrong* with her?" Raisa was trying her hardest not to get angry. She knew it wasn't Aileen's fault her mother was here. It was hers.

Aileen's face drew blank, "I don't know Raisy, sometimes we don't have all the answers."

An unsuspecting doctor stood at the nurses' station a few feet from where they stood. Raisa had had enough with vague questions and nondescript answers, and marched over to him.

Aileen simply walked back into their mother's room. They stopped trying to rein Raisa in many years ago.

"Doctor, can I talk to you, please?" Raisa sounded very polite but her voice carried a firmness that dared the doctor to ignore her.

"Certainly, Miss Coen, what can I do for you?" he smiled in a very professional manner.

"What is wrong with my mother? Why isn't she getting better? What are you doing to help her?" Raisa's voice raised a level higher and louder with each question.

The doctor placed a hand on her shoulder and led her to a couple of chairs a little more out of the way and had her sit down with him. He spoke to her gently, "We don't know exactly what is causing the troubles that your mother is having –"

"Well, how and when are you going to find out?!" Raisa actually hated confrontations but she hated evasive doctors more. She could feel herself starting to shake.

"Raisa," the doctor's voice became even gentler, "we could do a lot of tests that might prove daunting for your mother, to find out exactly what the medical reasons are for your mother's failing health. But it might not make a difference *why*, at this point. Raisa... I don't know if your mother is going to get better."

Raisa felt the blood drain from her face. "What?" her voice was quiet now. "What are you saying?" She looked at the doctor pleading with her eyes for him to not continue.

"Your mother's body appears to be shutting itself down. We've tried to stabilize her to get to the root of the problem, but her body has not responded. It's as if she does not have the will. She is at the tipping point right now. A few more hours and there will be no turning back."

Raisa instantly felt a war rage inside her. One side wanted to fall apart, bawl her eyes out and fade into hysterical oblivion. This side wanted to take no responsibility, it only wanted to be angry and vengeful. She could scream at the doctors and throw a fit with her siblings, blaming them for allowing this to happen, for not being around when their mother needed them most. The other side knew that there was strength in her that did not exist in her brother or sisters. It was calm and careful. This side would take all issues into consideration and make the best decisions for her mother. No one else could.

She glanced down the hall toward her mother's room and spoke to the doctor with quiet resolve. "Does she know?"

"I think she suspects, Raisa, but, no... we have not told her."

"I'll take care of it, Doctor. Thank you for being candid with me." Raisa turned her eyes back to the doctor in acknowledgement for just a moment, and then headed back to tell her brother and sisters that their mother was dying.

He could tell that the sun had set by looking through the four-inch wide window next to him. Devon sat in the small waiting area in the critical ward a couple of halls away from Lona's room. It was the only way in or out of this floor so it served its purpose as a lookout point. He knew Raisa needed this time with her family so he was giving her space. He couldn't help feeling though, that in the last few days there was a distance beginning between them. When he looked at her a couple of weeks ago, it was like her light shined for him, because of him. In the last few days the light rays had scattered and lost much of their energy. He couldn't blame her though. There were at least six reasons he could think of off the top of his head that Raisa should be questioning why she was involved with him at all.

"Hey, Devon," Corli waived a bag of food in greeting.

"No, it's Dudley today… let me introduce you." Pen smirked at Devon.

Corli looked a tad confused but shrugged it off. "We brought burgers. Should we take this stuff over to Raisa and make it a foursome?"

Just as they were heading to find Raisa, Evert, Aileen and Charlotte came around the corner. Their red eyes and dejected expressions brought the three up short.

"What's happened?" Devon asked urgently.

Aileen and Charlotte shook their heads; they were in no condition to have a conversation and kept moving toward the elevators.

Evert stopped, his face cast down. "Our mom is dying. Raisa is going to tell her now. She wanted to do it alone. We're going home and coming back tomorrow." His voice cracked and he brought his hand to his mouth because the sound embarrassed him. Evert locked eyes with Devon for a few seconds; he wanted to ask a question, many questions, but he didn't know how to ask. *And what would this kid know about me, or life or death or anything.* He dropped his face again and walked onto the elevator with Aileen and Charlotte.

Corli pushed the bag she held in her hand into Pen. "You two stay here. I'm going to wait for Raisa outside her mom's room."

Raisa opened the door and quietly shut it behind her. Her mother was on a lot of medication to make it more comfortable for her to have a tube down her throat that lead to her stomach to keep her fed and alive. Lona stirred though, as Raisa pulled a chair up close to the bed. Raisa took in the sight of her mother. Her bruised cheek was now multiple shades of green and blue, her cut's only thin black lines. Her hair was matted to her head and she looked altogether miserable.

Lona brought her hand up and touched the tube that hung in her mouth and rendered her unable to speak. She made a slight grunting sound and looked at Raisa with pleading eyes.

"You want me to get that out?" Raisa gently touched her mother's arm and rang the buzzer for the nurse.

Lona's eyes closed in relief and a tear rolled down her cheek.

A nurse came into the room within seconds. "Can I help you?"

"My mother would like you to remove this tube... now." Raisa was not unkind but as she heard the sound come from her mouth, she thought she sounded like someone else... or maybe herself, just many years older.

"I can't do that without the doct –"

"Call him please. Right now."

The nurse excused herself to make the call and Raisa held her mother's hand securely. She was struck with the reversal of roles at play in this moment. She was taking care of her mother, just as her mother had taken care of her.

The nurse came back and brought a helper with her. Raisa stood back as they unhooked everything attached to this tube and then watched as they pulled it from her mother's mouth. It made Lona's body heave and gag. Raisa realized that she had never seen her mother in any kind of compromising scenario. She was always the picture of grace and poise. Her heart broke knowing how this must make her feel.

Raisa sat back down after the nurses finished cleaning away any evidence of the feeding tube. They also turned down Lona's medication and already she was more alert.

"Hi, Mom." Raisa took her mother's hand again. "Don't try to talk, it will just hurt."

Lona nodded gratefully.

I'm here, Raisa. Your mother and I love you very much. I know this is hard, but there are many things in life and death that are difficult. Even this experience will help you. Raisa took a slow deep breath in and then out again.

"Mommy, I need to tell you some things. Are you ready?" Lona nodded very slightly. "That tube wasn't working. Your body doesn't seem to want to accept any food or treatment. They can't figure out why, exactly, you aren't getting better." Raisa paused to swallow the knot in her throat and check her tears. "And... now... it looks like things are shutting down. You're probably not going to get better, Mommy." She searched her mother's face for the effect her words were having. The exact emotion she didn't know if she could handle was written into every line and feature of her mother's face. Lona was afraid. She looked weak and vulnerable and young, like a four year old, lost in the woods, only in an old and failing body. "I love you so much, Mommy. You know that, right?"

Lona closed her eyes and let a few more tears run down her face as she squeezed her daughter's hand. She wished that at this moment she could do away with her lifelong fear of physical and emotional pain so that she could be truly strong for Raisa. But she couldn't conquer it, especially now. She let the sadness of that failure settle into her bones. *But just maybe... after*, she thought. She opened her eyes and looked at her beautiful daughter, "I'm scared," she whispered. "I want to go home."

Devon was using the time at Raisa's house to study the Edward Brayden shows. It kept his mind occupied and allowed him to be near Raisa and protect her, even though they barely spoke. He told himself that the strain between them was only because Lona was dying, but every once in awhile, doubt would overtake him and he would agonize over the thought of losing her. He would have thought it was juvenile to be so upset over the prospect of losing a girlfriend if it weren't for the ever-growing knowledge that there was something they were supposed to *do* together. That's what he told himself anyway.

Pen split his time scouting the area, spending time with Corli and working on deciphering the shows with Devon. He let himself into the house and found Devon by himself, as usual, sitting in the living room with a notepad and pen, an episode of Edward Brayden on pause. "Same report as normal... no bruel activity today," Pen joked with a quick salute. "How's it coming with the show?"

Devon was clicking the pen on the notepad, "Well, here's one bizarre thing... I have no clue why it would be relevant but it keeps coming up. Something about the poles."

"Being one of Polish descent, or of the North and South type?" Pen quipped.

"Well, there is a reference in every episode of some kind... like polar opposites, bi-polar, tides and weather being affected by the poles, polar bears, polar heart rate monitors... I have no clue what that is. And several references to magnets." Devon had a picture flash into his mind of him and Raisa standing, pressed up next to each other. He wondered where *that* came from and shook his head to clear the image. "So, I would say the reference is to the North and South poles."

"Hmmm, that is interesting." Pen's looked was quizzical. "I bet that it's about the magnetic North and South poles. You know there not in the same place as the physical poles."

"No, I didn't know that." Devon looked sideways at his friend. "You're just a plethora of information," he grinned. "Okay, we'll keep an eye on any news about the magnetic poles."

130

Pen rolled his eyes. "What else?"

Devon went solemn again, "There is this part at the very end of every episode where they flash some inspirational quote up on the screen for about a minute, like they want to give you time to write it down. I didn't think anything of it at first until I realized that after the first twelve episodes, they repeated exactly the same for the next twelve."

"Have you written them down?"

"No, I was just going to do that. Here," he tossed the remote to Pen, "you find them and I'll write."

1. *It is a far, far better thing that I do, than I have ever done; it is a far, far better rest that I go to, than I have ever known.*

2. *Is it true? Is it kind? Is it Necessary?*

3. *You are what you think.*

4. *The best things in life aren't things.*

5. *Last, best hope.*

6. *Heir of all things, by whom he also made the worlds.*

7. *That which does not kill us makes us stronger.*

8. *Must turn, each in its track, without a sound, forever tracing Newton's ground.*

9. *Save the world by saving one man at a time; all else is grandiose romanticism or politics.*

10. *Mankind should be my business.*

11. *From the Depths Sound the Great Sea Gongs*

12. *Destruction, an annihilation that only man can provoke, only man can prevent.*

Devon read through them quickly when they were done. "Wow, this is pretty heavy stuff once it's written all in one place."

Pen was nodding in agreement, "Yeah… and they repeat exactly the same, huh? I wonder if that has any more significance other than to draw attention to them."

Devon heard Raisa walking down the stairs and changed his train of thought. He had heard all the members of her family taking these steps many times now, and he knew the soft step of Raisa the second he heard it.

The last thing he learned in the show was something that he had not shared with Pen yet. He discovered a reference to rays of light that he knew had to be about the same dancing light that shone from her. There was another reference though, that spoke of a completely different light, that he gathered was orange-ish in color and circular, not in rays. He was dying to ask Raisa about it on the off chance it was something she saw on him.

He looked at her face as she reached the bottom of the stairs and saw the same solemn look he had seen for days. She tried to smile at him but Devon saw that the smile did not reach her eyes. It was more like the sort of smile you gave someone you were passing on the street, not the kind you gave someone you loved. Devon felt his heart slump.

Hospice came twice a day to administer a morphine patch and record Lona's vital signs. They pointed out to Raisa and her sisters the pooling of fluid in Lona's limbs, saying that this was an indication of her vital systems failing. Evert only visited once, the day they brought their mother home, and Raisa thought it was unlikely that he would come back. Boys, especially her brother, didn't handle this sort of thing well.

132

Each girl gravitated to the tasks of caring for their mother that suited them best. Aileen was best at the dirty jobs, cleaning Lona and changing bed pads. Nothing ever grossed Aileen out to the point of inaction. She knew, too, about their mother's affinity for keeping up appearances, and Aileen was happy to know that what she did would make Lona happier to the end. Charlotte kept up with any physical needs. In the first day, she tried to give Lona some broth but when it didn't stay down, she switched to ice chips and the lemon swabs that hospice brought to keep her mouth from drying out. She would rub lotion on her mother's hands and brush the front of her hair. These tasks when done always brought many thanks from their mother, when she was awake for them. Raisa was the caretaker of their mother's feelings, staying with her most of the time, only leaving to eat or shower when Aileen and Charlotte were there. Raisa even began sleeping with her, since on the first night home, Lona awoke, frightened, not knowing if she were alive or dead.

Raisa now only heard the older, more mature voice coming from her when she spoke to her mother. "Just think, Mom, you have some wonderful things to look forward to... you get to be with Dad again. I bet he'll want your help designing your mansion in the sky."

Lona smiled. She couldn't speak much but could still give quiet one word answers.

"Are you in any pain, Mom?"

"No." It seemed an easy and honest answer.

"I think you have angels ministering to you, Mom. Dad won't let you be in pain, I'm sure of it." Raisa spoke with conviction. She thought that if she could see past the veil between this world and the next, they would be surrounded by loved ones, their hands on Lona, taking that pain from her.

133

Raisa spoke to her mother about a lot of things, memories of childhood, things she hoped her mother would look down on from heaven when she was gone, the mother and sister she would reunite with on the other side.

One topic that Aileen and Charlotte thought she went too far with was the planning of Lona's funeral. But Raisa thought that it was therapeutic for her mother to be involved in the planning of this one last thing. It seemed to calm her.

"What color paper do you want the program printed on?" Raisa asked lightly.

"Green, that mint color," was her mother's amazingly coherent response.

"Hmmm, that has always been your favorite color hasn't it." Raisa thought about how the whole lower level of their house was painted with it. "Only, if we're going to put your picture on the front, you might look sick in it." Raisa raised an eyebrow. She felt bad trying to change her mother's mind on a last request but hoped her mother would see the logic.

"Peach."

Raisa smiled, "That will work beautifully. What picture do you want on the front?"

Lona's eyes glazed as if she were having an old memory. She spoke slowly and her throat rattled but she was determined to make sure Raisa knew the one she spoke of, "You know that picture of when I was young, it was black and white but then they colored it? It was the only professional picture I ever had done. Do you know the one? I felt like I was pretty in that picture."

Raisa was startled by this burst of fluid conversation and could tell it was important. "I know exactly the one. You have been beautiful in all your pictures, Mom, but you're right... that is an especially beautiful picture. I'll make sure it is on the cover

134

and framed with flowers. Also, I think that Aileen, Charlotte and I are going to sing your favorite Primary song... I'll print the lyrics in the program too."

At this Lona's eyes glossed up and she closed them. "Can you sing it now, Raisa?"

Raisa knew she probably wouldn't make it through, but she started anyway.

> *I often go walking in meadows of clover,*
> *And I gather armfuls of blossoms of blue.*
> *I gather the blossoms the whole meadow over;*
> *Dear mother, all flowers remind me of you.*
>
> *O mother, I give you my love with each flower*
> *To give forth sweet fragrance a whole lifetime through;*
> *For if I love blossoms and meadows and walking,*
> *I learn how to love them, dear mother, from you.*

Raisa had to whisper the last few lines through her tears. It didn't matter, though. Her mother had drifted off to sleep, her chest rising and falling with an easier breathing than she had before. Raisa wondered how many more times she would hear her mother speak.

Charlotte walked into the room, "Raisa, why don't you go spend some time with Devon. He has to be feeling neglected."

Raisa gave Charlotte a worried look. "I have to stay with Mom. What if..."

"I promise I won't leave her alone, Raisa. And I don't believe she is going to go tonight. *Go*. Go get out of the house."

Raisa sighed, "Okay, but let me know if she asks for me. *If* we leave the house I'll have my cell." Raisa got up from the chair beside the bed, looked at her mother's sleeping face, just in case, and then headed for the stairs.

135

Devon stood up in surprise when Raisa walked toward him instead of toward the kitchen like he thought she would. "Hi," he said a little too breathlessly. "How is your mom?"

"She's sleeping. We had a good talk today." Raisa looked at the floor. For some reason it was difficult to look into Devon's eyes. *Char is right, I have been neglecting him.* A copper ring near the floor moved into her field of vision. She looked up to see if Devon had moved closer to her but he hadn't. The rings were just growing in strength as he stood there. She realized just now that the light around him had been much more dim and subdued in the last week or so. She speculated that it must be her that affected them. *A negligence monitor, great.* "What do you think about going out for dinner, would it be safe?" She surprised even herself with the question.

Devon's mouth was slightly open for several seconds. He was caught off guard. He marveled at how a simple dinner proposal could feel like redemption. *Okay, I have to actually think about this… not make a selfish snap decision.* "Um, yeah, I think it will be… okay." He looked over at Pen to involve him in the plan. Pen's expression was half concern, half amusement. "Why don't you go pick up Corli and meet us over at Mario's." He looked back at Raisa with renewed hope in his heart. He was searching her face for a sign that he was saved. "Is Italian good?"

10

Raisa noticed that both she and Devon had their hands stuffed in their pockets as they walked from the parking lot up to Mario's. Devon stepped quickly to the restaurant door and accidently turned his pocket inside out in his rush to open it for her. Raisa smiled and felt a zing fly through her body as she remembered how attentive she thought Devon was. His arm slid around her waist as they stopped at the front of the dining room to wait to be seated. Raisa's breath caught at his touch. *How lucky am I to have this feeling all over again.* She looked up into his eyes as he stood next to her. The copper flecks were shining bright. They reminded her of laser beams she'd seen at night clubs.

The hostess had to repeat herself to get Devon and Raisa's attention. They both smiled awkwardly and followed her toward a table for four at the center of the back wall.

As Devon followed Raisa, his hand placed at the small of her back, he was struck with the notion that this was a real date; something he wished he could have done sooner. *What a poor showing, Devon. You'll have to make up for that*, he thought. He quickly surveyed the table, and decided that Raisa needed to sit next to him and not across. He pulled out a chair for her. "Here you go… I like to sit facing out so I can see what's going on." He walked behind her after she sat down, dropped his hand to her shoulder and left it there as he pulled out his own chair. He sat sideways instead of facing the table so that he could look at her.

137

The hostess was good. She knew when she wasn't needed and made her greeting quick. She winked at them as she retreated.

Raisa wondered if she was being fresh. "What do you think that was for?" She turned to look at Devon and was surprised when she saw his face a few inches from hers.

"What was what for?" he said softly as he discreetly moved Raisa's hair back and slowly touched his lips to her neck just below her ear.

Raisa suddenly felt dizzy. She moved her hand to his leg and had a mad desire to maul him, but tried to concentrate on breathing instead. "You are so not fair…" she barely managed.

Devon didn't leave his hiding spot at Raisa's neck. He ran his lips across her ear and then his nose along her jaw and into her hair. His broad hand was around the back of her neck. "Never said I was fair," he breathed.

All Raisa could do was close her eyes. She felt like she could take this for about two more seconds. "Devon," she whispered, "Why don't we – "

"Are we interrupting? I guess we could get our own table." Pen had a sideways grin and one eyebrow cocked. He was holding Corli's hand. Corli was smiling and biting her lip as she took in the sight of her friend melting into her chair.

Devon casually sat up and grabbed a roll from the basket that had just been dropped off at the table. "I was wondering where you guys were… what took you so long?" Other than the grin on his face, there was no evidence of what he had been doing. He took a bite of bread.

The waitress came and took everyone's order. Raisa's head was starting to clear. As the four friends sat and talked, nibbling on the bread with olive oil and balsamic vinegar, Raisa's thoughts returned to her mother for a moment. She made a conscious effort to push away the sadness and decided to try and enjoy herself for at least a little while.

Devon was trying to decide whether or not to order a glass of wine, "I wonder if their Chianti is any good-" when the hair prickled on the back of his neck. His face shot up and he quickly canvassed the room. His eyes landed on a couple that had just walked into the bar area at the opposite side of the restaurant. Raisa, Pen and Corli felt it too and followed Devon's gaze.

The couple appeared to be drunk already as they stumbled, laughing loudly, to the bar. The girl was dressed in an outfit that collected looks of lust from most of the men in the room and disgust from most of the women. The man was groping her shamelessly. He started waiving at the bartender to order a drink and suddenly froze. His face turned from gregarious to frantic as he spoke urgently to the woman hanging at his waist. Panicked, they both turned to look across the room, a green flash licked from their eyes. They froze for no more than two seconds, then turned and barreled out of the door.

Devon and Pen were up and out of their seats the moment they saw their eyes. They moved quickly and carefully through the dining room to the bar and then out the door to pursue the two bruels.

After half a block, Pen caught up with the woman but left her for Devon and turned on the speed to quickly span the additional twenty yards to catch the man. Neither bruel put up a fight once they were caught. They hung limply like a rags in Devon and Pen's hands. They pulled the couple back into the shadows of a closed office building and held them against a stucco wall.

Devon's voice was calm but full of authority. "What are you doing here and who sent you?"

Both the man and the woman stood slumped and mute not willing to make eye contact. Pen and Devon pushed their arms harder at the bruels necks.

"Answer me!" Devon demanded.

The woman whimpered, "We weren't looking for you...we were just out having a little fun –"

"Shut up, Sandy!" the man growled. "We don't owe them anything."

Devon reached into his pocket with his free hand and produced a knife. In one swift motion he opened it and brought it to Sandy's throat. He pierced her skin with it and watched several drops of blood run down her neck and onto her nearly bare breasts. "Funny, I thought it would be green," Devon sneered inches from the woman's face.

Pen watched Devon. He wasn't shocked by his friend's actions but had hoped that this part of Devon was being tempered by having Raisa in his life. "You better give up something. My friend here is looking a little unstable. Wouldn't want your girlfriend to get hurt," he warned the man.

He spit in Pen's face and scoffed, "I don't give a shi-"

"Wait, wait!" The woman was panicked; Devon had pushed the knife further into the skin of her neck. "Really. Nosh ordered us to stay away from you, I swear."

Pen and Devon looked at each other. They had a name. In the split second that they were distracted the man and woman tore free from their captors and ran like scattering cockroaches. They started in pursuit but stopped after a few feet. They both knew that these bruels were no threat.

Raisa's heart jumped into her throat at the sight of the two bruels. Before she could collect her thoughts, Devon and Pen were out the door and Corli was standing with her handy switchblade held

140

down at her side, watching after them. After a few minutes she sat back down but turned her chair to watch the doors of the restaurant.

"I don't think I'll ever get used to this," Raisa sounded shaken. "They have always made me nervous, but now…. How do you stay so calm and think so fast, Corli?"

"Honestly…I don't know," Corli answered. "It's almost automatic… like it's something that has been a part of me all my life and I just didn't know it."

"Well," Raisa grabbed Corli's hand and squeezed it, "I don't think I will ever be able to repay you for everything you have done for me. I couldn't ask for a better guardian, or a better friend."

Devon and Pen walked back into the restaurant as several of its patrons stared at them. They arrived back at their table at the same time their food was delivered. Devon caught Raisa's nervous look. "It's okay. They ran off. They weren't after us." He bent and kissed Raisa's cheek.

Raisa let some pent up air out of her lungs. "So, did you catch them? What did they say? Did you… hurt them?" Raisa realized that as much as she hated any form of violence, she would not be upset if they had suffered just a little.

Devon's mouth was already full of chicken piccata and nodded to Pen.

Pen saw Devon's guarded nod, which meant, 'tell them what happened but leave out the parts I wouldn't want Raisa to hear'. "Yeah, we caught them. They came in here on accident. They weren't looking for us. We… had to persuade them a little. They have been ordered by someone named 'Nosh' to stay away from us."

Raisa gasped. The memory of the night that Garik stabbed her flooded back. She clutched her hand to her chest.

141

Devon dropped his fork and both of his hands came to Raisa's body. He didn't know what was wrong but was doing his best to try and figure it out.

"I've heard that name," Raisa exclaimed. "Garik…" she choked on the name. She had never hated anyone more than she hated him. Not as much for herself, although that was plenty, but for what he did to her mother. "He said that 'Nosh would be proud' when he… well I don't remember if it was before or after he……." Devon wrapped his arms around Raisa.

"So, he's the one," Corli stated, "the one that is in charge of all of them. Take him out and all this nonsense would be over." She took a stab at her food and popped it in her mouth rather nonchalantly.

Pen, Devon and Raisa looked at each other with surprise and then back at Corli munching her food.

Pen half chuckled, "She does have a point."

It was 8pm when they got back to the house. Corli fetched Charlotte and Aileen and brought them downstairs to eat the food they brought home for them.

As Charlotte reached the bottom of the stairs she stopped next to Raisa. "Did you have fun?" she said, regarding her with a kind smile.

Raisa saw no need to go into detail about which parts were extremely fun and which weren't. "Yeah, it was great… thanks." She gave her sister a hug.

Charlotte hung onto Raisa and spoke softly into her hair, "Mom asked where you were about five minutes ago. I think she was happy when I told her you were spending a little time with your friends. I'm sure she's anxious to hear about it." Charlotte finished the hug with a squeeze and let Raisa go, knowing she would want to get upstairs. She joined Aileen in the kitchen.

142

Raisa looked at her friends with a little concern. She didn't want to be rude. "Are you guys okay?"

Devon spoke up. He looked at Pen and Corli first, "You know, I have a pretty good feeling that those orders to leave us alone will apply to all the bruels. Why don't you guys take off... go do something fun? We'll be fine."

Corli thought that sounded too good to be true, but had her concerns. Her brow wrinkled a little. "Are you sure?"

Pen chimed in with a smile, "Well, I think he's right, they don't want to have anything to do with us. Let's go catch a movie... or something." He stepped closer to Corli and pulled her into a waltz pose. Then he dipped her.

Corli pulled herself up and softly smacked him on the shoulder with her open hand. "Quit it, Pen" she scolded. But she couldn't help the smile that crept to her lips.

Pen reached over and grabbed something from the narrow table in the entryway and presented it to Corli.

"It's beautiful!" Corli took the paper rose that Pen held up for her. "How did you do this?" She turned the flower over in her hand.

"Just a napkin... from the restaurant," Pen answered. "I'll show you how to make them." He smiled and kissed her forehead.

"Okay then, we're out," Corli said decidedly.

She gave Raisa a hug, socked Devon in the stomach, grabbed Pen's hand, and led him out the door.

Devon turned to Raisa. He didn't want to let her go, but was prepared to tell her good night. "I'll watch more of the show and settle in on the couch while you take care of you mom-. Instead he got a surprise.

"Come on." Raisa grabbed his hand and pulled him up the stairs and into her room. She flipped on a miniature table lamp, giving them just enough light to see where they were going. "This will be more comfortable for you than the couch. I'll be sleeping with my mom anyway. You have the bathroom and here's my iPod if you want to listen to some mu-"

Devon grabbed her hand and pulled her to him forcefully. Raisa took in a surprised breath. He didn't kiss her. He looked into her eyes, pulled her hands to his neck and put his hands on her waist. He held her gaze as he slipped his hands under her shirt and felt her soft skin. His eyes blazed into Raisa's as he gradually felt his way to her stomach then around again to the small of her back. His fingers dipped the slightest amount under the waist of her jeans, which sent Raisa's heart slamming against her chest. Raisa dropped one hand along with her eyes slowly down Devon's chest. The perfect rise and fall of his muscles under her hand made her knees weak. Raisa spoke, surprised that she had any air left to do it. "You enjoy torturing me, don't you?" She trailed her gaze back to Devon's face. *What is that look?* His eyes were lazy and smiling; his mouth was slightly open and turned up at the corner. *It's.... devilish!*

"Actually," his eyes twinkled and smoldered with copper embers, "I'm torturing myself." He took Raisa's hand from his chest with both of his, brought it to his mouth and kissed it. He surprised Raisa again when he spun her around with the hand he was holding till she was facing away from him. He pressed himself against her back, wrapped his arms around her and kissed her neck. Then he whispered to her, "Go see your mom... I'll be here if you need me." He let her go and gave her a pat on the butt.

Raisa spun around, "Ahhh!"

Devon was trying not to smirk as he went and stretched out on the bed.

Raisa grabbed her tank top and shorts. She tried to glare at Devon, but she was having an equally difficult time keeping the smile from her face.

As she left the room, she thought of something that made her happy. *My dad used to do that to my mom – exactly the same.*

Raisa changed into her pajamas and sat in the chair next to her mother's bed. She had an impression that she and her mother were not alone. The room felt full of people somehow, even in the silence of it. She wasn't even close to tired and Lona was sleeping. Raisa took in the dark stillness of the room, and listened to her mother's irregular breathing. She heard the rattling in her chest and knew that meant fluid was settling in her lungs. It was difficult to listen to the pattern, or lack thereof. On occasion there were several seconds between breaths and Raisa's heart raced in alarm till the next breath came. Raisa hadn't slept much in the last few days.

Lona roused, her gulp of air indicating that she was a little panicked.

"I'm here, Mom." Raisa took her hand. "I'm right here."

Lona settled immediately and drifted off again.

Raisa tried lying down, but between listening to her mother and her inability to turn off her brain, sleep was very far away. She listened and stared into the darkness for several hours. She heard Charlotte and Aileen go to bed, in their old room that they used to share, a couple of hours ago. The house was quiet.

Her mind turned to Devon and a quiver ran the length of her body. She was so physically attracted to him that it almost hurt. She decided to try to distract herself from that line of thinking by pondering his other qualities. *He's obviously a born leader, he is strong and agile, he can fix things, he loves his mother deeply, he is chivalrous, he is intelligent, he's not a quitter, he's got a*

145

snarky, sarcastic side... that he doesn't use too *often,* Raisa smiled in the dark, *he carries himself beautifully... almost like royalty, he is utterly gorgeous, his kisses are amazing, his touch is so tender it melts me and at just the right times he is strong, he has a 'bad boy' side.......* Raisa saw an image pop into her head of her and Devon standing in an embrace............ *this isn't working!* Raisa peered at the clock, it read 1am. Raisa's heart sped as she carefully climbed out of her mother's bed. *What am I doing?!*

Her bedroom door was wide open and she was glad that she didn't have to open it. She was not so glad, though, that she didn't want to risk the noise of closing it behind her. *No one is getting up now... don't worry about it, Raisa. And that way you won't do anything you're not supposed to,* she told herself. She came to the edge of her bed to see Devon with her headphones in his ears, and his eyes closed. She wasn't sure if he was asleep but she leaned down to hear what music he was listening to. *Soundgarden, Forth of July,* she smiled.

She bent down to kiss him, placing her hands on the bed at either side of his shoulders as she did. His lips were still for only a moment. His eyes opened as he kissed her back and pulled the music from his ears. He touched her face and slid his hand down to her bare shoulder. Raisa pulled back from the kiss and sat down beside him. Devon took the sight of her in, staring at every inch of her in the dim light, the form of her body in the thin tank top, the bareness of her legs in her shorts. He wanted to touch her but somehow restrained himself and remained still.

Raisa was amazed that she didn't feel self-conscious as Devon looked at her. It made her happy that he did. She wanted to touch him. She reached for the edge of Devon's t-shirt and slid her hands across him, pushing his shirt up. She bent down and kissed his stomach, letting her hands wander up to his chest.

146

Devon moaned softly. He let the feeling of Raisa's mouth and hands on his body sink into his skin. Before he could think about what he was doing, he pulled off his t-shirt and pulled Raisa by her waist on top of him so that he could feel her against him. Her hair draped onto his shoulders. As he kissed her deeply, he felt a floating sensation that told him he was losing control.

Raisa's head was spinning. *Is this really happening?* Abandon replaced the question in her mind. She felt herself gingerly lifted up, flipped and tossed lightly on her back. Devon pressed his body on to hers. She felt his hands in her hair and then searching her body. Devon moved his mouth from hers to her neck and worked his way below her collarbone. Just as Raisa was thinking that the slightest step further would be the farthest she had gone, the light bulb popped on her desk.

Devon and Raisa both froze. An electrical current hung in the air that continued to snap and flash for the next few seconds. They listened for any other sound or reaction from anywhere else in the house, and then both started to carefully breathe again, unable to contain it. The electrical phenomenon that plagued them when they were together didn't faze them much anymore, but it definitely stopped their momentum.

Devon, his control regained, sat up on the edge of the bed and pulled Raisa up next to him. He brought his hand to her cheek and rested his forehead on hers. "That was... amazing," *excruciating and all together crazy...* "What got into you?"

Raisa bit her lip. She couldn't decide whether she was sad or glad that they stopped when they did. "I couldn't sleep, and I couldn't stop thinking about you.......... I think I was possessed."

Devon chuckled and kissed her forehead. "Well, we better get you out of here and back to your mom's room. I know for

147

certain that I would not be able to handle that again right now… you drive me crazy." He stood and helped her to her feet.

They turned toward the door and both stopped short, their eyes popped wide. There, outside the doorway, stood an image of Raisa's mother, floating a foot off the ground, almost glowing in the dark hall. She wore an old-fashioned white nightgown. Raisa recalled that it was not the one she had on in her bed.

Where did you go? Raisa thought she heard her mother's voice in her head. She blinked her eyes. In a split second, she tried to decide if what she saw was solid, and questioned herself as to whether this was a hallucination brought on by guilt. She did feel a little like she was caught doing something wrong with Devon. Then the image was gone.

Raisa grabbed at Devon's waist. "Did you see that?" It was sinking in, what it might mean, if it was real.

Devon took her hand and started to lead her out of her room, "Yes."

He dropped Raisa's hand as she stepped into her mother's room and waited outside the door.

Raisa knelt down next to the bed at Lona's side. She held her own breath and listened for the jangling sound that would tell her that her mother was still alive. She waited what seemed like an eternity, leaning in closer and closer to her mother's face. Lona sucked in a jagged breath. Raisa slumped to the floor.

Raisa took a minute to regain composure and walked back out of the door. "She's… fine." Raisa couldn't think of a better word.

Devon wrapped his arms around Raisa and held her. "Okay, you go get some sleep." He pulled his arms away to let her go.

Raisa stood there, not moving in any direction. She looked up at Devon. She didn't want to be away from him. She also felt

148

that under no circumstances could she leave her mother. This place that she stood was the only reasonable place to be.

Devon took in her expression and reached for her hand. "Here, have a seat," he whispered. He pulled her down onto the carpet, there in the hall just outside her mother's room. "I won't be able to sleep either," he smiled.

Raisa felt relieved. She could see and hear her mother from here, and she had Devon right in front of her.

They sat indian style facing each other. Devon took both of her hands and spoke softly, "You said I could have these anytime I wanted." Devon thought it seemed ages ago, not weeks, since he held Raisa's hand in the hospital while she slept. "This is perfect, actually." He leaned over and propped his elbows on his knees. "Whenever we're alone I get distracted by you." He smiled the devilish smile and then continued, "I've been wanting to ask you about something." He looked into Raisa's eyes and saw something he hadn't seen before. In the dark like this, her eyes actually had a light of their own that created faint rays. He realized this must be why her eyes were so fierce.

Raisa remembered when she asked Devon about his mother and her father. That had turned out to be some pretty heavy stuff. And now she was a little nervous about what Devon wanted to know. *Not that I have anything to hide.* "Oh, right, I haven't told you about my sordid past. Well, ask away… if you must."

Devon's eyebrow lifted. "Sordid past… uh huh… we'll get to that another time." Devon paused. He realized that he wasn't quite sure how to broach the subject. "You know how Pen and Corli and my mom all have that light above them?"

Raisa relaxed a little. "Yes."

"Well, you know Edward Brayden has that light above him too… and I've picked up that they are talking about another

149

energy and light as well." He peered at Raisa, here in the dimly lit hall, hoping that she would help him out and just say what she knew so he wouldn't have to sound foolish and explain the whole thing.

"Oh..." Raisa breathed with a slight exclamation. *He's found out about* his *light!* "So... can you see it? The energy around you?" Raisa felt a thrill run through her.

"No. I wasn't sure if I had one... I mean, I didn't think I did. But I can see yours." Devon leaned back on his hands so that he could take in the energy flowing from her. He followed it from her chest up to the ceiling. It was completely renewed from how it had been diminished just a few hours ago. He hadn't ever studied it like this before, so close to it. It was brilliant and fascinating.

Raisa was stunned. "*My* light? *I* have a light?"

Devon leaned back toward Raisa and smiled. "Yeah, I've seen it since the first day I saw you, sitting with your family at your father's service. It took me awhile to get used to it, to see you through it. It almost blinded me at The Rabbit Hole."

Raisa had thought before about discussing his energy with him, but this was a shock. She had never considered that she might have something similar. "What does it look like?" she asked in wonder, her eyes still wide.

Devon let his eyes see the full force of the energy coming from her. He touched her bare chest where it seemed to start. "It comes from all around here." He traced origins of the moving rays along her chest and neck with his fingertips, "and shines out in bright white rays and spirals... towards heaven... always up." He dropped his hand and readjusted his eyes so he could see her face again. "It's beautiful."

Raisa was astounded, but she thought about how Devon must be insanely curious about his, now that she knew for sure that he couldn't see it. She suddenly couldn't wait to tell him about it but was considering how to describe it to him. She stood and reached for his hand. "Stand up so I can tell you about yours." He took her hand and let her pull him up. "Yours is the color of copper." She took his arms and held them out a few inches from his sides, at an angle and told him to leave them there. Then she moved the palms of his hands so that they were slightly more parallel with the ground. "There. Your energy is in rings around you." She pulled her hand through them, along the edge of them, circling around Devon. "They're not solid, they're kind of misty and they reverberate with your heartbeat and move with you." Raisa stared at them outright and close-up for the first time. She felt the energy in them when her hand passed through. "They are smaller around you up here, "She touched his bare chest where she could see the first one and let her arm wrap around him as she continued following the rings around him, "and they get larger till they reach the ground. They connect you to it… to the earth." Raisa stopped circling him when she was back in front of him. She placed herself inside the rings and brought her hands to Devon's chest as she looked up into his eyes. "They are mesmerizing, and I could stare at them for hours." The light in Devon's eyes was shining brighter than ever. She thought about telling him about it. *No… this one I want to keep to myself for now*.

Devon was awestruck. But he couldn't help the thought that came to his mind now; that someone good should have this gift, not him. One thing he knew for sure though, it was part of what bound him and Raisa to each other, and that was a very good thing.

151

11

Raisa had the sensation of being shaken awake. Her eyes flew open to see that she and Devon had fallen asleep in the hall outside her mother's room. It was very early morning and the house was rumbling. Devon pulled himself up onto his arms and looked wide eyed back at Raisa.

"Earthquake," Devon said, startled but evenly. He scrambled to his feet and grabbed Raisa. They moved to the doorframe of Lona's room to assess the severity of the situation. "It's not stopping." His voice escalated with the growing noise. He clung to Raisa, checking around them for anything that might fall and hit them.

Aileen and Charlotte came through the door of their room, teetering as they walked. "It's getting stronger!" Aileen shouted as she grabbed at a wall to keep from falling.

"You guys get out of the house!" Devon was gesturing to Raisa and her sisters. Aileen and Charlotte quickly headed for the stairs.

"No," Raisa yelled defiantly. She turned and stumbled toward her mother. The strength of the trembler continued to increase. She heard the first crash of glass falling to the floor in the bathroom, followed by the sound of objects falling throughout the house. Raisa threw herself over the top half of her mother to shield her from anything that might strike her.

Devon knew it was useless to try to get Raisa out, so he set to the task of trying to keep her safe. He figured that it had been about five minutes now and the quake showed no signs of stopping. Besides shaking slightly harder with each minute, the house began to sway. The walls groaned under the stress. Devon's eyes flew to the window that was only a few feet from the bed and directly behind Raisa. He quickly scoured the room for something he could use to shield Raisa and her mother, trying to keep his eyes focused on what he was looking at through the jumping objects in the room. He spotted a blanket thrown across a chair and grabbed it. Just as he had managed to spread it out over Raisa and her mother, the windows shattered with a blast and sent glass shards flying through the room. Several hit his bare torso.

The sound was deafening now, an unearthly groaning and grinding noise filled the air. Anything that was not too heavy, but heavy enough became a shooting bullet through the room as everything bounced. Devon reached for the edge of the comforter on the bed opposite of where Lona was laying. He quickly pulled it over and sandwiched the three of them inside of it. Once he was covered, he made his way under the next layer to Raisa and her mother.

Raisa opened her eyes as Devon dropped to his knees beside her. "You're bleeding!" She screamed.

"I'm okay," he yelled back at her over the roar.

The house continued to shake, sway and groan. Though they couldn't see it, Devon and Raisa could hear by the cracks and crashes that the house seemed seconds from ripping apart. The bed that Lona was laying on had jumped across the floor so far that they were practically pinned to the wall under the shattered window.

Raisa held one hand over her mother's face and the other reached to touch some part of Devon. And though this was probably the most scared she had ever been in her life, she refused to shut her eyes. She would hold on to the sight of Devon even if the earth cracked open and swallowed them.

Devon grabbed Raisa's outstretched hand and pulled it to his chest before he reestablished his grip on the bed to make sure that it didn't crush them, pushing it back away from the wall with every bounce that it tried to move toward them. The quake had to be the equivalent of a seven-point-five by now and it wasn't letting up. Though the world was shaking, Devon kept his eyes on Raisa. "I love you." He didn't say the words very loud. He could have made no sound at all for all he knew. But he knew that Raisa needed to know it, if this were to be the last chance he would have.

Raisa saw Devon's words. She clutched her hand at his sholder.

At least fifteen minutes passed before the intensity of the quake declined. The house sounded like a one-hundred-year-old rickety wood gate now but it was miraculously still standing. At about eighteen minutes, everything was still rumbling, shaking and rolling, but Devon felt that they could risk removing the blankets. There was still too much movement to stand but both Raisa and Devon leaned up to check on Lona. She lay perfectly immobile on the bed, but her eyes were wide open, looking straight out to something that they couldn't see.

At twenty-four minutes, standing and walking was an option but not a good idea. At twenty-seven minutes, all that was left was a constant swaying and rolling. At thirty minutes, finally, everything was still.

Raisa quickly checked her mother over. "Are you okay, Mom?" Lona didn't respond. Raisa laid her ear to her mother's chest. She heard a faint heart beat, felt the slight rise and fall of her chest and turned to Devon. "She's alive," Raisa breathed with relief. She quickly moved closer to Devon. She needed to see the sources of the bleeding. She picked up a chair that had toppled. "Here, sit down in the chair –"

"I'm fine," Devon said softly as he considered Raisa's distress. He was planning to go and check things out but her expression stopped him.

"Sit!" Raisa demanded.

Devon sat. He would have teased her about being bossy under different circumstances. As it was, he was starting to feel some discomfort from the glass pieces that he now saw sticking out of his body.

Raisa grabbed a first aid box that was dumped on the floor from the cupboard in the bathroom. As Devon held pressure on the worst of his wounds, Raisa removed glass, and began to sterilized and bandage his cuts.

"Raisa!" Charlotte called from the entryway. "Are you guys alright?"

"We're up here," Raisa shouted back as she finished a bandage on Devon.

Charlotte and Aileen appeared moments later in their mother's bedroom doorway. Charlotte's expression was one of wonder, "I wouldn't have believed that you guys were okay after the way we saw the house twisting and shaking!"

Raisa cut the last piece of tape. "Yeah, it was pretty intense," she answered in a dazed tone. She bent and kissed Devon on the lips. It wasn't a long or mushy kiss, but it was a couple seconds longer than Aileen and Charlotte would have thought appropriate, she thought, under the circumstances.

Devon's brow creased. He didn't understand the family dynamic that was unfolding in front of him. Raisa sounded like she was in shock and her sisters seemed way too cool for the situation. He stood and wrapped his arms around Raisa.

155

In Devon's embrace, Raisa suddenly began to quiver and tears spilled from her eyes while she took hard and staggered breaths.

Devon held on to her till she relaxed and breathed easier. He kissed her temple then pulled her back to look her over. She seemed to have steadied.

"I'm going to go turn off the gas and check this place out. You guys please don't move around the house till I know it's safe." Devon squeezed Raisa's hand and walked carefully around the scattered debris and out of the bedroom.

Aileen and Charlotte stood staring at Raisa. "What?" she said defensively as she felt her face change a shade. She bent over to pick up a figurine lamp that dropped to the floor and was amazingly still intact, just one chip off the green ballroom gown of the woman that had always donned a lampshade for her shelter. Raisa's mind was scrambled, and she thought about how this plaster figure resembled her mother... at least how she looked when she was young.

"Nothing..." Charlotte answered as she moved to begin the clean-up with Raisa.

By the time Devon reappeared, the girls had straightened the room and vacuumed the glass with a small chargeable hand vac. He recovered his shirt from Raisa's room and pulled it over his head. "The house is leaning a little but I think its fine. The gas is off. Just be careful turning anything on... and wear shoes, there's glass everywhere." He had his cell in his hand and hit redial to Pen.

"What about your mom?" Raisa asked with renewed concern.

"I got through to her on the third try. She's a little traumatized, but fine. I've tried Pen and Corli a few times each. Here," Devon held the phone out to Aileen, "you try your family

156

first." While Aileen placed the call, Devon looked at the TV on the dresser. It was an old tube style and only about twelve inches wide with a giant crack diagonally across it. "Does this thing work?"

"It used to," Raisa answered. "It was all the way over there." She pointed to the opposite corner of the room. "I'm not sure now."

Devon stood back as he clicked the 'On' button. The TV buzzed to life –

"...event of global proportion. Reports are coming in from every geological site over the world. It appears that every major fault on the planet was affected by this event. Some initial reports have indicated readings as high as ten point seven on the Richter scale and all have been over seven. The devastation in third world countries is presumed to be unfathomable and many nations that do not typically have earthquakes have not fared well according to early reports...."

Charlotte finished her call and handed the phone back to Devon absently as she listened to the TV. He dialed Pen again but got a busy signal. "Are your families okay?"

Aileen nodded and spoke without taking her eyes off the TV, "Yes. And I called Evert too. They're fine. Are you guys hearing this?"

Raisa sat next to her mother and laid her hand on her shoulder. Lona's eyes were closed again. No one left the room and they settled in to watch more of the broadcast.

"...with me is Dr. Sanchez from the headquarters of the USGS in Reston, Virginia. Doctor, does the USGS have any speculation as to why an event like this would occur?"

"We are still correlating data and it may be awhile before we can answer such a broad question... we may never know."

"I see. Well, can you tell us anything about what effects this event will have on the people of the world?"

"Well, our initial theories presume that at a minimum the weather and tides will be majorly upset. Every time there is a major earthquake, it moves the position and shape of the planet

157

a small amount... but we're talking inches... we still have many calculations to do but this event may have changed the position of our North and South poles by hundreds of yards... and the magnetic poles are another issue altogether..."

Devon's phone rang. He lifted it to his ear in a daze. He couldn't believe what he was hearing on the television, but relief colored his voice knowing who it was. "Pen... you okay?" Devon was still staring at the small cracked TV screen.

"Yeah, I'm good and Corli is with me... are you watching?"

"Yeah."

"We're on our way over. It might take awhile."

"K." Devon shut his phone. He looked at Raisa. *I have not had a chance to tell her anything...*

Raisa had never seen this expression on Devon's face before and was trying not to be frightened by it. *Is it shock? Fear? No, I don't think fear... is he overwhelmed?* "Devon, you okay?"

Before Devon could answer, a loud intake of breath sounded in the room. They all looked at Lona. Her eyes were open and her expression was lucid. She reached out her hand for Raisa and looked back and forth between her and Devon.

Raisa quickly took her hand. "I'm here, Mom. What's wrong? We're going to be fi–"

"Raisa," her mother's voice was urgent, "It's started. Get the money... on the table... all of it. Take it and go. You have to go." Just as quickly as Lona had become aware, she closed her eyes and drifted off again.

Exactly twelve women lay dead and mangled in pools of blood that ran into each other. The entire floor was littered with shattered glass. The sparkling prisms shining from them reflected the green hue of the mist that was caught near the ceiling and the maroon red of the spreading blood on the floor, making the scene look like a sick and twisted wonderland. A bitter cold wind whistled through the drawn shutters and threatened to clear the stifling stench in the room. Twelve women stood silent, in a half circle at the edge of the room, tranced as usual, with no apparent knowledge of the ones that were dead.

Nosh sat reclined on the lounge in front of the fireplace, his face, chest and hands covered with blood. An occasional breeze caught his matted hair but gained no response from him. He held a crystal glass of scotch in his hand and the bottle was on the floor next to him. His eyes looked catatonic and he was mumbling to himself, "The southern Lasteires can go to... what good will they do... when they are not matched by the north." He powered back the scotch in his glass with one shot and poured another. "One will fall... and none will succeed. He'll come to me. He'll come... on his own.............. All will be well."

Charlotte sat with her mother. Lona hadn't responded for several hours to anything. It seemed only her body remained, still breathing a rattled sound and her heart lightly pounding out irregular beats. Hospice called and said that they couldn't come due to the circumstances and were not certain when they would. Aileen worked her way through the house, straightening and filling trash bags with fallen plaster and their parent's broken possessions.

Devon, Raisa, Pen and Corli sat around the kitchen table. Pen had a bandage wrapped around his head and a small amount of blood was showing through the gauze at his forehead. Devon seemed totally unaffected by his injuries. Raisa was thinking about how genuinely lucky they all were to be alive. She had always been afraid of earthquakes but having lived through this one, she thought it might no longer be a phobia. Corli had that

159

same 'let's-get-on-with-it' look that she had worn so often in the last few weeks, for the first time in her life. Raisa hoped that everything that happened hadn't taken the 'fun' out of Corli. She always thought that was her best quality.

"There are some things we need to talk about," Devon addressed everyone but glanced at Pen in particular. "Pen and I have pulled a lot of information from the Edward Brayden shows that seem to be especially relevant today. We can continue to go over the things we have discovered, but I think it is more important than ever that we go to see him… Edward Brayden… in person… now."

Raisa instantly felt a pang of alarm. "But, my mom! I couldn't leave her!"

"Raisa, I know this is not what you want." Frustration and tenderness both colored his voice. He took her hand from the table with both of his. "But we *need* to go, I feel it in my bones. And after what your mom said a few hours ago, I think she agrees."

"We don't know what she was talking about," Raisa snapped as she yanked her hand from Devon's. "She could have been delirious for all we know; with all that nonsense about the money on the table… she doesn't know anything about Edward Brayden. How could she want me to go see him?" Raisa realized that she sounded angry, and she was. Her father had died alone. She would not risk the same fate for her mother. Her mother needed *her*.

Corli had been quiet since they sat down at the table, with nothing in particular to add. She was game for whatever Devon and Pen decided was right. She knew she would be able to help Raisa come around if she could get her alone for a minute. She was casually perusing the stack of papers on the table they sat at, flipping them like the pages of a magazine. *Money on the table,*

160

huh? She dropped them from her hand. The white paper on the very top caught her eye, so she picked it up. Her eyes grew wide as she read it. She turned it and held it out to Raisa, "What is this?"

Raisa took the paper from Corli. "I don't know, I think it's some paperwork that my mom had to take care of after my dad died. She's been looking it over for awhile." She dropped her eyes to the paper. "It says 'Certificate of Sale for the property at 973 Noble'... that's *here!* And down at the bottom in my mom's handwriting is a bank address. It's the bank over on the corner outside our tract. And there's a number... SDB1013."

"That's a safe deposit box," Corli added. "But where's the key?"

"Hold on." Raisa felt a sudden rush of adrenaline. She sprung up the stairs to her parent's room. There was a drawer at the top of her father's dresser that had always fascinated her. It had so many odd little treasures from her parent's lives that she would sometimes spend hours looking through it. If her parents wanted only her to have something, this is where the key would be. She yanked on the drawer, it always stuck, a good thing too after the events of the morning, and reached to the back corner for a little, very old jewelry box with a spring top on it. She held her breath as she opened it.

Raisa walked back down stairs and into the kitchen. She lifted her hand in the air and between her fingers was a shiny, large key with the number 1013 engraved on it.

12

The inside of Raisa's house served as a haven of ignorance. Though they had the television on all day, watching stories of destruction and people behaving badly unfold, it was nothing that prepared them for seeing it first hand when they left home.

A glance up the street of the similarly constructed houses exhibited that one in every ten or twelve had collapsed to some degree. Emergency vehicles and debris littered the streets.

Devon, with an empty backpack slung over his shoulder turned to look at the others. "I think we better walk."

"Told you it was pretty crazy," Pen added as they stepped around the rubble that used to be a mailbox pagoda that Raisa's father had built.

As they walked, Raisa noticed that Pen was the only one with a visible injury. "So, what happened to your head?" she asked curiously.

Pen glanced at Devon as he answered, "Let's just say that Devon's NHRA clock has shined its last neon number... I lived, it died."

"Bummer," Devon said with a grin.

As they rounded the corner to the main street, Raisa was struck with how many people were on foot and how strange it was to see so few cars on the road. When they approached the beginning of the strip mall, they saw that some of it lay in ruin. They heard several alarms still sounding from businesses that had their windows blown out and no one attending to them. Raisa saw a woman that she guessed was in her early thirties, darting suspiciously from one of the darkened store fronts, her arms full of goods from inside.

"Did you see that?!" Raisa wasn't really asking a question, she was merely shocked at what she saw. Just as she said it a group of boys exited another deserted store, bags touting the stores logo full to bursting in their hands. "It's so sad," she said to no one in particular. Raisa tried to imagine how it would feel to rob one of the stores. She concluded that she couldn't imagine even stepping through one of the broken windows with that intention in her heart, let alone actually taking something.

"An example of the true character of man," Devon said with a disgusted look on his face.

"I don't believe it is as broad as 'all human nature', do you?" Raisa's eyes looked almost hurt, not wanting to believe that was true, but seeing for herself that it may not be far from the mark.

Devon didn't answer but continued to walk.

They arrived at the bank parking lot. There was a line of at least thirty people outside the bank and several armed guards kept the group immediately in front of the bank in order. As they took their place in line, Pen and Corli flanked Devon and Raisa. *Protection mode*, Raisa thought.

"And then there's people and their money," Pen said under his breath as he perused the parking lot. Everywhere they looked people were fighting, couples were having loud and heated arguments and several customers left the bank only to be robbed. Some fought back, others simply allowed the theft and regained their losses by stealing from someone else. The whole ordeal went on unchecked. What happened outside of the bank was obviously not the guards' concern.

The line moved quickly. Several angry customers were turned away because the bank had run out of cash. When they reached the front of the line, a man with a uniform and a gun asked what their business was.

"We need to get into a safe deposit box." Raisa held up the key.

"Only two," the guard replied.

"We'll wait here for you," Corli said as she grabbed Pen's hand.

The guard placed a hand on Devon's shoulder as they stepped to enter the bank. "I need to check the bag," the guard said gruffly.

Raisa saw a look on Devon's face that surprised her. Devon clearly resented the guard placing his hand on him and saw that he was struggling to not react.

"Sure," Devon managed. "It's empty... safe deposit box?" he sarcastically addressed the guard. The guard, unaffected by Devon's attitude, checked the backpack and waived them in.

Raisa entered the vault with the teller while Devon waited in the little room inside the buzzer gate. *Wow, this is kind of cool,* she thought as she looked at the stack of locked boxes that reached to the ceiling, *I feel so grown up... get a grip, Raisa... you are grown up, now pay attention.*

The teller led her to one of the larger boxes on the bottom row and put her key in. "You put your key in here," she directed when she realized that Raisa wasn't familiar with the procedure.

Raisa carried the heavy box to the room and shut the door. Even though her mother's words had played in her head all morning, she was still shocked when she opened the lid. "Wow..." was all she could say.

It was full to the rim with cash. Various denominations were showing but the bulk was in hundreds.

"You should count it," Devon said carefully. He felt a little weird. Though he didn't want to presume any ownership of the

164

bucket of cash, deep down he knew that Raisa's parents had intended for it to help both he and Raisa, to accomplish whatever it was they needed to do.

Raisa sat, doe eyed. "Can you help me?"

Devon smiled and leaned in to kiss Raisa's forehead, then placed his hand on her cheek. "It's going to be okay," he whispered. He held her eyes with his until they looked a little less frightened.

By the time they reached the bottom layer of cash they were at five hundred and twenty five thousand dollars. Devon reached into the box to scoop up the next bundle and heard a clink as something dropped back to the bottom.

Raisa leaned over to get a better look at what it was. Her eyes widened and pooled up as she reached in and pulled out the objects that had made the noise. She held them up for Devon to see. "These are my parents' wedding rings."

Both Raisa and Devon sat still and quiet for awhile in this little room with the rest of the world buzzing outside, looking at each other, looking at the rings, wondering what their lives were going to look like in the next few days, the next few months, the next few years.

Corli was on Raisa's laptop at the kitchen table while Pen was building sandwiches. "I'm amazed that internet connection hasn't been an issue," she mused.

"Yeah, and you know what else is weird?" Pen asked while he licked some mayonnaise off his finger. "No aftershocks... it's like the planet did exactly the shifting it wanted to do and stopped dead."

"Got it!" Corli was staring intently at the screen. "This Edward Brayden site says that his last public appearance on his tour was at this hotel in Seattle, Washington. That was over a

165

month ago, though. I wonder if he is still there?" Corli left the table and walked over to help Pen, now that she found what she was looking for on the computer. "So, what do you think it means... the no-aftershock thing?"

"Who knows what any of this means." Pen stopped slicing tomatoes to consider the thought and turned to face Corli. He took her hand. "But it's obviously bigger than anything any of us could speculate, if we are going to assume that the geology of the entire planet is involved somehow." Pen tucked a lock of Corli's shiny black hair behind her ear. "Corli," Pen's voice was soft but it sounded rough, as if he was having a hard time keeping it even. He looked down at her hand in his then back to her dark eyes. "I am 'all in' for this thing. I think it is going to get pretty dangerous. I have to be there for Devon. But, you..." Pen stammered a little, "you don't have to do this. You can stay here where it's safe and–"

Corli held her hand softly up to his mouth. "I'm part of this too. Raisa needs *me*. They are obviously the important ones. They need to be protected so that they can do what they were born to do. And I was meant to be with you. I never would have found my courage without you. So... sorry, you're stuck with me."

Corli stood on her tiptoes and kissed Pen. She hadn't intended on delivering more than a simple kiss, but Pen suddenly bent down and wrapped his arms around her and scooped her off the floor, keeping his lips on hers. He kissed her tenderly and with a sentiment that made Corli feel joined to him, like they were sharing something very special and very private. She felt something wet on her face.

Pen set her down gently and bent down low to hide his face on Corli's shoulder. She knew that he was using it as an excuse to wipe his eyes before he looked at her. She smiled into his hair and her heart melted.

"So," Pen cleared his throat as he stood up, almost fully recovered. "We jump into the unknown abyss together."

Devon sat with Raisa at Lona's bedside, but a few feet away in a rocker. He didn't feel comfortable hovering over Raisa's mother. She still had not opened her eyes since the previous day. Her breathing was so shallow that it was barely perceptible. Devon listened to Raisa as she spoke to her mother about the 'other side', who was waiting for her, that her father was busy getting everything ready for her, and that it was okay to go. Devon's heart squeezed in his chest for Raisa. He knew how hard this was for her, but he was in awe of the emotional strength she was exhibiting for her mother.

"I haven't heard your dad for awhile." Devon almost didn't realize he had said this out loud and looked at Raisa to make sure the comment wasn't upsetting.

"He's here... he's just taking care of mom. I can feel it." Raisa rested her hand on her mother's arm. It wasn't very warm.

Charlotte walked in. "Pen made sandwiches for dinner. I'll sit with Mom for awhile. You two go eat." She pulled Raisa from the chair just in case she considered objecting and handed her to Devon.

"I think I found Edward Brayden," Corli broke into what was a very silent meal.

Devon looked at Raisa. He saw that she couldn't lift her eyes from her sandwich. "I think we should leave in the morning," he said as softly as he could.

167

Raisa nodded. As much as she didn't want to go, she felt the gravity of the situation as much as anyone. "Where is he?" she asked quietly as she picked at the lettuce in her sandwich.

"Seattle. At least that's where he was a month ago. I'm sure we'll find a way to get a precise location." Corli knew that the best way to help Raisa come to grips with leaving her mother was to speak plainly. It would appeal to Raisa's rational side.

"We'll have to drive," Pen added. "Regular air traffic is grounded, only emergency flights are allowed right now. And I doubt we could convince anyone that it's an emergency." Pen only half smiled.

"How far is it… exactly?" Devon knew it was far. He wondered just then if time was as issue with anything. He had a feeling that there was not an infinite amount of it left.

Corli leaned over the computer and typed in the cities. "One-thousand-one-hundred-and-eighty-five miles, or eighteen hours and twelve minutes… give or take."

"And we may have to double that considering the condition of… everything," Devon mused.

Corli pulled USGS on the computer. "I can see all the faults on this site. I'll check it out to see where we might run into problems." She clicked on an article about the recent event. "Hey, listen to this…

"The USGS in analyzing the data that it has gathered from around the globe, has determined that this unprecedented event showed a unique characteristic. Typically, the sheer size of these earthquakes if occurring individually would have created several large fissures in the earth's crust on or near the major fault lines. But because all of the tectonic plates and therefore the faults moved with similar timing, these fissures did not occur. Most of the damage of structures worldwide was due only to the shaking, not from displacement of earth. This also explains why there have been no aftershocks. The pressure that builds from

168

one fault moving independent of another and forcing its neighbor
to move did not exist."

"That's good isn't it?" Corli wasn't sure but thought that
optimism was the best approach.

Devon appreciated her effort. "Well, I guess we'll find out.
The sooner we get started, the sooner we get there. Why don't
you guys go chill tonight. You're going to get tired of us soon
enough. Pack light… we'll take one car. We'll try to hit the
road at about 8am."

Raisa felt her stomach turn inside out. She wasn't sure how
much of that was about leaving her mother and how much of it
was fear of their unknown mission. *As long as I'm with Devon,
it will be okay,* she tried to convince herself.

As they were finishing up, the doorbell rang.

"Were we expecting someone?" Corli asked even though the
look on everyone's face indicated that no one did.

"I'll get it." Devon was up and moving, Pen a few steps
behind. Devon saw through the glass and happily opened the
door.

Gloria stood with a cautious smile on her face. "I hope that
it's okay that I came unannounced."

Devon wrapped his arms around his mother. "I didn't think I
would get to see you," he said, relief coloring his voice. He
closed his eyes and hugged her tight. He was surprised at
himself for thinking that this might be the last time he'd see his
mother, ever. He wondered what it was that would make him
think that. They were just leaving town, not hopping a shuttle to
outer space.

Pen and Corli left and Raisa excused herself to her mother's
room as Devon and Gloria settled in the living room.

"I know you're leaving," Gloria started.

169

"How…" Devon let his question trail off. He looked at the soft light above his mother. He had seen enough to know now that part of this gift of light also meant varying degrees of a connection to an information source of some kind. He also realized that, although he didn't know why, information was shared with him and Raisa as needed. There was no point in asking a bunch of questions. Devon took his mother's hand and smiled. "Tomorrow morning."

"I brought you something. I want you to take it with you." Gloria took her hand out of Devon's, but patted his hand so that he left it in her lap. She pulled a small velvet bag from her purse. "It was your father's," she said hesitantly as she carefully emptied the contents of the bag into his hand. "He gave it to me when we found out I was pregnant with you." Sitting in Devon's palm was something that looked almost like a pocket watch. Gloria picked it up from Devon's hand. She pushed a small latch on the side and it popped open. She clicked another latch and the center of the piece detached. She set the center part back in Devon's hand.

"It's a compass," Devon said flatly. He wasn't sure how to feel about this. He didn't know that anything from his father existed, other than the picture his mother had. He felt a mix of revulsion and gratitude that his mother had kept it all these years.

Gloria held the gold shell that had held the compass up to Devon. "There's an inscription," she said quietly.

""So that my Love and my Son will never lose their way and always return to me."" Devon read aloud. It almost made him wretch but he tried to hide any expression from his mother.

"Hey, Ed, where do you want this stuff?" David's arms were full of boxes labeled 'Patagonia'.

170

Edward Brayden sat in an office style roller chair pulled up to a long folding table, the kind you saw at church potlucks. He was looking intently back and forth between a television that was stationed to CNN and his computer screen, the current search was for private plane pilots.

"Ed?" David's misty light above him jittered as he repositioned a box that almost fell from his arms.

"Sorry, David," Edward looked up, "there should be some space left in the storage room behind the kitchen."

The mess hall of the campground with its sturdy wood beam construction showed little to no damage from the earthquake. It had been transformed into the nerve center of the operation. It was buzzing with so many people that their mist's swirled and mingled with each other. Edward thought it looked like God was stirring the Aurora Borealis with a stick to create a beautiful light show.

They were situated a few miles from the base of Mt. Rainier. The site itself was not very well known since it had been privately owned. It was donated to The Assembly during the last of the show productions over a year ago.

A couple that was holding hands and had anxious expressions walked into the chaotic mess hall. They saw Edward at his makeshift desk, his purplish light a contrast to everyone else in the room, and walked toward him, waiting hesitantly for an appropriate moment to interrupt him.

Edward felt a warm charge enter his body from his back. His face softened and he smiled as he turned to see the bright glistening rays and warm electrical rings attached respectively to the couple.

"Such a beautiful thing," Edward said reverently as he stood and offered his hand to the young man. "An honor to meet you. I'm Edward Brayden."

171

"I'm Landon, and this is Evetta." The warm greeting calmed the two considerably.

"Hold on." Edward sat at his computer and quickly pulled up a document and began entering their names into a list. "Your last names?"

"Landon Watson," the boy directed. He looked at his girlfriend, offering her the chance to get into the conversation.

"Evetta Marino," she said kindly as she looked lovingly back at her boyfriend.

Edward motioned for them to pull up chairs from the table near them and have a seat. "Now, tell me about yourselves," he began with much more fervor than before. "What do you consider your greatest talents? Or what do you love most in life?"

From the conversation that followed, Edward learned that Landon was a teacher by nature and loved to work with children and Evetta was a horticultural genius.

"So, do you have any questions for me?" he asked.

Landon and Evetta's faces turned more somber. "No," Landon answered. "David filled us in pretty well last night I think."

"Okay then. But if you think of anything at all that you want to ask me, don't hesitate. I'll answer if I can," though his tone clearly denoted that he would probably rather not. He handed them a piece of paper with some information on it. "Do you think that you two can make it to Spanaway Airstrip? You'll ask for a pilot named Mills. I'm afraid you'll have to pay him... he'll fly you to Thule. You'll wait for the rest to arrive there."

"We should be good." Landon sounded strong and frightened at the same time. He stood and held out his hand to Edward. "Thank you for everything."

It was late in the evening. As was now the norm, Aileen and Charlotte were in their room asleep and Raisa sat in a chair next to her mother, the only light spilling from a crack in the attached bathroom door. Another day had brought no noticeable change in Lona. Though Raisa could swear that her breathing was even shallower and her limbs even less warm, if that were possible for a living body. She knew that this would be the last night she would spend next to her mother. She wondered why her mother was holding on to life when there was virtually none of it left in her body. She caught herself wishing that her mother would die now so that she wouldn't be making the choice to leave while she was still alive and was mortified by her selfishness and insensitivity. *You're a horrible person, Raisa.* It was her own voice she heard.

Her thoughts turned to Devon. She wondered what he would think of her selfishness. But mostly she was thinking that she couldn't stand it that he wasn't within touching distance. As she was considering leaving her perch next to her mother just long enough to find him, she saw two pillows fly through the air and land on the carpet outside the door.

Devon appeared in the doorway, a hesitant smile on his face. "Care to share the carpet tonight?" he whispered to Raisa.

Raisa looked at him. His hair was damp and he wore an old t-shirt and drawstring pants. She was struck by how no level of dumpy clothing could hide his beauty. She also had a mad desire to feel his wet hair. She sighed and stood up. "Yeah, this is great."

They positioned the pillows next to each other outside the door. Devon was reconsidering, thinking about going head to head so as not to risk lying next to her, but Raisa instantly plopped to her stomach and propped her head in her hands, elbows in the pillow, so she could look into the room. Devon shrugged to himself and laid down on his back.

He wasn't sure what to say to her. He wanted to tell her about the compass that his mother brought to him, but when he looked at her, he knew that she was only thinking of her mother. He turned towards her and wrapped his arm around her back and kissed the hand that propped up her chin.

Raisa dropped her face towards his and breathed him in. She loved the fact that he smelled like her shampoo. "Thank you," she whispered.

"For what?" he smiled as he softly kissed her cheek.

"For... taking care of me," she said sweetly.

"My pleasure," he whispered in her ear.

Devon looked into Lona's room. He wasn't sure of the reason, exactly. It may have been a reaction to the fact that he wanted to wrap his body around Raisa's or it could have been to check the room before he put his head down to sleep. Either way, what he saw surprised him. "Raisa, look!" he said softly as he pulled at her and gestured towards Lona.

Raisa lifted her head and peered into her mother's room. She instantly felt a swelling in her heart. With wonder and an overwhelming affection taking hold of her, she looked at her mother lying so still, as a golden mist hovered above her.

13

At 8am Catalina Island was rarely visible from Raisa's favorite hill overlooking the reservoir. This morning was no exception. There was a thick haze in the air from the marine layer brought in by the ocean. Raisa thought she could almost smell the sea. She felt Devon's hand in hers and wished that she were bringing him here to watch a sunset, not to say goodbye to her town. She wondered why it felt like she would never stand here again and quickly dismissed the thought as being overdramatic. Pen and Corli sat a couple of yards away on top of a picnic table huddled together to stay warm in the damp morning air. They all looked out over the misty, grey landscape of hills and tract houses. They surveyed the damage of the earthquake and wondered if they would ever call this home again.

"We better get moving," Devon said, breaking the reverie. He helped steady Raisa as they walked down the uneven grass hill to her car. He opened the front passenger door for her.

"Why are we taking this car again?" Corli questioned a little sarcastically as she hopped in the back seat. "My vote was for my dad's beemer."

"Hey, I thought you liked my car," Raisa chimed playfully. She was trying her best to not be the wet blanket on this trip and saw the opportunity to lighten it up. She knew she didn't sound authentically cheerful but she hoped to get an 'A' for the effort.

"Sure, for running around town, it's the coolest. But a long trip? Not so much," Corli smiled.

Devon knew that Raisa's heart was aching and was proud of her for not being mopey. He knew that he would have been a nightmare under these circumstances. *She has the perfect temperament for me. She could quite possibly be the only girl on the planet that could put up with my crap... I really don't deserve her.* His thought struck him full force. He had to work more than he would have liked to push it out, to keep his head in the game.

"Actually," Devon added, purposefully changing his train of thought, "this car has the most seat surface space of any of our options. And if it breaks down there is a better chance I'd be able to fix it... and... this is the only car that Pen's guitar fit in," he smirked sideways at Pen.

Getting out of the local area wasn't so bad. Their community withstood the earthquake relatively well due to its newer construction. As they hit the older areas though, the highway detoured off and on many times, sending them through neighborhoods they would never have gone through intentionally. It was clear, after three hours of working their way toward Los Angeles, that there were many thousands of people in dire need of assistance. About every third house or business had some kind of noticeable damage. It was also clear that no help would come, a least not for a long time.

When they hit the downtown LA area after about five hours of driving and came to their first detour off the freeway, Devon made sure that everyone's windows were up and the doors were locked. "Just so you guys know," he said in a low voice, "the back seat has a storage area under it. The cash... and the guns are under there. Except for the pistol, which I have."

As they wound their way through the streets and damaged neighborhoods, they noticed a larger concentration of people the further in they went. They turned onto a street named Darwin

176

and saw that traffic was being stopped one block ahead. Devon looked for a way to turn around but found that they were boxed in. As they inched forward they saw more clearly what was happening. Some of the locals had set up their own blockade, harassing the people in the vehicles for whatever they could get. The sidewalk was speckled with women's purses, duffle bags and empty, plastic groceries bags that lifted and floated, like mini ghosts, with the slightest breeze.

Raisa's nails dug into her seat as fear settled into her.

"Heads up," Pen said under his breath.

"Nice and easy…" Devon replied.

Corli pulled out her switchblade and slid it under her leg.

Devon rolled down his window about three inches as they pulled into first position and stopped. The man in charge of the road closure railing pulled it back in place behind the last car through. Devon didn't speak, he only very slightly nodded to the man that approached his window.

"Hey, ese… what are you doing here?" The man feigned a friendly tone. He wore a bandana around his head that was partially covered by a sideways black ball cap. He put his hands on the top of the Mustang and leaned down to look into the car. "Mmmm, your girlfriend is nice bra… why don't you come and party with us?"

Devon's blood instantly boiled but he kept his expression even. "Mira carbon," Devon mocked, "we were just passing through… move the f-ing gate……..… please."

The man didn't appear to think that Devon had shown enough respect, which he obviously hadn't, and jutted his head back for reinforcements.

Raisa held her breath.

Pen, seated behind her, saw someone run toward the car with a baseball bat. With perfect timing and agility, Pen opened his door, closed it behind him and sunk a knife into the runner's stomach before he could take a swing. His aim had been for Raisa's window. Devon reached behind his back, pulled his gun, and pointed at his new friend's face as he opened his door and stood behind it. Corli noticed the man reach behind him so she jumped from the car and held her knife against him, sticking him just enough for him to feel it in the side of his chest. Several other onlookers began to close in, supposing that anyone defending their car so adamantly must have a lot to steal. Corli thrust her knife into the man's side, knowing that he would collapse, which freed her to take on the next person that approached. Her stab seemed expertly placed because the man fell and didn't get up.

They were in a standoff. Devon, Pen and Corli firmly planted outside the car, two attackers down and many more slowly moving in.

As Devon swept the group in search of the leader so that he could take him out, Raisa screamed, "*Devon, in front!*" The man at the roadblock pulled a gun. Devon turned, faster than seemed possible, and fired once, hitting him squarely in the center of his forehead.

Raisa was stunned. She watched the body of the man in front of her fall in slow motion. She felt like she was stuck in some gangster horror movie. While half of her brain was blurry and short-circuiting, the other half was concerned for Devon. Would the fact that he killed a man incapacitate him? How were they going to get out of this nightmare situation?

"Who's next?" Devon said as he returned his eyes to the side of the road.

Raisa clearly had her answer; he was cool as can be.

The advancing group hesitated, but some were undeterred, almost zombie-like and continued forward.

Devon saw a man, surrounded by a small group, watching the situation unfold as if he were watching a movie. He was only about five foot-eight but completely muscle bound and he wore the nicest clothes of the bunch. "Got you," Devon said to himself. Just as he was about to pull the trigger, a boy wearing a hooded sweatshirt, ran to the muscular man, throwing his hood off his head as he went. He glanced at the car before he spoke to the leader and Corli and Devon squinted because of a green flash that met their eyes before he turned away.

"Hold up," the leader yelled, not panicked in the least, just loud enough for everyone to hear. "Move the gate. Let them go," he ordered.

Devon still pointed the gun at him. Pen and Corli held their ground until the crowd backed up, then jumped back in their seats. Devon waited until the gate was removed to drop his aim and get back into the car. He gunned the motor and sped the Mustang away. The freeway onramp was only fifty yards up the street and he took it at seventy-five miles per hour.

"M-M-Master... S-Sir... H-Hello... Sir..." a black robed woman stammered, her voice echoed through the thin cold air and rose in volume above those on either side of her.

Nosh waived his hand severely above his head as a signal to the others to be silent. He had not heard a voice from this medium for over a week.

The floor of the office was cleaned, the bodies moved and the glass swept, although the reddish-black stains on the wood floor were still there, creating a perfect stencil of where the circle of women stood when it was complete. Boards were nailed in place of most of the broken windows. One was left with only the shutters so that Nosh could look outside if he wanted to. He had

179

been tempted on several occasions since the windows shattered to drop someone off the edge of his perch just for the sport of it.

The constant breeze through the cracks in the shutters now kept the air clear in the room. The second the misty sludge steamed up from a green flame, it was torn back and forth until it was gone.

Nosh's shoes still had glass in them and his steps crunched as he moved closer to the woman that spoke. "State your name. And quit sniveling," he commanded.

"My name is John, Sir." He didn't stutter but his voice was still shaky.

"John... HA! What a name for your kind. Are you going to prophesy for me? Tell me of the second coming? What do you have to report? I don't have all day," Nosh barked.

"I'm in LA, Sir, and I just thought you would want to know that the boy, Devon, just came through here. He would have been killed if I hadn't told them to stop –"

"Where was he headed?"

"North, Sir, is all I know. He had that Raisa with him and another girl and boy with him." John waited patiently for a reply. When none came and he had not been dismissed he spoke, "Sir?"

Nosh didn't hear him. He had walked toward the window, consumed by the news. He felt almost... giddy. Devon was on his way. He opened the shutters and a gust of cold air burst through it, forcing him back a step. He moved to the edge of the floor that dropped off the side of the building with no fear of the height. It was as if he could simply step outside with no consequence. He looked out over the gloomy Portland city landscape and smiled. "Devon is on his way."

It seemed that the worst was behind them. As soon as they passed the highway cut off to Bakersfield, the road improved

180

dramatically. Corli mentioned that she thought the rest of the drive through California would not be on top of any fault lines so the roads should be good.

They stopped to fill up the gas tank, at ten dollars a gallon, and shook off the stress of Los Angeles. Raisa put in a CD of Stanley Clarke to further calm herself. It was her favorite track, "Funny How Time Flies" that she clicked it to. No one was in the mood to talk so the music was a good distraction for everyone.

Raisa's mind was now free to wander. The first thing she thought of was Devon and the way he acted in LA. She admitted to herself that there was obviously more to him than the sweet, caring and good Devon that she had come to know. She understood better, now, a couple reasons that he might compare himself to his father. *So, he has a dark side. I've still never seen him hurt someone in malice or conspire to do something evil. He is a man that knows when the situation requires a tough exterior and precision decision-making... that's a good thing. He is not his father.* Having resolved the issue in her mind, unsure of how much she was rationalizing and not wanting to decide either way, her thoughts turned to her mother and her sisters that she left behind. The picture of her mother lying still and lifeless in her bed filled her mind, Aileen and Charlotte sitting next to her as Raisa said goodbye to them.

Her sisters didn't have many words for her. They seemed genuinely stumped as to why she chose to leave at that time, just before their mother was going to die. But they also seemed to realize that it was important to her. And for the first time, she felt like her sisters supported her and didn't judge her or treat her like an eight-year-old. At this moment, she physically felt the love she had for her sisters grow in her heart.

181

As the song finished, Raisa's cell rang. She automatically popped the stereo off as she reached for her phone. In the seconds it took to get to it, Raisa's heart started sinking. Her premonition was all but verified when she saw that it was her home number calling. She stared at the phone for a few more seconds before she answered it. "Hello." *What is the appropriate way to sound when you're getting a call like this?*

"Raisy, its Char," was all Charlotte could get out at first.

They were both choked-up, unable to speak for about a minute.

Charlotte regained enough composure to speak first. "Raisa, I think for some reason, Mom was waiting for you to leave before she could go. Within an hour after you left, she started going through periods of not breathing for a long time. She finally stopped doing that about an hour ago. We wanted to make sure before we called you. Don't you worry about not being here, Raisa. She never woke up again and it's obvious she wanted you to go. We love you, Sis."

"I love you too," Raisa murmured through the silent tears and lump in her throat. It was all she could say, and hung up the phone. *Daddy?* She called out in her mind, but there was no response. *Of course, he's busy taking Mom home.*

Devon reached over and took Raisa's hand as he drove. There was no reaction to his touch but he held on anyway. He tried to imagine how he would feel if this was him and his own mother and the thought nearly made him sick. He tried to think of something he could do for Raisa, something that would at least clear away everything else that was going on, so that she could mourn in peace.

Raisa's eyes hurt from not blinking. Devon freed her hand as he pulled of the highway. She looked down. It was sweaty and

182

dirty and she hadn't even realized that he was holding it until he let it go. The last while had been silent. Raisa wasn't sure how long it had been since her sister called. It could have been one hour or five. She felt bad that everyone else had to suffer because she couldn't cope. *Maybe if I just go to sleep it will be better.*

As if on cue, Devon pulled into a hotel. Pen and Corli looked at each other and then back out of the window at the property they were approaching. It was definitely at least a four star hotel and probably a five. The lights in the fountain at the front came on exactly when Devon helped Raisa from the car. He knew that this time it was only a timer synchronized with the setting of the sun and not the electrical charge that followed them. Her light was dim and scattered and he was certain that his followed suit.

They pulled their bags from the car, including the ones under the back seat. Pen carried his guitar as they walked into the lobby, and passed the four armed guards that the hotel employed.

"Devon," Corli whispered, "I've never stayed in a place this nice." Both she and Pen were taking in the marble floors and walls, the plush velvet seating and the soaring ceilings. A few pieces of marble had cracked off of the walls in several places but those areas had been roped off with the same brass and red velvet posts that adorned the line for the front desk. Even their rubble looked classy.

After they checked in, Devon pulled Pen aside, spoke to him in his ear and stuffed a wad of cash in his hand, along with the room key for him and Corli.

Corli looked back at Raisa as Pen pulled her away by the hand with him. She wanted to comfort her, to be there for her like she had every other time before. But that was a job for Devon now. She felt sad and happy about that. Under different

183

circumstances, this would have been an exciting and carefree teenage moment, the two of them checking into a posh hotel with their boyfriends. They would have gone on about how gorgeous the boys were and hint at just how far they would go with them. Corli sighed, "I don't feel like a teenager anymore," she said barely loud enough for Pen to hear.

Pen looked over at her as if he had been caught thinking what she had said. He pulled her over closer to him and hugged his arm around her as they walked to find the hotel sundries store.

Raisa was vaguely aware that the hotel was beautiful. She let Devon guide her to the elevators and up to their room. "Thank you, for taking care of me," she murmured to Devon and looked into his eyes for the first time in hours. She knew she was being redundant but she also knew that she was a catatonic mess, and that Devon was in fact, taking care of her. She saw Devon's eyes light up from her exhibited sign of life, as short lived as it was. He led her to the edge of the bed and sat her down on the end of it. He took off her sweater and shoes, kicked off his own, then set to busying himself around the room.

Raisa fell to her side on the bed and pulled her knees into her arms. A picture developed in her mind of the scene that Charlotte described to her. She imagined herself sitting with her mother along with her sisters while the last minutes unfolded, waiting anxiously with them for her mother to breath or not to. She pictured herself crying with them and hugging them, comforting and being comforted. She thought about how her sisters had to call for the coroner who came and took her mother away. She was suddenly grateful for the experience she had at her father's viewing. *It's only a shell*, she reminded herself. Her mother was no longer in that body.

She had called for her father every so often in her mind but had received no response.

She heard water running in the bathroom and was glad that Devon was doing things without her and not doting on her. *I'm glad he's not trying to make me feel better.* As quickly as she had that thought, another thought replaced it, *I wish he would come and just be next to me....*

Devon answered the knock at the door almost before it happened. It was Pen. He handed a bag to Devon through the door. "Thanks, man," Devon gave Pen a quick fist bump, closed the door and disappeared into the bathroom.

Raisa tried to get her eyes to close. She wanted to escape with sleep. But remembering how that never really worked for her anyway, she gave up and stared at the armoire across from her, following the wood grain from one end of the cabinet to the other.

Devon's outstretched hand came into her view. She let him pull her up and lead her to the bathroom. Raisa felt a wave of warmth flow from his hand and into her body. She felt her muscles soften and relax as he opened the door and pushed her gently in, in front of him. Raisa had no words for what she saw.

The light was off but all along the edges of the bathroom, candles were lit and giving off the scent of sandalwood. A bottle of wine sat in ice on the counter with a single wine glass next to it. She heard a drip from the faucet in the bathtub and saw a bath drawn with lots of bubbles. There was a vase of various beautiful white flowers next to it. "Gardenia's," Raisa's whisper broke the silence and echoed against the damp tiled walls. Raisa knew that she should feel anxious, but she didn't.

She heard Devon close the door behind him. She also knew the sound when he pulled off his shirt.

185

Without turning her around to face him, Devon began, slowly and carefully, to undress Raisa. Finally, with relief, Raisa closed her eyes. Devon didn't touch his body to hers. He didn't kiss her skin. She only felt the occasional brush of his hands or his arms, like a graze of static over her.

She wore a simple white t-shirt and her arms easily rose when Devon touched his fingers to the hem of it. Without hesitation he gently pulled it up and over her head, watching her hair fall back to her shoulders as he did. Raisa brought her hands to the top of her jeans, but Devon's hands reached around her and gently stopped her, pushing them slowly back down to her sides. He unbuttoned and unzipped her jeans with little effort, then bent down and easily peeled them off. Raisa had only to lift each foot for a second. She felt the slightest pressure of his touch at the back of her bra. She wondered again, why she wasn't frantic. But all she felt was Devon's tenderness. She trusted him, completely.

As Devon pulled the straps of her bra down and let it fall into his hand, he looked at her breasts from behind her shoulder. He watched as the air affected them. He was struck with her beauty. Looking at Raisa like this, right now, was like considering a work of art. He dropped his fingers to the lace top of Raisa's panties and ran his eyes up the sway of her back, and then back down the curve of her legs as he carefully removed them.

Raisa felt Devon's hands in her hair as he pulled it off her shoulders and clipped it. Then he took her hand and led her as she stepped into the water and slid into the bubbles.

Devon moved to the counter and poured a glass of wine. He pulled a stool next to her as he handed her the glass. She took a sip and felt the cool sweetness of it run down her throat, turning warm as it went. He started humming a tune with a beautiful baritone voice that shot adoration into her soul. It was a lullaby.

She looked at him, with the candles glowing behind him, the others barely lighting his eyes and saw the most beautiful expression on his face. She couldn't find any words that would do it justice. She watched him as he submerged a big thirsty sponge into the water and brought it to her shoulders and neck. He saw her scar, small and pink on her chest and made this one exception. He touched it lightly with his fingers, looking at it almost quizzically.

Raisa's composure washed away. Her emotions lay open and raw. Tears streamed down her face. She clutched at his hand with both of hers and held it to her cheek as she let everything come out.

14

The blackout drapes of the hotel room were pulled shut with the exception of a one quarter inch space that allowed a narrow beam of early morning light to break across Devon's chest. Raisa opened her eyes to see his face in front of hers, the beam of light illuminating his peaceful countenance. She became aware that she was wrapped in a terrycloth robe with nothing on underneath it and the previous evening flooded her mind. Raisa was so grateful for what Devon had done for her, how selfless and thoughtful he was. She knew that he would protect her physically and emotionally in the face of anything. *I'm such a basket case sometimes… it's a wonder that he puts up with me… I don't deserve him,* she thought.

She didn't remember coming to bed, and she slept so soundly she was amazed. She figured that she must have been so relaxed that Devon had to carry her here half asleep.

Raisa didn't move a muscle. She wanted to watch him sleep for as long as possible. She was fascinated by his fluttering eyelids, made more pronounced by his beautiful long dark eyelashes, and the deep breaths that made his chest rise and fall. Just as the rhythm of it threatened to lull her back to sleep he opened his eyes by just a sliver.

A sweet smile broke across his face. "Hi, Sunshine," he whispered. He rolled slowly toward Raisa and without the slightest pause slid his arm under the robe and around Raisa's back. He pulled her next to his body, closed his eyes again and reveled in the feeling of her skin.

Raisa's pulse instantly doubled. Last night she had been totally naked in front of Devon and completely calm, but this was different. Now she was lying in a bed with him, he was practically naked next to her, just wearing underwear she thought, and there was absolutely nothing to stop them from doing whatever they wanted to do.

Devon felt Raisa's heart race against his chest. He almost suppressed his smile. "What," he said softly, "did you think that after my Herculean effort last night to not touch you I would have any resolve at all left this morning?" He kissed the tip of her nose.

Raisa had no clue how to respond. "I….." she let the attempt go.

Devon pulled his arm out from around her and brought his hand to her face, brushing her cheek with his thumb. He looked in her sleepy but panicked eyes and held them in his gaze until they turned calm again. "You are so beautiful, Raisa," he whispered. He softly kissed her lips.

Her caution washed away. *I love him... I'm going to be with him forever. This is perfectly natural.* She kissed him back with more enthusiasm than she had ever shown him before, holding his face with one hand and running the other through his hair and down his neck to his chest.

Devon sensed a level of energy take hold of him that he had never felt before. He opened his eyes as he kissed her and drew her closer to him again. He wasn't able to look through her shining rays though. He wanted to close his eyes and melt into Raisa, but what he saw was more than he could ignore. As their kissing became more intense and he felt Raisa's body press on his, part of her white light broke away and began to bend toward him. It wasn't that he could just see it, he could feel it, like an electrical current melding his body to hers. But what he saw next

189

brought him up short. He pulled away from Raisa abruptly, breathless. "Wait...."

Raisa was startled. "What... what's wrong?" she asked, still reeling from kissing him.

"I just saw... something." Devon's eyes were wide-awake now.

"What... what did you see?" Raisa felt a little rejected at this particular moment but was trying not to show it. She made the move to go further and he was stopping. "Did I... do something wro—"

"No! No... trust me... nothing like that." Devon could see what she was thinking. He grabbed her hands and brought them to his mouth and kissed them. "Trust me."

She saw in his eyes that he meant what he said and waited for him to explain.

"Your light," he began, "part of it bent away from the rest... toward me. And then I saw... I think I saw *mine*. I saw an orange-ish sort of rim of light, moving up to meet the light that was bending from you. It just startled me, that's all." Devon could see that his description of what happened surprised her as much as it did him.

Raisa looked into his eyes and saw the copper flecks burning. A knowledge of something hit her, and it came out of her mouth without a second thought. "We were made for each other," she said quietly and confidently.

Devon stared at her, knowing it was true. They both let that soak in for a minute. "I guess this is a pretty big deal then. It feels like it would be a consummation.... if we... had... made love." Devon had never felt bashful about sex. Not that he had a lot of it, but he was a confident man and it was never an issue for him. But this was entirely different. He knew he loved Raisa more than anything. He also wanted to be with her more than he ever wanted anything in his life. But it had to be right, and he needed to figure out what 'right' was in her case.

Raisa felt more than ever, with this knowledge, that there was no reason for them to stop themselves. She watched Devon work it over in his head and saw that he was reaching the opposite conclusion. "Really? *You* are going to go all *proper* on me?" she said, a bit agitated.

Devon smiled and chuckled low in his throat, "You are *cute* when you're frustrated. I've never seen you like that before." He grabbed her, outside of her robe, and rolled her over on top of him and clamped down on her when she struggled.

"*You...*" Raisa was past irritated and on to mad. She squirmed and wiggled but it was no use. "You're not fair!" She was trapped.

Devon's smile went wide and full of beautiful teeth. "Never said I was."

He tickled her, she chased him around the room, they had a pillow fight and they kissed passionately without going too far. The world was far away for about an hour.

Pen and Corli sat in a booth in the only open restaurant inside the hotel. Both had their elbows on the table with all four of their hands clasped together between their faces, laughing and chatting quietly. Devon had been teasing Raisa all the way from the room by chewing on her ear, her neck caught in the crook of his arm so that she couldn't get away. As they approached the table both Devon and Raisa stopped and looked at Pen and Corli, who had not noticed their arrival. "We could get our own table," Devon teased.

Corli looked up in surprise, like she'd been caught. She glanced at Raisa, but only long enough to realize that she was blushing and her eyes instantly shot down to the surface of the table.

Raisa tried to suppress her gasp, a small part of her exclamation made it out of her mouth. *Oh my goodness... she did it... she slept with him!* she thought to herself. Raisa bored a hole into Corli with her eyes, willing her to look back up and verify what she already knew. She caught one more sideways glance from Corli and all was confirmed. *I'm happy for her... but I'm jealous too,* Raisa sighed. She'd catch her sometime later to talk.

Devon received a nod and a suppressed smile from Pen. Devon smiled and nodded discreetly back.

They ordered breakfast and began discussing their plans for the day and whether or not they could make it to Seattle by nightfall. It would all depend on the condition of the roads, and whatever natives they encountered. Corli said that the earthquake faults would not interrupt them again till Salem or Portland, Oregon which was only two or three hours from their destination.

They were only a few feet from the bar area of the restaurant. It was 9am and already several people were drinking and watching the big-screen television, all with sober expressions despite their inebriation. CNN was showing live footage from inside an emergency United Nations meeting. The increased intensity of what was happening on the screen caught Pen's attention. "Check it out guys!" he said in a low but urgent voice.

"...as you can see, the floor has erupted into several shouting matches. The state of each Nation, all having been affected by the earthquakes and their inability to calm and contain their people and consequently their governments, is precarious at best. Some are saying that it is time for control in the form of a global government. Others are demanding that the richer nations support the lesser ones unconditionally. We have even heard threats of nuclear retaliation against those that will not come to aid. In an unprecedented move, several media organizations have moved onto the floor, trying to talk to the leaders, bringing messages from the people calling for action... Uh... as you can see, it's getting pretty heated down there... wait – the back doors just opened and armed soldiers are pouring in and moving to the perimeter of the room... Hey! That man over there has a gun! No! The soldiers have drawn their weapons! Get down! Get-"

The screen went silent and the CNN logo appeared. They all sat stunned. Pen spoke quietly, "This is unbelievable... our society is degrading faster than I ever would have imagined."

"It won't be long now till the media is the ruling government," Devon said sarcastically under his breath. "We need to get moving."

Edward sat staring at his computer screen, his chin in his hand and tapping his pen on his mouse pad. He was watching the television. Reports from all over the world showed that the damages from the earthquake were not particularly bad, especially as they related to others in history. But because of the number of countries simultaneously affected by one earthquake, there was mass hysteria. People feared the disaster signified something more cataclysmic to come, that it would trigger a domino effect of prophetic events. It was humanity that was breaking, not the planet.

The mess hall was very quiet compared to any of the previous days in the last few weeks. Only one or two rallys were moving about, setting up for the next meal. Most of the preparations for their move to Thule were complete. They were only waiting for the last six Lasteires, three couples, to arrive to get whatever they needed to move on to their next destination. Whether it was supplies, money – although there was not much of that left – or just explanations and reassurance, this is where they all came before they started the next part of their journey. Except for the Southern Lasteires, they were different.

David walked into the room and behind Edward, checking the computer screen to see what he was looking at so intently. "Staring at that list isn't going to make them come any faster." He pulled up a chair and sat.

"I know," Edward sighed. "Allowing them to come here on their own with no interference is such an important part of the process. But sometimes I wish I could cheat a little and at least find out who they are before they get here... maybe keep an eye on their progress."

"No interference?" David chuckled. "Is that what you call all the rigging you put into the show?"

Edward's face tweaked to the side. "They have to have *some* clue to go on. *Some* rallys appreciate my efforts," he jibed at David. "Plus, we're running out of time," he said more seriously.

A door to the hall crashed open, *"Help! I need help!"*

David and Edward jumped out of their seats and rushed toward the door. They reached the young man, who looked like he had been beaten and cut, just before he fell to the ground. They helped him move to a chair. Edward saw that his light rings were scattered and pulsing with his speeding heartbeat. "What's happened? Where is the girl?" Edward asked urgently.

"They have her!" The boy was on the verge of tears, "You have to help me!"

"David, gather everyone up, quickly," Edward ordered. He turned back to the boy. "What's your name, Son?"

"Brian, and my wife's name is Kara. The wicked men killed our friends two days ago. We almost made it here... but outside of your campground, they caught up with us. They took her!

194

She's still alive though… I can tell. Please… *please*, help me get to her!"

David reentered the hall, twenty others were behind him, all armed with knives, swords, bats, anything they could use to fight, and some with guns.

Edward walked through the group and David handed him a blade as he passed. "Let's go!" Edward commanded as they burst out the door.

Pen decided to keep his guitar with him in the back seat now that Raisa was feeling better. He was feeling pretty happy too, randomly breaking into unsolicited smiles when he looked at Corli, or thought about her, or thought about the night they spent together. *Life's too short, especially with everything going on… keep busy living.* He had no regrets, especially where Corli was concerned.

They were making good time and even though the world seemed to be crumbling around them, Pen felt like the mood in their own little bubble was pretty optimistic. *Music always makes things better,* he thought. He was picking away at Blackbird by The Beatles.

"I love this song. My sister Aileen is really good at it too. I have always thought that it looks really hard, but you play it beautifully," Raisa smiled at Pen.

"Do you know the words?" Pen asked eagerly.

"Are you kidding?" Corli smirked at Raisa. "She knows every word to practically every song… she's like the friggin 'Music Encyclopedia Britannica'."

Raisa glanced at Devon. She had never sung in front of him before and was a little anxious about it. He nodded at her expectantly. She smiled back a consenting smile.

Pen had been looping the intro. When he returned to the verse, both he and Raisa began to sing, breaking into harmonies as they went.

> *Blackbird singing in the dead of night*
> *Take these broken wings and learn to fly*
> *All your life*
> *You were only waiting for this moment to arise*
>
> *Black bird singing in the dead of night*
> *Take these sunken eyes and learn to see*
> *all your life*
> *you were only waiting for this moment to be free*
>
> *Blackbird fly, Blackbird fly*
> *Into the light of the dark black night.*
>
> *Blackbird fly, Blackbird fly*
> *Into the light of the dark black night.*
>
> *Blackbird singing in the dead of night*
> *Take these broken wings and learn to fly*
> *All your life*
> *You were only waiting for this moment to arise,*
> *You were only waiting for this moment to arise,*
> *You were only waiting for this moment to arise*

Pen smiled big at Raisa. "Wow, you're really good. We should take it on the road."

"That would not be me... I'm more the choir director type, but I do love it," Raisa admitted. Then she had a thought. "Hey, do you know any songs that Devon can sing too?" She looked at Devon to make sure this question didn't get her in trouble, her forehead raised in anticipation of a backlash. The memory of his incredible voice humming that lullaby to her made her want to hear more. She had a feeling that he was a really great singer with a naturally good ear that just didn't know it.

Devon slid down in the driver's seat a little lower, exaggerating that he was comfortable and turned his head toward Raisa. "I'm not afraid of you, Rai."

Raisa saw the confidence on his face, the slightly sarcastic grin and the sparkle in his eye. *He called me Rai... nobody has ever called me that. I love it!* She felt butterflies in her stomach. *How does he do that to me?* "Okay… so what's it gonna be?" she countered.

Devon looked in the rearview mirror. "Pen, you know a bunch of Clapton, right? How about Layla?"

"I love Eric Clapton…" Raisa murmured a little surprised.

Pen looked back at Devon in the mirror with a comical 'dead pan' look. "You're serious," he mocked.

"Feel free to join in, everyone." Devon wasn't going to back down, but a buffer of other voices would be nice just in case.

They all sang a rousing version of the song together. Raisa didn't have a problem hearing Devon very distinctly through the other voices, including her own. She was right. He had an excellent ear and an earthiness to his voice that was extremely sexy. Raisa felt like a prayer had been answered. His voice only cracked once and even that was endearing. *That's it... I think he's perfect.*

They had been driving in Oregon for a couple of hours. The world seemed untouched up here with everything so green and beautiful. They avoided large towns and stopped as infrequently as possible but it was time for food and gas.

"Curtin." Devon read the name of the town from the sign out loud as an indication that this would be their stop. "Everyone on your toes."

They pulled off the highway and into the town that appeared to span only two blocks. Two men sat at the corner of the first and only stop sign, their chairs backed up to the wall of a small country style store. The men stared at the newcomers, sizing them up to determine if they were trouble or not. The consensus appeared to be in the negative when they smiled warmly and one lifted his hand in a greeting.

Across from the store was a gas station/drive up Dairy Queen combo that Devon pulled into. He looked at the one and only gas pump as he came to a stop by it. "Wow, only four dollars a gallon. Do these people own any televisions? They could charge triple that and get it." Devon hopped out and reached for the antique handle.

"We don't believe in ripping people off for the sake of ripping people off 'round here. Here, let me give you a hand with that." An older man with a warm and wrinkled face had emerged from the station portion of the building. He was wearing old and dirty coveralls and wiping grease from his hands with a blue rag as he reached for the pump nozzle. "She's a little temperamental."

"Thank you," Devon said a little surprised. It seemed a rarity to run into anyone genuinely nice these days.

"I bet you kids are hungry," the man spoke as he lifted the hood of the Mustang and began to check the oil while the gas was pumping. "Mazy here makes a mean fried chicken. Hate for you to miss out on the fresh batch she just took out of the fryer. I know I'm gettin' me some."

At that, Pen and Corli hopped out of the car and walked over to the DQ window, taking deep breaths to fill their noses with the wonderful smell. Raisa got out and moved to Devon's side. "Should I order the chicken for all of us?" she asked Devon as she curled her arm around his.

"Sounds fantastic," Devon grabbed Raisa's hand and kissed it before she walked to the window to order with Pen and Corli.

"I'm Calvin. What's your name, Son?" the friendly mechanic/gas station attendant asked as he held his hand out to Devon.

"Devon, Sir," he replied as he took Calvin's hand.

"Well, Devon, there's a real nice park just past town on the left there that has a couple picnic benches. Real' pretty spot for you to eat your lunch... called 'Pass Creek Park'."

"Thank you, Calvin." Devon felt an instant respect for this man and it didn't seem right to call him by his first name. He immediately realized that Calvin reminded him of Vince, and then wondered if he and Raisa would hear from Vince again, or if that was over.

Calvin noticed that Devon wandered off in his head and returned the gas nozzle to the pump and closed the hood of the car. When he came back around the car, he saw that Devon was present again. "That'll be fifty-eight dollars," Calvin smiled at Devon.

Devon pulled out eighty and stuffed it into Calvin's hand as a wad so he wouldn't try to give some back. "Keep the change. And thank you."

"That's mighty nice, Devon, thank you." Calvin didn't see exactly how much Devon handed him, but he knew it was more than he had asked for. He didn't need the extra money in the least but he decided not to make a stir about it. *It'll teach the boy a valuable lesson.* Not that he could figure why the lesson needed to be taught. *To be gracious about the gifts you get by takin' em willingly and not insultin' the giver by tryin' to refuse it.* Calvin saw strength in Devon. Years of meeting people that stopped in their little town on the way to somewhere else gave him a unique perspective on human nature. It was one of his favorite things to do, to guess the character of the man or woman he was speaking to even though he may never see them again. He was sure that Devon would do great things some day. *The world, especially now, will need a boy like this,* he thought. "You know, Son, this is likely the last friendly place you'll run

199

into headed north. Most of the world has lost their minds, if you take my meanin'. It starts up pretty bad come Salem, or so I've heard. You best be careful." Calvin sounded genuinely concerned about sending his new friend on his way.

Devon held out his hand to Calvin. When he took it, Devon lifted his other hand as well and held Calvin's warmly. "Thank you for your kindness, Calvin. We won't forget it. And I promise that we will be careful. Our trip is very important. You've helped more than you know."

They purchased their meal from the friendly Mazy and drove back a block to the country store to browse while their chicken cooled. They purchased sarsaparillas from the warm and friendly, bright-eyed teenage boy that manned the cash register, then headed for the park. As they sat under the shade of a maple tree eating the most wonderful fried chicken that any of them ever tasted, Devon was lost in thought. During the last couple of years his general impression of the human population had degraded. Currently it was that they were unbecoming in character at best, with the exception of his close personal friends and his mother, of course. It put a kink in his theories to meet what seemed to be a whole town of genuinely good people that weren't jaded or cynical, ignorant or self important. What had seemed like a foolhardy journey to discover his purpose, now seemed that it might have some merit. That there may actually be some good people and some good things left. And if this tiny town in the middle of nowhere had good people, how many others were there that he didn't know about. His stomach knotted when he realized that he had been ready to write off all human kind without having all of the information he would need to make that kind of judgment.

Corli finished her food and was looking out at their surroundings and enjoying the cool breeze in her face. Each rise of the wind sent a rustle through the leaves that made the trees sound as if they were communicating with each other. "These trees are so beautiful. I wish I knew what their names were."

"You mean like Tom or Bob? Or I know... Russell," Pen joked.

Corli rolled her eyes.

Pen stood up and gave Corli a peck on the lips, then pointed to the tree they were sitting under. "This is a bigleaf maple, and those over there," he pointed behind them, "are red alder. The ones over there," he pointed toward an area that sloped up, "are red cedar and I think some noble fir... like the Christmas trees." Pen looked pleased with himself.

"I never knew you were such a nerd." Corli was looking at him with her head tilted sideways.

Devon saw Corli's disbelief and chuckled. "Hours and hours of the Discovery Channel. He's a sponge for large amounts of useless information."

"Not so useless," Pen played resentful, "who told you about the magnetic poles?"

For at least thirty seconds all that could be heard was the crackle of wind around them. Pen's jest had snapped everyone back to reality and abruptly ended the lightness they all felt while sitting in the midst of this haven of trees.

Raisa sighed. "It's so peaceful here. I wish we didn't have to leave."

A man named Jude sat bound to a chair at the far end of the mess hall, several people that seemed annoyingly 'good' were watching him to make sure he didn't try to escape. He seethed with the indignation of it and tiny green flames leapt from his

201

eyes whenever he caught one of his captors looking at him. He was loosely gagged to keep him from spitting.

Brian and Kara sat with Edward near his desk while David and a girl named Renee tended to their injuries. "It's amazing that you weren't hurt worse, considering that you were his captive," Renee said as she continued to look Kara over. "How is it that he didn't kill you?"

Brian looked at his wife with a knowing smile. "Kara has a gift with people. She can lead you to look into your soul and question your very existence. She can convince the worst of us to do the right thing. I had no doubt she would be safe if only she had the chance to speak."

"Counselor," Edward said it as if it were Kara's new title. Then he turned to his computer and typed it in next to her name. "And what about you, Brian, what do you do?"

"He is a brilliant engineer and inventor," Kara praised her husband.

As she spoke, her light became so brilliant that Edward had to squint. He slowly turned to type next to Brian's name and as he did he was overcome. His head bent and his eyes glazed over to the point that he could not see well enough to type. He felt honored to be the one to meet and guide all of the Northern Lasteires. In all of his travels through his career and life, he had never seen couples so connected as these Lasteires, or so in love. They all seemed to have an admiration for their partners that seemed to transcend what the world knew of relationships. From what he knew of their future, it would be of paramount importance that they be united. He turned back to face the couple. "I am hoping that you won't be in Thule long before we catch up with you. Then we will move the entire group to our final camp. We have verified that the earthquake did in fact create a small land mass at a location close to the current

202

magnetic north pole, which varies daily, but it may not be large enough for all of us to camp. We'll have to go at the last minute."

The sky was beginning to cloud over so they rolled down the windows of the Mustang. The air blowing through the windows was a nice change from the air conditioner.

Raisa was thinking how it had been about twenty four hours since her mother had died and wondered what she would be doing up there right now. She imagined a kind of heavenly processing station where her mother would have to check in at various locations (meeting up with the deceased relatives, accounting of your deeds, receiving instructions for what you'll be doing now) traveling to each with only a thought, and of course being accompanied by her father all the way. She thought back to her dad's passing and tried to calculate how long it was from when he died to when she first heard his voice and felt his spirit. *Just over three days,* she figured. *That would be an appropriate amount of time for processing.* She sighed out loud and hoped that it would be only another two days till she heard from her father again and hoped that she would be lucky enough to be able to hear from both of them.

Devon was lost in his own thoughts about the town of Curtin and the effect the people there had on him, when Raisa's heavy sigh broke him out of his head. He grabbed her hand. "You okay Rai?" He kept his eyes on the road but smiled into the kiss he planted on her hand.

Raisa considered the question and felt surprisingly confident about the answer. "Yeah… I'm good, actually."

Corli pulled out the computer and reviewed the maps that she saved. "Well…" she broke in, "I'm glad you're feeling better because it looks like we'll most likely be hitting bad roads again soon. It was so stressful back in LA... I hope it isn't anything like that was." Her forehead wrinkled as she reflected on the previous day.

"Yeah, we're just south of Salem and that's where Calvin told us to be careful," Devon added.

In the next mile, they passed several road construction cones and posts that were haphazardly placed in or off to the side of the road. It wasn't clear if there was a purpose to them; they didn't seem to mark anything in particular, but they definitely gave the impression that something ahead might be trouble.

Fortunately, Devon had slowed down or they might not have stopped in time before they hit several road gates that were pulled across the highway over the opposite side of a small hill. Devon put the car in park and got out to see what it was blocking. "See that? The whole road is gone where it went over that creek bed. Guess we'll have to turn around and get off at the last exit."

As Devon found his way to the frontage road that continued to take them north it started raining. By the time they reached the creek bed next to where the highway ended, the rain was falling considerably harder and there was enough water running through it to cover their path with about two inches of overflowing stream. Devon stopped a few yards from it. The image of a flash flood carrying them away down a river ran through his mind. He felt an edge of concern creep over him. "I don't like this." He backed up the hill a ways and pulled over to the gravel shoulder.

The sky continued to darken as they all peered out of their now securely rolled up windows. To their left, the highway was barely visible through the trees. To their right the trees were much thicker. The forest seemed to hug a sheer rock face that blocked their view of whatever lay on the other side of it. They watched as the rain darkened the color of the stone, miniature waterfalls cascading from the top of it. The leaves on the trees danced with the beating rain and wind that was whipping up. In front of them they watched the creek water swell up and over its banks.

The increasing downpour and the darkness of the sky made it difficult to see more than a few yards so their gaze automatically adjusted to their more immediate surroundings.

"Look at that!" Pen pointed to what would be considered a trail at best, which went up to their right and into the trees. They all scanned the incline to see if it led anywhere. Lightning flashed. "*Did you see that car*?!" Pen was pointing up the trail with such enthusiasm that he was practically in the front seat.

They all saw it for barely a second through the trees. But the lightening strobe that flashed directly into the trees beside them was enough to make it a very clear picture. A dark, blue, older model sedan of some kind with three of its doors flung wide open and a mist of exhaust still coming from the tail pipe had been hastily parked in what looked to be a small clearing about twenty yards up the trail. Suddenly a second flash revealed a man running past the front of the car being chased by another.

Devon threw the car into gear and shot up the inclined trail, spewing gravel behind them. He had barely enough room to pass the blue car and pull into a flatter and more open space. They all held their breath as they scanned the opening and its tree lining through the rain. "*There!*" Devon pointed. They saw two women, their backs to the rock, preparing to engage three men in a fight. Devon had his hand on his door latch. "*Raisa*," his exclamation held more than urgency in it. He saw coming from one of the women a bright streaming light that was exactly like hers. But it only distracted him for a second. "Stay here!" He pulled his gun from his back as he ran. Pen and Corli had their knives and were running behind him.

Raisa sat stunned for a moment. She had known exactly what Devon's inflection meant because she saw it too. Many thoughts rose in her mind about how the rays looked coming from her and if they were exactly the same as her own, but she couldn't think of that now and pushed them away. There was something else. "The man... where is the man?" Raisa popped open the glove box and pulled out her gun as she looked through her rain-streaked window in the direction she thought she saw him run. It was opposite of the direction that Devon had gone. The thought of venturing out of the car without him to protect her sent a surge of dread through her. She saw movement near the ground several yards away that wasn't the same as how the bushes and grasses danced rhythmically with the wind and rain. Her heart leapt in her chest and the pulse of her blood in her ears deafened her as she yanked her door open and dashed toward what she saw. Her grip tightened on the handle of the three-fifty-seven, partly because she was full of adrenaline and partly because she was getting drenched and worried about the gun slipping from her hand. She blocked out the feeling of the rain and reminded herself that her grip should be firm and steady but not strained. She slid her finger to the trigger and was vaguely aware the she had raised the gun in aim as she approached two men that had fallen to the ground in a struggle. One was on top of the other with his hands to his opponent's throat. He was unaware that anyone had come up behind him. She looked at the man on the bottom and saw jittering coppery rings plunging frantically into the ground around him. She looked at his face and realized that he was a young man. He also was not going to last much longer. *Can I do this?!* Raisa's mind was trying desperately to work it out. *I need to see his eyes!* "Hey!" she yelled.

The startled attacker turned without releasing the young man's neck. His eyes flew wide with a green flash of terror. He didn't have time to react before he heard the crack of the firing revolver. His head snapped back with the impact it took to the face and his instantly lifeless body fell to the side of his prey.

Devon, Pen and Corli made sure that the two women they helped were not injured. Five against three had made it an easy fight that was over in seconds. Devon chose not to use his gun so that they might avoid killing the bruels unless it was necessary, but the new girl with the yellow mist had insisted on killing them. She thrust her knife (the biggest hunting knife that any of them had ever seen) into each of their hearts herself, just to make sure of it.

Just as they turned toward the clearing, a loud shot rang out. Devon instantly recognized it as Raisa's weapon and broke into a run.

He didn't have time to think, only react. But now it felt like each of his steps forward were in slow motion, like a nightmare where you are running and can't move at all. He pushed the panicked thoughts of Raisa being injured, or worse, out of his head with almost complete success. The sliver of fear that was left was enough to drive him mad. What took seconds but seemed like an eternity finally ended when Devon found Raisa. As he burst onto the scene, what he saw was somehow not what he expected at all.

Raisa sat on the ground, her gun on the foliage at her side. A bruel lay next to her, dead, with a mutilated and bloody face. She was leaning over a young man, his head in her lap, and brushing the water from his face with her hand, speaking to him gently as his coppery rings of light beat with his heart.

15

Raisa didn't hear Devon's arrival over the rain that still battered the hillside and her own voice that cooed for the boy. Devon surveyed the scene for several seconds before he found his voice. He was relieved beyond expression that she was unharmed. His heart soared with pride that Raisa stopped this attacker with an obviously well placed shot. He watched her tenderness and kindness with this stranger and loved her even more than he had a moment ago for the tenderness he saw her exhibit. But he also felt a stab in his chest and nausea rise up into his throat. This physical reaction was new to him. He felt the ground slant and he didn't know how to right himself. "Are you okay?!" he managed. As he waited the mere seconds for a reply, he watched as the boy's rings of light, with his head still in Raisa's lap, grew in strength and depth of their coppery color.

Raisa looked up at Devon with relief that he was there. "He was almost strangled to death," she said in a small voice, as if it would have been a grievous atrocity, as if she had a great love for this stranger.

The boy coughed and opened his eyes.

The rest of the group arrived. The girl with the bright white spirals and rays ran to her partner's side and dropped to her knees. "Thank you," she said as she looked earnestly into Raisa's eyes before looking down and scooping him into her arms.

"Good job with this one." The other girl nudged the bruel's shoulder with the tip of her tennis shoe. "I'm Morgan," she said

209

rather nonchalantly for the circumstance, and held her hand out to Raisa, both in greeting and to help her up.

"Great to meet you," Raisa took her hand and popped up. She couldn't help but gawk a little at Morgan, who was striking. Besides her beautiful misty light that hovered over her like Pen and Corli's, she had radiant, deep brown skin, an extremely toned physique and defined features that reminded Raisa of some kind of warrior princess.

The injured boy recovered enough so that he stood, his partner holding on to him as he rose. The rain began to subside and patted lightly against the wet leaves on the ground.

"I don't suppose you all have had time for introductions," Raisa blurted. She felt strangely invigorated. She moved over to Devon who had not moved since his arrival. "This is my boyfriend, Devon," she said evenly. *Wow... that is the first time I have said that out loud. It sounds strange... but amazing!* She looked tentatively up at Devon as she grabbed his hand and used it to throw his arm around her.

Hearing Raisa refer to him so confidently eased the pain and nausea in his gut. He held out his hand to Morgan and squeezed Raisa closer to him at the same time. "Hi," he managed. "And these are our friends, Pen and Corli," he gestured to the pair.

Morgan greeted them and then looked over to the couple that was her honored charge to keep safe. She was about to introduce them to their new and well deserving friends but stopped short. She saw that an unspoken communication between them had already begun.

They were looking intently at each other. It was clear that the four of them could see the lights and mists on the other that before then had only been seen on their own partners.

The girl ventured forward first, holding her hand out to Raisa. "I'm Julia, and this is Scott. Thank you again for what you did." She took Raisa's hand with both of hers and held it.

Raisa looked into Julia's bright blue-green eyes and felt their intensity. In the past, a person locking eyes with her like this might have intimidated her, but in this case it almost seemed like they were passing strength to each other. Julia stepped in front of Devon to shake his hand. Out of nowhere a pang of protectiveness hit Raisa. She wanted to step in between them and it was almost impossible to keep herself put. She watched as Devon and Julia took each other's hands and felt herself go off balance.

"And thank you for saving me," Julia smiled warmly at Devon.

"We didn't do much," Devon replied a little impishly as he dropped his arm from around Raisa to address her.

Raisa's vision tunneled. She looked at the two of them, Devon with his earthbound energy and Julia with her rays reaching to the sky. She looked at her straight bright blonde hair and beautiful figure. She saw that her beauty was natural, *no make-up*, she noticed. *What if I'm NOT the only possible girl for him?* Just before that thought consumed her, her vision widened again to see the boy, Scott, step up to her.

Scott appeared to be mostly recovered but Raisa could see the bruises starting to surface on his neck. She reached out to shake his hand since that seemed the method of greeting for the day but was surprised when he embraced her in a hug instead. "I was a gonner." His voice was raspy and quiet in her ear. "Thank you for saving my life."

Veins were bulging from the forehead of Nosh's scarlet colored face. "That stupid bitch with the knife!" They were the last four

211

on their way to see Edward Brayden, and they were slipping through his fingers. Nosh was near madness, though that was not unusual. It was becoming more and more difficult for him to reign in his anger enough to function. The only thing he had for him now, that kept his grip on sanity, was that Devon was closer. But now the two couples were joined. "What if that Julia dissuades Devon from coming to me? She has strong words and authority in her... AH!"

Nosh grabbed at his upper left arm with his right hand and started clawing at it. He stood in the center of the circle of women and blood stains, willing his feet to move but they would not. His face flew up in panicked anticipation.

NOSH MEGEDAGIK. He heard the voice in his head, though it could have been booming from the rafters of the ceiling, he wasn't sure anymore. *The 'one who kills many' does not seem an appropriate title for you any longer,* the power of the voice resounded off the walls of the room, or was it the insides of his skull.

Nosh's knees cracked and bent suddenly in forced supplication, his palms smacking the floor as he fell. His forehead hit as well and as he raised his eyes again he felt blood dripping into them, stinging. "How dare you force me to submit," he snarled low in his throat, "without me you have nothing."

With you, I have little more. Time is short. You will show me a victory soon.

Nosh's head bowed without his consent. He pushed against the unseen force till blood trickled from the open wound on his forehead as well as his eyes and nose. He shook furiously with the effort but made no progress. As he sunk to the floor, losing consciousness, he heard an echoing laugh that froze in his bones just before his vision blurred and went black.

It was a caravan now, Devon drove the Mustang in front and Morgan drove their blue sedan behind. The two groups spoke enough, forgoing the obvious, to know that they were both heading for the same hotel in Seattle and in comparing notes, Corli had the most information about the route they would take. The roads grew a little worse but the state of Oregon secured an advantage over any troublemakers. Most every time they exited the highway and detoured, they saw armed forces along the way, swiftly handling any disturbance that occurred. Devon thought about Calvin and wished that he could update his friend on the travel conditions. Corli offered that it would probably take four hours to get to the hotel from where they were and at the rate they were going.

Raisa turned toward Pen who was sitting behind Devon now. She glanced at Corli who was watching the scenery go by out her window. *It doesn't look like I would be interrupting anything...* "Hey Pen, switch spots with me." She didn't really give him a chance to respond before she expertly slid over the seat and sat in between them.

Pen smiled. "Sure, that's cool!" He was just lanky enough to fold himself sufficiently to make the move without any trouble.

Both Raisa and Corli's faces were bright with smiles. "I feel like we haven't talked in *forever*," Raisa breathed as she grabbed Corli's hand with a feeling of relief and squeezed it.

"I *know... boys...* they make us forget the important things," Corli giggled.

The sound of Corli's laugh wrapped around Raisa like an old familiar blanket. She knew that Corli was trivializing things for the sake of lightness and appreciated it immensely. Raisa was glad at this moment that they hadn't brought any other car. She and Corli could have a conversation in the back seat and the sound of the engine would cover for them.

Devon had an idea of what Raisa was trying to do so he turned the radio on low; a classic rock station was playing "Black Water" by the Doobie Brothers. He also struck up a conversation with Pen about Discovery Channel content.

Raisa leaned up and threw her arms around Devon and kissed him on the neck before she retreated back to her crouch next to Corli.

They talked about the boys for awhile. "You've had a very special gleam in your eyes since last night," Raisa teased.

Corli blushed. "Oh, Raisa... I can't explain it... Pen is so amazing. We talked for hours. We both realized that... well, you know." Corli didn't look up at Raisa until she realized that she didn't get a response. Between friends of ten years or so, a facial expression can pretty much say it all and Corli instantly knew why Raisa hadn't said anything. "What? Why not," she exclaimed a little too loudly. Pen and Devon broke off their conversation mid-sentence and turned to look at Corli. "Sorry... it's nothing." She waved a hand at them and they obediently turned back and resumed their discussion. Corli smiled apologetically at Raisa and leaned in to hear her answer.

"He wants to wait," Raisa sighed at the back window of the car.

"But why?" Corli sounded incredulous.

"I know, right?" Raisa huffed. But then her face softened and smiled as she replayed the other parts of the hotel stay in her mind. "It's okay... he is being very sweet. I know that when it happens it will be perfect."

Corli was babbled. She saw the connection that Devon had with Raisa. It made no sense. But rather than press the issue, she decided a change of subject was in order. "So... what do

214

you think of our new friends?" she asked as she glanced behind them. "They're very unique, don't you think?" Corli lowered her voice even more. "I think Devon is jealous of Scott," she whispered in Raisa's ear.

"What? That's absurd," Raisa said skeptically. Her eyebrows crinkled.

"Didn't you see the look on his face that whole time? I'm telling you, he was tortured."

Raisa was surprised. She certainly had not seen it. *Maybe it's because I was too busy being jealous of Julia*, she surmised. "He is pretty cute. I've never been attracted to anyone like that before but I can definitely see the draw." Raisa had to think past the bruises on his neck to remember any details. She recalled that he had very pale skin, his hair was almost shaved and he wore a goatee. "I like that cap he put on when they got in the car… he seems very artsy." Raisa thought about discussing Julia with Corli but it made her stomach turn so she opted against it. "What do you think of Morgan?" Raisa's smile went wide.

"I LOVE that chick, don't you?" Corli held her hands out for effect. "You should have seen her with that knife… fearless! I would never want to be on her bad side, that's for sure. And what about you, Raisa, with that kill shot! I honestly didn't know you had it in you."

They chatted more about their new friends and Raisa's heroic shot. They pulled the boys into the conversation. Raisa noticed that it was never herself or Devon that spoke of Scott or Julia. *I hope this doesn't turn into a 'thing'*, she thought.

Devon realized that Raisa was not saying anything directly about Scott even though she had been the one to save him. He couldn't keep from wondering if she avoided talking about him for a specific reason. *Maybe she likes him and doesn't want to spill it*, he thought at first. Before the stabbing in his chest got

215

too bad he chastised himself. *You're an idiot Devon... she probably just saw how stupid you were about the whole thing and doesn't want to hurt your feelings... I hope... that would be in her character anyway.* He shook his head and tuned back into the conversation just as Corli was saying how well spoken Julia was.

"She seems almost like a politician. Or a young and unspoiled one anyway... the way you *wish* politicians would be."

Devon thought about Julia and how the light came from her the same way it came from Raisa. He thought it seemed different though, he just couldn't figure out how. Raisa's energy drew him in, made him want to stare at it, stare at her, be close to her, revel in it. He knew logically that Julia was attractive, but even with her light, she was just a girl with a bunch of cool stuff coming out of her neck. He agreed that she had some skill with speech and that she was nice, but that was it. His brain automatically went back to Raisa in a comparative way. His heart beat faster. All he wanted was to be alone with her, to check their connection, feel her touch, now. But that would have to wait. He pushed the gas pedal down just a little further.

The sun had been gone for at least three hours when their little procession entered the Seattle area. They passed through Portland with no trouble at all, short of the time consuming detours. Devon called Morgan's cell to see if their group was as hungry as his. An advertisement on the radio for "Walter's Waffles – open late" caught their attention and since it was not too far from the hotel, everyone agreed on the eatery.

"Oooo, I hope they have chicken and waffles," Raisa said hopefully. She held her hand to her stomach as it gurgled. "Although, nothing could beat the chicken we had for lunch. Maybe just the waffles."

216

"Oh, man… did you have to say all that?" Pen threw his head back on the seat and Corli reached up to sooth him, petting his hair.

Devon chuckled, "We're almost there guys."

They spotted the small neon sign a couple of blocks up. Raisa considered how the sign contradicted the old town feel of the brick buildings, scrolled wood and stone around them. She couldn't see any earthquake damage in the dark but assumed that there had to be some. "This town is beautiful," she breathed at the window. It created fog as she spoke. "I can't wait to see it in the daylight."

They pulled into a tiny parking lot next to the restaurant, the blue sedan right behind them. As they left their cars and headed the few steps to the restaurant door, Devon felt an edge in the air. He looked around him instinctively and noticed that everyone else felt it too. They didn't lag outside but hurried through the door. Once inside, the edginess subsided a little and Devon stretched. "I think we're good," he said low enough for their group to hear. There were only a few people in the restaurant and he didn't feel any anxiety from them.

The seven of them filed into a big, round corner booth as the waitress handed out menus. Raisa ended up next to Devon, of course, but was a little uneasy about the fact that Scott was on the other side of her. *At least Julia is on the other side of him and not next to Devon.* She felt Devon's hand clamp down on her leg and pull it next to his tightly. Raisa's lips curled up behind her menu. *I guess Corli was right… this should be interesting…. Okay, menu, food.* Raisa tried to ignore the silence and the electric buzz emanating from her side of the table. It was similar to the warmth she felt whenever she was near Devon but it spiked and almost burned every now and again. Finally something on the menu caught her eye. "Fresh pineapple and coconut syrup... yum!"

"I knew you were going to get that." Corli helped end the lack of conversation by chiming in.

Raisa lowered her menu and smiled. Then she looked at Devon who she swore was boring a hole through his menu with a crinkled brow and unseeing eyes. She quickly looked back at her menu. "And, Devon, I bet you're getting the chorizo and egg waffle, right?

Devon's face smoothed as he looked at her. "Yeah, how'd you guess?" He let a smile break through and Raisa's heart skipped a beat.

The waitress returned and took everyone's orders. She also took away the menus that had served as the excuse for not looking anyone else in the eye. Corli shared a glance with Raisa that said 'see how uncomfortable Devon is? I told you.' She glanced at Morgan, who pretended that she didn't feel the tension, her eyes on her fingernails. She emanated her desire to be left out of the situation. Raisa looked at Devon. He was typically the one that started conversations but she could tell by the downward curve of his lips that nothing on his mind would be coming out of his mouth. She tried to think of something light as a conversation starter when she saw Julia, out of the corner or her eye, pull her hand from her lap and bring it to the back of Scott's neck. Scott leaned forward and pinched the bridge of his nose with his fingers.

"Are you okay?" Raisa had to resist the urge to reach up and touch Scott's shoulder beside her. She was concerned, but there was no way she would intentionally give Devon any heart ache.

Scott looked up from his hand, his eyes weighted with an unknown opposition. "Voices... they're getting really rough."

"Oh," was all Raisa could say. But her tone was knowing.

218

Devon seemingly snapped out of his mood and looked across Raisa to Scott. "Okay, so there's another thing we have in common… but we haven't heard any for quite some time," he said thoughtfully. He looked at Raisa to check that his statement was still correct and Raisa nodded. "We weren't sure why. It's interesting that you still are." He leaned out to look at Julia. "What about you?"

Julia's mouth spread to a snide smile, "No, they don't bother me anymore. I talk back." Small chuckles escaped from the group, some of them uneasy, hoping they weren't perceived as rude. Morgan just smiled warmly at her fingernails.

Scott seemed to recover and the food was delivered. The conversation flowed a little more freely after that. Devon seemed to feel more comfortable as well and posed a few questions to their new friends. It was discovered that Julia had a political science degree from UC Berkley, ethics and accountability in government, a minor in communications. Scott was an accomplished artist. He had no formal training but had been able to capitalize on his talent. His favorite and most sought after style was 'surrealism' but according to his partner, he could do anything. Julia was twenty-five, Scott twenty-seven and Morgan was twenty-four.

Raisa felt small and insignificant as the discussion continued. She watched Devon, who seemed completely un-intimidated by their accomplishments and was glad for it. *They've had a few more years than us to accomplish their goals,* she thought. But she couldn't quite make herself feel better. *Who am I kidding… I wasn't even registered for school.* She pouted internally.

The mood was warm as they finished and paid for their meal but as they left the restaurant the watchful edge returned. Devon stopped by the cars and motioned for everyone to gather. "I have a feeling that we are being watched." Everyone seemed to agree.

219

"Keep your eyes open. We'll only stay at the hotel if it seems safe, but no matter what, we need to get in there to find out where Edward Brayden is. When we get there, I want Morgan to take the lead and Pen and Corli to take the rear."

It was after eleven and chilly outside. They pulled up to the Santino Hotel and saw that the streets in the area still hummed with night life. They each canvassed the crowds of partiers to determine if there were any 'unfriendlies' but they couldn't quiet catch anyone's eyes.

Devon looked at the hotel to size up the situation. It was fairly small and quite old, made of brick like most of the surrounding buildings. They were only separated from the entrance by the narrow sidewalk. There were no armed guards but two attendants on either side of the one door. He squinted to see them in the shadow of the awnings. "Raisa, look!" He pointed at the attendants. Raisa turned from scanning the other side of the street and smiled. A light mist hovered over both of their heads.

"We're in the right place. I can still feel the bruels though," she shivered.

Pen and Corli hopped out and stood at their respective sides in protection mode. Devon and Raisa gathered all the bags. Morgan followed Scott and Julia the few steps to them and then took the lead. The attendants opened the door for the group. Pen, at the very rear, turned and walked in backwards, scanning the street. He stopped just before entering the hotel to take one last look. An attendant stepped close to him and spoke, "Yes, they're there... several of them. We'll be watching." Pen nodded and turned into the building.

Devon looked around the small and cozy lobby. It looked more like an old fashioned living room, maybe from the late-eighteen-hundreds, than a hotel. The ceilings were low, the walls dark green and a fire burned in a rock fireplace, dark wood carved couches around it. He wished that he was bringing Raisa here on vacation rather than into some unknown and potentially dangerous situation. It seemed like a romantic place.

The small concierge podium near the door was manned by another person with light above his head and one of the clerks behind the check-in desk had it too. This is the one he would talk to. He walked to the desk and saw that the boy's name tag said Nigel. He was Asian, slight of frame, with a swath of black, straight hair covering one of his eyes. He looked up and smiled a warm and slightly excited smile as Devon approached. "Can I get you guys some rooms tonight?" Nigel asked as he flicked his head to uncover his face. The phone rang at the desk and the other clerk answered it. Instead of answering Nigel, Devon felt compelled to watch the other clerk from the corner of his eye. The clerk with the phone in his ear nodded and glanced up at Devon but seeing that he was being watched, turned to face the other direction. He said something too quiet for Devon to hear and hung up the phone. Then he made himself busy in a very close proximity to Nigel.

Devon realized that his question wouldn't really matter, even if the annoying clerk played for the wrong team. So he spoke, but in a low voice. "Nigel, I'm looking for Edward Brayden, is his show still on location here?" He could tell that the meddlesome clerk was listening.

Something in Nigel's eyes told Devon that it was all under control. "I'm sorry, Sir. They left us over a month ago. Sorry you missed it. He does put on a great show though, doesn't he?"

"Do you know where they went?" Devon knew that Nigel had the answer to this. Why else would all of these people like Pen, Corli and Morgan be here.

"I'm sorry, Sir, I don't. But I might be able to find out for you in the morning." Nigel smiled and winked with the eye that was mostly covered by hair.

Brilliant, Devon thought, and smiled.

"Let me get you a couple of rooms, though. And, unfortunately, I can only do two together. Will that be okay? Believe it or not, we are almost full. All of a sudden, people want to spend their money."

Devon turned and looked at his friends. This was a democracy and he wanted to make sure that they all weighed in. They all agreed that this seemed a good place to stay the night since it seemed to have extra protection. "Sure, two rooms will be great."

After typing in the necessary information and collecting cash from Devon, Nigel held out two room keys, the old fashioned kind, with actual keys and numbers on the attached plastic rectangle. "That will be rooms two-eighteen and two-nineteen." His gaze was steady.

Devon reached to retrieve the keys and barely glanced down at them, only really looking at them when he realized that Nigel did not let go of them easily. He saw that the numbers were three-twenty-four and three-twenty-five. When he glanced up again, Nigel's expression remained unchanged. Devon caught his drift. "Thank you, Nigel. Good night," he said smoothly.

When Devon pushed the button for third floor in the elevator Raisa questioned him. "Um... wouldn't two-eighteen and two-nineteen be on the *second* floor?"

Devon held up the keys for everyone to see. Silence followed.

After they were all in their rooms, Julia knocked on the adjoining door. Devon opened it. Raisa watched Devon's face carefully to see if she could pick out any partiality to Julia and

222

was gratified that she didn't think she saw any. Even when Devon invited them into the room so that they could all talk together, he was immediately back at her side and finding some way to touch her. *I was just being stupid, I guess... I wonder though... if he wasn't worried about Scott, would he notice Julia then?* Raisa sighed out loud.

"Rai?" Devon noticed. "Don't worry. I think Nigel has this whole process down."

Raisa smiled in answer to Devon's concern. Better for him to think that was why she was sighing. Raisa got up to check out the room. Her eye went to something electronic. "iPod jack!" she exclaimed happily. She plugged in her iPod and selected her night-time playlist, making sure the volume was low. It started with, *Sting, Sister Moon.*

"Ah, sweet." Pen smiled at Raisa.

Then the room broke into several small vignettes.

Morgan told Corli about the two men that they lost. Corli listened intently, her eyes welling up when she saw the sadness in Morgan's eyes. "We married young. Mark was a star running back in high school and then in college. We were a perfect pair. He just got signed to go pro!" Morgan's voice was proud. "You would think with all that training and muscle he would be indestructible... but one moment of carelessness, or *thinking* that you are invincible........." She snapped herself out of her own reverie to continue, "Sean was Scott's friend, they grew up together. It's only been a couple of months...." Her voice trailed off again.

Devon and Julia were having a discussion about various political stances. Both seemed content that for the most part, their views were similar, only disagreeing on some enforcement issues. Raisa's attention never left their conversation for long, gauging whether or not she thought they were flirting. She felt pathetic for doing it, but couldn't stop.

Pen was quietly picking his guitar with each song that came on the stereo, occasionally glancing at Corli in case she needed him. He could see that she and Morgan were going to be good friends.

Scott had a sketch pad and seemed to be engrossed in a new creation, completely oblivious to anyone else in the room.

Raisa hummed along with Pen for awhile but was curious about Scott's work. She finally decided to go sit next to him and check it out. Devon seemed to be over whatever he felt before, and besides, he was still involved in a conversation with Julia. *Hmm... no, don't trip Raisa. It can't get more boring than politics.* She went and sat next to Scott.

Raisa took in an audible breath when she saw what Scott was drawing. It almost felt sacrilegious to put it on paper for anyone to see. There was an arcing line of couples, each in a kind of embrace, though not a romantic one, per-se. It reminded her of a flash she had seen in her mind of her and Devon. Each couple had the energy that she and Devon, Julia and Scott had. It was wildly stronger in intensity than the energy that Raisa saw though. Scott's drawing had the copper rings raising higher and wider, the white rays and spirals more substantial than she saw them on Julia, and some of them bending off in another direction rather than just up. Raisa thought about the fact that if regular people saw this drawing, they would think it was surrealism, not realistic. "Is that what you see?" she murmured, her hand automatically reached to Scott's arm and she gently laid it there, anticipating his response.

Scott looked up, "No, not like this... this is what I dream." He smiled and his expression lingered for a moment, then his attention returned to his sketch pad.

224

Devon had been keeping an eye on Raisa too. Though he made sure she never caught him looking. When she went to sit with Scott, something twisted in his stomach. When he saw Raisa's reaction to Scott's art, the bottom dropped out and allowed the twisting feeling to wreak havoc on his entire being. He watched Raisa's hand rest on Scott and saw an extra glow of light where their skin connected. Then he saw the way Scott looked at her, they had a connection, he was sure of it.

Devon realized that he had not heard the last few sentences that Julia had spoken. He wrapped up the discussion point he was on as quickly as he could, not quite making sure that he did it politely.

Julia watched his eyes dart to Raisa and smiled to herself. *They must still be a new couple.* She had no concerns at all. She knew how strong the bond was between her and Scott. She decided to make it easy for Devon. "Well, it's getting late. Scott, are you ready?"

"Yes, that sounds good," he said happily. Scott looked at Julia with an infinite regard as he stood and joined her to leave.

They agreed that the door adjoining the two rooms should stay ajar and Devon reminded everyone to be 'weapons ready' and packed for a quick exit if need be.

Devon saw the uneasiness in Raisa's countenance and smiled. He planned on slipping down to his underwear and quickly under the covers, but opted for drawstrings and a t-shirt so that she would be comfortable. He realized as an afterthought that this would be more respectful to Corli anyway. He washed up and changed in the bathroom and everyone else followed suit.

Raisa thought the situation felt a little strange, like a coed sleep-over, which was something that she had *never* done. It didn't seem to bother anyone else though. *I guess we're all*

225

basically clothed. But getting under the covers with a boy, and having Corli in the next bed over doing the same thing? It was weird.

Pen turned out all of the lights except for a small desk lamp, then promptly did a belly flop on the bed. Corli giggled.

Once everyone was settled, Devon pulled Raisa to him under the covers and closed his eyes. "Ahhhh," he quietly groaned. "I've been waiting for this all day." He looked at Raisa's face then, just an inch from his. Her eyes sparkled like blue stars in a dark, summer sky. A warm feeling flooded through him. "Can you feel it?" he whispered.

Raisa saw a new expression on his face. His eyes were devastatingly clear, even in the dark. There was the slightest wrinkle in one spot in the center of his forehead. His lips were slightly parted and expectant, not for a kiss or even air, just waiting. "The current?" she breathed.

"Yes," his eyes closed. "Our connection."

♦♦♦

Raisa stood in the middle of the street in front of her home and watched a car that belonged to one of her neighbors drive slowly down the street away from her. She was about ten years old. *I haven't had this dream for awhile… I wonder why now?* She felt something in her hand and turned to see a boy, just older than her, with warm maple colored skin, holding her hand. *This is new.* Suddenly another boy, it was Garik, *I'd never recognized him before*, ran by them, a flaming arrow drawn in a bow and aimed at the car. Garik waited for the precise moment when the car drove over a manhole cover in the street to release the arrow. It flew far and straight, striking under the car, the gas tank. The car exploded into a gigantic fireball. Panic instantly overtook

Raisa. She had an urgent premonition that the fire from the car would ignite the natural gas lines under the street. She yanked the boy that held her hand. "Come on! We have to run!" They only made it a few feet before the next explosion ripped through the concrete street, knocking them to the ground and rendering them deaf. Then the two houses on either side of the street where the car burned, exploded, becoming engulfed in flames within seconds. The explosions continued up the street, two houses at a time. For some unknown reason, Raisa scrambled, dragging the boy with her, till she reached the entry way of her own house. Raisa knew that this was the wrong thing to do... it would be seconds till her house exploded too. *This is what always happens in this dream. I wonder if it is because I think that I can stop it somehow...* The next explosion tore through her house, her damaged ears barely registering the blistering sound. The force of it tore through the foundation, creating chunks of floor that tilted at various angels, making it impossible to move anywhere. Flames ensued.

♦♦♦

"Fire!" Raisa's eyes flew open. The exclamation was a scream in her dream but was barely audible in reality. She relaxed when she realized where she was. It was the same moment she always woke in that dream. She started to close her eyes again when she sniffed the air. *That's not a dream... smoke!* "Fire!" she said, loudly this time. It woke everyone up, and a second later the hotel alarms peeled.

16

Sirens were heard approaching the hotel. A minute later they were all up, gathered in one room and ready to go. Devon peeked through the curtains and saw that the first light of day was barely on the horizon. An urgent knock came at the door.

Pen held out his hand as everyone else froze. He walked to the door and looked through the peephole. "It's Nigel." Pen jerked the door open.

"Let's go!" Nigel exclaimed dramatically. He waived his hands with urgency, his eyes wide and bright. He seemed more excited than any other emotion that might have been more appropriate for the situation. He led the group quickly to a set of stairs at the far end of the floor and led them down. He spoke quickly, never looking back to see if all his guests were following, "They've surrounded the hotel... I've never seen so many of them at once! They set fire to the rooms you were supposed to be in and then jammed the doors shut. We don't have a handle on the fire yet – glad it's on the other side of the building, eh?" The proud smile in his voice was evident.

They reached the ground floor but Nigel unlocked another door with more descending stairs on the other side of it, ushering everyone through.

"Where are you taking us?" Devon's question didn't sound alarmed, only curious and a little breathless from the rush.

"Underground." Nigel did his best Vincent Price impersonation, and then chuckled.

228

"I've heard of this, the Seattle Underground." Pen sounded excited too.

"Yep!" Nigel closed and locked the door behind them. He didn't continue down the steps and Devon could see that this was where they would part ways.

"How far are we going?" Devon asked quickly.

"Just two city blocks," Nigel began. "You'll go till it ends, then up some stairs. Look out the door but don't come out until you see me pull up. I'll bring a van. Here," he said and quickly stuffed some paper in Devon's hand. "This is a map to the campsite where Mr. Brayden is. Hurry! We have to get you out of here. God speed." Nigel turned, unlocked the door and dashed through. They heard the lock click again.

It was dark and dank in the underground path. The musty smell was strong, like earth and stagnant water, and air that had not been disturbed for fifty years. They rushed single file down what was once an old cobblestone sidewalk, passing what used to be the ground floor of the buildings above. Most were dilapidated and crumbling, boarded up to keep vandals out. Opposite the old buildings, on the street side was simply a damp dirt and concrete wall that leaned into the walkway. Occasionally unseen roots reached from the wall and the ceiling and brushed their arms and faces like craggy spirits from another century, grasping at something that might carry them away from their crypt. Trickling water could be heard dripping into unseen pools. At fairly regular intervals, light seeped through thick purple glass tiles that were set in the sidewalk above them which gave the group just enough light to keep from stumbling over the uneven surface.

Raisa was not going to be the one to interfere with their silent getaway. Everyone was concentrating on their footing. But regardless of the danger they were in, and the anxious adrenaline from it, she was dealing with an ache in her heart. *I can't believe I'm leaving the Mustang behind...* It made her feel foolish and materialistic. But it also made her think of her father. She mulled it over in her head. *He would want me to get away and be safe... maybe I can come back and get it sometime...*

Corli felt like they were missing something, she just couldn't figure out what it was. Everyone carried their small bags. Devon had the extra backpack that she knew was the cash, and she knew that they had divided up the firearms so that each person carried one. They were finally approaching the stairs at the end of the creepy tunnel when she realized what it was. She broke the silence. "Pen, your guitar! You didn't bring it!" Her expression was pained. She knew how important it was to him.

"S'okay, Love." He turned and smiled a little wistfully at her. "I knew it was just gonna slow me down from here on out. Still got the pipes." He pointed to his chest. "They'll do just fine."

Corli grabbed his hand with her head lowered and nodded. It was obvious that things were heating up. She realized that more than the issue of traveling light, there might not be much occasion for a sing-along on the horizon.

They huddled together on the stairs as Devon cracked opened the door, early morning light streamed through. The street corner was only a few feet away from them and the van would be easy to see. As Devon kept watch, Raisa turned her attention to Scott, Julia and Morgan. She watched their expressions and saw that the situation they were all in together right now didn't seem to affect them as much. They had been here before, metaphorically, and had lost their friends and lovers. They seemed resigned to the journey, knowing that they were called to do it, but there was no happiness left in their eyes. She thought it seemed that only duty drove them.

The van squealed to a stop at the corner and Nigel hopped out, the motor still running. "Hi guys!" He waved for them to come out, a large and confident smile on his face for the fact that his plan was working.

"He's here, let's go!" Devon ordered calmly. He stepped outside and turned to usher everyone else out. Morgan was the first one through the door after him.

Another car screeched up behind the van and the door flew open. In an instant, a man with sickening green eyes flew at Nigel, landing a knife blow into his back. Nigel hadn't seen the man, it happened so fast. His face changed from happy excitement to inquisitiveness. The man pulled his knife from Nigel's body that was stiff with shock and turned on his heels to face his real targets.

"NO!" Devon cried as he lurched toward Nigel, catching his head just before it hit the ground.

Morgan, who was a step closer, heaved herself at the man, pinning his body to the van with hers. The speed and stealth that she did this with didn't look particularly deadly. It wasn't until she stepped back, pulling his knife from his abdomen – as well as the tip of it from the metal face of the van behind him, that anyone knew what she had done. His body slumped into the gutter. The curb was so high that he almost disappeared.

Devon and Morgan pulled Nigel into one of the back seats of the van while everyone else piled in. Pen slid into the driver's seat. He pealed out; checking his rearview mirror to make sure that no one else had followed Nigel, and left the trash in the gutter.

Devon knelt on the floor of the moving van, holding Nigel's hand. Morgan sat on the other side of them, her expression as smooth as stone, only her quiet streaming tears giving her away.

231

Nigel looked up at Devon with half seeing eyes. "Did we get away?" He sputtered blood out of his mouth, but he smiled expectantly.

"We did. We're going to get you to a hospital... just hold on." Devon sounded strong and reassuring.

"Huh? Naw... don't waste-" Nigel tried to cough but more blood just gurgled from his mouth.

Devon squeezed his eyes shut for a moment. *No, no, NO!* But he knew that it was pointless. Nigel was too badly hurt.

"Besides..." Nigel found enough air to continue, "not like I'll be around much longer anyway." He looked at Morgan then and smiled wide. His teeth and lips were covered in blood but he still looked – excited, "I'll see you on the other side! Come find-"

"Dev, where am I going?" Pen called behind him. "The hospital?"

Devon felt the hand in his go limp.

"No."

"It feels strange to be going south again," Devon remarked. He had moved up to the passenger seat next to Pen after wrapping Nigel's body in a grey wool blanket they found in the van. He held the paper that Nigel had given him. It was smudged with Nigel's blood and looking at it, Devon wondered exactly how much blood had been spilled for this cause. How many were there like him and Raisa, Julia and Scott, and how many had died trying to defend their friends. He ached to know the point of it all, to find out what his part was and to give meaning and reason to the seemingly senseless death that came of it. He tried to imagine an end to the madness, a way for life to be different than it was today. A life where he and Raisa could grow together as a normal couple, but he couldn't conceive how. "It should only take about an hour to get there from here – if we don't run into any trouble," he continued absently. *But "trouble" will undoubtedly find us*, he thought.

Raisa sat at the back of the van. This was the farthest in proximity she had been from Devon for any length of time in days. She still felt their buzzing connection though, like an arc of energy across the van. It seemed to be growing stronger every day. She was almost surprised that she couldn't see it. She squinted her eyes, focusing and unfocusing them to see if she could catch a glimpse of anything in the air, but all she saw was Devon's energy rings, moving slowly, resounding with his pulse. She regarded Devon outright then, looking at his beautiful concerned face. She thought of him with pride today, as she did most days, the way he led everyone, and the way he cared for Nigel. It was obvious that Nigel's death was affecting him, as it was all of them. *But with Devon*, she thought, *it actually changes his path. He allows his experiences to mold and shape him, to turn him into a better man.* Her thoughts turned to Nigel then. Part of her was curious, almost jealous of Nigel's death. She knew if she voiced this thought, her sanity would be in question. But, she wondered what it would be like. *Nigel certainly wasn't afraid.* Raisa realized at that moment that she was changed. Death and pain used to terrify her. But now, since her father and mother had died, she wasn't afraid at all. She knew now that there was a life after this one and nothing could convince her otherwise. It would be an adventure to follow after her parents. "Exciting," she murmured to herself in wonder.

"Now that we're out of the city we should get some food. We have no clue what we're in for when we get to the camp." Devon paused, "And we need to find an appropriate place for Nigel."

Edward called breakfast two hours earlier than normal and asked for everyone's attention before they started their meal. "I've heard from Nigel," he began. "It seems that our last two Lasteire couples are together. They're leaving the hotel this morning." The group seemed encouraged and began a low chatter amongst themselves. Edward raised his hand. "Though this *is* good news, there's more." He waited for everyone to quiet down. "Nigel said that there was a large group of wicked men at the hotel, larger than he has ever seen. He seemed certain that he could get them and their friends out undetected." His voice lowered then and his eyes cast down. "But I'm certain that they will not give up. It's only a matter of a very short time till they assume that our friends have gotten out, and will try to follow them... here." He paused, thinking of the best way to word what he would say next. "We have always known that this whole thing would fail if even one of the chosen is killed. You all have worked and fought bravely to protect them, and many have given their lives. What I believe we will face now, is the last desperate attempt to overtake us. They *will* come here... all of them, at least any that can get here, to try and stop us. We must not waver; we must not let them win!" His voice rose till it filled the room. "Now........" he barely stopped the knot rising in his throat. "Eat your breakfast," he choked then dabbed his forehead with a napkin, composed again. "And *pray*." He started walking up the isle as he finished. "David will fill you in on strategy and weapons. Be ready within the hour."

A drive-through in the town of Auburn had produced a round of hearty breakfast sandwiches for the group. But everyone ate in silence, barely tasting their food as Pen pulled onto the four-ten toward Mt. Rainier. The mountain loomed in front and to the left of them the entire drive, it seemed to jut from the earth as a warning of some kind, singular against the blue morning sky. After a turn at Enumclaw they began to climb and the mountain didn't look quite as ominous as it had before. The forest was beautiful and thick, but the warning remained.

The groups thoughts were almost audible above the noise of the road: *Such a beautiful place, a place we have to go, to learn about something we need to do, into certain danger, a place we really don't want to go to right now.*

"Pull onto the next dirt road you see, Pen." Devon's voice was quiet.

Pen pulled off the highway and drove into the trees for about a mile till their path was little more than a trail.

Everyone helped. A spot was selected under the shade of a beautiful pine tree that grew at the top of an incline overlooking a small and quiet valley. A dogwood was in bloom at its base. They removed as much earth as they could and gathered rocks to cover and protect his body. They worked together quickly and quietly.

When the task was done they all stood in silence. Some looked out onto the serenity of the valley, some at the beautiful flowers hovering over Nigel's grave. No one seemed to feel the need to speak. It was a peaceful place.

Devon broke the silence. He sounded like he was talking only to himself, "We didn't know him very well... and yet he was willing to give his life for ours."

A breeze moved through the trees and the smell of pine and wild flowers caused everyone to breathe in deeply. Morgan quietly began to sing; Pen and Raisa accompanied her with soft harmonies. At the refrain, a lump rose in Raisa's throat, tears streamed from her eyes. She was grateful that Morgan's soulful voice continued strong, she couldn't make any more sound.

Why should I feel discouraged, why should the shadows come,
Why should my heart be lonely, and long for heav'n and home,
When Jesus is my portion? My constant Friend is He:
His eye is on the sparrow, and I know He watches me;
His eye is on the sparrow, and I know He watches me.

I sing because I'm happy, I sing because I'm free,
For His eye is on the sparrow, and I know He watches me.

"Let not your heart be troubled," His tender word I hear,
And resting on His goodness, I lose my doubts and fears;
Though by the path He leadeth, but one step I may see;
His eye is on the sparrow, and I know He watches me;
His eye is on the sparrow, and I know He watches me.

Whenever I am tempted, whenever clouds arise,
When songs give place to sighing, when hope within me dies,
I draw the closer to Him, from care He sets me free;
His eye is on the sparrow, and I know He watches me;
His eye is on the sparrow, and I know He watches me.

No one seemed willing to move from this spot on the mountainside. The moment was too serine.

Devon ventured a step and took in the other's faces to let them know it was time to go. They all had moved only a few feet...

"Aaaahhh!" Scott suddenly fell to his knees, his hands clasped to his ears, groaning in pain. His breathing came as if he were being tortured. Julia, standing next to him, would have dropped to help him but was frozen in her spot, her face grimaced and her eyes unseeing.

"Raisa! Quickly!" Devon motioned to her as he rushed to Julia's side. Raisa had already started to reach for Scott. She didn't know why, but what they did next seemed automatic, like something you already had planted in your head to do in case of emergencies. And though she never thought of it before, it happened just that way.

Raisa bent down to Scott and wrapped her arms around him, lifting him up from behind, under his arms to a standing position.

She felt his energy prickle her skin. Devon put his arm around Julia's waist and held her toward Raisa and Scott. Then he reached for Raisa, locking hands to enclose them between the two of them. A static SNAP cracked in the air above them, and Devon and Raisa watched as the energy from Scott and Julia doubled in size and melded together, buzzing loudly, creating wholly unique patterns as it merged. They stood like this for only seconds till both Julia and Scott seemed to regain control. The light show slowly subsided.

"What just happened?" Pen sounded more puzzled than worried, but he, Corli and Morgan were wide eyed and gaping. "Looked like you made an electrical storm sandwich." He rubbed his arm and realized it felt all tingly. He turned to Corli and Morgan. "Do you guys feel that?" Corli started shaking like she had a sudden shiver and Morgan slowly stamped her feet to work the stinging out.

"Are you guys okay?" Raisa sounded out of breath as she and Devon dropped their hands and moved to the side.

Julia and Scott now held each other in a loose embrace. Scott saw a pained look in Julia's eyes and lifted his hand to her cheek. He leaned in to kiss her lightly. "You heard them this time," he whispered softly to her, his lips thin with concern for her. Julia only nodded.

Raisa watched their exchange and was taken with the thought that for the first time, Julia looked, vulnerable.

Devon reached across and gently placed a hand on Scott's shoulder. "What did they say?"

"They were taunting... and laughing, cruelly. It was so loud I thought my head would explode." Scott's brow creased at the memory. "They said we were trapped, and that everyone would die. But... I don't think they meant just us. I mean, not just all of us here...." he trailed off and looked toward the mountain peak.

Devon nodded and stepped back. He turned a little to place his hand on Julia's back. Before he could ask, she started shaking her head quickly, imploring with her eyes that she didn't want to have to explain. "I know it's difficult, Julia, but it's important." Her head dropped forward. Devon looked to Scott. He knew that if the connection between the two of them was anything like the connection that he and Raisa shared, that his comfort, and even more, his proximity to her, would help calm and reassure her.

Scott seemed to know exactly what Devon was asking for and took Julia up in his arms, holding her tightly to his chest, securing her in his energy.

Julia held her cheek to his shoulder and took a deep breath in. Then she exhaled and felt Scott's energy thrum through her body. She relaxed. She kept her eyes closed and her face pressed into her partner as she spoke. "They were laughing at me too. But they didn't say anything... they showed me...." A tear leaked through her closed lids. "A horrible vision." Her voice dropped to a whisper. "I saw Morgan and Corli....... die....... a horrible death."

Devon's eyes flew to Pen, who instantly wrapped his arms around Corli.

"I won't let *anything* happen to you." Pen reached out and grabbed Morgan's hand, "any of you."

Devon looked at Raisa then, her face was grayish white. "We don't know that this vision is certain... you know that, right? They are blind. They can't tell where we are unless a bruel sees us. It's only a scare tactic." He put his hand on the back of Raisa's neck. She nodded. "We need to get moving... we should be only thirty minutes or so from the camp ground."

Devon drove now so that Pen could be close to Corli.

"I'm alright, really." Corli was trying to convince Pen.

As they neared the road and the trees thinned, Devon suddenly hit the brakes. Everyone peered through the trees toward the road. "They're close." Devon said this for general purposes. Everyone felt the proximity of the bruels. Two cars raced by, going the direction they were headed.

"This could get pretty dicey, Devon." Pen cautioned. "If we go that direction, we will undoubtedly have bruels in front of us, blocking us from the camp, *and* behind us... we'll be surrounded."

"We've chased trouble before. And I won't leave whatever folks are at the camp to fend for themselves. For all we know they aren't expecting the bruels, and we don't know what kind of defenses they have. The sooner we go, the fewer there will be between us and the camp," he mused. "Is everyone in?" Devon turned to get everyone's reaction.

"We're in." Morgan placed her hand on the hilt of the knife in its sheath at her belt, a determined smile swiped across her face.

"Yes, let's." Julia shared the smile with Morgan.

Devon received nods from Pen and Corli. His eyes rested on Raisa where she sat in the passenger seat. "Are you ready for this?" He grabbed her hand and felt a spiky warm rush flow through him.

"I guess so," she answered nervously.

One corner of Devon's mouth turned up. He could feel her adrenaline.

Raisa pulled her three-fifty-seven from her bag. "Let's go."

Devon punched the gas and they broke onto the road. The inside of the van was busy with preparations while he drove.

Raisa took over the map. "It's only been fifteen minutes but the next road to the right should be our turn-off."

"I don't think I was supposed to go seventy miles per hour. The camp entrance is only a mile after the turn, right?"

"Yeah." Raisa's breathless reply gave away her nerves. She knew she would be better once they got there. It was the anticipation that always got the best of her.

Devon reached over, grabbed her hand and made her lean almost off her seat so that he could bring it to his mouth and kiss it. "Love you," he said in a low voice.

"I love you," Raisa breathed back. She had to resist the desire to stay locked in his gaze and looked unwillingly back to the road. "Here it is!" She pointed to a poorly paved road on their right. A slightly obscured street sign was on the far corner. "Assembly Way."

Devon kept the van at a low speed after the turn. Unfortunately it was not a straight road and every turn in it mounted their anxiety. After climbing the mountain face on four switchbacks with no consequence they all wondered if they might have been imagining the danger. "Maybe they didn't know where they were going," Devon wondered aloud as he began the next blind turn.

But as they rounded the corner they learned that this was not the case.

17

Devon guessed that these were the two cars that sped past them when they were hidden in the trees off the highway. The cars were pulled across the road making it impossible to pass. The doors to each vehicle hung open but its occupants were nowhere in sight. Where the road straightened out beyond the cars, a brown painted sign on a post marked the entrance to the camp.

"Everyone get low," Devon ordered as he threw the van into park and slid off his seat to squat on the floor of the van. He pulled Raisa down with him. A shot came from somewhere off the side of the road and struck the outside panel of the van somewhere around the second row of seats. It pinged loudly as it tore through some of the metal but then ricocheted away.

"They're crappy shots," Pen remarked as he pulled his gun and released the safety mechanism while sitting in his crouched position. "What's the plan, Dev?"

Devon mused for half a second. "I'll leave the van from the passenger side, since it's up against the mountain, and draw their fire. Then you guys will be able to pinpoint their location and take them out from the cover of the-"

"The hell you will," Pen interrupted.

"I agree," Morgan added, shaking her head.

Pen and Morgan locked eyes and nodded at each other. Pen looked back at Devon. "No offense but that kind-of defeats the purpose here. Morgan and I will draw the fire. Then Corli, you and Raisa can get your target practice."

241

Devon nodded painfully. "Okay. Then, your goal will be to get to the other side of their vehicles. I'll take a place at the front of the van, Corli, you take the back. Raisa…" Devon didn't want her involved at all but he knew she was a good shot. "You stay in the van and use the window. Stay low and wait a minute before you look for them. They'll think we have all left the van and it might give you an advantage."

"What about us?" Scott spoke for himself and Julia.

"*Only* if it seems safe *and* necessary, sneak from the back of the van across the road to get them from behind after their attention has been drawn away."

"Got it." Scott and Julia squeezed each other's hands.

"Okay…" Devon slid the door of the van open, "go!"

Hearts pounding, everyone sprang into action. Shots were fired from three places across the road at Pen and Morgan as they ran. Devon and Corli returned fire in the bruels general direction, they were hidden well. But, Pen was right; they were not accomplished marksmen to say the least. Devon's plan seemed to be working.

Until Morgan reached the other side of one of the abandoned cars. Her focus was on the trees across the road as she bent down for cover behind one of the open car doors. The next second, someone had a fist full of her hair, some of it ripping painfully from her scalp, and was drawing a knife near her throat. He had been hiding on the floor of the back seat.

As the bruel raised Morgan up in front of him, Pen saw another man stand from his hiding place in the foliage, aiming for Morgan. He instantly dashed from behind the car and past Morgan to distract the shooter. In the instant he passed her, he thought he heard, "Oh, no you didn't". He was trying to decide if she was referring to the man that held her, the man that was taking aim at her, or *him*, when he heard the crack of a bullet entering the space between the shooter and himself.

At almost the same moment, both Corli and Devon fired at the standing bruel. Both of their shots found their mark and he fell at almost the same time as Pen.

Morgan made quick work of her captor. The distraction that Pen caused gave her the one second she needed to twist neatly out of his grasp and pull her own blade from her belt. Her movement didn't stop till she stood over his dead and bleeding body. She ran to Pen and looked to the trees as she prepared to pull him to safety.

Scott and Julia had exited the van at the very beginning and were able to cross the road undetected.

Corli was wracked with the urgent desire to run to Pen. When she saw Scott and Julia emerge, guiding a disabled bruel in front of them she disregarded the fact that there may still be someone that might shoot at her, and ran to him and Morgan. Devon kept his aim on Scott and Julia's new prisoner.

Raisa watched most of this happen from the driver's side window of the van. She knew that one bruel was unaccounted for. Now that her friends were in the open, she pulled herself up to sit in the window frame, and scanned the trees. "Where is he?" she said to herself as the site of her weapon moved along the edge of the forest. She saw some movement in the bushes at the bottom of the turn in the road. "Running away are we?" she murmured as she twisted in the window to take a good aim. Thinking that he was far enough away to escape unscathed, the bruel leapt from his cover to run down the road. At step number two, Raisa's shot rang out, and the coward fell to the ground.

"I'm fine," Pen argued as he stood against his audience's wishes. "It just grazed me." Corli had already torn a sleeve off

243

of her own shirt and started wrapping it around his bleeding arm. "We need to get off of this road... Devon, help me out."

"You're right. Morgan, can you move one of these cars?"

"And what do we do with this one?" Scott waved a hand at the bruel they had restrained and sat on the ground against the van. He was blubbering like a baby.

"Do you think we should make sure the one down there is dead?" Raisa asked as she pointed down the hill.

Morgan was moving the car that had the keys left in it. Everyone else's eyes followed Raisa's pointed finger and froze.

Suddenly they realized that the forest was not as quiet as before. There were vehicles, lots of them, driving up the road. Some of them could already be seen through the trees.

"Morgan!" Devon shouted, "Stay in that car! Pen, Corli, go!" He turned and pistol-whipped the crying bruel, knocking him out cold. The sound of cars approaching was more pronounced now.

Pen and Corli jumped in the back seat of the car. Morgan was moving toward the camp entrance before the doors were shut. Pen twisted in the seat to look back. He watched as Devon, Raisa, Scott, and Julia hurried into the van. "C'mon! Get moving!" he urged, willing the van to move. He watched as the first car rounded the corner behind the van. "Something's not right! Morgan, turn around!"

Raisa was in the driver's seat. She turned the key in the ignition. It made one click and then nothing. "It's dead! It won't start!"

A dark and low laugh echoed off the walls of the penthouse. Nosh stood staring into the flames of the fireplace. Each of the twelve women behind and across the room from him displayed tall continuous yellow-green flames above them, the sick green smoke now erupting from each in plumes and sparks. A tangible energy rumbled through the air of the space, the following event would determine everything.

And Nosh was torn.

He had opened his mind and soul to evil long ago, leaving nothing on the inside of him private. Each thought, each intention, each emotion laid itself bare to be scrutinized, twisted and used by malevolence even greater than he himself would ever achieve. Fear. Fear was the greatest tool of evil, he knew, and he had endeavored for many years not to show that most powerful emotion so that it could not be used against him. It was a task he had mastered. The dilemma he faced now felt like it would rip him in two. He dared not allow the full thought enter his mind. But it played on the edges, threatening to undo him, to show his weakness to evil.

Nosh listened to the rantings of the men through the half dead voices of the sickly women. He could hear their bloodlust as they rushed the mountain, eager to be gathered together in a strong force, ready to fight, ready to kill.

During his momentary distraction the thought leaked in. It came as a blistering stab in his head. *Devon... let Devon be unharmed....* Nosh's hands flew to his skull to squeeze the thought out.

The four in the van gaped through the windows at the six vehicles that came around the corner, the first of which was less than fifty yards away. There was no telling how many more would come from behind the turn. A snap of static ripped through the van as they all tensed.

"I've seen this movie and it doesn't end well if we stay in this van," Scott said. His knuckles were white as he clutched a hand full of vinyl seat. "Let's get out of here!"

245

"You're right, let's go." Devon threw the sliding door open again. He and Julia jumped out. But Raisa and Scott left through the driver's door. By the time he and Julia made it around the van to run across the road, Raisa and Scott had already jumped into the foliage. Devon and Julia's faces flew to look at each other and in that second they shared a common anxiety. The first car arrived, and they were separated from their partners. Regardless of the panic they both felt, they had to move. They darted across the road, neither of them daring to look back at who would follow them. As their feet hit dirt they heard the first angry snarls. Devon grabbed Julia's arm intending to run down the uneven hillside. After only five steps, they heard their pursuers enter the forest behind them.

Morgan slammed on the breaks and pulled the car into a spin to reverse their direction. Halfway through the spin she gasped and then pulled the car to a stop after the perfect one hundred and eighty degree turn. They were suddenly surrounded by people, people with weapons. But they weren't stopping, they were running.

"They've come to help!" Corli cried out. "Go, go, GO!"

"There must be at least thirty!" Pen exclaimed.

"That ought to even this up a bit," Morgan said as she stepped on the gas and headed back down the road.

"There!" Pen pointed as he saw Devon pull Julia over the embankment in the distance. "Sh-t!" Pen felt helpless and irritated as he watched three bruels follow only steps behind them. His hand moved to the car door, preparing to jump out. "We should never have left them." His voice was hard, especially for Pen.

The cars stacked up on the road behind the first that had stopped. Only two or three could fit across, so the men jumped from their cars and directly into the brush at car length intervals along the road.

"At least they aren't too bright," Edward commented in a rushed and low tone as they ran.

David followed his gaze and looked at the men spilling into the forest. "They're all spread out."

"Yep." Edward grinned.

Morgan slid the car expertly to a stop behind the group on foot at an angle perfect for Pen to tumble out without losing any momentum.

Edward and David led an assault on the first men they encountered, defeating them and then moving on down the hill to the next stumbling group of wicked men. Morgan and Corli kept to the rim of Edward's group. They seemed to fall into a comfortable fighting pair, anticipating each other's movements and protecting each other's backs. Together they picked off any bruel that ducked the main attack.

Pen almost fell as he hit the ground running. The car was moving faster than his legs could compensate for. But he willed his lanky frame to stay upright as he charged into the brush where he saw his best friend go. The dimming sound of fighting behind him turned his thoughts to what was happening on the road and his hand flew to his chest. For a split second he felt panic for leaving Corli behind. But he quickly reassured himself that she was surrounded with allies and quite frankly, could take care of herself.

He slowed to a walk and began surveying his surroundings, listening intently, hoping for a sign that would lead him to Devon. He concentrated on slow even breaths as he peered through the trees. Far off and up near the road, he saw a couple of bruels taken down by some of Edwards group but he knew that Devon would not have traveled that way. He turned and strained his eyes to see into the shadows of the forest below him. "C'mon Dev, help me out," he mumbled. His level breathing suddenly cut off as he saw a running bruel in the distance disappear behind a tree. Pen took off at an angle down the hill to see if he could cut the expanse. The rough terrain made it necessary for him to watch his footing but he continued to look up for any clue as to where Devon was. Then he saw. There were three men running in a line. Just two feet in front of them, Devon was pulling Julia behind him. Pen took off at a full sprint, no longer looking anywhere but at his friend and praying that his feet would find solid ground as he let the downward slope propel him forward. He watched with horror as the first bruel dove for Julia. In the next instant, a burning band of electric copper, white light and prisms seemed to separate the air above them and arc across the sky. He pulled his gun from his belt.

Raisa knew that Scott was running behind her. She assumed that Devon and Julia were not far behind that, but she didn't dare take the time to look back. They scrambled downward but Raisa decided to start turning to the right, away from their assailants, so that they would eventually climb again and hopefully return to the road at the entrance of the campground where she thought Morgan, Pen and Corli would be. She heard a commotion in the distance but couldn't bring herself to slow their pace. She watched only the ground in front of her and could not guess how long they had been moving when Scott's voice broke her concentration.

"Raisa, wait," he blurted out as he reached for her arm to stop her. "They're not behind us. We have to go back!"

Raisa's foot caught in a tree root. She would have hurtled forward if Scott had not already securely taken a hold of her. He

248

threw his other arm around her to keep her from falling to the ground. As Scott drew her back up to a standing position, Raisa was suddenly and acutely aware of being held tightly in his arms. His chest was a smooth plain and the muscles in his arms were strong and sinewy against his thin frame. She couldn't help the automatic comparison that popped into her brain. Simultaneously, the bottom dropped out of her stomach. "Devon!"

They stood and dropped their arms to their sides, looking back the way they had come. What would have been an awkward moment in another circumstance, swiftly morphed to dread as they realized a large distance separated them from their partners.

"No, no, NO!" Scott yelled as he dropped to his knees.

Raisa's first thought was that Scott had been hurt, but there was no one around them to inflict any harm. His hands clawed into the dirt as if he were in agony. At the same time she saw his energy rise up over his bowed head, as if it were reaching out to something but could not break free because of its attachment to the ground. It took only a second to realize what was happening. And just as it had been natural for her and Devon to help Scott and Julia before, she knew what she needed to do and quickly pulled Scott up from his tormented crouch on the ground.

If the origination of lightening had a sound it would be like this. The instant that Scott had his bearings and Raisa was in his circle of energy, holding his arms, a fire and white light shot out and instantly bent back to the earth. Blazing and buzzing, beautiful and terrible, Raisa knew that what they created together was connecting them to Devon and Julia. "C'mon! Let's go!" Raisa spoke over the noise of the energy as she slid an arm around Scott and started to follow their arc. As they ran, as quickly as they could while still staying together, Raisa felt power leaving Scott, like a battery losing its potency. Scott began to stumble. "We're almost there! Look!" she pointed just a few yards away where the light stopped, but she couldn't see Devon. *Where are they!*

Suddenly, Pen came into Raisa's view, running like a gazelle from above them. He came to a stop at the end of the arc seconds before she and Scott did, holding his weapon up and moving in a circle to see if he could find *someone* to take a shot at.

As she and Scott came to the scene at the ground, Scott stumbled forward till he was kneeling at Julia's feet while Raisa stopped and took in the horrible sight. Julia lay on her side, the handle of a large knife protruding straight up from her body just where her elbow would normally lie. Her white light was barely visible, and fading. Devon held her head up with one hand to keep it from lying in the dirt and was trying to determine what he could do with the other hand to help her.

The arc was gone but Raisa could still feel a tangible connection to Devon. And in that connection she could feel that Devon was in pain. Not physical, she could tell, but emotional. *He feels responsible…* Devon's eyes met hers and the anguish in them told her that she was right.

"Julia… baby… no… hang on," Scott pleaded through his tears.

Raisa pulled her eyes away from Devon to look for help. She was relieved to see a group of people working their way quickly down the hill, followed by a hovering mist and headed in their direction. Corli and Morgan were with them and as they came closer she recognized Edward Brayden. Two of the group instantly knelt at Julia's sides, laying their hands on her and bowing their heads. One quickly looked up to Edward, "I don't know…" was all he said. Several more were there and Julia was lifted from the ground so carefully that her position did not change. Scott held her feet while Julia came up the hillside, as if she were floating.

The air was clear again and the breeze began to drift around them. Raisa thought she could hear a low and soft singing above the trees as they made their way to the camp -

There is a balm in Gilead to make the wounded whole....

18

Most of the group that entered the camp ground had dispersed, hurrying off to prepare for the clean-up of the battle, grabbing supplies to join those that were pursuing the bad men that had gotten away, and those that were caring for the wounded. A small group hesitated at the entrance to the main hall. Devon reached for Raisa's hand as they watched Julia being carried into a small cabin not far from them, Scott and Morgan directly behind her. His forehead was creased and his voice broke. "Tell me that she will be okay, Raisa."

It was Pen who answered as he laid his hand on Devon's shoulder. "I'm certain of it," he said.

"It may not seem like it, but we have some of the best care available here." It was David who was leading them to the hall. He turned and extended his hand to Devon. "I'm David. I'll show you guys around a little and show you where you can clean up. You'll need to rest a little. It's doubtful that you'll get much of it after tonight... rest, that is." He led Devon, Raisa, Pen and Corli through the door. "This is our mess hall and meeting room. We'll come back here for lunch. Edward will want to meet with you after that. I'm sure you have a lot of questions."

"*There's* an understatement," Corli said only half under her breath.

David smiled at Corli who blushed in return for her snarkiness. "Renee," David looked to the girl that had been walking with them, "will you show... is it Corlis and Penley?" David looked back at Corli, still smiling.

"Corli. And Pen." Corli stammered a little.

"Will you show Corli and Pen where to go while I take our Lasteires to their room?"

"Sure. Come on guys." Renee gestured to Pen and Corli and they followed. "I'll show you where the rallys hang."

"Rallys?" Pen questioned with a tilt of his head as they walked. "We have a name? Like a species? Or is it more like the rally monkey? And what's a Lasteire?" Corli gave him a stern look and an elbow in the side as they followed Renee through a door at the back of the hall.

David closed the door softly, leaving Devon and Raisa in a modest room that was only a few steps down a hall from the main room. The air was cool and smelled of earth and forest pine. A small window across from the door with white eyelet curtains let in light that filtered through the large boughs of pine trees just outside. The walls were bare timber and the floor cement. A full size bed with fresh linens took up most of the room and a door to a tiny bathroom was open.

Raisa turned and looked at Devon. Butterflies fluttered in her stomach and she shivered. She knew why she felt the butterflies… that happened all the time when she looked at him. But she was trying to decide if the shiver was because of the temperature of the room or the look on Devon's face. *Concern? No… more than that. Guilt*, she thought. He seemed glued to the spot where he stood and undecided as to whether he should turn around and walk out, or just sit down. She slowly turned and reached with the intention of delivering a supportive hug. But before she could complete the movement she was scooped up in his arms, leaving her toes dangling over the floor.

Devon pulled Raisa as tight as he could to him. He squeezed his eyes shut and his breath came out heavy as if he had just been holding it. Without letting go, or looking at Raisa he started talking with an intense whisper into Raisa's hair. "It was my fault, Raisa. I should have protected her. I should have had her in front of me instead of behind me. I should have turned and killed those bastards before they had a chance to hurt her. What if she…" Devon held his breath.

Raisa pried herself back a few inches and found the ground with her feet. Her hands came to Devon's face and forced him to look at her. "No. She won't die." Her voice was low but even and clear. "Just like I was protected when I should have died, she will be too. As much as we would like to think that we can do all of this on our own, that we are in control, we are almost powerless ourselves. Don't you see? Any of us could have gotten in a car accident or something and died at any moment in the last twenty years. But we didn't. We have a purpose, and we are being spared for it. And our fates are the same as Julia's, and Scott's. She's going to live, Devon."

Devon's eyes were willingly staring at Raisa's now and what felt like hysterics before was replaced with calm. "How do you do that?" he whispered with clear admiration in his voice.

Raisa smiled and took a moment to find a copper fleck in his eyes. "Faith."

Devon held on to Raisa but wandered off in thought for a moment about this word. "You know, that was never a real concept to me before… you. I remember listening to how you think, when you were in the hospital. It was like a glow stick snapped in my mind… and my heart too, I guess. Something that had always sounded absurd to me, the whole religion thing, turned into something that made perfect sense when I saw it from your point of view. And then when we met Calvin… I guess I feel like there is a chance. Like we can really affect a change of

254

some kind in this stupid, mixed-up world." He paused with a quizzical look to the side. "Is that faith? Do... I have it too?"

Raisa's body felt warm and light. She took note of the swirling copper lights around them and noticed a prism effect she had never seen before. "Yes, I think you do." She smiled and reached for Devon's face again. This time she was determined to finish what she intended to do.

They kissed for several minutes. Never moving from the spot where they stood. Never feeling the need to do any more or any less, until Raisa grunted.

"What? What's wrong?"

"We're sticky!" Raisa had suddenly become aware that they were both covered in drying cold sweat and dirt. "Gross." She peeled herself quite literally away from Devon. "Showers. You first," she ordered.

"Okay, bossy." Devon moved quickly around the bed to avert the flying hand he knew was coming. And he was just quick enough.

As Raisa heard the shower spring to life a soft knock came at the door. She opened it to find a young man that she thought she recognized from their walk into the grounds. He held three bags in his arms and a soft mist hovered above his head. "Here are your bags from the van, Miss. We've pulled it onto the grounds. Here are the keys." He held the contents of his arms out to her but seemed too shy to make eye contact.

"Thank you so much." Raisa took the keys, their bags and the backpack of cash. *Of course these people must be honest to a fault and they would never dream of keeping the money for themselves... they probably didn't even look in it. But, they must have to figure out who the bags belonged to...* she nodded to herself with appreciation for their new friends.

"Lunch is at eleven-forty-five, Miss." He glanced up for a split second, then turned and left.

Raisa closed the door and turned to see that the bathroom door was still open. "I have our clothes. And lunch is at eleven-forty-five," she called to Devon above the sound of the water as she unloaded their bags to the bed.

"What time is it now?"

Raisa could here that Devon was talking through the water in his face. Her skin warmed and her butterflies took a frantic flight as a picture filled her mind; Devon's copper colored skin and toned muscles sheeted with warm soapy water. She shook the etch-a-sketch again and walked to the bathroom door, trying to make herself sound as nonchalant as possible, "I'm not sure, do you have a watch?" She rounded the corner and saw the curtain of the shower with the outline of Devon's body behind it. Her eyes darted to the floor to keep the blush from burning darker.

"Don't you have your phone?"

Devon was washing his hair now and Raisa was trying to concentrate on what it was that he had just asked her. She looked at his empty jeans and t-shirt on the floor. *That doesn't help.* Her eyes went to the little sink and the shelf just above it. She saw the contents of his pockets including a round gold piece with a chain. It looked too big to be a watch but she reached for it. "What's this?" Raisa took it in her hand and sat on the toilet seat next to the shower.

Devon poked his head through the curtain.

Raisa studied the object she held. She was so intrigued that she completely forgot her thoughts from a moment ago.

"Oh, I've wanted to tell you about that. There just hasn't seemed to be a good time. I guess now is good though." Devon let the curtain fall closed again and started rinsing his hair. "It's a compass." Devon paused. He wasn't sure how to go about

256

telling Raisa where it came from. After a short internal deliberation, he thought it best to keep it simple. "From my dad."

Raisa sat without speaking and listened to Devon recount the visit that Gloria had made to her house before they left. She popped it open when Devon told her about the inscription and read it to herself, *"So that my Love and my Son will never lose their way and always return to me."* A shiver ran down the length of her spine. She tried to discern Devon's feelings about this object but decided that he was putting considerable effort into sounding detached. She barely noticed when the water turned off and the shower curtain pulled back.

Raisa held the compass up and looked at Devon, intending to ask him to show her how it worked. But instead an entirely different thing happened. First her eyes grew wide as she took in the sight that she had imagined only minutes ago. Then with no hesitation, which surprised her, her eyes relaxed and her body melted as she surveyed every inch of his wet, tanned and muscular body. "Oh my," escaped her lips without her cognition.

"Rai... I'm shocked," Devon chuckled as he reached for a towel and wrapped it casually around his hips. "I feel almost violated," he teased as he stepped out of the shower. He bent down and held a finger under her chin, lightly closing her mouth and kissed her softly. "Your turn," he said as he smiled and left the tiny room.

Raisa was watching Devon's face as they entered the mess hall for lunch. She saw it cloud over when Devon saw Morgan at the table with Pen and Corli. Morgan's eyes were swollen and red and her posture was bent with grief. They sat down with their friends and ate the modest lunch with no conversation; Devon's

257

eyes never left his plate. He was listening to a recording in his head, playing over and over about what he should have done to protect Julia. But he also couldn't help but listen to everything being said at the tables around them, his brain automatically filing away information for future consideration. When they finished and the tables cleared, Raisa broke the silence with the question she knew had to be asked. "So, how is Julia?"

Morgan sniffed and took a deep breath. "They removed the blade with surgery. She's lost a lot of blood and is still unconscious. Her vitals are not great but they say that they have repaired all of the damage that they could see. They are worried that they might have missed something or that she has slipped into a comma. They are monitoring her and said that they should know within twenty-four hours if she is going to pull through."

"And Scott?"

"A wreck of course. He is so tied to her that I don't think he would live if she died." Morgan turned and looked out the window toward the cabin where Julia and Scott were as if she was waiting for someone to call her name. "It's strange," she said absently as she kept her gaze on the cabin. "It almost feels like she's not there."

Raisa instantly thought back to when she was in the hospital for her stab wound. *I wasn't there either… I was visiting with my dad.* She considered the conversation that she had with her father. *I wonder if the same thing is happening to her. Daddy? Are you there?* She heard nothing in return. *I miss you.* Being lost in her thoughts she barely noticed when Pen, Corli and Morgan where called away. It wasn't until Devon took hold of her hips and turned her toward him on the bench that she was aware of her surroundings again.

"Raisa, I need to ask you something." The expression on Devon's face looked more tortured than ever, to the point that Raisa was startled when she saw it.

"Devon, I thought we talked about this. I know that Julia is going to be okay. As a matter of fact, I think I know why-"

"No, it's not that," Devon interrupted. "Well, not exactly anyway." He was straddled across the bench and he reached down and pulled Raisa up closer to him so he could speak quietly. "I know you saw the light that went between us before, when we were on the side of the mountain, right?" Raisa nodded. "Well… it was… interesting that it wasn't just between you and I. It was connected to all four of us." Devon took a couple of labored breaths before he continued. "I was wondering… I mean… do you…" his voice lowered to a rough whisper. "How do you feel about Scott?"

Raisa was so caught off guard by the question that she couldn't think of anything to say. She was trying to follow his line of thinking when he continued in an unbroken string of what had been on his mind.

"I mean, I would understand if you chose him over me. You guys have so much more in common and now we know that this energy thing isn't just you and me and you obviously have a connection with him because I saw it the first time we met them and if Julia doesn't make it I know you would be there for him and-"

"Stop." Raisa held her hand up to his lips. She was going to tell him how idiotic the whole idea was when David approached them.

"Devon, Raisa," he nodded a greeting. "Edward would like to see you now."

259

Edward stood from his makeshift desk, straightened his shirt and watched David lead Devon and Raisa across the room toward him. He saw the stress on their faces and took a deep breath in and out as he wondered how much they knew and what questions they would ask. His heart ached every time he went through this process with the Lasteires, for the terrible and amazing burden that these young people carried, and for what lay ahead of them.

This is our leader… and the woman that will be beside him. A smile started to spread across his face but then faded a little. *This is it, Ed. This is the last piece.* He looked up for a moment as if asking for reinforcements. *Please, guide my words for these young people and give them strength and peace.*

"Welcome, Devon, Raisa." He shook each of their hands slowly and warmly. "Please, have a seat." David and Edward nodded to each other and David left them, clearing the rest of the hall of stragglers as he went.

"You brought quite an entourage with you this morning." Edward realized as soon as this escaped his lips that the effort which he intended, to make light, had the opposite effect. His eyes shot up again. *A little* more *help…*

"You look nervous," Raisa thought out loud as she looked at Edward and the jittering, misty pink crown above his head.

"You're very intuitive," Edward said wryly. His nerves calmed instantly. He turned and rolled up to his computer and began typing. "That will be a great asset to Devon."

Devon seemed to snap out of his thoughts and spoke for the first time, "Asset for what?"

"Well, we've gotten a little ahead of ourselves haven't we… let's start again." Edward rolled back from the computer and close to Devon and Raisa. "How about you two tell me what you know and we'll go from there."

Devon took a deep, frustrated breath. *That's why we're here, isn't it? For you to explain this madness to us!* He closed his eyes for a moment and gathered his civility before he spoke. He looked Edward squarely in the eye. "We're different," he said. "We've seen things all of our lives that have led us to believe it. But recently, the shi-..." He took another breath. "There has been a lot more, and it has led us here, to you, because of some great purpose. We've gathered that evil has been plotted against good, in an enormous way. And... *whether I am worthy of that... or not,* we are in the middle of it."

Raisa watched Devon as he spoke and saw him transform before her eyes. The tortured mantle melted from his face, his posture straightened and his eyes gleamed. The challenge, it seemed, pulled him out of his reverie. His energy was full and steady, and in answer, her own energy thrummed inside of her. The space where their energy met had a steady soft glow.

Edward leaned back in his chair. "Your connection is beautiful... so strong." He watched the dancing rings, plumes and arc for a moment. "But, let's continue." He leaned forward with his elbows on his knees. "So, you watched the shows?"

"Yes," Raisa replied. "Very clever... but cryptic. We didn't start to pick up on the clues till a few days ago. And I still don't think we really got much, other than the fact that we needed to find you."

"Well, yes." Edward scratched his head. "It was difficult to do without making the network suspicious. Did you decipher the quotes?"

"We had them all written down," Devon replied, "but we couldn't find any significance other than what each phrase said on its own... which sounded pretty epic all by itself."

"That will be where we start then. Here," Edward grabbed a sheet of paper with the quotes written on it and handed it to Devon and Raisa. "Read the first word of every quote."

Devon read aloud, "It – Is – You – The – Last – Heir – That – Must – Save – Mankind – From – Destruction."

Devon and Raisa sat, speechless. The enormity of what Devon had read left them unable to consider what their next question would possibly be.

Edward recognized the expression well. It had been the same for so many of the other couples. He began the explanation of the details. "There are twenty-four couples in total, like you, twelve for the north and twelve for the south. You have been aptly named Lasteires because the forty-eight of you will inherit the earth." He paused to evaluate the level of shock on Devon and Raisa's faces and continued. "I have been honored to be chosen to help guide the twelve northern Lasteire couples to your destination at the northern magnetic pole and have you ready at the appropriate time."

Devon found his voice. "What, exactly, is going to happen?" Devon spoke evenly but the paper he still held in his hand began to wrinkle. "And why have the bruels been trying so desperately to stop us? And who is their leader, Nosh?" Devon let the paper fall to the floor and pulled Raisa's hand from the grip it had on the edge of her folding chair.

"Bruels?" Edward's eyebrow curled into a question mark.

Raisa answered, "Brute – cruel, bruel. Nickname. Easier," her impatience evident in her voice.

"Ah, I see. Well, the dark side," Edward's fingers quoted the air, "is led by Nosh Megedagik. His name means "Father" "kills many" in Algonquin. I guess you could consider him my counterpart. We have learned from Jude that he uses women that he has tortured into submission as some kind of vessel that

262

communicates his will to the... bruels, as you call them." Edward paused, remorse coloring his face. "They call it "The Scouring". We have not given it a specific name. We only know that it is an event that will change the face of the earth. It will be facilitated by the energy that you have, connected together. Any existing evil will be eliminated so that the world can start again. It is the evil that is killing the world. Nosh's survival depends on our failure."

"With a name like "The Scouring" it sounds a little more drastic than just eradicating evil," Devon probed.

Edward bowed his head. This was the worst part. It never got easier to deliver. He lifted his eyes and squared his shoulders. "From what I've been shown, it is my belief, that the forty-eight Lasteires will quite literally repopulate the earth. I don't know exactly who or what will survive besides you."

"No..." Devon's voice was choked and came in a desperate whisper. "There has to be another way."

Beside him, Raisa sat silently, with tears beginning to stream down her face.

"This is the only way, Devon. And it is your destiny to guide them. You are their leader," Edward said firmly.

Edward knew that he needed to end this meeting now. He could not let any more questions arise that would create more dialogue. This was the fact that they all faced and nothing was going to change it. Now they needed time to process the information and solidify their resolve.

"Now," Edward's tone became businesslike. "We should leave for the camp at Thule tomorrow, but that will depend on whether or not we can move Julia. I have faith that we will." He stood and held his hands out toward Devon and Raisa. "Be with each other now. Talk, mourn, love, and build your resolve in your purpose together. We are in the home stretch. David will be available if you have any other questions."

As if on cue, David reentered the hall as Edward nodded and left. He approached the astonished couple still in their seats. "Hi guys," he spoke softly. "Why don't we get you back to your room to rest?"

Devon and Raisa rose to their feet as if the suggestion made it happen. Raisa felt numb. She could swear that she was outside of her body watching it move, not feeling the progress herself. She leaned into Devon and felt an intense heat radiating from him.

Devon felt the blood in his veins race from his feet to his hands as he balled them into fists, and rise up his neck and face. *This isn't right. What kind of God would obliterate billons of people like that? And why would I have any part of it? It's horrific, it's heinous, it's....* Devon did not believe that there was a word that existed that could explain how wrong it was for so many to die.

"Wait," Raisa gasped and grabbed David's arm as if she had just woken from a nightmare. "If Edward Brayden is the leader of the northern Lasteires, then who is the leader of the southern Lasteires? Can we talk to him... or her...? ...whatever, but maybe this isn't exactly right... maybe...." Raisa knew she had heard the truth and was grasping for anything other than what her heart was telling her, but she couldn't help it.

David turned. He still spoke softly, almost soothingly, "They have no one but themselves. There was not a need for someone to guide them."

"No need? How could that be possible? How do they know what to do?" Raisa wasn't even trying to keep her voice from sounding hysterical.

"They have an enormous amount of faith. They were told in various manners what they were to do, and why, and they just, *went*. Amazing people, those in the southern hemisphere... nothing could deter them. They have been at their destination and waiting for us, and the selected time, for several days now." David turned and resumed his walk across the hall.

After they followed a few uneasy steps, Devon spoke angrily at the back of David's head. "Where is the bruel you have in custody? I know one is here. I heard someone talking about it at lunch. I want to speak to him."

"That's probably not a good idea right now. I think you should do as Edward suggested and spend some time alone together. Here we are." David opened the door to their little room.

Both Devon and Raisa felt like they were being sent to their room by a parent. They passed David with obvious resentment and he closed the door behind them. Devon half expected to hear a lock turn, but all they were left with was stillness, and their despair.

They sat on the edge of the bed for several minutes. As their emotions subsided some, Devon spoke first. "My mother," he whispered. "And your sisters." Raisa leaned her head onto Devon's shoulder, wrapping her hands around his arm. "And Calvin...." Devon's voice trailed off.

Raisa sat up and looked at Devon. "What about Pen and Corli? I'm sure they'll make it, right? I mean, they were called to help us... certainly that means they are supposed to survive this, right?"

Neither Devon nor Raisa dared to guess the answer to the question out loud.

19

"So the term 'all in' had a little more behind it than we thought, didn't it Babe," Pen said, sounding resigned. He and Corli sat alone on a blanket of pine needles under a giant sugar pine tree. The warmth of the afternoon brought the fragrance of the forest to them on a soft breeze. Pen touched Corli's wet cheek with his thumb and cupped her face. "It's hard to believe there is so much doom and gloom going on while it is so peaceful here, right now. Too bad we can't just stay together right in this spot. I would love that. Wouldn't you?"

Corli only nodded. She had a lump in her throat that no sound could get past. She nuzzled her face into Pen's chest and watched the drops from her eyes make little wet marks on his t-shirt.

"Tomorrow, we'll be off again, to some frozen wasteland. But today we're here. I... love you, Corli. Thank you for giving that to me."

Corli closed her eyes and tried to memorize everything about this moment. The sweet pine mixed with Pen's smell of the ocean and lemon scented soap, the rise and fall of his chest as he breathed and the sound of his voice from the inside where her ear pressed against him. The first boy she really loved telling her that he loved her. She wished as he did, for the world to go away. She was agonizing over the thought that she should get up and go find Raisa. She knew that by now she would know everything too. But, then Pen began to sing quietly. The world could wait.

You and me and rain on the roof
Caught up in a summer shower
Dryin' while it soaks the flowers
Maybe we'll be caught for hours
Waitin' out the sun

You and me were gabbin' away
Dreamy conversation sittin' in the hay
Honey, how long was I laughing in the rain with you
'Cause I didn't feel a drop 'til the thunder brought us to

You and me underneath the roof of tin
Pretty comfy feelin' how the rain ain't leakin' in
We can sit and dry just as long as it can pour
'Cause the way it makes you look makes me hope it rains some
more

The light became dim in the tiny room and Devon listened to Raisa's steady breathing. The heartbreak of the afternoon exhausted her. He had listened to her spill her soul until her words ran together. As soon as he convinced her to rest her head on a pillow, her eyes became heavy and in seconds she was asleep.

Now his mind sped. *There has to be another way... I have to figure this out.* He wracked his brain for any possibility of a solution. *I need to talk to that bruel... what was his name? Jude... that's it.*

Devon carefully lifted himself off of the bed. Raisa didn't move at all. He could tell she would be out for awhile, although he knew that was rare for her. *It takes the prospect of the end of the world to wear her out enough for her to sleep...*

As he noiselessly closed the door behind him, standing alone in the hall, he was struck with a horrible and physical pain. A tether that he had not realized was so tangible to Raisa felt like it was being twisted and wrenched. To leave her side and not

267

discuss his plans with her felt immoral. He leaned his forehead on the door with his eyes squeezed shut. *I have to protect her.* He pulled himself away from the door and continued down the hall away from the main room.

He passed several doors, some closed and some open. They were living quarters, storage rooms – all but empty now, and what appeared to be lock-ups, metal doors with heavy locks, the doors open just enough to see a set of bars a few feet into the room and empty cells. Devon saw that the hallway was about to bend around to the other side of the building, probably dropping him off at the other side of the mess hall from where he left it. He was about to turn around when he saw one metal door, closed and locked. The hair stood on the back of his neck.

He looked around him for something to break the lock. Just when he considered getting brutal with a fire extinguisher, he noticed a ring of keys on a nail directly across from the door. *Wow…. Nice Devon… remember to use your head next time.*

The click of the lock echoed down the hall and Devon paused before pushing the door open a few inches. He saw that this room was like the others with a cell so he slid inside and pushed the door almost closed behind him. The room had a single, high window and the late afternoon sun that streamed in made it difficult to see below it. As he moved closer to the bars, he saw a figure lying on a cot, arms leisurely tucked behind his head and feet crossed, an uneaten sandwich from lunch still sitting on a table at the foot of his bed. The man's face was in shadow but a flick of green from his eyes sparked and lit a broad smile for a moment.

"Hello, Devon," the bruel said in a low but happy voice. "How kind of you to visit me. Of course, I knew you would come. He's waiting for you, you know…. It is your destiny, after all."

268

Devon, confused by what the bruel said but determined not to seem caught off guard, replied, "Hello, Jude. I see they are treating you well. Obviously, they didn't ask my opinion."

"Oh, don't be that way, Devon. I have been helping my new friends here in the woods." Sarcasm laid thick on Jude's words. "But that's almost done. I only needed to play along long enough to speak with you. Now, we'll see how many prissy, little rallys I can take out before I go." Jude suddenly sat up on his cot. "Unless, you take me with you... I could show you the way." His eyes flared with the prospect.

"Where, exactly are we going?"

"Why, to see Nosh, of course... in Portland. You'll love the penthouse. It overlooks the city! And he'll be so pleased with me!" Jude sounded almost giddy.

Devon processed all of this quickly. *That's it! I go, take out this Nosh, hunt down the rest of these idiots...* "Okay, Jude. You've got a deal. I'll be back for you tonight. Not a word. Or I'll kill you instead."

Corli knocked softly on Raisa and Devon's door. *I hope I'm not interrupting anything.*

Raisa startled awake. She instantly looked for Devon and was confused that he wasn't next to her. She heard a second soft knock. "Come in." Her voice was scratchy and faint so she cleared it. "Come in...."

Corli cracked the door and peeked inside. She saw Raisa sitting on the bed alone and straining a smile back at her. As she walked in she felt like her heart hurt for her best friend, like she hadn't seen her for weeks. "I miss you," she said, as she sat and wrapped her arms around Raisa.

"I miss you too." Raisa hung onto Corli. "So... I'm assuming that we're both pretty up to speed on what's going on."

Raisa dropped her arms and grabbed Corli's hand. "But, do you know when we're leaving here tomorrow? And is everyone going? Do you know how Julia is doing? How are you and Pen?"

Corli smiled at Raisa's mini panic attack. "It's going to be okay, Raisy. We're all leaving together tomorrow. They say Julia is still touch and go but... I don't know, I just have a feeling that she's alright. We're supposed to leave at 9am tomorrow, after breakfast and getting everything here at the camp packed." Corli squeezed Raisa's hand to reassure her. "Let's not talk about that stuff right now. I'm getting you out of this room. It's beautiful outside. Let's go for a little walk."

"Do you think it's safe? And I don't know where Devon is." Raisa looked around the room as if he would appear from thin air.

"We won't lose site of the camp. And, I'm sure Devon is fine without you for a few minutes. Come on." Corli pulled her off the bed and out the door.

They both took deep breaths as they walked out of the back door of the mess hall. "I hear water," Corli delighted as she pulled Raisa into the trees. Soon they were navigating a short pine needle covered slope to the edge of a rocky stream. The late afternoon light only escaped the cover of trees in a few places on the water where it revealed the mossy, green rocks below the sparkling, clear surface. The shadows, where they met the water changed the rocks to hues of black and blue and you couldn't tell anymore whether the stream was shallow or deep. Corli pulled Raisa to a small sandy opening next to the water. "This reminds me of that camp ground you used to go to with your family every summer, doesn't it? It made me so happy, the years that you took me with." They sat down in the sand and started looking for smooth flat rocks to skip on the water. "Remember that boy you met up there once? He hit you in the stomach with his lunch bag?" Corli and Raisa both laughed.

"He was really cute though," Raisa recalled. Her features relaxed and her voice softened. "I was only fourteen… I think he was fifteen. I couldn't believe he liked me. Then I thought I must have had it all wrong when he swung his sack lunch into me. But then when I talked to my mom, she chuckled and said 'don't worry, he likes you'. But, of course then she added that she didn't think he was a good boy for me." Raisa smiled with a roll of her eyes. She looked down at the sand and lifted some in her hand. "I never understood my mother," she said softly. "But now I see that she was probably just thinking so hard all of the time… trying to do the right things for me, to prepare me. Not far off from my original notions as a child," she smirked at Corli. "That was only a few years ago. But it seems like a dream… or someone else's life," she finished quietly.

Corli watched Raisa's face and saw how the weight of what lay ahead had changed it. She determined right then to make these minutes count. "Do you remember when you tried out for your first singing group? What was it… Madrigals, right?..."

Corli and Raisa digressed to happy times. They reminisced while they played in the sand with their fingers, skipped rocks and listened to the happy babbling of the stream.

Pen knew Corli's mind well enough to know that she had been aching to see Raisa. He also knew that she wouldn't say anything because as strong as she was, she needed him right now too. It felt good to be needed. But he sent her off to find Raisa anyway. That would make her the happiest right now.

He wandered through the grounds for a few minutes, expecting Devon to emerge from the mess hall after being booted for Corli and Raisa's "girl time". When he didn't show, Pen wondered for a moment what kind of trouble Devon might be getting himself into. Then his eyes came to rest on the medical cabin and he automatically walked to it. Whatever was going on in there had a lot of bearing on what the next few days would look like. He carefully pushed the door open and saw Morgan sitting in a tiny makeshift waiting room in front of a set of hospital curtains drawn across the entire width of the cabin.

"Hey," Pen said softly as he sat next to her. "How's everything going?"

"Not much change." Morgan sounded exhausted and was obviously not in the mood for a conversation. Her eyes never left the arm of the chair she sat in.

"Is Scott in there? Can I go in?"

"Yeah, I'm sure it's fine," she replied simply.

Pen slid between the curtain panels. There were five hospital beds lined against the back wall and another small area separated by more curtains. Pen assumed that was a surgical area. Julia lay in the center bed, the only one occupied, under the only window. Scott sat in a chair at her side holding her hand. Pen suddenly wondered how many movies he had seen that looked exactly like this. *Dozens... maybe it will turn out like the movies. Ninety-five percent of those people wake up and have a miraculous recovery, right?*

Scott looked up but said nothing.

Pen thought he looked like it would cause him actual pain to open his mouth and speak, so he didn't give him any reason to. He just walked over and pulled a chair to the foot of the bed. In opposition to Scott's tortured expression, Julia's face was peaceful. But also vacant. Her only movement was a very slight rise and fall of her chest and the drip of an IV that was taped into the back of her hand.

"It's only for nutrients," Scott answered Pen's gaze with a rough and desperate whisper. "They say that physically, they think she's fine. I tried talking to her but I didn't get any response. I should be able to pull her back... wake her up... right?"

Pen put on his best 'everything is going to be fine' face. "I'm sure she can hear you, Scott. Don't give up." Pen watched Julia's face for several minutes as they sat in silence. He hoped he might see something the others missed but no matter how hard he looked, nothing changed. He started to feel a little awkward, staring at Julia this way. So he stood and moved to Scott's side, intending to pat him on the back, tell him to hang in there, and make an exit. As his hand came to Scott's shoulder he looked down at Julia again.

"Did you see that?!" Pen exclaimed with surprise. "Her eyes... you can see her eyes moving behind her eyelids!" Pen pointed and leaned in to look closer.

Scott shot up straight in his chair and stopped breathing. He clutched tighter at Julia's hand.

Then, as they both watched with anxious anticipation, Julia's lips parted. "Devon?!" she called anxiously. Her eyes didn't open but her voice was remarkably clear. A moment later she was completely still again.

An involuntary gush of air came from Scott's lungs as if he had been punched in the stomach. He doubled over. Pen simply hung onto his shoulder to keep him from falling out of his chair.

Devon sat alone in the mess hall at one of the long picnic tables. He had walked through the hall of doors and found himself back in the main room, as he suspected he would. He considered returning to Raisa or looking for Pen but decided against both. It would be easier to do what he intended if no one suspected

273

anything. And Raisa and Pen could read him too well. *I'll just sit here, consider my options, and wait for dinner. Hopefully the room will be busy.* Lost in his thoughts, he was startled when a man in an apron emerged from the kitchen and started banging a big, metal spoon on the back of a pan as he walked out the door. Dinner.

Rallys filtered into the hall, some of them going to help dish out food. Devon watched Pen enter through the main door. He was able to join him without Pen seeing that he had been sitting in the room the whole time.

"Oh, hey Dev. Where's Raisa and Corli?" Pen asked casually.

Devon wasn't sure how to respond. Should he have known that Raisa and Corli were together? Were they supposed to be with him? Luckily, the pair appeared at the door before Devon had to reply. He exhaled with relief and didn't like the guilty feeling that was left behind.

Raisa moved directly to Devon's side. She slid a hand under his shirt at his back. Pulling herself close to his side, she looked up to his face, "Sorry I crashed out on you. I can't believe I got so sleepy. Did you go for a walk? I missed you when I woke up."

Devon loved it when she sounded a little pouty. It was such a direct contrast to her inner strength. It made her seem vulnerable, and made him want to take care of her... forever.

"Yeah, I went for a walk." *It isn't a lie...* he thought. He pulled her tighter next to him as they moved up the line. He looked down at her and into her eyes, taking a second to find a few bright shining blue flecks. *I can do this*, he thought. *All I have to do is think about being with Raisa right now and nothing else.*

"Are you okay?" Raisa was surveying Devon's expression.

"Perfect." Devon didn't smile but bent down and gave Raisa a short but passionate kiss.

"Get a room. Oh, wait. You have one," Pen quipped.

Raisa blushed and was glad they arrived at the head of the line so she could grab a plate and concentrate on the food.

The dinner conversation stayed fairly light. No one seemed to want to discuss the tough subjects, which was fine with Devon. His plan to concentrate on Raisa was the easiest thing he had decided to do in a long time. They shared loving glances and squeezed each other's hands under the table while Pen made jokes about what might be in the goulash they were eating. Corli watched Pen and smiled at every remark.

As they finished up, Pen stood and reached for Corli's hand. "Hey, why don't you and me bring food trays to Morgan and Scott?"

"Sure, that's a good idea," Corli agreed happily. Then she took on a more serious tenor. "How are… they… doing?"

Pen hesitated for half a second. He hadn't thought about how everyone else would react to what Julia said. He knew that it tore Scott up, and now he thought about how it wouldn't do much better for Devon or Raisa. *What could it hurt to leave it out?*

"Pretty much the same," Pen replied.

"Should we go too?" Raisa looked from Pen to Devon.

A shadow threatened to return to Devon's face. He thought again about how he should have kept Julia from harm. But before the thought could bring him down Pen answered.

"No! I mean, no. It's pretty quiet over there. We're just going to slip in and out… no need to make a production out of it."

Corli cocked her head sideways and crinkled her brow at Pen as if to say 'what was that all about?' Pen turned to the side and

275

mouthed 'I'll tell you later' back to her. She shrugged and moved to join him.

"I guess we'll see you guys tomorrow morning then," Corli said cautiously. She wanted to back Pen up even though she had no idea what was going on.

Devon didn't need any persuading. He had already dropped the matter in his mind and had switched back to Raisa and spending the evening with her.

Raisa pulled her bag into the bathroom with her. *Old tank tops and ratty shorts… could I look any less attractive in these rags? Ugh!* She grabbed the cleanest ones she could find from the mix and threw them on, brushed her teeth and splashed water on her face. She tried to imagine what else she could do to look her best, considered a little makeup, then realized that was ridiculous since she was going to bed. Her eyes unfocused while she looked in the mirror and her mind took her back to the first time she saw Devon, standing at the back of the church for her father's service. It seemed like so long ago. So much had unfolded in a few short weeks. She felt that no matter how much tragedy was behind her or what horrific events lay ahead, anything would be bearable as long as he was with her. She knew that deep connected love was a rare thing, somewhere in the range of three percent of all committed relationships was her guess. But she got the fairytale, albeit in the midst of a nightmare. She couldn't imagine being any more ready to give herself over to a man, mind, soul and most importantly right now, body.

A soft knock came at the door.

"What's taking you so long Rai?" Devon didn't wait for an answer to the knock and slowly opened the door. Raisa looked in the mirror and saw that his eyes were smoldering and his

276

energy was thrumming a deep dark rust color. Her tummy did a flip. She tried to pull her eyes back to her own face in the mirror, to check to make sure she looked okay, but she couldn't stop looking at Devon's tousled hair and bare chest. Even after seeing him so many times, his beauty still left her completely disarmed. She couldn't move.

Devon pushed his body into her and put his hands on the sides of the sink just behind hers. He felt a warm static buzz as his skin touched her arms and her back. Every nerve ending in his body was alive. It was all he could do to move slowly, but he was determined to take his time and enjoy every second he had with *his* Raisa.

Raisa could feel Devon's skin and muscles in his arms and chest around her shoulders. The sensation was at least a hundred times more intense than any butterflies she had ever felt. *He wants me… he* really *wants me… as much as I want him.* The little room seemed to spin and be completely still all at once.

Devon pushed her hair aside with his nose and slowly moved his mouth up and down her neck, his breath leaving her skin warm and moist. He never took his eyes off of her staring back at him in the mirror.

Raisa nearly melted into a puddle and her eyes began to involuntarily close. But Devon breathed into her ear, "Look at the contrast of our skin… it's beautiful… you're beautiful."

Raisa forced her eyes to focus and looked down at their arms. "Like maple syrup," she could barely whisper the words.

"And milk," Devon finished with a murmur.

His hands went under the hem of her top to her stomach, sending a thrill through his own body, and pulled her back to him as he continued to kiss her neck and shoulder. They stepped backward together, slowly, out of the bathroom. Devon's hands were exploring now. He slowly pushed her shorts down at her waist just far enough to feel her bare hip and exhaled as he grabbed her hip bone and pulled her hard into him.

Raisa gasped, but not with surprise. She could feel every part of him. Her eyes were closed now but she would not have known if they weren't. All she could see was bright white light behind her eyelids. Her hands reached behind her, grasping for Devon. She had to feel Devon's warm skin and hard muscles under her hands, to touch his face and feel his hair in her fingers. She had one hand full of boxers and the other hand full of the hair at the nape of his neck when they reached the bed. Her breath came faster and her heart pounded furiously.

Devon pulled his hands from Raisa's body and laid them on her shoulders. He brought her arms to her side, running his hands down till he held her hands then lifted them up high and twirled her around to face him.

Raisa let out a small laugh. "I remember the first time you did that," she whispered. "Only you were sending me the other direction. You won't send me away now, will you?" Raisa's voice was teasing and she kissed his neck, adding a little bite at the end.

"Wild horses…" Devon's breath caught even though he was doing his best to remain suave. "Never," he finished. Then he lifted her up and laid her down gently on the bed. He stood for a moment admiring Raisa as he held her hand. Then he bent down and brought her hand to his lips. "I'll love you forever, Raisa." He was overwhelmed by the power he felt in these words. He did love her, more than he thought it was ever possible for one person to love another. And it had happened despite himself. Every cell of his body was incomplete before Raisa and was now absolute. He marveled at how it all happened in such a short time. He realized that it was simply a blessing, there was no other explanation, that he was chosen for her.

278

"I'll love you forever too," she whispered. She thought it sounded silly. Like she couldn't think of something as epic to say as he had. But it was the simple truth. As she looked up at him, she thought for a moment that she saw a tortured look in his eyes. The gravity of their future and what they were about to do showed on his face. But there was more, she just didn't know what it was. Something made her feel the need to grab onto him and not let go. *That can't be a bad thing right? It's because I want him so much.* She pulled gently on his hand, inviting him to lay down with her.

Devon hesitated. *Oh, god... what am I doing? What if I don't come back? I can't take this from her if I'm not going to be the one that is with her.* But he wanted her so badly his whole body was aching. He let her pull him down on top of her, a low and breath- filled sigh escaped his mouth, and their bodies entwined. The energy they created together, bright arcs, misty copper rings intermixed with brilliant spirals, cast a glow to the room that they amazed at together.

Devon watched Raisa's peaceful, sleeping face. Her rays and spirals were faint and misty and they danced lightly around her. He knew she wouldn't wake up. They had been awake for hours into the night and he knew she was exhausted, because he was too.

But it couldn't matter. What he needed to do gave no room for exhaustion. A lump rose in his throat and his eyes welled. Maybe it was her beauty or the prospect of leaving her side that affected him. Or the idea of not telling her. Or the thought that he might never see her again. He wasn't sure which caused this feeling... probably all of them.

He pulled himself up and got dressed. He emptied his bag of everything but weapons and some of the cash. A switchblade

279

went in his back pocket, the keys to the van and his compass in front.

As he closed the door behind him, the wrenching of the tether was so strong he could barely breathe. His feet felt like sand bags as he moved down the hall. He thought that, like earlier today, as he got further away, the weight would lessen. But it didn't. *It's my decision, isn't it?* He looked up into the darkness. *I'll be carrying this with me always. It's okay.* He dropped his head and continued to walk.

Devon checked his phone. It was three-forty in the morning. He pulled the keys from the nail on the wall and quietly unlocked the door to Jude's prison. Jude was standing and waiting, his hands on the bars, his eyes glittering with excitement.

"It's about time," Jude whispered a little too exuberantly.

Devon said nothing. He stepped up to the bars, slid the key into the lock and swung the door open causing Jude to take a step back.

He stepped forward again, eagerly toward Devon. "Come on, let's g-"

Devon's blade sunk to the hilt into Jude's heart.

20

The road down the mountain was only vaguely familiar in the dark, but it wasn't difficult for Devon to find his way. His mind was wandering as he went. It was hard to believe that less than twenty-four hours had passed since he arrived on this mountain – the place he had tried so hard to get to and now was leaving. He was surprised that he made it out of the camp without anyone noticing. Maybe that meant that this was what he was supposed to do, that it was ordained or something. And then always the image returned of Raisa's face, a burning in his heart coming with it. He fought down the sudden nausea…. He wondered how long she would sleep and consequently how long it would be before everyone knew that he was going against the "master plan". He wondered if they would consider him a traitor. Or if they would think he just chickened out – that was more likely. He grunted a little to himself when he thought about the fact that he really had no *plan* whatsoever. He knew approximately where he was going, thanks to Jude, but he had no idea how he was going to figure out *which* tall building in downtown Portland he was going to, or what exactly he would find when he got there. He tried to picture in his mind what Nosh Megedagik, "father-who-kills-many" might look like… probably tall and very large with a twisted face. *Who knows, maybe he'll have horns and a tail… a monster…* "the devil", he thought out loud.

Out of nowhere he felt a pinch in his leg under his pocket. Suddenly he wasn't comfortable and adjusted in his seat. He stretched out enough to reach into his pocket, pulled out the compass and threw it on the dash of the van with a four letter exclamation. It popped open where it fell. Devon could just make it out in the reflection from the headlights off the windshield. "Huh," he grunted. *The stupid thing doesn't even work. That's the north hash pointing straight at the windshield. And the little arrow is right on top of it. And I am definitely not going north.* A moment later, Devon happened to arrive at Highway Five. He knew he would be turning south. He watched the compass as he maneuvered the interchange and entered the highway. The needle still pointed the direction he was going.

♦♦♦

The courtyard in the middle of the old Mediterranean style house was full of warm sunlight. Raisa sat at a small, old, worn and rustic, dark wood table. She was alone. *Wait a minute... this isn't right.* The stucco was the color of cantaloupe and she could see into the richly decorated kitchen, living room and through to the windows in the front of the house. But the house was empty. Completely void of any life.

♦♦♦

Raisa shot straight up in bed and frantically felt next to her for Devon. Her eyes tried to focus in the utter blackness of the room. It seemed impossible that he wasn't there. She felt confused as she pulled back the sheets. They were cold and stiff and she saw only the white glow of them. No warm and familiar body lying beside her. She took a deep breath to get her bearings. Maybe he was just in the bathroom, or stepped out for air. And even though she checked those things, she felt a pain in her gut, like a torn umbilical cord. She knew he was not there. Not anywhere close.

She turned on the bathroom light that seemed to blare out mockingly at the darkness in the room and threw on jeans and a sweatshirt. She ventured out to find Pen and Corli. Maybe they would know where he was. As she walked outside, the first light of morning was barely beginning to show off the side of the mountain behind the tips of the pine trees, but it was still very dark at her feet and she stumbled more than once over rocks and divots she couldn't see. The forest was quiet around her except for the creek that she and Corli had visited. She thought about how the water went on, rumbling endlessly over the slippery rocks even as everything else slept, except for Devon in this case.

"I have no clue which cabin they're in", she murmured to herself. She stopped walking and closed her eyes for a moment. *Corli, where are you?* She waited for something, she didn't know what, to steer her in the right direction. When she opened her eyes and looked toward the cabins scattered in front of her, she mused for half of another minute. She scanned the outlines of the small structures against the dim light and landed on one that was two back and to the side from the one she knew was the medical cabin in front. She made her way to this one, stepped onto the creaky, wooden porch step and slowly opened the door. What she saw made her feel guilty that she and Devon had a room to themselves. The one-room cabin was filled with cots and sleeping bodies. She could barely tell in the darkness where one left off and the other began.

"Corli," she whispered at what she hoped was an appropriate level.

"Raisa?" she heard Corli's sleepy voice answer back from somewhere amidst the group.

"Corli," she whispered back. "Where's Pen... Devon's gone. I need to know if he knows where he went."

Pen woke up when he heard Corli's voice. Both of them got up and made their way to Raisa and stepped outside.

"Gone?" Pen questioned. "He didn't say anything?"

"No, nothing." Raisa said with embarrassment. Her face fell. What did this mean about their relationship? She thought everything was okay. Especially after-

"I thought he might be up to something... he was being so 'Dudley' earlier. Did he take anything with him?"

"I don't know. I didn't look. I just came to find you."

The threesome emerged minutes later from Devon and Raisa's room, determining that he had packed light, taking a weapon – and the van. The sky was a little lighter but still not close to sunrise.

Someone from Corli and Pen's cabin had decided to wake Edward after they heard what Raisa said. Edward and David were walking toward them from the back side of the mess hall.

Edward spoke first. "So it's true? Devon is gone?"

"Yes," Raisa answered softly.

"And Jude is dead," Edward remarked as he looked at the other three. "Do you think Devon could have done that?"

"Yes," answered Pen.

"But... why? He was not a threat to anyone," Edward questioned accusingly. He was trying to understand without sounding judgmental – and failing miserably.

"I'm certain he had his reasons," Pen said coolly. He looked directly at Edward when he said this, his eyes clear and warning even in the dark. He would defend Devon's moral character to his death, even if he was wrong.

Edward nodded several times. "Okay, okay.... Do you have any idea where he's gone?"

Raisa, Pen and Corli stood silent as the question hung in the air like a circling vulture. Raisa felt like she *did* know, but just couldn't locate the file in her brain to open and reveal the answer. And none of them wanted to guess what was probably going to be an extreme hazard of a guess.

"I do." A clear voice came from behind them.

They all spun on their heels to see Julia, helped along by Scott and Morgan, walking toward them.

Raisa's head snapped up and her eyes locked with Julia's as the other group came to a stop in front of them. Even in the dim light Raisa saw perfectly Julia's bright, hazel green eyes. They reminded her of a storm tossed ocean. She thought she could actually see the play of the waves moving behind her gaze. They drew her in. For a moment, she felt like she and Julia were the same person, seeing a mirror image of herself in the other girls eyes. Then she understood.

"They showed you, didn't they?" Raisa spoke softly. "I knew you were there, on the other side, visiting. It's hard to come back, isn't it?" Julia only nodded. She understood what they shared.

"Well?" Pen said, somewhat impatiently. He saw the significant moment happening between Raisa and Julia but decided to be the voice of haste.

Scott hung at Julia's side, his face cast down and looking like he was awaiting a death sentence. It was debatable as to who was doing the supporting.

"I was shown a large room at the top of a business building. The building itself is made of orange stone or brick and the top is in the shape of a pyramid that is grey or green."

"Koin Tower," Edward interjected. "It's in downtown Portland."

Julia continued, her words spilling quickly as she relived the vision. "They showed me Devon talking to an older man in that room. It sounded like... like he was striking a bargain with him. I was confused. I asked them why they were showing this to me. It made no sense." Julia paused. Scott sunk lower at her side but no one was paying attention to his agony. "Then they told me that... it was... Nosh that Devon spoke to."

Raisa gasped.

"I tried to call out to him, to tell him to stop," Julia said, as if she was still pleading for Devon to listen to her.

Scott's head snapped up, his back straightened and his copper rings bloomed like a flower in time lapse. She hadn't called out to him because she wanted him... it was a warning! Scott was delivered, while everyone else simply remained intent on Julia's words.

"But they told me it was not yet a reality, just one of the many paths that Devon might take. They showed me many things. But I'm thinking that we don't have time to discuss them right now. You have to go after him, Raisa. You are the only one that can fix this." Her light was steady and beaming from her chest. It melded and connected with Scott's.

As they rushed to leave the camp, Edward followed them to their borrowed car. "We're clearing out today - flying to Thule," he told them in a matter-of-fact tone as he tossed a bag in the front seat. "A man named Otis Wright will be waiting for you at Pearson Field, a small airport in Vancouver, Washington. "It's only about seven miles north of downtown Portland. Bring lots of cash."

Corli twisted in her seat and asked, "What if we can't get Devon?" Raisa lost the ability to breathe and froze where she stood hanging onto the open car door, waiting for Edward to reply. The thought was inconceivable, and the question, she knew, was rhetorical.

The answer was blunt. "Then, don't bother."

Pen drove much faster than he should have as he took the hairpin turns down Mt Rainier in an Impala. Under different circumstances, Corli would have asked him to slow down but instead she and Raisa kept their hands securely in the OMG straps over their windows where they sat in the back seat together. Pen had maps, scribbled notes, a pistol, the backpack of cash and the bag of sandwiches piled in the seat next to him.

"How far behind him do you think we are?" Pen wondered out loud.

"Less than an hour, I think," Raisa replied as if she had just checked the direction of the wind. "I don't think I was asleep for very long before I realized he wasn't there."

Corli watched Raisa's face in the growing morning light. It was changing every few moments and Corli knew that Raisa had drifted off somewhere else in her head. From a creased forehead and thin lips; to a smooth brow and the edges of her mouth starting to turn up; to eyes closed with her lips slightly parted; then back to worry. As Corli watched this myriad of emotions cross her friend's face, she felt the red start to rise up her neck and onto her cheeks. She tried not to speak but her anger bubbled over. "How could he leave you? How could he think that he should go and do this? And without telling you! Or any of us! What, he just 'does' you and then goes off to get himself killed-"

"Corli!" Raisa cut her off with a shocked exclamation. "Don't. I know it doesn't look good…" she took a deep breath. "But I'm certain that he believes he is doing the right thing. And besides… we didn't… I mean we haven't… not all the way, anyway," her voice was quiet at the end. Raisa stared at her hand in her lap. "That must be why he stopped… why he held back… why he kept stopping *me*." *Because he doesn't know if he'll survive this.* The thought stabbed at her heart. Raisa looked up, not knowing what reaction she would get from her best friend.

"Oh." Corli's mouth hung open after she finished the word. "I'm… sorry." It sounded like a question.

"It's okay." Raisa blushed and lowered her voice. "It really was amazing… we made out for hours… and I had some… feelings I've never had before." She felt her face flush deeper.

"*Uh hum*," Pen coughed and cleared his throat. "I know this is about a three hour drive, so it will take awhile, not that I plan on going the speed limit… anyway…….. do we have any idea what Devon thinks he is doing, talking to Nosh and all? And more importantly, do we have a plan? I'm just sayin', maybe we should put our thinking caps on."

On a hunch, Devon pulled off the highway at Hawthorn Bridge toward downtown Portland, when the compass needle started jiggling erratically. *It's not so unreasonable that something that came from evil would lead me to evil, right,* he thought to himself, ignoring the feeling in his gut that there was a greater significance. He wound through a couple of the city blocks, trying to follow what he thought the compass was telling him. *This is ridiculous…* he considered. Until he saw looming in front of him, a tall building – not the tallest, but the most stylish by far, even with several floors of boarded windows. *This is it.* He knew it was true, somehow.

It was past eight now. He couldn't tell if the building was of the business sort, or condos, or both - and wondered if he would be able to get in. He couldn't even remember what day of the week it was.

He cut the engine and dug for his resolve. He pictured Calvin with his gentle spirit and soiled coveralls, the face of his loving mother with her graceful countenance, his goofy, best friend, Pen, and then Raisa. He would save this world mostly for her – whether he died doing it or not. An adrenalin and electricity mixture rose from the bottom of his feet to the crown of his head. He sighed heavily, the weight of being away from Raisa still bearing down on him like the hydraulics of a trash truck compacter. He blinked as he realized his vision had turned orange.

He tucked the hand gun he had sort-of inherited from Raisa's father into the back of his jeans, pulled the compass off the dash – not entirely knowing why he would bring it with him – and walked into the lobby marked 'Koin Center' and straight to the elevator well. He half acknowledged that the security station sat empty.

Devon looked at the compass in his hand before he called the elevator. It was spinning endlessly and fast. *I guess that means 'straight up'*, "or down to hell," he muttered, *one of the two*.

When he reached the penthouse floor the elevator doors opened to a small landing. He stepped out, his hand behind his back clutching the gun, the compass thrumming in his pocket, and stopped short. Two large mahogany carved doors, the only thing in the space, stood closed not more than six feet in front of him. But that wasn't what made him freeze. What stopped him was the music. He recognized the song that blared in the room behind the doors. Nessun dorma. Luciano Pavarotti.

The air wouldn't move in or out of Devon's lungs. How many times had he heard this song and watched his mother close her eyes and sway to the powerful opera. For half a second he tried to remember the meaning of the Italian words; something about 'no one shall sleep' and 'I will win'. Devon shook his

289

head to clear it, trying to pass yet one more thing off as coincidence, and clenched his jaw. He registered that the song was coming to its loud, dramatic end and pushed the doors open wide. He was blasted by a gust of air that was both fresh and putrid at the same time.

His gaze landed instantly on the back of a grey haired man who sat on an ornate lounge, facing a fire that burned low in the fireplace. *One old man? How hard could it be*, he thought. He walked steadily forward, planning only a few more feet before he shot this guy in the head and asked questions later.

Unmoving, Nosh spoke as if he were greeting his favorite neighbor. "Good morning, Devon." Then he stood, smiled, and turned to face his guest.

Devon cocked his gun and aimed for a shot to the forehead. The eyes in the face he was about to shoot opened wider, but not with fear, more with surprise... or sheer glee? Devon paused to take in the whole face, searching for the meaning of this old man's reaction. And choked.

The floor rocked under Devon's feet. Or at least it seemed to. His arms fell to his sides unconsciously and he no longer felt the metal of the gun in his hand. He felt his own face twist into lines of furry but there was a disconnect with his brain. In his head was only confusion. *Where is the monster with the tail...* fizzle, snap. *Miguel Castaneda is dead...* His neural pathways blazed haphazardly searching for some sense to what he was seeing and never finding a solid thought to land on. His brain retrieved the image of the photograph his mother kept in a frame behind a closed cabinet door, the picture of his father, Miguel Castaneda, and compared it to this man standing in front of him with this wide grin on his face. This man was much older, the lines that existed before were now deep crevasses. The hair that had only wisps of grey above the ears was now mostly all of the silvery

290

color. But the eyes, the way they were shadowed under his brow yet still pierced through you like daggers, were the same... exactly.

"No..." he heard a voice mutter, "it can't be." But the old man hadn't spoken. The words, he realized, had come from his own mouth.

"Welcome, my son." Nosh lifted up his arms; the smile still plastered to his face, and walked the rest of the distance to close the gap between them.

Devon regained the feeling in his hands and raised the gun to a few inches from his father's face. He felt the years of anger against this man, for what he had done to his mother, for what he had done to countless other women, culminate like the point of a tornado in his chest. He forced the only words he could find out of his mouth.

"What are you doing here?" Devon's voice was trembling and thick.

"Why, Son, the same thing you are," Miguel's voice cooed. "We both want to keep this beautiful world from being destroyed, don't we?" His arms were still wide and gesturing. "Hear me out, Son... let's not be so hasty." He reached his hand over and rested it on top of the nine millimeter pointed at his face and gently pushed it down.

Devon wasn't sure why he didn't just fire, why he was letting this fiend push his arm down. He couldn't keep the feeling of curiosity, the chance to get answers, from creeping into his head, slightly muting his determination and cooling the color of his vision.

"That's it, Son," Miguel said proudly. "Why don't we come and sit by the fire." He gestured toward the ottoman, inviting Devon to walk the few steps by his side.

"Stop calling me that," Devon sneered. "Just because I haven't killed you yet, doesn't mean I won't. Or that you would ever, in this life or any other, deserve to call me your son."

"As you wish... Devon. The words make no difference," he shrugged, "it doesn't change the truth." He flipped the fingers of his hand as if to hurry Devon along.

Devon cautiously walked to the open end of the ottoman. He waited for his father to sit before he did.

"I see you used the compass," Miguel said with delight. Devon became aware of it again as it whirred away in his pocket.

"Might I see it? It has been so very long since I gave it to the beautiful Gloria..." he seemed to be reminiscing.

Devon fought the revulsion and nausea that ripped through him for hearing this man, or whatever he was, speak his mother's name in such a manner. But he pulled the compass from his pocket and tossed it at him, hoping that the couple of feet it had to travel would be too short for him to react, hoping he would fumble and miss it.

Miguel snatched the compass neatly out of the air. The thing instantly stopped its noise. Miguel sighed and opened his hand to look at it. The smile on his face twisted darkly. *So many years. So many plans laid. And here we are.* He looked up at Devon, preparing to launch into the sermon he had been preparing for precisely this moment.

Devon noticed the change in his face, realized that he was about to speak and cut him off before he began, "Save it, preacher... you have no following here. Just cut to the chase. As a matter of fact, why don't we start with a couple questions?"

"As you wish, S-... Devon. We have all the time in the world." Miguel chuckled darkly to himself. As long as Devon was here with him, that was the wonderful truth.

Devon eyed him warily as he spoke, "So... you're 'Nosh'? It sounded more like a sarcastic statement than a question. "You have been the leader of all of these evil people bent on killing for all of these years?"

The corners of Miguel's mouth bent down drastically and then leveled again. "Oh, Devon," he began and sighed, "Yes, I suppose I am Nosh. But you have to understand that trying to save this insipid human race isn't easy. The greatest gifts do not always have the prettiest wrapping. There are always compromises that must be made. And some must die for the greater good. I'm sure that you understand that concept, don't you? And, I will take some credit for the work that has been done here, but the leader? No. I cannot take the credit for all of that."

"Well, if you are not in charge, then who is?" The suspicion was clear in Devon's voice. He didn't believe his father's sing-songy dribbling, but on the off chance that there was someone else he needed to get to, he humored the conversation.

Miguel's voice took on a stronger, dual note and his back straightened. His face glowed blood red and his eyes opened wide. "I'm sure that you know by now, Devon, that there are things in Heaven and below that are far stronger than us. The one who I serve wants everything for us, for our lives to be rich. You would be wise to listen to me now... to choose your path carefully. Your strength will be paramount in the coming weeks. Together we can put everything back in order. We can make everyone happy and live out our dreams in the process."

Except for the warning in Devon's heart, this sounded right, like the exact thing he was trying to accomplish, to put everything back together. But what did Miguel know about his dreams. Until recently he had never even had any. For just a split second, he considered though, the option of joining with this

293

man, compromising for the greater good, to see if it would reconcile in his head. It might work.

Then everything changed.

Devon's face shot up to see his father's. With a maniacal grin it seemed to spiral toward him even though he knew that neither of them had physically moved. The weight he had felt on his body for the last few hours was almost completely lifted but replaced with a groggy, sick feeling. What used to be orange and full of depth and light in what he saw now had the visual texture and color of a newspaper photo. But worst of all, he felt a presence in his mind that he wanted to cower away from but lacked the ability. He pushed back with all his mental strength, like screaming at himself, only for the sound to fall on his own deaf ears. He could only just keep the presence from taking his mind entirely. And though this internal struggle continued, Devon heard calm and emotionless words come from his mouth.

"That sounds like a good thing," Devon droned. "I'd like to hear more."

"Ahhh, ha ha ha," Miguel stood and clapped his hands together. "Excellent! Wonderful! You've opened your mind! We have so much to discuss-" His cheerfulness cut short, he turned sharply toward the entrance of the penthouse when the elevator dinged to announce an arrival.

Pen and Corli stood next to each other and protectively pushed Raisa behind them as they peered from the elevator through the open doors into the penthouse. Raisa allowed it for the moment.

"Devon!" Pen's voice was filled with joy and concern at the same time. He could see Devon and had the proof he needed that his best friend was still alive, but Pen knew instinctively that something was very wrong; his stomach wrenched and he could sense the evil spilling from the room. His arms rose automatically in protection of the girls.

They advanced as a unit and Raisa peered between her protectors, catching her first glimpse of Devon. His eyes found hers for a moment, and her body tensed as she realized he had no intention of coming to her. A chill ran the length of her spine.

Devon stood and moved in front of his father.

"Welcome, friends!" Miguel sang.

"We're not your friends," Corli said flatly, her knife twitching in her hand.

"Devon," Pen said low and urgently, "what's going on here?"

Raisa's moment of restraint was over; she had to get a clear look at him and pushed between her guards. She saw him. Frozen where she stood, she took in the sight. He was pale and his head was bowed. His copper rings were almost completely gone and replaced with a murky mist that moved like fingers and hovered at his feet, webbed and clinging to his legs, attaching him to the floor.

Miguel moved to Devon's side and wrapped his arm around his son's shoulder. "We're going to clean up this mess and restore all to order," he stated. "Isn't that right, Son?"

"Devon…," Raisa said in a low confused voice to no one in particular. "Devon…" clearer and resolved now she moved to run to him, to take him out of this place, but Corli grabbed her arm and held her.

"Raisa, no," she warned. Corli exchanged a quick look with Pen and saw that he agreed with her.

Pen moved their threesome further into the room and looked around as much as he could while keeping his gun trained in the general direction of the man at Devon's side. He saw that Devon held his pistol down at his side but seemed almost unconscious of the fact. He saw the boarded windows with a gap several feet wide in them letting the wind whip into the room. Everything besides the damaged windows seemed to be indicative of a normal, posh but sparsely furnished penthouse office. Until his eyes landed on a large heap in the front corner of the space that was covered with a dirty painters tarp. A draft of air carried a rancid stench to his nose.

Devon still stood motionless at Miguel's side. Watching his friends move into the room with dead eyes. Miguel watched them too, seemingly amused.

"Devon," Pen spoke as he continued toward the mound, keeping his eyes on him. "Talk to me, man. We know you were coming here to talk to Nosh. Is this him?" Pen looked at Corli and signaled for her to check under the tarp. He took Raisa's arm from her as she ducked behind and carefully lifted the edge of the tarp with the tip of her blade. Corli let out a stifled cry and raised her arm to cover her mouth and nose as she let the covering fall back into place.

"Dead bodies... women." Corli strained to keep from retching, her eyes watering as she moved back to Raisa's side. Raisa's forehead was creased as she looked from Devon to Corli and back again. Pen moved them into the stream of fresh air closer to the window opening.

"Devon!" Pen's frustration over Devon's lack of response wore through. "We need to get out of here, man! They're expecting us at the airport-"

"Oh my God," Raisa had finally looked away from Devon long enough to look at the man that stood next to him. Her eyes instantly sprung up silent tears as she spoke. "You're Miguel... Miguel Castaneda! You're Devon's father! You *bastard*!" Pen and Corli weren't quick enough this time as Raisa ripped her arm away and propelled herself forward. But just before she could

296

throw herself on Miguel, Devon reached out and grabbed her around the waist and held her back with an iron grip. Raisa struggled, "Let me *go*, Devon! What are you doing?! Why…" her voice strangled away. She knew quickly that there was no possibility of escape. Devon's strong arm around her felt familiar but cold and foreign at the same time. But he wouldn't harm her, she didn't think. He had to be in there somewhere. She twisted under his grip to look at his face. His eyes were pale muddy colored glass. There were no bright shining copper flecks, and he stared back at her like he knew her but couldn't understand what she could be upset about.

"It's alright, Raisa. Everything is going to be fine. You'll see," Devon's voice was like a recording, plastic. There was no part of his soul in the words.

Pen and Corli moved closer, trying to calculate the possibility of snatching Raisa back but didn't dare test Devon's state of mind while the gun still hung in his hand.

Raisa turned her face to Miguel and felt it twist and burn. "What have you done to him?" she breathed between her teeth.

"I've done nothing." Miguel sounded almost hurt by the accusation. "Devon simply saw the logic in my… *our* plan." He stepped toward Pen and Corli, his face taking on a more sinister smile. "And you want to live don't you? Rather than having the flesh melted off of your bones… because that *is* what will happen." His voice raised and the room seemed to darken. A low and throaty laugh filled the air. "Everyone, all your friends, your loved ones, everyone on the planet will melt by fire delivered from the heavens on bolts of lightning! *Nothing* will be left!" Then he smoothed his face and transferred his weight as if he were changing characters. "Unless… unless you join with us," his voice suddenly sing-songy again. But there was still a dark rumbling noise filling the rafters of the space. Miguel

297

straightened and lifted his hand as if to address a throng of followers, "You'll live like kings! Masters of all you see!" Then his eyes leveled on Corli and Pen. *Insolent children*, he thought, *they care nothing for power*. He spoke again, examining them like mice in a plastic box, "What will you do as you watch your mother die, Ms Fairchild? Mr. Gray, now that you have found, love," the word twisted as he spoke it, "how tragic it would be to die. Surely you all can envision what you will gain in this new era-"

"*No!*" Corli shouted, shaking her head. She couldn't take it anymore. What was he saying? "You're *evil*! You *lie*! You're talking about yourself, *not us*." She was crying now and didn't care how loudly she did it. Pen pulled her to him by her waist.

"You need to free Devon from whatever you've done to him, *now!*" Pen's voice was shuddering. The gun, still held up was shaking in his hand. "You are a liar and a murderer! We *will not* listen to you-" The gun suddenly flew, simply plucked from his hand by an unseen force. It landed inside the fireplace and scattered embers on the floor. The gun heated. The bullet explosions started. Miguel was laughing in unison with the rumble in the room, Corli was screaming for Pen to get down, and Pen was yelling, calling to Devon. Devon was silent and still.

Raisa put her hand on Devon's arm that was around her and whispered up at him through the madness.

"Let me face you, I won't run."

His grip softened just slightly and he allowed her to turn toward him. She reached up and touched his face, searching his lifeless eyes, checking for any connection at all.

"I love you, Devon. It's all that matters." Her eyes pooled but did not spill. "Are we giving up?" she asked softly. And even though the rumbling continued to grow louder she knew

298

that he heard her. "Is this it? Do we die now? Or are we servants to this madness, to Nosh, forever?" She almost felt like it wouldn't matter as long as she could be with him. But would he ever be "*him*" again? Her forehead dropped against Devon's chest. She couldn't tell if he responded or not. She squeezed her eyes shut, still listening to the deafening chaos of the room. "Dad... Mom..." she whispered.

Raisa felt a tremendous thrum through her body at the same time she heard a very loud noise. Not startling so much as all-encompassing, like standing in the center of the giant bass pipes of an enormous church organ. Her eyes shot up to Devon. He was shaking his head like he needed to break it open. Raisa, no longer restrained by Devon, spun on her heels.

Vincent and Lona stood several feet off the floor as sparkling white visions across the room from each other, their arms cast up in the air. The rumbling laughter silenced.

"Behold!" Vincent and Lona spoke together, the sound both terrible and absolutely lovely at the same time. A shining image sprung up that filled the space between them and lifted to the ceiling. It was like the one she had seen back at the Taco Shop but much, much larger and more corporeal. She could see that everyone in the room could see it too.

"Evil and darkness would tell you that this world can be saved," their voices thundered in unison. "But, look and see what will come if the Lasteires do not complete their task!"

The translucent screen began to darken in the center and spread almost to the edges. Images began to flash across it. Images of suffering and torture. Nothing was green. Everything burned and bled. At first the pictures were general and random, people in anguish that they didn't know. Cities that they had never seen, burning. But then one came that they knew. Calvin, clung to the edges of a muddy and toxic ditch while being whipped for no apparent reason by a huge laughing man.

Corli gasped. Raisa tried to look away but couldn't tear her eyes from the scene.

It changed then, to their own neighborhoods. Violence that they couldn't imagine any human was capable of was rampant. A picture flashed of Charlotte, folded up and holding her legs, hiding in a tiny closed space, filthy and crying, shuddering at every noise she heard. Then came Devon's mother, Gloria. She was not dirty, and was even in a very lovely room. But when the picture zoomed in, you could see that her cloths had been partially ripped from her body. She was bound mercilessly to a metal bracket attached to the floor and she was crying quietly.

A pain filled huff escaped from Devon.

"Enough!" he begged.

The visions in white lowered their arms and the screen disappeared. Vince and Lona both turned and looked at Raisa. Even as they did, they began to turn into more mist and begin to fade. She saw them gaze at her till they both disappeared. But then she heard them. *Love*, was all they said.

Raisa turned back to look at Devon, holding her breath, hoping.

She was practically blinded by the light she saw there between them, all orange and white and golden. And the connection, it felt as strong as bridge cables. She let the air out of her lungs in relief as she reached to wrap her arms around him, forgetting everything else.

The next seven seconds happened all at once and yet to everyone in the room it was slow motion.

Miguel, in a rage and with a guttural cry lunged for Raisa and Devon. Devon, just in time, pushed Raisa out of the way. Miguel and Devon struggled for a moment. Miguel howled and

300

pushed Devon with all his might, grabbing the gun from Devon's hand at the same time. As Devon fell back and Miguel spun to shoot at Raisa, Pen saw. And leaped.

The gun discharged as Pen flew, the bullet entering his chest at his heart. His body went limp while he was still in the air and when he hit the floor he was sliding. The momentum carried him quickly across the slick wood the short distance to the opening in the glass and plywood face of the building. Corli screamed. And Pen was gone.

21

Devon was on his feet in the same final second. Filled with rage, he moved on Miguel. Miguel cowered at the sight of his son, who was glowing from head to toe. A fire had started from the spilled coals and it had enveloped most of the wall. The rug in front of the fireplace was beginning to burn. Devon took the gun from his father's shaking hand. And took one step back.

"*You can go to hell.*" Devon barely choked out the words.

Devon kicked.

Raisa thought she heard bones crunching as she watched his foot connect with the monsters neck and chest. Miguel flew across the lounge and into the fireplace. As he shrieked and writhed in the flames, Devon grabbed Raisa and Corli and dashed for the elevator, slamming the large wooden doors to the penthouse behind him.

The elevator didn't move fast enough. Corli clawed at the doors as she heaved air in and out of her lungs as if she were drowning. Devon stood motionless, staring at the shiny metal elevator doors, his arms wrapped tightly around Raisa's waist. Raisa had one hand clutched tightly into Devon's shirt, the other raised and reaching toward Corli, her breathing escalating to match her best friends. The ding of each of the 34 floors below the penthouse ridiculed them, stretching time to its limits.

By the time they reached the bottom floor, Corli had already begun to pry the doors open with her fingers and squeezed through them before it seemed possible that she could.

Devon and Raisa emerged from the building only seconds after Corli to find her pacing and looking up the side of the building. Smoke was beginning to billow from the top floor.

"Where is he? *Pen*," she called out for him like a mother calling a child for dinner. "He's hanging onto the side somewhere, right? We have to find him so we can get him down."

"Where is he?" Devon asked himself quizzically. He was staring at the concrete sidewalk. He walked toward the street, expecting to see that Pen had landed lightly on his feet, farther out, imagining that he would jump out from behind the van to surprise them. *A sick joke*, Devon thought, *but I wouldn't put it past him.*

Raisa stood watching them, tears streaming from her face.

"What are you doing?!" Corli half screamed at Devon and Raisa as she realized that they weren't scanning the side of the building with her.

"Corli," Raisa choked, "I don't think... I don't think he's here."

Corli walked back and stopped in front of Raisa, searching her face. Then she dropped to her knees, her hands spread on the sidewalk as if she could pull Pen up through it. Devon looked and Raisa too. His knees began to buckle.

Devon felt an arm gather him around the waist and his head cleared. Corli felt a soft arm around her shoulders and fingers pushing the hair gently from her eyes. They all heard Vincent speak and knew that Lona was there too. *Pen is gone. We have spared his body from hitting the earth and took him away so that none of you would have to bare the sight. He has given his life here for you completely. That will not be forgotten. Go now. You have much to do. We will watch over Penley for you.*

The three of them stayed motionless and quiet, the bustle of the city around them totally insignificant. Vincent and Lona were gone and had taken their friend.

Death.

Raisa thought back to when her father died and how just like then, there didn't seem to be an appropriate reaction. But, she took hope in the thought that she knew her mother and father lived on, and Pen would too. *Pen...* she thought aloud in her mind, *thank you for saving my life*.

The sirens of fire trucks were the first sounds that had an effect on them. Raisa pulled Corli up from the ground.

"We have to go," she said and looked at Devon, coaxing him to help her get Corli into the front seat of the car.

Raisa drove, which separated her from Devon. But he sat behind her, his hand on her shoulder and neck, unwilling to be parted from her. The ride to the airport was silent, except when Corli read from Pen's scratched notes on how to get there. She folded the paper carefully when they arrived and tucked it inside her shirt.

"Come again, Otis? You want *how* much?"

Raisa had taken the lead and Devon and Corli were keeping up as best they could. While Raisa dealt with logistics from one side of her brain, the other side wondered if it was horrible that she was functional while Devon and Corli weren't.

"I'll tell you what," Raisa bargained, "Forty thousand now and thirty-five when we get to Thule."

"Alright," Otis nodded, "but we better get going or the price is going up. It's a long flight, over twenty-five hundred miles, and we'll be lucky to have any light left as it is." Despite the urgency in his voice, Otis didn't move, short of lifting his palm up toward Raisa. She pulled the backpack off her shoulder with a sigh and crouched down to find four bundles of hundreds inside. She glanced around. No one in the sparsely populated room seemed to be paying any attention to their transaction. She placed the money in his hand and he tucked it into his coat as he turned and started walking. "Follow me," he muttered.

Otis was out the door of the terminal, which was actually more of a makeshift office in the front corner of a large metal garage, in three steps. They gathered their bags and hurried after him.

Devon perked up for the first time since they left the city as they walked onto the airfield.

"Wow." He stopped and looked at a row of old planes pulled close to the building. "Your dad would love this," Devon said with a little whimsy in his voice. He looked ahead to see that Raisa had stopped and turned.

"What?" Raisa said incredulously. This was not what she thought his first coherent comment would be. She grabbed Corli's arm who hadn't heard a word anyone said, and would have kept walking if she didn't.

"These are World War II planes," Devon explained. "Your dad worked on these." He started up again and skipped a little to catch up with Raisa and Corli.

Raisa wasn't exactly sure how to respond so she kept walking, pulling Corli with her, and checking Devon's face to see if he was going to say something else uniquely bizarre.

They stopped a few feet further in front of a much larger plane.

"Wow." Raisa exclaimed flatly. "This is nice." She could see up the stairs and into the cabin. Otis had already disappeared inside.

"Yeah, it's a Cessna. A Cessna Citation Sovereign, I think. It has to be this big to make the trip without stopping for gas."

The very corner of his mouth tried to tilt up as he looked at Raisa but no smile could come. Under different circumstances Devon would have been proud of his knowledge and want to brag a little; the engine size, wingspan and weight capacity, but it seemed so entirely trivial now.

"How do you know all this stuff?" Raisa asked, wondering if he was in shock, as she led the silent Corli through the door and to a tan leather seat that was already in a reclined position. She buckled Corli in, grabbed a blanket from overhead and tucked it around her friend. Corli's eyes closed almost instantly. Raisa kissed her forehead. She turned back to see Devon already sitting, very still and watching them. She could tell he was processing Corli's behavior. She took the seat across from him and reached for his hand.

"Vince," he said as he took her hand and pulled it to his lips. Raisa visibly shuddered and a light beam shot so brightly from her that Devon wondered if it would damage the plane. "Your dad," he continued as he looked at her, "he taught me a bunch about planes."

Otis popped in suddenly from the cockpit and startled them. Raisa became aware that she needed to breath. He spoke quickly while he closed and locked the door of the plane.

"Just so you know, folks, this is going to be about a six hour flight and I'm supposed to have another crew member but no one was crazy enough to come with me. I'm leaving the cockpit door open in case I need you." He turned and disappeared into the pilot's seat. Moments later the engines roared to life.

Corli slept through the takeoff. Devon and Raisa, lost in their own thoughts, stared out of the window as they climbed to their cruising altitude. Raisa peeked over at Corli often, worried, but she seemed to be sleeping peacefully enough. The silence wasn't

306

awkward for Raisa... it seemed appropriate after the events of the last forty-eight hours. They all needed time to process. She soon noticed though, that Devon was not having the same reaction to the quiet. He looked like he would wear a hole in his seat if he didn't speak soon.

"Raisa," he half blurted, then took a deep breath. "I... I know you're not going to yell at me for what I did. I can see that you're not angry. But what I don't understand is, why? It was obviously a very bad idea, and..." his head dropped, "It's my fault Pen is dead."

Raisa dropped to the floor in front of Devon and took his hands. She bent lower to see his face and make him look at her. "Have you not learned yet that everything happens for a reason?" She could see the pain in his eyes; it appeared to be a physical pain, pain that she thought she understood. She continued as gently as she could, "Look at everything we have gained. We know more about Nosh than anyone now because he is, or was your fa... Miguel. We know he destroyed his clairvoyants so any bruels we find will be acting on their own. And, we know that as much as we may have wanted things to be different, we have no choice... we have to do this." She squeezed his hands, asking for a response. When she didn't get one she continued. "Even Pen..." a knot formed in her throat. "If he hadn't saved me... everything would be over. And the only thing we would have to look forward to, are those awful things that mom and dad showed us."

At this Devon looked up from his lap at Raisa through some of his hair that had fallen into his eyes. "You said mom and dad."

Raisa looked back at him confused. Hadn't he seen them along with everyone else? "I thought you saw-"

"Yes, I saw them... but you didn't say 'my' mom and dad."

"Oh." Raisa's heart skipped a beat. "Well, they love you too and… I imagine at some point…" she flushed and lowered her face.

Devon lifted his hand and pushed a lock of Raisa's curly hair away from her eyes. "So… you still want to be with me?"

"I don't think there is anything I want more," she whispered.

Devon's eyes turned glassy. Raisa could see that he was doing his best to not let them fill up completely. His rings thrummed and reverberated around her. She wondered if the energy would create a magnet and draw the plane down to the ground.

As Devon looked at Raisa's face and the light from the blue in her eyes, an image of the future conjured in his mind; Raisa by his side in some unknown future, in a place he didn't recognize and a small group of people looking at them with questions written on their faces. He half expected to hear a voice at that moment. When it didn't come, he said to himself what he knew the voice would have said. *You really think that you can lead these people into the future, Devon Castaneda? Who are you? You are nothing.*

"I know that the path is set, Raisa," he whispered. "And I know that you and I will see it through, but… how? How am I going to come out on the other side of this and be a leader? How will I know what to do? Just because I can run a construction crew doesn't mean I can be Moses. How do I tell them that it's okay that everyone on the planet is dead but we'll be fine?"

"Theory?" Raisa sat back on her legs. "How did Moses do it? I can't imagine that we'll be entirely on our own… I have faith that we'll have help."

Devon exhaled long and sat back in his chair, releasing Raisa's hands. "Faith," he said, closing his eyes. "You have to be meant for me. I have virtually none, but you seem to have enough for both of us."

Raisa watched Devon's eyelids to see if they would reopen. When his chest began to rise and fall with deep breaths she stood to grab another blanket. As she bent to drape it over him, her mind vacillated between wanting to leave it off so that she could look at the outline of his broad shoulders and chest, and trying to calculate how many hours of sleep any of them could have gotten in the last two days. When she realized she was too tired to figure it out, she dropped the blanket in place and walked up to the front of the cabin.

"How's it going up here, Otis?"

"Just fine, Miss. Well, all except for these instruments." Otis leaned up and tapped on the glass of one of the gauges. "I don't get it. These usually only act up when there's real bad weather, but the skies are clear."

Raisa struggled to keep the concern from her voice but it came out with a much higher pitch than normal, "Are those gauges super important? Are we going to end up in Mexico? Or over no land at all? Or-"

"No, no. We're fine Miss. Plenty of back-up instrumentation and communication with the ground. This isn't my first walkabout."

Raisa exhaled and took a moment to re-establish her emotional grip.

"Otis? What did you mean by 'no one was crazy enough to come with you?'"

He turned away from the window to look at Raisa for half a moment before answering. "It's a frozen wasteland, Miss."

"Please, call me Raisa," she interrupted.

"Raisa. Okay," Otis agreed, though Raisa didn't think it mattered to him one way or the other.

"There's an air force base there," he continued. "That's where we'll be landing. But besides being all ice and blizzard, no one knows exactly what's going on with the fly boys there. Some military bases are all rogue, considering themselves enforcers' of the law. Some are abandoned – people wanting to get back to their families since the earthquake, some are a combination of both – fighting against each other."

"Which one is Thule like?" Raisa wasn't sure which one she was hoping for.

"Don't know," Otis replied. "Crap shoot."

"Ah," was all Raisa said. She was too tired to contemplate the consequences of any of the scenarios. And, being too tired for niceties, she turned and sluffed back to her seat, grabbing a blanket for herself before she plopped down in her chair.

Corli knew she was dreaming in a loop, but it was comforting so she didn't try to break it. She was standing and waiting on a rural sidewalk in front of a church – the feeling was that someone would arrive to get her. The air around her was light and hazy and she heard a buzz in the air; the way the power lines on her street at home used to buzz in the damp morning. A hand appeared a few feet in front of her, reaching out to lift her up into the cloud that hid the rest of the person that the hand belonged to. She reached out, she knew it was Pen, and thought how cute it was that he was probably trying to surprise her. As soon as they touched, she felt the soles of her feet prickle. She looked down and her feet were beginning to disappear. Tiny lights like sparklers appeared to be burning her away, but it didn't hurt, it only made her lighter. She lifted up into the mist with a sigh of relief.

The dream would end, and start all over again.

310

Corli wasn't aware of how many times she was carried away by Pen but she did notice when it changed. Bright blue, magenta, green and sometimes gold began to flash against her eyelids. She tried to will the distraction away so she could continue her curative dream, to no avail. She opened her eyes just a sliver to assess if the light was part of the dream or reality and gasped. If she didn't know better she would have assumed that their plane was flying through fireworks.

"Raisa! Devon!" Corli was on her feet and shaking both their legs at the same time. "You gotta see this!" She dropped to her knees and pressed her nose to the window between them.

They sat up slowly, Devon rubbed his eyes and Raisa yawned but both of them straightened in their seats when they saw the colors swirling around them as the light spilled in through the windows of the plane. "Whoa…" they said in unison as they moved to peer out their windows on either side of Corli.

"It's like someone has a giant brush," Raisa said with awe as she stared out the little window, clutching the edges of it. "And we're watching them paint the sky. It's so unbelievably beautiful… I feel like there has to be music in it. I wish we could hear. Rachmaninoff, I think."

"This means we're close," Devon spoke, sounding almost reverent. They watched as distinct waves of separated light bloomed into vibrant colors chasing each other across the darkening sky. As one would roll away, another would spike into existence to replace it. It moved fluidly, like water, but with no weight to it, their plane slicing through the edges of the color and light as if it didn't exist. "The Aurora Borealis originates from the atmosphere above the geomagnetic poles. I've seen pictures… but nothing even close to this. I would bet there are scientists going crazy right now, wondering why it's so much bigger and brighter."

None of them had to say out loud what was clearly so obvious, and each knew they were all thinking it.

The time was close.

"Can one of y'all come up here for a minute?" Otis called from the cockpit.

Devon pulled his gaze from the window and walked to the front of the plane. "What do you need, Otis?"

"Sit down here." Otis indicated the co-pilot position. Before Devon's back side hit the seat, Otis was standing and leaving the cab.

"Hey!" Devon exclaimed as he grabbed the control column and looked wide eyed at the glass in front of him. "What are you doing?! I can't fly a plane!"

"Gotta take a wiz... and find the landing strip," Otis called back over his shoulder as the lavatory door shut. "And don't worry, it practically flies itself," he yelled so that his voice carried through the shut door.

Devon knew enough to know that he shouldn't make any sudden moves or touch anything other than the controls in his hands. He could feel the tug of resistance and held the yoke even. As the initial thrill of what he was doing subsided, he looked down at the switches, buttons and gauges on the dash. He also knew enough to know that something was wrong. The trim, speed, direction, all of the gauges that indicated where and how they sat in the sky were clearly wrong and changing often. The fuel gauge though, held steady, at near empty.

Otis emerged from the tiny toilet hoisting his pants and tucking in his shirt. He walked back to the cabin where Corli and Raisa sat still watching the light show in fascination.

Raisa caught sight of him looking toward the ground through a window and startled. "Otis! What are you doing?! Who's flying the plane?!" Corli turned and gaped at him as well.

"I'm lookin' for the base. Instruments are all kooky and there's no one on the horn." He moved to the other side of the plane and looked out again. "Devon took over for me." At this he turned and grinned at the two girls. "Scared?" Raisa and Corli only stared blankly back at him, trying to decide if they should be.

"There she is." Otis stood and clapped his hands once before heading back to the cockpit.

"Don't ever do that again," Devon announced as Otis took his seat.

"Don't see as there'll be a need," Otis replied with the slightest grin as he adjusted and turned the plane. He tipped the nose down toward the blackness below them.

"I don't see any runway lights. How do you know where to land?" Devon asked while straining his eyes into the black glass in front of them. They seemed to be pointed away from the northern lights now.

"Best guess," Otis replied nonchalantly.

As the plane dipped lower and lower Devon thought he could see one or two lights on the ground, but they looked like lights from random buildings. Nothing substantial enough to indicate they were near a runway. Visions of the plane smacking into a tree or a building or the side of a hill and breaking to bits filled his mind.

Otis began to whistle 'Pop Goes the Weasel'.

Devon looked at him, stunned. *Is he crazy? Is this what 'Otis under stress' looks like?* "Ay, Dios mìo," Devon whispered as his knuckles turned white from their grip on the armrests of his seat. "You guys get your seatbelts on, now!" he

313

yelled back to the girls. He relaxed only a little when he heard two clicks.

Otis continued his whistling, now it was 'Rock-a-by-Baby', as Devon continued to strain his eyes, looking for their strip of asphalt. Everything was pitch black or the eerie glowing white of snow. He couldn't tell how far off the ground they were. Otis flipped a few switches and started into 'The Itsy Bitsy Spider'. The plane slowed considerably.

Devon knew Otis was landing the plane now. And he still saw nothing out of the front of the plane. His hand flew and slapped to the wall at his side and his heels dug into the floor as if he could brace himself for a crash. And then-

Little blue lights sprung up in a wave on either side of them. Ten seconds later, they touched down. Devon was frozen in place, staring at Otis, his mouth still open, as they came to a stop.

"You all right, Son?" Otis asked casually.

22

David sat in a hard folding chair in a little room next to the chapel at Thule Air Force Base. It was early evening and he waited quietly and patiently as he watched Edward having an animated conversation with the air above them. For the last two days since they arrived it had been like this. Three times both days, Edward had asked David to follow him into this tiny room that had only a few chairs, a book case filled with hymnals and bibles and a small television mounted high into the corner, conceivably for close circuiting a service from next door.

"I need help," Edward said as he looked up in the general direction of the blank TV screen. "And please don't say "the Lord helps those who help themselves," Edward worked hard to keep frustration from coloring his voice.

Not exactly a burning bush, David thought as he looked up at the television and continued his speculation as to whom, exactly, Edward was talking to. He had not yet heard a response to anything Edward had said. Yet the "conversation" continued.

"I *know* the time is short," Edward said, exasperated. He covered his eyes with a hand and rubbed them, then gestured at the air again. "I have the plane... big enough for everyone."

Tentative silence followed.

"No. No one here that can fly it," he exhaled as if he were saying this for the tenth time. "The base is all but deserted. It seems that it was more of a tactical missile warning place for the government. We're lucky the plane is here."

David felt an electric buzz in the air. The hair stood on his arms.

"My apologies, forgive me, of course it is not luck," Edward said humbly. He bowed his head, the purple mist settling down around his ears.

Several couples ambled around the room. The airman's club was lit with old florescent lights behind plastic, but it had pool tables, darts and a bar. Though there was no one there to serve anything. A menu board with push-in letters for drinks and snacks hung unlit on the wall, some of the letters having been rearranged to spell out several words that clearly had nothing to do with food. For the last two days, the Lasteires and rallys spent their time here, at the library, the mess hall, or occasionally at the small chapel on base. Invariably, they spotted Edward walking purposefully from one place to another, bundled in his parka and David on his heels, and tense for a moment - wondering if the time had come - only to breathe a sigh of relief when he passed them by without a word.

Devon, with Raisa wedged at his side, sat with Corli, Scott, Julia and Morgan in low couches at one end of the room, with little to say. Corli was twisting white paper napkins into roses, one after the other. The room was littered with them.

"I wonder how many nationalities are represented here?" Julia pierced the silence of their little group.

They all lifted their eyes to peruse the room.

"It could be most all of them," Raisa remarked. "All except Australia, right? That's pretty much the only country that doesn't have a piece of it in the northern hemisphere."

"I wonder if the group near the South Pole looks similar to ours," Julia questioned, quieter than she had before.

316

Devon looked around the room with the others at the young adults of varying features and color. For several minutes he regarded their different skin tones and eye shapes, statures and builds. Then he switched to their various mannerisms and in this he saw only similarities. He was struck with how many couples were sitting in this one room. And, regardless of where they came from, each had their complement of rings and rays, just like he and Raisa, that all looked the same. He looked through the energy and saw their fondness for each other. One boy whispered into his girlfriend, or wife's ear – a smile on his face that would make you think there was not a care in the world to be had. Another couple sat, simply holding hands, but their contentment to be with each other was clear on their faces. Still another, leaning against a wall in a slightly darker corner, would make anyone blush if they watched for too long... they never stopped kissing.

He looked at Corli, then. She was finishing another rose that she dropped into a pile of them. He felt his heart contract as he thought of Pen, his best friend, who was gone. He missed him. This had happened for the last day and a half since they arrived – random thoughts of Pen – watching Corli's sorrow and matching it in his mind with his own grief. He breathed a frustrated sigh. *Why am I so aggravated?*

He answered himself.

Because. Pen would not want me to be Dudley. He would want me to do something phenomenally great in his absence.

Devon's gaze moved to Raisa's face in the crook of his arm. He felt like he could ignite a flame where their eyes met. His jaw set so hard that the muscles twitched around his cheek bones.

Raisa had looked around the room at all the other Lasteires when her friends did, but found nothing to hold her attention. Her eyes landed on Devon within seconds. She watched his face

317

and did her best to read everything that passed through his thoughts. She thought she had each notion figured out until his expression, while he watched Corli, changed. She knew the expression where he recognized Corli's pain and then felt his own, but then it morphed into something completely indecipherable. When he looked down at her she felt almost guilty for watching him because of the intensity in his eyes. And what he asked her next seemed completely out of context with how he looked at her...

"Where is the backpack? The one with the money," he whispered.

"In our room," Raisa answered, but it sounded like a question. *What could he need with that?*

"Corli, can I talk to you for a sec?" Devon gently moved Raisa away from his side on the couch and stood.

Raisa frowned.

Corli hopped up and accompanied Devon to the exit. Raisa saw Devon bent over and speaking low to Corli before he quickly left the building.

"What was that about?" Raisa asked suspiciously. She was curiously eyeing Corli as she rejoined their group.

"Nothing." Corli's answer was a little too high pitched for Raisa to believe her. "Hey, Raisa, why don't you and Scott shoot a game of pool?"

"Um... okay?" Raisa stood up and looked at Scott, wondering if he was as perplexed as she was. He shrugged, not appearing to have an ulterior motive (like Corli), and went for the rack of pool cues.

Raisa didn't notice the people filtering out of the club. And she didn't notice Corli gathering up the paper flowers from the room and leaving her. She was having fun doing something normal

318

instead of thinking about death and purpose and responsibility. She was laughing with Scott at her beginner's luck; she was up four games to two. As she racked for the next game, Corli appeared and tapped her on the shoulder.

"Thanks Scott," Corli smiled at him. He shrugged again.

"You." Corli pointed at Raisa's nose. "Come with me." She grabbed Raisa's hand, pulled her to the foyer and donned her with her thick and furry jacket.

"Where are you taking me?" Raisa asked easily. She felt lighter than the last time she had felt the bitter cold on her face and gladly followed Corli up the little street, her newly borrowed snow boots crunching on the frozen gravel.

"We're taking you to your room to get dolled up. You have a date," Corli said with a happy inflection.

"How lovely," Raisa responded lightly with a skip. She loved surprises, and the thought that Devon had orchestrated one made her warm inside.

They sluffed off their jackets as they entered Raisa and Devon's room. Raisa looked at the bed and blushed. It was obvious that one side was being slept on over the top of the covers. *Why didn't I make the bed this morning*, she was thinking. Then her eyes landed on a blouse that had been laid out on the un-rumpled side of the bed.

"Where did this come from?" Raisa wondered out loud. She fingered the delicate blue sleeve of it. "It's really pretty," she whispered as she looked over the draping cut and the embellishment of white satin trim that edged the V neck.

"It's a loaner, from the Danish girl, Larisa," Corli pretended to be busy fixing her own make-up - though she wasn't wearing any - not wanting to answer questions.

319

Raisa held the blouse and turned to look at Corli. She knew that Corli could see her in the mirror but was intentionally not turning around. "What's going on here?" Raisa's eyes squinted.

Corli deflected. "Just put it on, girl! We're in a hurry."

Corli led Raisa by the sleeve of her jacket towards the small collection of buildings that she knew were the theater, library and chapel.

"Did they get a new movie?" Raisa deduced as she breathed out white fog in the frozen air.

"Nope."

"Well, I'm not in the mood to read-"

"Stop trying to guess! You'll ruin it," Corli ordered and tugged a little harder to pick up there pace. They passed by the theater. Just as Raisa was about to protest about a wild goose chase, Corli turned to the door of the chapel building, and stopped to face her best friend, since forever.

"What are we doing-" Raisa's eyes popped open wide and her mouth felt dry. Her mind jumped quickly through the various surprise scenarios she had considered, and then formed a new one based on where they were standing now. Shock kept her from believing she could be right.

"I'm so happy for you Raisy," Corli whispered. "I love you!" She threw her arms around Raisa and squeezed her tight, then took her hand and pulled her into the foyer of the church.

As soon as Raisa stepped inside, a thrum of energy thrilled through her body from her core to her fingertips and toes. Her eyes still wide and unable to speak, she absently let Corli pull her coat off, smooth her frizzing hair and warm her cheeks with her hands. Her stomach started to jitter.

"Is this what I think it is, Corli?" Raisa could barely breathe.

For the first time, she heard music coming from the small double doors just ahead of them. "To Make You Feel My Love," she whispered.

"Stay right here," Corli raised one finger then disappeared behind the double doors. Seconds later she was back, and handed Raisa a bouquet of two dozen white paper roses.

When the rain is blowing in your face
And the whole world is on your case
I could offer you a warm embrace
To make you feel my love

When the evening shadows and the stars appear
And there is no one to dry your tears
I could hold you for a million years
To make you feel my love

I know you haven't made your mind up yet
But I would never do you wrong
I've known it from the moment that we met
There's no doubt in my mind where you belong

I'd go hungry, I'd go black and blue
I'd go crawling down the avenue
There ain't nothing that I wouldn't do
To make you feel my love

The storms are raging on rolling sea
And on the highway of regret
The winds of change are blowing wild and free
You ain't seen nothing like me yet

Raisa stood at the back of the tiny chapel hanging on Corli's arm while the song played from a small karaoke machine next to the podium in front. She looked around at the smiling, packed in

321

faces of what she thought must include all of the northern Lasteires. The energy in the place was completely tangible and a rope of light continually materialized and misted away connecting the couples to each other in varying patterns. There was a solid white, burning arc though that did not dissipate; the one she saw connecting her to Devon down the short aisle. She looked at him and flushed. He was glowing; his coppery rings were so vibrant and strong that they enveloped the whole front row of seats. His eyes were expectant, his smile a little crooked. He was glorious.

She wasn't sure how long she stood there, taking in the scene and staring at Devon. She wanted to go to him, to sprint up the aisle. But she couldn't help but think of how she wished it could be a little different.

Then, she felt a familiar hand on her back. It gave her a little push. *Go Raisa*, she heard in her father's loving voice.

She closed her eyes for a couple of steps so she could see her dad in her mind's eye, and there he was, smiling brightly at her. Her mother was there too, on his arm and beaming. *Now everything is right. Thank you for coming.*

Corli deposited Raisa with Devon, relieved her of her paper bouquet, and took her seat in the front row just as the music ended. The chair next to her was left empty, regardless of how full the little chapel was, a single paper rose on the seat.

Devon took both of Raisa's hands with his and their arc became a circle. Devon lifted her hand to his mouth and kissed it, taking a deep breath in and out while her hand was still there. Raisa felt his breath on her wrist and a warm wave washed over her. He dropped their hands and looked into Raisa's fierce blue eyes, pulling her closer to him. Only a sweet electric buzz could be heard in the room, until he spoke.

"Raisa," Devon's voice was clear and soft as velvet. "Will you marry me... right now?"

Raisa couldn't feel herself inside her body. Was she really hearing Devon ask this? Whether she was dreaming or awake, she knew the answer.

"Yes... *yes*. Absolutely I will," she said eagerly.

He wrapped his arms around her and buried his face at her neck.

"Thank you," he whispered.

Raisa's body felt fluid and light. She was sure that she would lift from the ground if Devon wasn't holding onto her.

The priest, who Raisa had not noticed until now, cleared his throat. Several happy chuckles answered from their audience.

David sat as before but with his head bowed. Edward had been praying off and on for the last couple of hours, sweat running from his forehead despite the chill temperature of the room. When Edward stopped mid-sentence, David looked up... and heard a voice.

Let me ask you Edward Thomas Brayden, do you have faith?

"Yes," Edward answered steadfastly. He straightened up where he stood and let his arms fall to his side with his palms forward. He knew this was it. In whatever form it might come, the answer, the means to complete their journey, was going to be revealed to him now.

The little TV buzzed to life and snapped to a tight shot of the front of the chapel next door.

Neither Devon nor Raisa heard much of what the priest said short of the question they were waiting for that they each wanted to answer.

"I do. I have never felt as sure of anything in my life," Devon said intensely. As the words left his mouth he felt his heart fill completely.

"I do." Raisa felt her face warm and her eyes fill. There was a sensation that they were physically mixing together, like pouring a glass of milk and maple syrup back and forth into each other till the inside of each glass looked the same.

"Oh... wait," Devon blurted. He dropped Raisa's hand on top of the other so that he didn't have to let go of either, while he dug into the front pocket of his jeans.

For half a moment Raisa felt panicked. "Wait for what?" she asked incredulously.

"I can't forget these!" He pulled his fist from his pocket and turned it over, opening his hand to reveal two gold rings.

"My parent's rings... I'd almost forgotten..." Raisa whispered.

Devon slid her mother's delicate garnet and diamond ring onto her finger, making it truly hers now. And handed the simple brushed gold band to Raisa. She pushed it onto his finger and thought about her father in her dream, of the cantaloupe colored courtyard, where he told her that Devon was meant for her.

"You may kiss your bride," the priest said.

Devon's mouth touched softly to Raisa's. He cupped her face in his hands.

Raisa reached up and curled her fingers into the hair at the back of his neck, pulling him more forcefully into the kiss. She felt him smile on her mouth. Then something that she never thought she would ever do happened - she giggled - her joy bubbling to the surface.

The audience had just started to clap and chatter when the double doors of the chapel swung open. Edward walked in and stopped at the back with David landing just behind him.

"So sorry to interrupt," he said hurriedly. Edward's thoughts were so preoccupied that he was not completely clear as to what he was interrupting - but there was no time. "We're leaving early in the morning... 6am I think." He seemed to be calculating in his head. "Devon," he held his hand up to acknowledge to whom he was speaking.

Devon instantly felt horrible. Of course he should have sent someone to find Edward and make sure he was there when he married Raisa. Just as he opened his mouth to apologize, Edward finished his sentence.

"You'll be flying the plane," he announced.

The joyful atmosphere created by the wedding was abruptly broken. All but their small group had left the chapel after Edward exited, as quickly as he had entered.

"Everything changes tomorrow," Devon said solemnly as he sat, Raisa on his lap, with his friends in the scattered folding chairs of the chapel. "We will all leave this life behind... and start a new one."

"I'm ready," Corli said evenly. She straightened in her seat and set her jaw. "There are only a couple of options for how my day will end tomorrow." *And either way, I'll see Pen soon.*

"Me too," Morgan agreed. She was sitting next to Corli and grabbed her hand. They looked at each other. "We share the same fate, my dear." And they were bonded in the knowledge of it.

Raisa, though she tried, couldn't keep her thoughts from spilling out. "This is all so confusing and sad and torturous! And astonishing at the same time.... We've seen our friends and

325

family die," she looked lovingly at Corli and Morgan, tears instantly springing to her eyes, "And we've seen and heard their spirits, our angels now." She dislodged a hand from around Devon's neck to wipe her eyes before she continued, "We're intimately involved in the apocalypse...... and I'm *married*." They all laughed, and cried, together.

Julia squeezed Scott's hand and they shared a loving glance. Then she looked at her friend, Morgan. She knew her well from the time they spent together in college. "Morgan," she said, "I want to thank you for everything. I can't even begin..." her voice failed her momentarily. "Well, thank you." The corner of her mouth curled up. "Especially for that time you stormed in and saved me from the drunken debate team."

"Girl, you know I've always had your back." Morgan sounded tough as usual, but her voice broke at the end.

"Hey," Scott cut in, to everyone's surprise. "I want to hear favorite memories... something magical that happened in your life, from all of you... I'm going to paint them all."

They spent the next hour or so recounting special moments in each of their lives; Devon counting stars in the sky with his mother as a young boy, Corli watching her father cook massive Italian meals, Julia receiving honors in school that meant all of her hard work paid off, Raisa discovering how music moved her to tears at four years of age when she heard "Somewhere Over the Rainbow" for the first time, and Scott's own, when he was given his first art set for Christmas.

As the conversation died down, they all knew that as much as they wanted to, they couldn't remain in this reminiscent bubble forever.

Morgan was the first to give in. She stood and reached for Corli's hand. "Come on, You. We need to get our sleep." She led Corli out, waiving to Julia and Scott, and winked at Devon and Raisa as she left.

Julia and Scott were next. "Congratulations, Guys," Julia said as she stood and pulled Scott up with her.

"Yes," Scott added, "enjoy your night." He realized a second later how that might have sounded, considering their newlywed status, and felt his face turn red as he and Julia left.

Raisa suddenly felt short of breath and butterflies took flight in her stomach. She looked at Devon with round eyes. "I'm married," she whispered.

"So am I," Devon teased as the smile spread across his face. "Come on, Rai." He lifted her off his lap and set her down with his arms around her. "We should get back to our room. The things I want to do right now should definitely not take place in a church."

Raisa giggled. *There it is again! What's happening to me?* "Devon, I think I'm a little nervous," her voice jittered as they walked out of the chapel. Raisa pushed herself tightly into Devon's side.

He pulled her free hand up and kissed it. "You're talking about tonight aren't you, not tomorrow." He shook his head and grinned as they walked.

As their feet crunched along in unison, a ribbon of magenta ripped across the night sky in front of them. They watched the waves of light in the distance; the only sound was their breathing, till they arrived at their room.

The moment they got through the door all nerves seem to disappear. They were instantly kissing. Devon pulled so forcefully on Raisa's jacket to get it off of her that she thought it would have ripped had it not been so thick. Raisa's reaction was to push Devon onto the bed.

The room was beginning to resemble a corner yard sale when a loud knock came at their door.

Raisa fell to the bed next to Devon. "Really?" she groaned, breathing heavily.

They hauled themselves off the bed and hastily pulled the minimum amount of clothing back over their bodies. Devon pulled the door open.

Edward, again, without any apparent knowledge of what he was interrupting, stepped inside and shut the door behind him. He held out a large five-inch thick paperback book to Devon.

"It's a manual for the C-130j Hercules. I thought you might want to study it." He unloaded it into Devon's arms. As soon as he made his delivery he looked around, his eyes landing on Raisa, who sat quietly with a bright red face. Edward suddenly realized what he had walked into. His own face flared in embarrassment. "Oh... yes... well, congratulations to you both," he mumbled awkwardly as he quickly showed himself out.

Devon turned to look at Raisa, the massive instruction manual still in his hands. He looked down at the manual and back up at Raisa again. "Faith, right?" he said resolutely. He looked down and flipped a few pages. Then dropped it to the floor with a thud. "I'd like to spend this night with you instead of this book if that's alright with you."

"Yes... yes, please... with me." Raisa said breathlessly. Her heart sped again.

Devon moved to the foot of the bed and bent to his knees. He held Raisa's face in his hands. "*Te amo*, Raisa," he whispered.

The yard sale becoming complete, they melted together; fire and light, man and woman, milk and syrup.

23

It's time.

Both Devon and Raisa opened their eyes when they heard Vince's voice.

Raisa started to breath heavy and looked around their room.

"Hey, *hey*," Devon propped himself up on one elbow and brought his hand to her face. "It's going to be alright. I promise."

"No... I mean, I know it is... It's not that," Raisa whispered in a panicked voice.

"What is it?" Devon asked perplexed.

Raisa pulled the covers up to her eyes and answered from behind them. "Do you think my parents saw? I mean, what we did last night?"

Devon took a second to realize what Raisa was referring to. Then burst out laughing. He couldn't stop himself.

Her panicked expression gave way to a frown as she sat straight up. "It's not funny! It's embarrassing," she grumbled. She got up and headed for the bathroom, dragging all of the covers with her.

"Hey!" The chill air stopped Devon's laughter. "I'm sorry, Rai," he called after her with one last chuckle.

At this time of year, five-thirty was showing a little of dawn's light as all of the Lasteires and rallys emerged from their buildings; bags, suitcases and backpacks in tow.

"I wonder if any of this stuff makes it through." Corli mused curiously as she zipped her backpack. Morgan hoisted a bag over her shoulder and began walking with Corli but had no answer for her friend. It was an abstract question after all.

They merged into the groups of the others winding their way towards the massive runway that ran along side of the small military town. First Scott and Julia, then Devon and Raisa fell into step with them when they passed their building. No one said hello or good morning, but the looks that passed between them as their group gathered held sentiments. *I love you. I'll miss you. I'm frightened for you. I'm strong enough to do this. I'd die for you. I'm ready.*

The line of people slowed as they reached the clearing. The plane was on the frozen tarmac, the back of it open to form the ramp showing all the jump seats and supplies that were already loaded. David and Renee were handing out warm scrambled egg sandwiches to everyone before they climbed into the belly of the enormous aircraft. The steam rose from each person's hands like a magic potion.

Devon pulled Raisa to the side before she could step on the metal rise. They walked to the side of the plane where they could see the swirling lights in front of them. Raisa registered for the first time that she would probably be separated from Devon for the flight.

"Are you nervous?" Raisa peered up at Devon from inside his circling arms and copper circles.

"About the plane? No." Devon's voice was perfectly even. "I figure if Edward had some kind of vision then it's a done deal." He pulled Raisa in tighter to him. "It's just really strange that all of this crazy stuff is going to happen so soon… today. I wanted to make sure you are okay." He kissed Raisa's forehead.

330

"You better be careful," Raisa teased. Her lips cracked half a smile. "That sounds dangerously close to faith." She stretched up and kissed him on the cheek. "And I'm okay. I just wish I knew what's going to happen to all the rallys, to Corli."

They stood for a few moments more, locked in each other's arms, till they heard the last of the line boarding the plane. They walked in silence back to the ramp and up the incline. Devon held Raisa's hand while she sat down in a mesh jump seat, then pulled her fingers to his lips. He turned away and made his way to the front of the plane. Raisa watched as their electrical cable stretched across the space without diminishing. When he disappeared through a door, the energy just went through the wall. She could feel his heartbeat. She knew that nothing could break the connection they had now.

Devon successfully powered up the plane while Edward sat in the co-pilot seat feverishly pouring over another instruction manual.

"Ed, you can put that thing away," Devon commented cooly. "I'm going to need *you* not the book." Devon flipped a couple more switches, checked several blinking lights and engaged the throttle. They started to roll and Edwards face shot up in response. "Isn't that right, Vince," Devon said.

Edward watched, listened and took commands as Devon himself seemed to be taking direction while he taxied the aircraft to the southern end of the runway and turned it around. The sound was deafening as Devon brought the turboprop engines up to full power and started up the runway.

"Man, this thing is heavy!" Devon exclaimed. "It doesn't feel anything like a commercial jet. Do we have enough asphalt?"

Edward looked wide-eyed at Devon, desperately hoping that the question was not being directed at him. When he could see that Devon already received the answer he relaxed a little. As they sped by the buildings near the runway, Edward looked at them for a moment, wondering if this was the last time he would see civilization. *Of course it's the last time… you knew that.* He determined it was time to look forward, to the northern lights, to his destiny, and decided he would turn his face away, his time here was done. But just before he did it, he saw a row of green-lit eyes, at least a dozen or more, standing next to an open hanger. His hands grabbed violently onto the arms of his seat and he gasped.

"What?!" Devon responded to Edward's intake of breath without taking his eyes away from the runway. "What's wrong?! It's now or never, Ed!" he yelled over the noise.

"No, keep going," Edward yelled. "Nothing's wrong… keep going."

With what seemed like only feet to spare, the plane lifted off the ground and almost immediately they were over the black and white icy sea. As they climbed higher and looked at the light display in front of them, they could see that the ribbons of light were making a shape. The northern lights were nearly unrecognizable as such. They filled the sky with each color of the rainbow. Every color in the spectrum of light was separated into misty ribbons and spinning in front of them. It had created the illusion of a funnel.

"Like God stirring the Aurora Borealis with a stick," Edward murmured.

And though it didn't touch the earth, yet, it had a very distinct and constant point at its base.

"Guess we know where we're going," Devon said softly. He was awestruck by the sight.

"Yeah," Edward replied as he stared through the window in front of them.

Raisa sat in the noisy expanse of the cargo plane with the thirty-five other Lasteires and rallys, all buckled into their mesh chairs. She was a little surprised that she wasn't anxious about Devon flying the plane. She knew somehow that her father, who had an almost endless knowledge of anything with an engine and wings, was helping her husband. *My husband... that is going to take some getting used to.* It was a happy thought. But then her forehead creased and her heart seemed to double its weight in her chest. *That will be the very least of changes after today.* She let her mind glide over all of the pictures in her head of her family, of her home, and of her friends. As she willed her eyes to keep from spilling over, she felt a familiar gaze on her. She looked up to see Corli sitting across from her and looking back at her with the same sadness on her face.

Morgan put her hand on Corli's; she had been watching the both of them. Then she nodded her head toward the rest of the occupants of their cargo hold so that Corli and Raisa would look around at the rest of them, and it seemed that everyone else on the plane was having the same experience. Sadness and despair were everywhere in their tin-can airplane. Raisa wished that they at least had windows to look out of, it might have made the situation feel less dismal. *This won't do,* she thought. *We need to be strong if we're going to do this right.* She looked back at Corli and forced herself to smile, a smile that spoke of resolve. Corli straightened in her seat and returned the sentiment. Raisa looked over at Morgan's hand on Corli's. *We are in this together, all of us.* She reached over to grab the hand of the girl sitting next to her (Kara, was it?). Kara startled for a moment but then looked at Raisa, and Corli and Morgan. She took the hand of Brian next to her. In seconds each had joined hands with the person on either side of them. A strong current thrummed through the cabin.

"That went quick. About an hour and a half, right?" Devon said with surprise. He and Edward were staring out at the base of the funnel they had aimed for. It wasn't a point anymore now that they were so close. It looked more like the eye of a tornado but without the destructive wind and much more colorful and dreamlike. Devon had already slowed the plane and dropped considerably in altitude.

"We should be able to see a piece of land. I'm assuming it will be directly under the lights," Edward said as he strained his eyes at the ground in front of them.

"Land? Is there even any land up here? I thought it was all ice."

"What do you think the earthquake was for?" Edward replied absently. "There!" Edward almost broke his finger jamming it into the glass as he pointed at the ground.

There it was; perfectly round and flat and about ten yards in diameter. It looked like a giant chocolate cookie swimming in a sea of milk.

"Wow… well… guess we better put this thing down. *Oh, I'm freeeeee, free fallin', yeah I'm freeeeee, free fallin'…* "

"*What* are you doing? Have you lost your mind?" Edward asked incredulously.

"Worked for Otis. *Ohh I'm freeeeee…*"

The ramp of the plane opened and Raisa, being the last one on, was the first to walk down to the ice. She saw the circle of earth not forty yards from where they landed and the swirling light above it.

334

"Well done, Devon," she said to herself. She saw that the "platform" that had presumably been created by the earthquake was obviously volcanic. It was very dark, raised up only a few inches above the ice, and from this distance, it looked like a giant sponge floating in white foam. When she looked to the sky to regard the misty swirling light, it almost took her breath away. They were so close to the center of it here, where it came within twenty feet or so from touching the circle of rock, it created a ceiling of ever flowing colors; green, blue, magenta, gold, purple, silver. She wanted to reach up and see if she could interrupt the stream of it, or if it would flow right through her.

As each Lasteire couple walked down the ramp and passed her, their eyes landed on the round of dry, black rock and they walked to it without a thought. Electricity seemed to split the air with a snap and connect the colored ribbons, like pulling taffy down from the sky at the edge of the funnel, tipped with a bright flare, to the first Lasteire that stepped onto it. And then again to the others that joined him. Raisa was reminded of a tesla ball. The energy would connect, then disconnect and move to someone else. It was a disorienting feeling, Raisa could tell, because some would look at their hands and arms and some teetered a little, regardless of the flat ground, before getting their bearings. The rallys followed but stayed on the ice outside the circle; it seemed like the right thing to do.

"Hey, Rai." Devon slipped his arm around Raisa. She had been waiting for him at the bottom of the ramp.

"They look confused. And look at the light... it's so sporadic," she said, concern coloring her voice.

"That's because it's not complete. We're not there." Devon grabbed her hand and kissed it, then looked back to the circle. "Are you ready for this?"

A crack of lightening shot through the middle of the funnel that made every one jump.

Edward stood near the edge of the circle and held up his hands. "Alright everyone, this is it. Please make a circle on the land here," he called loudly. He turned to see that Devon and Raisa were making their way to the group assembled in front of him and then looked beyond them, to see if they were still alone in this frozen wilderness. As the Lasteires spread out around the edge of the land he returned his attention to them and continued, "I want you folks to know that…" he choked on his words. *That I'm sorry. That I'm afraid for you, that you will be all alone in this world when I'm gone…* "That it has been my distinct honor to help you get here. I want you to know that I think you are all very brave and amazing young people."

Raisa and Devon stepped onto the land. The air snapped loudly and a ring as thick as a bridge cable, formed connecting all of the Lasteires, but it didn't stay solid, it still randomly broke and reconnected with deafening pops of energy.

"May God bless you, guide you and keep you," Edward finished.

Devon looked around at their erratic electrical circle. The light from the girls was extraordinary, shooting out like fireworks and floodlights. But it was chaos; there was no direction to it. His coppery rings, that he could see very clearly now, were strong and steady, close to the ground and pulsing. He could feel himself being pulled down as if the gravity in this spot was double that of anywhere else on earth.

"I feel so weightless, like I could jump a hundred feet," Raisa said nervously as she grabbed on to Devon's hand. Julia and Scott were right next to them and she had the same compulsion at the same moment to hold onto Scott.

"Something's not right. Come closer, here." Devon pulled Raisa to stand in front of him, her back to his chest. It made a sound, when they came together, like a thud of something breaking the sound barrier. "Everyone," Devon called back over his shoulder, "like this, hold on to them." The sky cracked with lightening again and wind started to circle around them.

Morgan came to stand in front of Julia and Scott, her feet spread apart on the ice to ready herself for whatever was coming... she wasn't sure what that might be but she would be ready just the same. Corli stood in front of Raisa.

"I love you!" Corli yelled over the great sound that was building.

Raisa was struggling to stay attached to Devon; she couldn't move away for fear of the feeling she would float away, but she wanted more than anything to run to Corli and wrap her arms around her. She cried out, unsure if the pain she felt was her heart breaking while she looked at her best friend or the tork she was feeling on her body.

Edward moved to Corli's side, looking at Devon for some kind of reassurance that everything was going as it should. Devon was fighting so hard to hold on to Raisa that he couldn't see anything beyond her.

"Something's not right!" Raisa called back to Devon. She began to turn in his arms and as she did, she felt like her body was a spring lock dropping into place. "Ah!" she cried with relief as she finished her turn to face him.

Julia had just enough presence to see what Raisa had done and followed her lead. One by one each girl turned toward her partner. At the moment the last girl turned, the light shot out hard and fast from Raisa and all the other girls, their heads thrown back by the force of it. They all looked like they had been knocked unconscious.

337

"I have you! I won't let go!" Devon shouted. He caught Raisa as she was bent backwards, her torso being thrust away from him. He gathered her up at her waist and held on tight to keep her from lifting off the ground. The light poured from her neck and chest. At first he was terrified at how violently the energy was radiating from her. But then he felt her breath as if it where his own. He could sense her, he was joined with her mind, and he knew that she was okay. He watched the rays and spirals from their circle burn endlessly up and out into the atmosphere, now with perfect synchronization blooming like petals from a stigma. The misty ribbons of the northern lights began to give way, spilling downward to feed the strength of the energy coming from the Lasteires.

As Devon's eyes squinted from the brightness he tried to look into the light. His mind was drawn into it. "Scott," he yelled to his side, "can you see that?"

"Faces... in the light," he called back at Devon.

"It's them, the Southern Lasteires!" Devon suddenly became aware of his connection to everyone, all of them, all forty-seven people, and theirs to him. They all felt and understood each other, their power, their essence, their fear and their determined spirits, passing through the energy and into and through each of them.

The remnants of the Northern Lights began to swirl faster, pulling to the center of the circle, funneling down and ripping light from the sky as it emptied into the Lasteires.

Edward lifted his hands. His lips moved but nothing could be heard over the roaring wind.

Corli's tears were torn from her face before they could make her cheeks wet and her hair was plastered horizontally across her face. She stood there watching Raisa, bent backwards and shining like a star in the sky. "I'm ready... please, I'm ready,

Pen." She knew that no one on the ground could hear her, but she knew that Pen could. She suddenly felt her toes start to tingle. She closed her eyes and smiled.

Raisa had an overwhelming sense of peace despite the force that was running through her. She moved her consciousness from person to person, feeling the personality of each of the Lasteires she was connected to. She saw their faces as happy and content, not in their current condition. A familiar vision came to her. She pictured herself wearing a white dress and standing near a white bistro table decorated with the vase and pink daisy, in an expanse of white space, greeting each of her new friends with warm smiles. She thought it was odd that she would have this dream now, but everyone was there with her, and she was learning about them; their lives, their fears, their loves.

But a feeling of foreboding suddenly attached itself to her, as it had every other time in her dream. The darkness unrolled like thick smoky batting and it was full of dread. There was no air to breath into her lungs. The lack of sound was maddening. It rolled over her and the table and the flower and all of her friends in silence and simply replaced them.

Devon! She wanted to call out to him but she couldn't speak. She knew this feeling… it was evil.

As quickly as the wind had whipped up, it stopped dead. The funnel of light began to slow and fade. The sky began to take on a sickly green hue the color of murk and poison. The rays of the Lasteire girls became thin and weak. The boys were losing their energy and were drawn to the ground, the powerful feeling of depravity bending on them.

"No, No, NO!" Edward's hands were still above his head and now his eyes flew to the sky.

339

A deep guttural groan filled the air like thunder. Then it turned to a sinister laugh. The darkness left behind by the retreat of the mist and color became thick and heavy. Breathing was like inhaling damp burning soot.

Not a single one can die... Edward turned away from the circle to face his fear.

No one had seen the second plane land. Or the two dozen bruels spilling out of it. Wild and rabid green-lit faces were suddenly charging the ring of Lasteires.

"Look out!" Edward yelled to the rallys as he drew his sword and sliced down the first assailant.

The rallys who were standing in front of their friends turned now to protect them. The Lasteires were immobile, stuck to the spot where they stood. What they had started on that circle of land could not be stopped or broken as long as they were all still alive. Terror colored the boy's faces as they watched their friends being attacked. The girls, in their semi-conscious state, had visions of fighting and blood. Blades flashed and bullets flew as a battle ensued.

Edward fought in front of Devon and Raisa. His greatest fear was that this onslaught was fueled by not just evil itself, but by someone that would come for the two of them, and stop at nothing to kill them.

Morgan and Corli fell into their now familiar fighting partnership in front of Julia and Scott.

"Not now," Morgan declared as she brandished her trusty hunting knife.

"Not ever," Corli answered, her shoulders set and her switchblade swirling in her hand.

The bruels were still easily outwitted by the rallys, but they had an unnatural strength with them here at the end of their purpose. They attacked viciously and for the first time, without regard for their own lives. The entire ring of rallys was being tested to their absolute limits, losing blood, and life in the process.

At the back side of the circle, David and Renee turned to defend Kara and Brian. A particularly large bruel was headed toward them holding a hatchet in his hand and sneering grotesquely. Renee had a pistol and fired at him, hitting him in the arm, but it seemed to have no effect. He barreled toward her making her his first target for the insult of the shot she fired at him.

"Hah!" He backhanded her and sent her flying into David, knocking them both to the side. The bruel stepped onto the circle of rock and raised his weapon to hurl at Kara's head. Brian cried out and tried to pull Kara away but couldn't move her. He stared at the bruel in horror.

The hatchet came down but it did not entirely hit its mark because David had recovered just quickly enough to thrust a long knife into the bruels side. Kara bled from a shallow slice off her shoulder. The bruel turned and swung again, burying the ax into David's back, before he fell to the ground.

Renee pulled air into her broken chest and ran to David's side, but she was too late. She stood. "Die, bastard," she murmured. And fired a shot into the bruel's head where he lay.

Tears streamed down Devon's face as he watched the rallys, his friends, defending the circle and many of them dying doing it. He had been able to yell a warning to Morgan once that saved her, but Scott had been injured in the leg before she could take out the bruel.

"Edward!" Devon sounded like he was calling out through water. "They're so strong! What can we do?"

Edward turned his head for a moment and replied with a yell, "We will prevail, Son! Right is on our side!"

Before Edward could turn his eyes back around to face forward, he heard a loud bang and felt a warm thud in his chest. *Oh no*, he thought, *not yet…*

Devon watched as blood began to pour from Edwards back. His crown of mist began to fade. Edward Brayden fell.

And in his place, stood Nosh.

Half of his face and his arms were a twist of red and oozing flesh, charred black skin was where his hair had been on his head. But he was smiling, a brilliant and invigorated smile. He dropped the gun he had used on Edward to the ground. He drew a long black blade from a sheath at his side as he stepped over Edward's body.

He looked on at his little army and the damage they were doing. He was pleased.

But he said, "You imps! Kill the people on the land!" He moved a step closer to Raisa, her golden curls hanging almost to the ground. "Doesn't matter," he said to no one in particular and at the same time toward Devon, "they probably won't be able to kill any of you. But I will. *Nothing* and *no one* can stop me now." He laughed out loud and took another step forward, chopping down one of his own evil men that stumbled into his way.

"How will you protect her now?" he yelled at Devon as he eyed Raisa's neck, exposed and vulnerable, raising his blade as he walked.

"NO!!!!!!!"

Morgan and Corli had moved with the battle. They hadn't seen Nosh until they heard Devon cry out. Morgan ran like a

342

shot from a gun and spun into the space between Nosh and Raisa, hitting him hard, and taking a deep gash in her side as she knocked Nosh to the ground. His sword clattered at Raisa's feet. Corli, just behind Morgan, dove for Nosh's weapon, picking it up before he could pull himself up and reach for it. It took one second for fire to light hot in her body… this was it! She stood and whirled around, holding onto the sword tightly, striking out with all of her strength.

The blade was sharp.

Nosh's hideous head hit the ground with a thump.

A sinister roar filled the air and the powerful wickedness that was around them doubled. It bent all rallys that were still alive to the ground, making them helpless.

Corli crawled across the ice. "Morgan…"

"It's okay," she sputtered. "We saved them… and Nosh is…" she coughed.

But there were bruels left, and they weren't stopping. They're aggression increased, rising up even as the Lasteires were bent lower.

Raisa was dying inside.

Mom, Dad… Vincent! Lona! Dear God, help us!

A tremendous crack split the sky with a deafening thrum! Bright yellow light spilled through in waves that looked like horses galloping through the tumbled surf of an ocean that devoured the sickly haze. A reverberating and painful howl from the evil struck the air when a circle of bright white beings appeared, their white robes flowing in the fury of wind they brought. Their arms were outstretched and their eyes like fire as their presence spread, rolling the darkness back. Vincent, Lona and all of the other's that had faithfully guided their Lasteire children and helped them to this point were there, in their glorified form, forcing the darkness away.

A collective sigh escaped from the Lasteires as they were released from the oppressive power. They straightened slowly and warmed in the yellow glow. Their energy reattached to each other. It blossomed out in prismed light, circling the earth, and they felt their connection to the Southern Lasteires again. The Northern Lights were gone now, taking the light of day with it. Only the brilliant light of angles and Lasteires was blazing in the sky.

As Devon easily held onto Raisa now, his own energy seeming to reach down to the roots of the earth, he looked over at Corli where she sat next to Morgan's lifeless body.

But Corli was looking up at the angels. At Pen.

The live bodies of the remaining bruels began to burn and blacken, their shrieks lifting into the air and then cutting off. The dead ones on the ground turned to black ash and swirled away. Where Miguel Castaneda's body and head lay, a black hole opened. It swallowed him and closed again, healing itself with ice.

Music of trumpets and choirs poured onto the air. Edward's body began to lift from the earth and an angel came to retrieve him, carrying him into the heavens. The slain rallys began to twinkle with light.

Corli kissed Morgan on the cheek. Then she watched her fizzle and mist away from her side. Then Corli looked up, reaching her hand for Pen, who took it. Corli closed her eyes. She felt the sparklers start at her feet and cool electric currents fill her body.

And Corli was gone.

The energy current reaching from pole to pole and filling the skies pulsed in veins that ran faster and faster. It became so brilliant that even the circle of angels could no longer be seen.

Devon and Raisa, and each of the couples, burned and pulsed. Their minds and breaths and heartbeats became one and the speed and rhythm of the light increased until it was constant. The sound became so blaringly loud and the lights so blindingly bright that it was as if there was no sound or light at all. The Lasteires could see nothing, hear nothing.

Then, an explosion! So glorious that from space it must have resembled the birth of a star, or maybe the birth of a world.

A yellow mist hovered high in the air for only seconds.

And when it was gone, it left total darkness and total silence.

24

"Devon, I can't see you," Raisa whispered with a shaking voice. She reached her hands out and felt his chest, breathing out with relief when she felt his heartbeat.

"It's okay." Devon grabbed her hands in the dark. "I can't see you either." He reached up to find her face and kissed her.

They heard whispers and sighs and quiet cries from the rest of their group.

"The ground is warm," Devon said.

Raisa held Devon's hand and stretched with the other to the outside of the circle. "And the ice is still there."

"Everyone," Devon didn't need to speak very loudly in the stillness around them, "we'll make a human chain to get supplies from the plane and bring them back here." Then he leaned in to whisper in Raisa's ear. "I hope it's still there."

25

"I think it's been about a day." Devon spoke quietly to Raisa.

By the light of glowsticks, they had set everyone up with their own little campsite of sleeping bags and some food. He wanted to talk to Raisa about what to do next but when he looked in her eyes he could just make out that there were tears on her face.

"What are you thinking about?" He brushed her cheek with his thumb.

"Corli," she whispered. "I know it's selfish… everyone has lost so much."

Devon kissed her hand. "I saw the whole thing, Raisa. Let me tell you about how she looked when she took Pen's hand…" He pulled Raisa close to him and whispered to her all the wonder of what he had seen the day before.

26

"This can't last forever, can it?" Devon's voice was wrinkled with concern as he spoke quietly to Raisa.

Their group, with the exception of Scott and Julia who seemed to keep quietly calm, looking to Devon and waiting faithfully for his instruction, began to murmur their concerns.

"Well," Raisa considered, "if God holds true to form, it should be less than twenty hours – if we've calculated right, before something happens… three days, you know."

27

Twenty four young adults lying on a small patch of warm lava rock at the magnetic north pole of the planet began to stir awake after existing in darkness for sixty eight hours. The last of their glowsticks were barely visible, like ghosts that you wondered if you really saw, marking vaguely where each couple was.

Devon heard several people stirring and being much less quiet than before about their displeasure with their situation.

"What do you say we have a little faith with our breakfast," he murmured into Raisa's ear before he kissed her on the cheek and crawled out of his sleeping bag. "Scott, come help me find something we can burn."

With measured steps and near dead glowsticks Devon and Scott ventured off to the airplane and were back again within minutes. Raisa wasn't sure exactly what it was that they brought back, but Scott succeeded in starting a fire. It burned with a beautiful blue and green flame in the center of their giant rock sponge.

"Help me out, Rai," Devon said as he pulled a folded piece of white copy paper from his pocket and handed it to her.

"What's this?" She asked curiously. She unfolded the paper but couldn't read it this far from the fire.

"You'll see. Ed gave it to me before we left the cockpit of the plane. I'll have you read it in a few."

Devon walked back to the center of the group. "Hey guys, how about we all bring our food by the fire and eat together."

The Lasteires had various reactions to his request that ranged from heavy sighs and grumbles to happy replies and smiles. But they all complied. They didn't have any other plans after all.

"I know that many of you must have a lot of questions," Devon began. He actually had to speak a little louder in their dead quiet darkness to compete with the crackle of the flame. The fizzles and pops from it were disquieting, like they were announcing the groups' existence, daring to be heard by anyone or anything. "I'm not saying that I have all, or even some of the answers, but I thought it would be good to review what we do have. And that's each other."

"Are we going to die, here in the dark?" It was Evetta. The question spilled out of her without her own consent and she snapped her mouth shut as soon as she asked it.

Devon looked at all of the faces around their little fire, meeting their gazes with what he hoped looked like calm, empathy and determination. He hoped the light that the flames gave was enough for them to see it.

"No, Evetta. I don't think we have gone through all of this just to die in the end. Our uniqueness has served its purpose and now it seems we're regular people. But what an amazing group of regular people!" He turned to Raisa and squeezed her hand. "It seems that Edward kept a list of us as we came to him. Raisa, if you would read for everyone the paper that Edward gave me."

Raisa smiled, "Of course." She cleared her throat and read aloud the list of names from everyone that sat in their circle, and what Edward had determined were their special gifts to bring into their new life.

Northern Lasteires

Mark Slater – Chemical Engineer
Larisa Slater – Seamstress
Li Mar – Doctor
Kita Mar – Mechanic
Munir Banai - Accountant
Parvenae Banai - Journalist
Jacque Benoit - Chef
Cecelia Leblanc - Architect
Curtis Fairchild – Carpenter
Delani Fairchild - Veterinarian
Wuma Savo – Priest and Healer
Zekya Savo - Chemist
Nico Millares – Fitness Trainer
Trisha Millares – Dance Historian
Jae Hu – Mathematician
Soo Min Hu – Astronomy
Landon Watson - Teacher
Evetta Marino – Horticulture
Brian Nye - Inventor
Kara Nye - Counselor
Scott Meyers - Artist
Julia King – Government and Communications
Devon Castaneda - Leader
Raisa Coen - Musician

There was only a moment of silence after Raisa finished before small, quiet conversations stirred up amongst the group. The air didn't feel quite so heavy anymore.

"Do you think that's enough for now?" Devon whispered to Raisa.

"I think it was perfect." Raisa smiled. She looked at Devon's face as the light from the fire danced across it, highlighting the angles of his nose and jaw, the curls from his hair and his eyelashes casting deep shadows. She looked at his eyes that were shadowed slightly by his brow and thought she

351

saw just a glint of copper that stopped her breathing for a moment. *A gift,* she thought. She leaned and stretched to place a kiss on an eyelid.

Raisa saw Julia out of the corner of her eye, stand and walk toward them. She assumed Julia was coming to talk to Devon but was surprised when it looked like she was headed in her direction. It wasn't that she *dis*liked Julia, not at all. They had even shared some pretty strong connecting moments. But it seemed clear that Julia would be better friends with Devon. They, after all, would obviously be partners in the leadership of the new, free world... this thought was far grander than she was prepared to consider right now, but Raisa couldn't help but wonder where she could possibly fit in.

"Raisa?"

Raisa stood up. "Hey, Julia... are you okay?" The firelight was exaggerating her drawn expression. Julia always looked so calm and self-assured, but now Raisa had the urge to try and comfort her.

"I," Julia hesitated and pulled her hand from behind her back, handing a small rumpled piece of paper to her. "I asked Scott if he would do this for me... for you."

Raisa slowly took the paper from Julia's hand. It was thin and the firelight illuminated it completely, giving it the appearance of delicate gold leaf. It was a sketch in pencil. It was a picture of Corli.

"I," Julia hesitated again, only this time it was clear that it was only difficult for her to continue. "I asked him to make one for me too." She held up her sketch of Morgan. It glowed in the firelight just as Raisa's did.

The two of them watched each other's fire glinted tears spill over for a moment before they found themselves in a gentle embrace.

352

The flames had burned low. The voices around their little encampment grew quieter as the excitement of new friendships waned and the evidence of their circumstances crept back into their hearts. Just as Scott stooped to add another bundle of fuel to the fire, it snuffed out.

They stood in utter darkness, their eyes opened as wide as ever, searching for anything that could take away their blindness. No one spoke and barely breathed, there was a feeling of something pending.

A small sound, a faint buzzing in the air met their ears. It was the first sound they had heard that they hadn't made themselves in what would have been three days. They all turned toward it, and reached out blindly to hold on to whomever they were close to.

"Look! At the horizon!" Scott gasped and pointed, though no one could see him do it.

A copper fizzing glow was barely visible in the distance, but it was growing with the speed of a sunrise. As it rose higher a dim line could be seen and as it climbed into the sky it promised to be a complete circle. The burning light resembled what spills from the shadow of an eclipse, but it was very dim. Did a celestial body create the effect or was it simply a ring of fire? When it rose high enough for the circle to be complete, it appeared to stop.

"A copper ring, close to the ground," Raisa murmured.

A pop like the sound of a flare ignited came to their ears next and they watched a ray of light, like a shooting star blaze across the sky.

"Bright white light, from Heaven," Devon amazed.

The slice of space where they touched, the coppery ring and the blazing white spear, flashed a singular ignition and became a

353

steady glow. The glow grew to a blaze and then, like watching one firecracker in a bundle lighting the others, it filled the ring in seconds. The Lasteires hands and arms flew up to shield themselves from the brightness.

But a thrum of sweet and deafening noise made them abandon the protection of their eyes. A soft yellow mist poured into their presence and their angels floated through and stood with them in the new light of day.

The warmth from their little patch of earth was almost gone. Devon and Raisa spoke with Vince and Lona, who floated brilliantly a couple of feet from the ground in front of them.

Raisa was trying not to be disappointed that Corli wasn't there.

"But it's been three days, why couldn't she come?"

"Patience, Dear," her mother said to her in her now musical voice. Raisa thought that it sounded like wind chimes. "She has a lot to do. We have been preparing for this, but she has not. She is with Pen though, does that make you happy?"

"Yes, it does." She smiled remembering the picture she had painted in her mind from the description Devon had given her of Corli taking Pen's hand.

Devon was being much more responsible.

"What is our first step, Vince? Where are we going to go? Are the Southern Lasteires okay? Will we be meeting them? What is it like out there? Is everything gone? How will we...."

Vince raised his hand, and it worked. Devon stopped and took a breath.

"Your plane has been protected. All natural living things remain, but all things made by man have been... shall we say, sanded down." Vince smiled warmly at Devon and Raisa. "We will be with you, for a time, till you no longer need us."

"And our friends in the South?" Raisa chimed in.

"You will go to meet them, and live with them, and start civilization anew."

"Where?" Raisa said with wonder and curiosity. She felt a thrill run through her. "Where will we live?"

"That is up to you." Vincent gestured generally to all of the group but landed on Devon.

Devon's brow raised and then he looked at Raisa. "Where do you want to live, Rai?"

Raisa thought of home. Her heart ached to go there, but she realized that it would not be ideal if everything was "sanded". So she opened her mind to think of naturally beautiful places she had been and tried to consider climate and natural resources.

"I know," she said thoughtfully, as the perfect place came to her. "On the coast, just above San Francisco... it's really beautiful there." She beamed at her father. She knew he had taken a lot of fishing trips there.

"A wonderful choice," Vincent grinned. But his brow wrinkled a little and he lowered his face. It made Raisa wonder if angels could cry.

"Done!" Devon said cheerfully. He grabbed Raisa in his arms and twirled her. "Let's get this show on the road. I have to plan a date night at the beach with my wife."

Twenty-four young adults boarded a large plane, the last one in existence, while their angels hovered.

Devon followed Raisa to the metal ramp. Before she took a step onto the plane, he wrapped his arms around her and nuzzled his mouth to her ear, and started to sing...

The Beginning

Song list

Helplessly Hoping – Crosby, Stills and Nash
Nearer My God to Thee - Sarah Flower Adams
Saturday Night – Elton John
Atomic Dog – George Clinton
Wanted Dead or Alive – Bon Jovi
The Point of it All – Anthony Hamilton
Red House – Stevie Ray Vaughn (original by: Jimi Hendrix)
Nessun dorma – Luciano Pavarotti (by: Giacomo Puccini)
I Need Thee Every Hour - Annie Hawks
I Often Go Walking - Phyllis Luch and Jeanne P. Lawler
4th of July – Soundgarden
Funny How Time Flies – Stanley Clarke
All The Pretty Little Horses - unknown
Blackbird – The Beatles
Layla – Eric Clapton
Black Water – The Doobie Brothers
Sister Moon – Sting
His Eye Is On the Sparrow - Civilla D. Martin
There is a balm in Gilead – John Newton
Rain on the Roof – Lovin Spoonful
Rachmaninov – 18th Variation, Rhapsody on a Theme of Paganini
To Make You Feel My Love – Billy Joel (original by: Bob Dylan)
Over the Rainbow - Harold Arlen and Harburg
Free Fallin' – Tom Petty
For Sentimental Reasons – Ivory Watson & William Best

Raisa's Song for Devon

Sweet Darlin'

Sweet darlin' you saved me
I'm hummin' from the lovin' you gave me
You went so far where my feelings are
Breathin' heaven fire, sweet darlin'

I know you, I know that you stopped running
You knew I had somethin' to show you
The fever tamed like an angel came
Made music of my name, sweet darlin'

Early that mornin' we knew I had to fly
The engines were screamin' and still I was asking myself why,
oh why
High on the wind I was feeling my sweet darlin' cry
My heart was breakin', I closed my eyes

Darlin' can you hear me? We can't be wrong
The night song pulls you near me
Time just falls and distance small, I feel you all
Sweet darlin'

Sweet darlin'
My sweet darlin'

Ann Wilson - Heart

Proof

Made in the USA
Charleston, SC
02 October 2013